IMPULSE

DAVE BARA

IMPULSE

Volume One of the
Lightship Chronicles

DAW BOOKS, INC.
DONALD A. WOLLHEIM, FOUNDER
375 Hudson Street, New York, NY 10014

ELIZABETH R. WOLLHEIM
SHEILA E. GILBERT
PUBLISHERS

www.dawbooks.com

First Printing, January 2015
1 2 3 4 5 6 7 8 9

DAW TRADEMARK REGISTERED
U.S. PAT. AND TM. OFF. AND FOREIGN COUNTRIES
—MARCA REGISTRADA
HECHO EN U.S.A.

PRINTED IN THE U.S.A.

This book is dedicated to my father, Gene Bara, the pilot who never flew but gave so many others their wings.

ACKNOWLEDGMENTS

As with any first novel, this book is a product not just of my own ideas and talents but also of many others at many different levels.

First and foremost I would like to thank my agent Joshua Bilmes at JABberwocky and my editor Sheila Gilbert at DAW. Without the two of them this book would not be what it is today.

Secondly there are many others who have helped me in my writing along the way, from direct encouragement and support to a smart word or two about the business. These people include Tom Trzyna and Rose Reynoldson from SPU, Tony Daniel, Janna Silverstein, Mike Bara, Patrick Swenson, Mark Teppo, Brian Thornton, Kat Richardson, Steve Mancino, Johnna Berry, and Pat Bara. I'm sure there are others I've forgotten in the mists of time, but from the bottom of my heart, thank you.

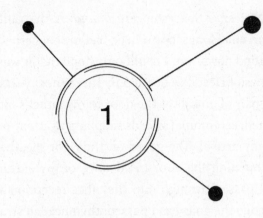

On Quantar

The long walk down the hallway to my father's office at the Admiralty had never seemed so endless. The only other time I had been here was three years ago, when I'd been told the news that my older brother Derrick had been killed in action. It was not a pleasant memory.

I pulled myself together one last time, hoping I looked presentable in my Quantar Royal Navy uniform. I hadn't even taken the time to shave. My father's message, when it had come, had been short and to the point.

Get here. Now.

I had grabbed my cap and uniform and rushed out of the navy barracks, hoping to catch the 0900 base shuttle across New Brisbane to the Admiralty. I shouldn't have worried. Outside I found a ground car waiting to take me to a private flyer. From there we had streaked across the New Briz skyline, weaving between the skyscrapers with our emergency flares lit, with me trying to squeeze into my uniform inside the cramped two-seater aircar the whole time.

The call, coming just a day before I was due to be commissioned

on Her Majesty's Spaceship *Starbound* as the ranking senior lieutenant and chief longscope officer, had me concerned. It couldn't possibly be good news, and I could only hope that it wasn't as disastrous
as the news of Derrick's death only three short years ago.

The pair of guards at the door to my father's office faced me as I
approached, ceremonial swords snapping to attention in acknowledgment of my arrival. The guard on the right sheathed his sword and
pivoted, opening the door in advance of my entrance, then held it
open as I passed through into the office reception area. I nodded to
acknowledge the guard as I passed, then headed straight for the desk
of Madrey Margretson, my father's secretary.

Madrey had been in my father's service for more than a decade,
and I'd grown used to her pleasant smile and warm hugs during our
infrequent social visits. She stood immediately as I came in, meeting
me well in advance of her workstation with a worried look on her face.
She waited until the guard had closed the door again before she began speaking, her tone all business.

"There's something going on, Peter. Something serious," she said.
"Your father's been in a conference with Admiral Wesley since before
0500. They've raised the alert status of both the Royal and the Union
Navies in the entire system to maximum readiness."

"Over what?" I asked.

"I don't know," she admitted, practically whispering. "But I do
know *Starbound*'s christening has been canceled and she's been put
on a twenty-four-hour launch clock as of 0800."

"Is that what this is about?" I wondered aloud. She shook her
head.

"I don't know. My instructions are to see you in immediately
upon your arrival. I'm not privy to the rest." She pulled and tugged at
my navy blue uniform, trying to take out the creases, and brushed it
with her hands to clear off any lint. She ran a hand through my
mussed black hair to smooth it and then took a step back to give me

one last look when her office com chimed. "He knows you're here," she said. "You'd best go in." She went around behind her desk and buzzed me in, the massive wooden double doors popping open as I stepped up.

"Be careful, Peter," she said to me, so quiet I could barely hear her.

"I will," I replied. Confused and more than a bit nervous at her tone, I stepped through the office doors and into my father's office.

Grand Admiral Nathan Cochrane of the Quantar Royal Navy sat behind his enormous redwood desk, his back to me as I entered. The face of Vice-Admiral Jonathon Wesley, Supreme Commander of the Unified Space Navy, was projected onto the longwave plasma viewer taking up most of the back wall. From the look of the room behind Wesley he could only be calling from his navy office on High Station Quantar, hanging three hundred miles above us in geosynchronous orbit. Wesley's gruff voice was magnified by the longwave and tinted with a heavy New Queensland accent. It filled the room as I came in and sat down on a sofa placed against the back wall facing the screen, I hoped out of range of the viewer. I could see my father's bald head sticking up just over the top of his office chair. From what I could glean they were in deep conversation about some sort of particulars regarding postings.

"... and then that should do it, Nathan. How long until you make the announcement?" asked Wesley.

"No point in waiting, Jonathon. I'll announce it via longwave to the cadet classes at noon," my father said. Wesley nodded twice, then looked up at me.

Not quite out of range, I thought.

"I see your son has stepped in. Time to get down to business," Wesley said.

My father swiveled his chair just far enough to catch my eye, then gestured to one of the two chairs facing the front of his desk. I walked over and sat down, fully aware of the fact that I was on duty and my father was my superior officer. I waited for him to speak or react, and started to grow anxious as the silent moments passed. Something was very wrong.

Finally he swiveled around to face me. His desk was by far the largest I had ever seen, and my father was every inch its equal. Wesley's oversized image peered at me from over my father's shoulder. I felt like I was in a fishbowl.

My father pulled off his old-fashioned wire-rimmed glasses and rubbed deeply at his eyes. When he pulled his hand away I could see his eyes were puffy, with deep red lines running through the whites. I'd only seen him look this way once before—when my brother had died. He reset the glasses, the silver of the wire offset by the white-tinged hair at his temples. I tried to remember what he had looked like with a full head of hair, but found that I couldn't summon the memory.

He looked down at his desktop and then up to me.

"As you may have guessed, son, there's been some news," he said. I shifted uncomfortably in my chair. My father took in a deep breath, then exhaled.

"There's no real way to soften this, Peter, so I'll just come straight out with it. There's been an attack on one of our Lightships." I felt a lump forming in the pit of my stomach.

Admiral Wesley cut in at this. "What I'm about to tell you is classified, Lieutenant," he started, then paused, clearing his throat roughly. "Five days ago, two shuttles from *H.M.S. Impulse* were on a First Contact mission to the Levant system when they were hit by a rogue hyperdimensional displacement wave that went on to hit *Impulse* herself. The damage was severe. Nine dead on *Impulse*, ten on the support shuttle and all twelve on the survey shuttle." His words struck me like a coil rifle round to the gut. Though *Impulse* was officially a Union Navy vessel, she was manned almost exclusively by Carinthian Navy personnel. The survey shuttle, however, would have been manned by officers from the Quantar Navy.

"All twelve?" I asked, looking to my father and then back to Wesley. "Our First Contact team?" Wesley nodded, a grim look crossing his face. I swallowed hard. Natalie Decker, my first and only girlfriend, was a member of *Impulse*'s First Contact team. She'd left only six weeks ago to join the crew of *Impulse*. But there could be a chance—

"I'm sorry, son, Natalie Decker was on that shuttle," my father said, cutting through my last, faint glimmer of hope. The knot in my stomach tightened even more. I leaned forward, elbows on my knees, and covered my face with my hands, fighting back tears.

Natalie and I had become close, perhaps closer than we should have allowed during our time at the Union Navy Lightship Academy. It had started innocently enough, studying in groups during late-night cramming sessions, expounding together on ethics in small group discussions and finding we had much in common. Then one night it had been just the two of us, alone in the dorm study lounge, and a long conversation about missing our family and friends back home had ended in kisses. From there, though we were always discreet, things had taken their natural course to greater intimacy. We found ourselves making time and space to be together while always keeping our training and duties foremost. She was my first lover, and I hers.

And now she was gone.

"Unfortunately, Peter," came my father's voice, "there's no time for tears." When I looked up, my father had regained his composure and sat with his hands folded on the desk. I wiped my own eyes clear and met my father's gaze.

"Yes, sir," I said, then took in a deep breath and let out a sigh.

"Understood, sir." My father nodded at me, pride evident in his grim smile. Wesley continued.

"Since natural HD displacement waves are extremely rare, we are assuming this was an intentional incident, either by an automated system still operating from the last war, or," Wesley paused here, "an active attack."

"Active?" I said, aware of the implications that statement carried with it. "The Corporate Empire?"

"Possibly," Wesley acknowledged. "We knew when we stepped back out into interstellar space that there could be remnants of the Corporate Empire of Man still out there. This incident seems to have confirmed our worst fears."

I thought about this. What I knew of the Corporate Empire was mostly from history classes. It had formed out of a loose coalition of planets controlled by merchant trading companies that started as a voluntary association, grew into a more formal government where participation by new colonies was encouraged with incentives, then finally became a force that was too powerful to contend against. It had grown to control nearly a hundred worlds at one point, but it was difficult to manage, and corruption was rampant. A system of royal peerage was instituted as a means of funneling responsibility through the most powerful of hands. It failed.

Then came the war.

Quantar was one of dozens of worlds that wanted out of the empire. One of my ancestors had even led the movement to form an Interstellar Republic with a constitution. This had angered the pro-Imperial families, who took up arms against the new Republic. The war raged for nearly twenty years. When it ended, at the Battle of Corant, all sides retreated back to their own systems for a century and a half, until the Historians arrived from Earth a decade ago with the gift of Lightship technology. Quantar had agreed to join with Earth and the most prominent of the pro-Imperial families, the Feilbergs of Carinthia, to form the Union. It was a fragile alliance, and never more so than now.

I turned my attention back to the conversation at hand. I wanted to talk about anything but Natalie.

"Don't we have defensive protocols for this sort of thing?" I asked as a way of sidestepping my feelings, my loss.

"We do," said Wesley. "Normally. But this was no normal First Contact mission."

My father cut back in here. "*Impulse* was sent into Levant because our automated probes had detected hyperdimensional anomalies in the system. Her mission wasn't just contact with the Levant government. She was also on an unofficial mission to determine whether the HD anomalies represented a potential threat to Union ships."

"A threat which we have now established," concluded Wesley.

I took in a deep breath, looking up at the two men I respected most in my life. "I've heard *Starbound* has been put on the launch clock. I want you to know that I and my teams are ready to go out there and face down this threat, sirs," I said. My father shook his head.

"I'm sorry, Peter. There's still more news, and I'm afraid it won't make you very happy," he said. I braced myself again. What could be worse than this?

"You won't be reporting to *Starbound*, son," he finished.

I was stunned. I had assumed we would be sending *Starbound* out on a rescue mission to *Impulse* and that I would be on her. I risked a glance up at Wesley, but his face was completely unreadable.

"But my cadet teams, we've been training for two years for this mission—" I started.

"That mission can be led by someone else," cut in Wesley. "You're needed elsewhere, Lieutenant," he stated in a commanding tone. I was having none of this.

"Where?" I demanded of Wesley, starting to rise out of my chair.

"What could be more important than serving on a rescue mission and bringing our countrymen home?" My father's hand on my arm put me back in my chair. Wesley wasn't my commanding officer, at least not yet. Technically we were still in different services, and I wanted answers, even if it meant pushing the limits of insubordination.

"There's no rescue mission, Lieutenant," said Wesley flatly. "*Starbound* is going out a week early as a show of force, and your new assignment is critical to the Union Navy."

I wondered if I was being taken off the line for my own protection. Before I could ask that question, my father answered.

"You'll be serving aboard *Impulse* as the senior Quantar Navy officer," he said, snapping me back to the business at hand.

"What?" I said. I was struggling with understanding these new orders and the grief of losing Natalie all at once. "But I'm barely a lieutenant. You're putting me in command of our navy's mission aboard *Impulse*?"

My father leveled his gaze at me. "Things have changed, Peter. Your brother has been gone for three years now. Natalie is gone. The responsibilities to the family and to Quantar have now fallen on you, whether you think you're ready or not. You're the only remaining son of the Grand Admiral, the son of a Duke of KendalFalk, a title that you too will someday bear. The son of a man who will soon become the full-time civilian Director of Quantar," he paused and let that sink in. He wasn't due to leave his post at the Admiralty for another year, but now . . .

"You'll have to step up, son, that's all there is to it," chimed in Wesley. "*Impulse* lost her XO and senior Quantar Commander on those shuttles. We're sending you out there as a replacement, to do a job for us."

"I don't understand, sir," I said, refocusing on my father. "You're leaving the navy?"

"To take a political position, yes, son. I have no choice. If this is the empire again, and they are stronger than us, then we have to be prepared to accept that the Imperial system might be reinstated. Quantar needs a leader, and so will our new team of officers on *Impulse*," he said.

"I thought you said *Impulse* was still in the Levant system?" I replied. It was Wesley who answered.

"*Impulse* docked at High Station Candle two days ago, Lieutenant," he said. "Repairs are already underway. You'll be on her when she heads back out, as the senior Quantar officer aboard." I didn't like that answer at all.

I appealed to my father. "My team has been together for three years training for this mission. Training for *Starbound*. And now, at the last minute, the navy is breaking us up? Why?" I said.

"Politics, son," said my father. The word made me feel sick, but I held my anger, and my tongue. "Word will get out soon enough about the *Impulse* disaster, and we have to be ready with the proper response." I looked to Wesley and then back again. I sensed his hand in this decision.

"And the proper response is sending the Grand Admiral's son to save the *Impulse* mission," I stated.

"Yes," my father said. He leaned in toward me with his massive frame, the way he always did when he was making an important point. "We have to face the fact that this Union is not strong, Peter. The Feilberg family of Carinthia and ours were at the axis of the old conflicts which led to the civil war and the collapse of the Corporate Empire. We can't risk that happening again. Remember, it was a century and a half of darkness before the Earth Historians came to Quantar and Carinthia. If they hadn't brought longwave technology and the Hoagland Drive we'd still be without a peace treaty."

"I know my history, Father," I said, rather more pointedly than I would have liked.

"Then you know we can't risk this new Union failing," he said. "Your presence on *Impulse* will send the strongest possible signal that we intend to stay in the Union for the long term."

I mulled this over for a moment, and didn't like what came to mind. "So I'm to be a political replacement, and the three years I've trained to serve on *Starbound* mean far less than my being seen as working with the Carinthians on their flagship," I said.

"Exactly," said Wesley from the longwave screen. "I'm sorry, Lieutenant, but considering the situation, you'll have to grow up much faster than you'd planned."

"I'm sorry as well, Peter," said my father. "I know how much you were looking forward to serving with your friends." That was true enough. But now it seemed fate had dealt me a different hand, one to a game I hadn't even known I was playing.

"What's the current status of *Impulse*?" I asked, changing the subject again. At least I could find out what I was facing. Wesley responded.

"Captain Zander has requested a minimum turnaround at Candle. He wants permission to go back to Levant and investigate the rogue HD waves," he said. "Lucius Zander is a man of many virtues, but patience is not one of them. If his ship was attacked by a First Empire weapon, he will want to take that weapon out. The Unified Space Navy's top priority is peaceful contact with the government of Levant and protecting the Lightship fleet. Zander is known as a passionate commander, if not a bit of a hothead. His actions once *Impulse* is back at Levant and he is in a combat situation are something we can't control. That's why the new detachment of Quantar officers is so important. Your team's task will be to shadow him and if possible deter him from his efforts to confront any First Empire weapon."

"Our *task*?" I sat there in disbelief, my anger growing at the implications of Wesley's words. "Exactly how are we to accomplish this *task*, sir?"

"Any way you can, Lieutenant," said Wesley. I looked to my father and then back to Wesley's image on the display.

"You're asking us to mutiny," I said. Wesley cut in sharp and angry.

"We're asking you to put your oath to the Union Navy above loyalty to your commanding officer," he said. "I'm not pretending it will be easy, but we expect you to protect *Impulse*, even with your own lives if you have to make that decision. The three ships in the Lightship fleet are all that stand between the Union and the tyranny of the old empire. If Levant is still defended by First Empire technology then we must avoid a conflict, or for that matter even contact, with Imperial elements at any cost. Do you understand your orders, Lieutenant?"

I looked to my father again. He was grim but silent.

"I do, sir," I said to Wesley.

"Questions?" he prompted sharply. I shook my head.

"Good," Wesley said, preparing to bring the conference to a close. I interrupted before he could finish.

"I'll want some of my cadet instructors with me on this mission, people I've worked with and know that I can trust," I said to Wesley. I may have been under new orders, but I still had cards to play. Wesley looked aggravated at me for interrupting him.

"I'll need names, Lieutenant," he said back impatiently.

"George Layton for one. John Marker for another," I said, naming my best helm officer and marine corporal. "I'll need a tech, Brice Devlin should do. Cort Drury from Propulsion, and Evangeline Goolagong as my Intel officer."

"Anyone else?" asked Wesley, obviously impressed with my forwardness.

"Yes," I said. "Jenny Hogan from Astrogation."

"No," cut in my father.

"But she's the best we've got," I insisted, and it was true. She also happened to be Wesley's niece.

"She may be," said Wesley over the viewer. "But I've got someone else in mind for that job." I wondered who he meant, but that didn't stop me from pressing him.

"So this mission is safe enough for the director's son but not the supreme commander's niece?" I said back to Wesley. He fumed in silence, turning different shades of red as he stared down at me from the oversized view screen, but I held my ground.

"Granted," he finally said. "I'll fill the rest of the roster with experienced spacers, Lieutenant. You won't want for good advice." I nodded. There was really nothing more to say.

"There is one more thing," said my father. He slid a box across the table to me. I opened the top. Inside, swimming in royal blue velvet, were two lieutenant commander's collar pins. "They belonged to your brother."

They're giving me Derrick's stars, I thought.

"This assignment comes with a promotion," said Wesley from the screen. "I know it's a small consolation." He was right about that. I shut the box again and stuck it in my pocket, then looked to each man in turn.

"When do I leave?" I asked. It was Wesley who spoke again. It seemed very clear to me now who was in charge of this mission.

"Effective at midnight tonight your commission is transferred from *H.M.S. Starbound* to *H.M.S. Impulse*. You have two hours to pack your gear and catch a shuttle to High Station Quantar, where you will have a forty-eight hour layover while you wait for transport. From there you will proceed to High Station Candle on the cloud rim and will report to the deck of *Impulse*, under the command of Captain Lucius Zander, at 0700 hours on twelve-dot-two-seven-dot-two-seven-six-eight. Do you understand your orders, Commander?" he said. It was the first time he had used my new rank.

I roused myself from my funk and stood, snapping to attention. "I do, sir," I said. He nodded his response.

"Now I'll leave the two of you to finish your visit in privacy," he said. "Good luck to you, Commander Cochrane."

"Thank you, Admiral," I said. Wesley nodded to my father and then the screen went to black, superimposed with the seal of the Quantar Naval Linkworks. My father turned off the viewer with the click of a button.

"I'm so sorry about all this, Peter," he said as I sat back down, sinking heavily into the chair, the weight of all that had just happened hitting me hard.

"No need to apologize, sir," I replied.

"I think there is," he said. Silence came over both of us then. I thought about Natalie, about how young and beautiful she had been. I had reconciled myself to losing her to the service months ago once I knew her assignment, but not permanently. Then thoughts of Derrick came. It had been his death in a shuttle accident, training new cadets, that had shocked me out of my immature pursuit of a professional soccer career and driven my decision to join the Union Navy and the Lightship Program. I had fought hard to get in, and made it on my own merit, but my mission now seemed somehow incomplete. I fingered the box with my—no, Derrick's—commander's stars inside. I wondered if somehow I had failed him by not making it to *Starbound*.

I fought off a wave of sadness as I looked at my father. We were both holding back tears as we sat in the quiet of the enormous office. I couldn't imagine what he had felt, having lost his wife, my mother, to cancer such a short time after the Historians had arrived from Earth. And of course they had both the knowledge and technology that could have cured her, but contact had come too late. Then he had lost his oldest son, the one he had staked all of his hopes and dreams on, and he was left with only me. I wondered if I even came close to Derrick in his mind. By my own measure I didn't. How could I? I had chosen the life of a second son, filled with sports and games and casual pursuits. Derrick had followed our father's path from the day he was born: the duty of a duke's son, the military and civil training, always focused on what was expected of him. I vowed in that moment, looking at my father, that I would do everything in my power to be the son that he wanted, the son that he needed to succeed him.

Finally my father spoke and broke the silence. "These are difficult and complex times, Peter," he said. "I was just thinking that before the Earthmen came with their technology and their science we led a much simpler life. Things changed so suddenly when I saw the Earth ships approaching Quantar. Our universe was smaller then, less complicated."

"Of course, sir," I said, unsure how to react. He leaned back in his chair.

"Those were good times, hopeful. Just you and Derrick and your mother and I. Now there's only the two of us left," he said, looking at me again. "I don't want to lose you too."

"You won't, sir. I promise," I said. I meant it down to my core.

My father accepted my promise silently, then he stood and came around the desk to hug me. He held on tightly for several moments before he let me go.

"Good luck, son. You're all I have now. I know you'll make us all proud," he said. I knew what he meant by *all*: all of the family, here or gone, and all the Cochranes of Quantar that had come before me. I took his offered hand and shook it.

"I will do my best, sir," I said, then broke the handshake. I acknowledged the conversation was over with a nod, picked up my cap and turned to leave. When I got to the office door I opened it and then stopped to look back at my father. He was sitting behind the desk again, gazing out of the window at the New Briz skyline. The sight of such a strong and forceful man reduced to such a state filled me with fear and anxiety. *It's all on me now*, I thought.

I stepped over the threshold without another word and shut the door behind me.

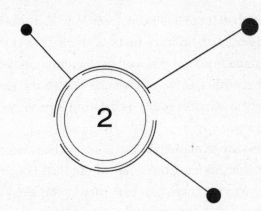

On High Station

Eight hours later, after a frantic packing session and a hypersonic plane ride from New Briz Airfield I was on High Station, in the quarters of *Starbound*'s assigned Earth Historian, Serosian. After throwing my bags onto my temporary bunk, I'd made my way here to be with my friend and mentor, hoping for some consolation and perhaps some wisdom from him as well.

I had spent many hours in Serosian's company during my three years of Academy training. He had taken me under his wing as his pet project upon my enlistment, for which I had always been grateful. I had known him a bit before—he had been Derrick's mentor as well— but not in anything more than a passing way. It seemed that I had always been off on some soccer foray or a social expedition with my friends when he had come calling. Then one day he'd arrived at my father's house with the worst possible news. We had talked that day, about what I don't remember; I was too numb, in too much pain. But I did remember calling on him a few weeks later and telling him of my desire to enlist in the Lightship service. It was the best decision of my life.

After that, there had been many long nights debating ethics and tactics, discussing military history, the battles during the Imperial Civil War and my struggles with my assignments, and relaxing, when I had time, with a game of chess. It was at the chess table that we found ourselves again today, pondering a game we would probably never finish.

"Chess is like mathematics," Serosian had once said. "Everything in the universe is an expression of physical laws, which ultimately break down to numbers." I wasn't sure I completely agreed with him. After all, how does one quantify or express emotions such as love, or for that matter, grief, in numerical terms? It was a question I had never asked and he would probably never choose to answer, even if he had one.

He had often told me that chess was his way of testing young cadets, to see if they could think critically and logically, yet also remain open to intuition and more esoteric influences. I'd asked him once why he had chosen to mentor me, besides my obvious family connections. His answer was simple: I was the first cadet who had ever beaten him at the game.

I pondered the formations on the board, my pieces always the white, his always the black. I had a bishop and four of his pawns, he a rook and three of my pawns. I wondered what the odds were of my winning, even if I did look to have a small advantage. From the positions on the board I put my chances at less than fifty-fifty.

"You won't win," Serosian said from across the room as he poured himself another glass of wine. "In case you were wondering. In fact I make the odds only thirty-three percent you'll manage a draw." He recorked the wine bottle and made for his chair opposite me at the table, scanning the formations. "You've already made one critical tactical mistake," he continued as he came back to our game.

"Yes," I replied, "that would be signing up for the naval service." He laughed at that, surprisingly loud for a man who had such a quiet, if deep, voice. Looking at us one would probably have assumed we were more brothers than mentor and student. We shared the same dark hair and deep blue eyes, as well as a similar set to the jaw. Serosian appeared perhaps a decade older and was a head taller than I, and I stood a firm six-foot-two in height myself. I knew the appearance of my friend was not an accurate measure of his age, however. The anti-aging regimens of the Earthmen had not yet been shared with either Quantar or the Feilberg family of Carinthia, and I suspected Serosian was close to twenty years older than he looked.

"I've been wondering about that choice," he said in response to my verbal foray, then made an advancing move with a pawn. "You could have chosen any career you wanted. Diplomatic Corps, the Merchant Fleet, even professional soccer from what I remember."

I responded by moving one of my knights. "We're a navy family, you know that. Derrick was an influence, of course. And besides all that, what career could offer me more than exploring deep space and rediscovering our lost heritage, a lost human empire?"

"Not many, I'd venture," he said, then made an attacking move with his queen. "I'll have you checkmated in five moves."

I smiled. "Remember your telling me about how important intuition is?" I said, then took his king's rook with my queen and put him in check. He frowned.

"Well, it looks like this game could go on a bit longer than I anticipated," he said. "No matter, we've other things to discuss."

"Yes we do," I said, and took another drink of my wine. Serosian magnetized the tabletop with the click of a button and then flipped it over to conceal the chess set. I took another drink of my wine, a shiraz from the Caderlands, then set my glass down.

"How are you feeling, Peter?" he asked. I contemplated his question for a moment. I wasn't really sure what I felt, but I did think I owed him an answer.

"Right now, numb," I said.

"The wine helps with that," he replied.

"Of course it does. But all day I've felt shock, anger, resignation, depression, more anger, the whole gamut."

"That's only normal. Natalie was a special girl."

"These circumstances are anything but normal," I replied. "First Derrick, now Natalie . . ." I looked down as my voice trailed off. "How many more times will I have to go through this?" I asked.

He didn't have a ready answer, so we sat together for a moment, each of us contemplating his glass of wine. "All I can say, Peter, is that space is a dangerous place. There will be pitfalls and failures and even disasters, but it is rare to lose two people so close to you in such a short time. You are unique in that."

"That gives me no comfort," I said, then turned a keener eye on my friend. He was as dark and unreadable as ever, the kind of man who never let anything slip out by accident.

"If I can make a suggestion?" he said.

"Please do."

"Perhaps it would help if you had a small memorial for Natalie before you left, with your close associates who knew her. Take some time to honor her and your love for her before you go."

"You know I don't believe the same way you do, Serosian, the way the Church teaches," I said.

"You don't have to have any specific beliefs to honor her and your loss, Peter. Just know in your heart that by your act you are honoring her memory."

I thought about that a moment, and couldn't really find any objections to it. In fact, it seemed like a good idea. "I believe I'll take your advice," I said, "Get Marker, Layton, the rest of the crew reporting for *Impulse* involved. Hopefully they'll all be here by tonight. But if I know Marker, he'll want to honor her with more than a quiet memorial."

Serosian smiled. "Then perhaps you should do both."

"I don't feel much like painting the station red right now," I said. He cocked his head at me.

"You're young. It may be the last time in a long while you get to enjoy yourself. I recommend joining in, if you can manage it," he said.

I thought about it some more. Marker would undoubtedly want to drink heavily. In some ways, it didn't seem like such a bad idea. And I did have another full day before my shuttle to High Station Candle would arrive. I changed the subject without giving any final answer.

"You invited me here to warn me, didn't you?" I said. "About *Impulse*. About Captain Zander." He nodded without saying anything for a moment, so I continued. "Do you know they've asked me to mutiny if I have to, to protect *Impulse*?" I said. He shook his head.

"That detail I didn't know, but it doesn't surprise me, knowing Admiral Wesley as I do," he said.

"He's certainly loyal to the navy," I said. Serosian's frown from the chess match returned.

"That's his one great fault, Peter," he said. "He's probably too old to adjust to the new paradigm. We all have to work together to succeed: Quantar, Earth, and Carinthia. The Union Compact is still very new and very, very tenuous. Things could break down at any time if the empire reasserts itself."

"I know my father trusts him." That elicited a sidelong glance.

"Indeed," he said, then let my statement lie. "I am sorry about the situation they've put you in, but in light of the attack at Levant, it's probably a sound policy."

"And what about the Historian aboard *Impulse*? What do you know of him or her?" The frown remained on Serosian's face.

"He's from a different school than I am," he finally said, as if that was enough.

"Different school? What do you mean?" I asked. Serosian seemed reluctant to answer, but did anyway.

"There are those of us in the Historian Order that believe that humanity is best served when each individual is allowed to fulfill his utmost potential. We believe in nurturing and growing our charges, the 'taking under the wing' idea. That's why I chose to mentor you, and Derrick before you. But there is another school of thought, another sect, that believes humanity is best served when individuals are sublimated to humanity as a whole, when the needs of the collective human society are put first. They believe that too much individualism, too much diversity, led to a breakdown of societal norms in the empire and created an atmosphere where corruption was allowed to become rampant as all behavior by individuals was rationalized. They think this led to the collapse of the Corporate Empire. They want humankind to be tested as much as possible, to be pushed and prodded into group action and knocked down when they fail the community or fall short of expectations. It's a delicate balance between the two philosophies, and the Church does not favor one over the other. Tralfane is of the latter school. He will push you in every way, Peter, and it will not be pleasant," he finished.

I took some time to soak this all in, as it was new knowledge to me. "I appreciate your honesty," I said, then turned my attention to the matters at hand. I eyed my friend. "This attack, is it the First Empire?" I asked.

"Unknown at this time," he said without hesitating, as if he expected the question. "Initial analysis of the Hoagland Wave indicates that it doesn't match any known First Empire frequencies. That could be because we don't have it in our catalog, or because it's a new type of wave. Either way I need the telemetry from *Impulse* to be certain."

"But if it's not the First Empire, in one form or another, then who could it be?" I asked.

Serosian's face went grim. "There could be other forces at work here," he said.

"Other forces?" I was surprised by the implication. "You mean the Sri? I thought your order wiped them out in the civil war." Serosian had told me many stories about the secret war between the Church of the Latter Days and the Sri during First Empire times.

"It's true that their home world of Altos was attacked during the war, but it was never destroyed, at least not militarily," he said. "We don't know where they went. It's always possible some of them survived on Corant, or perhaps on some other world."

The knot in my stomach returned at the mention of the old Imperial capital. Corant was said to be a mythic world of gold and bronze, of crystal lakes and flowing rivers, with only one major city. There was no industry allowed, everything was imported to the capital from other worlds in the empire. The countryside was said to be made up of massive estates for the wealthiest and most loyal of the emperor's vassals. So it was said.

The Sri themselves were another issue altogether. They were reputed to be a secret society of technological wizards that used their knowledge to make humans more like machines than men. The Church had outlawed their technology as unnatural and spent considerable assets to see that it was destroyed during the civil war. Apparently, they weren't as successful as the histories liked to portray.

"And if they are out there, what will they be like?" I asked.

Serosian's face became an emotionless mask that I couldn't read. "Pure science, with no accounting for the spiritual. Technology for technology's sake," he said. "It's a materialistic universe view, cold and soulless, and one that leads to enslavement." His hand went to his chin in contemplation as I waited for more. "If the Sri are out there, Peter, then they are far more dangerous than a revived empire. And if the Union cannot defend against them, then the Church will have to act."

"Act? What does that mean?" I asked, not sure I wanted to hear the answer.

"To destroy them, at any cost," he said. I didn't want to ask the next question, but I had to.

"And what about us? The Union worlds?" I said. "What if we just 'get in the way' of your private little war with the Sri?" Serosian averted his eyes from mine.

"The technologies that could be unleashed on the universe . . ." he started, then trailed off. "The weapons . . ." he hesitated again, and then shook his head. "This is why you must succeed, Peter, why the Lightship missions are so important. Any other scenario is unthinkable."

"And if the Sri are in league with a revived empire?" I asked. He leaned forward and met my eyes.

"If the First Empire still exists out there and it is under Sri influence, then none of us are safe," he said. "Watch your back, Peter. The heir to the seat of Quantar would be a welcome target for either of those potential enemies."

I nodded. "And what about this Captain Zander?" I asked.

"What of him?"

"He led *Impulse* directly into the attack that killed Natalie and my countrymen. Should I trust him? Should I hate him?"

Serosian contemplated me. "Whatever happened at Levant was no accident. Don't hate a man you've never met for Natalie's loss. Hate the ones who killed her with their machines. Hate the empire, Peter."

Then he stood up and walked away from the table and went to the window, staring out at the shining globe of Quantar.

I took another drink of my wine and contemplated what I had gotten myself into.

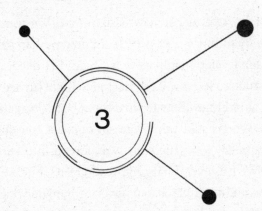

Exploring High Station

By evening, only George Layton and John Marker had arrived from my select team of cadet instructors, so I rounded them both up for the impromptu memorial service for Natalie and the others. I sent out a general announcement on the station com band, and by the time we gathered at 2000 hours about two dozen Quantar officers and enlisted ended up joining us. I was forced to lead the service, both by my rank and by my standing in Quantar society. I said the few words I could manage and we all lit a candle for those lost, followed by twelve minutes of silence, one for each of the lost souls. During that time I thought of Natalie, and then Derrick, and how much I had lost in such a short time.

At the end, each of the participants placed their candles on a makeshift altar I had prepared one by one, some adding photos of their friends who had been lost. When the crowd was gone I blew all the candles out, but I left the memorial where it was.

As I walked away with Marker and Layton I tried to clear my head and connect with what I was actually feeling. The fact was that I had emotionally broken from Natalie a few months ago, when she had first learned of her new assignment. We were being forced to separate by military necessity, so I knew we had to draw the line on our personal relationship as well. She didn't like it and neither did I, but we stuck to it. Now it felt like once I had turned my emotions off, I wasn't sure I knew how to turn them back on again.

Marker insisted we go out on our last free night together and Layton agreed, so in the end I was forced into carousing about the station. We hit several bars and restaurants, but eventually we ended up at a standing table at our favorite hangout, Paddy's Pub on the tourist deck, drinking our last beers together as cadets. From here on out it was going to be all business.

Corporal John Marker was a huge man with caramel-colored skin, an inheritance of his mixed descent from the aboriginal peoples of the Australian continent on Earth. I'd always wanted to tease him that I thought he looked more Maori than Aussie, but he was far too big to give stick to, and I was smart enough not to go there. Layton was like me, as Earth-English as they come and white-skinned as sheep's wool.

Marker was twenty-six, old for the cadet corps, and two years older than Layton, who was a year older than me. I had just turned twenty-three the previous month, so this was my last official drinking binge before assuming my station on *Impulse*. I'd come into the Lightship program two years late, but I made up for it by doubling up on my classes and finishing in three years instead of four. And becoming valedictorian of the class in the end, of course.

Marker raised his glass of stout. "For Natalie," he said. Layton and I repeated the toast, and I drank from my pint of beer. It was bitter for me in more ways than one.

"We're both sorry about this, Peter," Marker said. I nodded.

"Thank you both," I said. "Natalie was special to me, so we have to make sure we honor her with our performance on *Impulse*."

"Agreed," said Layton. "I just wish we were getting our first assignment on *Starbound*."

"We all do," I said, taking another swig of my beer. "But this mission is critical to the Union, and our performance is critical to Quantar. I'll miss *Starbound* too, and the adventures we could have had aboard her."

Marker stirred at this, and I could see the alcohol was starting to get to him. He'd been drinking far more than Layton or I had.

"And here's to *Starbound*," he said, loud enough for everyone in the pub to hear. "The finest ship in the Union!" The whole pub raised their glasses at that one.

"Here, here!" said Layton and I, lifting our beers and clacking them with Marker's. I was sticking to bitter, but Layton was going adventurous with a brown Belgian ale. Marker was strictly a stout man. We all killed our beers and then Marker called to the bartender for more.

"I can't believe they're breaking us up," said Layton in the intervening moment.

"Believe it," chimed in Marker. "That goddamned Wesley's a pillock. All he cares about is keeping his nose up the Carinthians' arses. As long as they're happy he keeps his job."

"Here, here!" said Layton, raising his empty glass just as the serving girl brought more. Layton tipped her heavily and then patted her gently on the bottom as she walked away. She turned and smiled back at him.

"I'll have that one eating out of my hands by midnight," he said. Marker looked down at him through glazed eyes.

"It's already 0030 hours, idiot," he said. I had to laugh at that. Layton took the insult affably enough and then turned his attention to me.

"Do the bloody Carinthians even drink beer?" he asked.

"I think they invented it," I quipped back, taking another big swig from my glass. Marker laughed so hard he snorted.

"Well, here's to 'em then," he said, taking yet another drink. On cue, three officers in Carinthian green came into the pub and made their way straight to the bar. One was an older gray-haired officer that I took for station staff, another a young red-haired man of ensign rank, and the third was an athletic-looking woman with the rank of commander.

"She's pretty," said Layton as the three Carinthians doffed their berets and started drinking in a corner of the bar. I watched her as she brushed out her regulation-cut hair with her hand and took a drink of a very dark beer. She was indeed pretty, but not overly so. I caught her taking a quick glance in my direction and nodding at me. I quickly looked away, not wanting to be seen staring at her.

Marker's booming voice interrupted my surreptitious observations.

"You know, Commander," he said, elbowing me playfully, his voice starting low but then rising. "You know goddamned well I'd follow you to the steps of the Emperor's palace!" he said, raising his glass. "If the goddamned Union Navy gave us half a chance!"

"I know, John," I said, trying to quiet him down. "I'm looking forward to having you both aboard *Impulse*."

"Well, I hope the cod-eating Carinthian Navy know what they're getting!" he said, practically yelling now. The bar was noisy but more and more patrons were paying attention to Marker's vocal exercises, especially the three Carinthians. He put his arm around me and started in again, this time in the clear direction of the Carinthian officers.

"This here's the best goddamned cadet graduate in the fleet," he said, tapping my chest repeatedly with his index finger while slopping beer on the floor. "Name's Cochrane. Peter Cochrane, and you'd better respect that!" he said, the slurring of his words increasing. "You're gettin' our bess!" Then he wrapped me in a huge bear hug.

"Thanks, John," I said, while waving apologetically to the Carinthians as Marker refused to let me go. The older officer looked miffed and the ensign had a disapproving look on his face, but the woman smiled a bit at me, more out of sympathy than anything else, I guessed.

"George, why don't you see if you can help me get John here back to his bunk," I said. Marker was still draped all over me.

"Sure thing," said Layton. He took one arm while I took the other.

"Perhaps you could use some help with your friend?" said a husky female voice from behind me. I looked around to see the Carinthian commander standing behind me.

"Um, sure," I said, pleased that she had come over to make my acquaintance, but worried about the circumstances. I was in fact quite unsure of how she could help with a man of Marker's size. She was around five-foot-seven from my guess, clearly in good shape but I couldn't say she was more than a hundred and thirty pounds soaking wet. Marker was a hundred more than that, easily, and he was starting to sway like a badly designed bridge.

"You're a cutie," he said to her.

She ignored him, smiling, and then turned to the young ensign from her group and waved him over. He put down his beer with a look of great distaste and reluctantly came over to our table. Without a word he slid in next to me and took my place. At first I didn't understand what was happening until he and Layton started walking the now-quiet Marker out of the pub. When I turned back the staff officer was gone and I was alone with the Carinthian commander.

"Um, what just happened?" I said.

"Your friend looked like he need some help home. In the interests of interplanetary unity I thought I would offer my ensign as assistance," she said. I smiled.

"I see," I said. "And your other friend?" She turned to look at the empty space near the bar where he had been standing a moment ago and shrugged.

"Probably home to his wife, I'd guess," she said. I picked up my beer as she pointed to a booth that had opened up.

"Perhaps we could get better acquainted?" I opened a path with a sweep of my hand and then followed the commander to the booth and sat down. She slid in across from me with her beer glass in hand. I noticed she also had a double shot glass with some kind of chaser.

I extended my hand. "I'm Peter Cochrane," I said.

"So I gathered from your friend. Pleased to meet you, Commander Peter Cochrane," she said, gripping my hand firmly in reply for a few seconds. As I pulled back, my fingers went to my new collar pins nervously, then I took a drink of my bitter. I had two full stars, she had three.

"And whom do I have the pleasure of sharing this drink with?" I said, trying to open up the conversation.

"I'm Dobrina Kierkopf, Commander, Royal Carinthian Navy, class of '74," she said. The same year that Derrick had graduated from our Academy. That would make her twenty-six, three years older than me. I took another sip of my beer to calm my nerves.

"Pleased to meet you, Commander," I said. "Kierkopf? Is that Carinthian?" I asked out of curiosity.

"Actually it's Slovenian," she said back. "We have a plurality of German ancestry on our world, with large mixes of other nationalities from Central Europe on Old Earth."

"Ah, fascinating," I said. Then without thinking I blurted out: "So, Commander, what brings you to High Station?" She smiled silently for a moment as I got redder and redder. It was an innocent enough question . . .

"That sounds like a pickup line, Commander. Do you use it often on superior officers?"

I swallowed hard, embarrassed at how my question had come out. "Forgive me, Commander, I didn't mean to imply—"

"Oh, so you *don't* find me attractive?" she cut in, a very stern look on her face. "Am I too old for you?"

"Certainly not, ma'am! It's just, I didn't—" She laughed hard and then covered her mouth as she giggled. "You're playing me," I said.

"Guilty," she said, then took a drink of her stout. I did my best shy-young-officer impression then and matched her with a drink of my bitter.

"You really should switch to something more robust," she said as I had a mouth full of beer. It took me a second to respond in kind.

"No thank you, madam," I said. "I've tried that motor oil before and once was enough!"

"You're sure?" she asked. I nodded.

"Absolutely."

"Then maybe I could interest you in trying some of this." She slid the double shot glass across the table to me. "It's a family favorite back home, especially in New Wurzburg, where I'm from," she said.

I looked down at the nearly full shot glass. The drink was clear with a slight green tinge and looked harmless enough. She sat and waited patiently, her hands clasped together.

"Aren't you up for the challenge, Commander Peter Cochrane of Quantar?" she said, teasing me. I had no intention of backing down now. I took the glass in a swift and casual motion. Raising it to my lips, I hesitated only a second before taking an ill-advisedly large drink. For a second I tasted the pleasant flavors of apple and pear mixed together, then the viscous fluid started burning my lips and tongue. It crawled down my esophagus like a worm on fire. I coughed and choked, my eyes watering as I struggled to catch a breath of air without burning my lungs.

"My . . . God!" I choked out, "What *is* that?" She reached across the table and snatched the glass from my hand, then downed the rest of it, more than half a glass full, in one quick gulp, snapping her head back at the finish and exhaling.

"We call it schnapps," she said in a normal tone of voice. I was still coughing. "As I said, a family favorite back home."

"I'm glad I'm not in your family," I said. She smiled wryly.

"Yes, well, I should answer your original question, Commander," she said.

"I've forgotten what it was," I said, wiping my mouth with my uniform sleeve. "But go ahead."

"You asked what brought me to High Station. I've been assigned as a strategic attaché for the Carinthian Navy for the last three months, although my commission has recently been transferred to the Union Navy Command."

"I see," I said, finally recovering from the schnapps. "Now I suppose you'll want to hear all about me?" To my surprise, she shook her head no.

"No need. You were born the second son of the Grand Admiral of the Quantar navy, who will soon be retiring to assume the honorary title of Director of Quantar. Since the untimely death of your brother in a Union Navy accident, you are now first in line to succeed to the chair after your father, should it ever be offered by the empire again. Your official title is Viscount of Queensland, but when your father becomes Director you'll become Duke of KendalFalk. You've just graduated at the top of your class of thirty-six cadets as a certified longscope officer, and your aptitude rating was off the charts. Your best friend is the Earth Historian, Serosian, who will stay with *Starbound*, and you'll be serving under Captain Lucius Zander aboard *H.M.S. Impulse* beginning in a couple of days. Did I miss anything?"

"I don't think so," I said, then thought about Derrick and how I had come to be in my current position. In many ways I didn't feel worthy, but that was something to deal with at another time.

I was a bit taken aback by her knowledge of me, and somewhat offended. It was clear she had extensive information on me and my family, some of it high-ranking intelligence. I didn't much like being put on the defensive and she had certainly done that. Frankly, I was more than a bit angry. "You Carinthians don't miss much, do you?" I said as I finished my bitter and then stood to go without saying anything more, my evening's fun waning. She tapped the table.

"Please stay," she said.

"Is that an order, Commander?"

"No."

I sat, letting her know by the look on my face that I was upset with the direction of the conversation. "I'm afraid I don't like having my private life so . . . well known," I said. She sighed, in sympathy, I thought.

"I don't believe you have a private life anymore, Commander. That's something you'd better get used to," she said. I contemplated her. Clearly she was much more knowledgeable about me than I was comfortable with, and the conversation seemed as if it had been arranged. I wondered if she knew about Natalie and my relationship with her, and what had happened with *Impulse* at Levant.

"In earlier times between us you would have been thought a spy," I said. She tilted her head slightly at me.

"Those times are over, Cochrane. What happened in a war fought a century and a half before we were born has no effect on us or how we behave. Quantar and Carinthia are allies and equal members of the Union," she said. I waved off the serving girl as she came past our booth. I'd had quite enough alcohol and quite enough of being lectured.

"As you said, madam, a war fought so long ago shouldn't affect us today. But you should also know that wounds can take a long time to heal, especially fresh ones." I thought of Natalie again then, and for the first time I began to feel a great sadness at her loss. There was an awkward silence as we sat together. I had no idea what she knew or didn't know about me, and at that point I didn't care. I just wanted a graceful exit from the conversation.

Then she broke through the silence in a quite unexpected way.

"Do you fence?" she asked. I was surprised by the question.

"Fence? Well, I suppose so. I took a quarter of it at the Academy."

"Excellent! I've been looking for a partner all week. No one seems interested in taking me on. Are you game?" She leaned forward as she said the last. I was a bit taken aback by her aggressiveness; that was something new in a woman for me. I found it intriguing, and she had certainly shaken me out of my funk.

"Well if no one on High Station will offer you the honor of a challenge, then I must accept. For Quantar, of course," I said. I also thought the exercise would do me some good after the stress of the last few days.

"Of course," she smiled widely. "You're a brave young man, taking on a challenge so quickly without even knowing your opponent. So tell me, how did you do in your fencing class at the Academy?"

"I ended up sixth," I responded.

"Ah, so you have some skill then! Excellent!" she said again, then got up suddenly to take her leave. "I have a court reserved at 0700 tomorrow, or should I say today, on the recreation deck. Don't be late." She said the last as if it were an order. I looked at my watch.

"But it's nearly 0100 already and I've been drinking all night!" I protested. She smiled again, turned to go, then turned halfway back.

"Oh, and, Cochrane, I should probably mention I was Champion my final year at the Academy."

"Academy Champion?" I asked through the fog of my beer. She shook her head negatively.

"World Champion," she said. I swallowed hard.

"*Carinthian* World Champion?" I asked.

She just smiled again.

"See you at 0700."

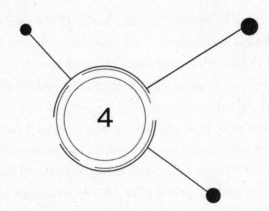

Fencing with Dobrina

I got up early and arrived at the rec deck by 0630, thankfully nursing only a slight hangover from my previous evening's adventure. After confirming which court Commander Kierkopf had reserved, I checked out a fencing suit and mask and sorted through the foils, finally settling on one that I hoped would help me to use my weight and muscle to advantage. After dressing I scurried out to the court, ten minutes early.

Commander Kierkopf was already there, stretching and flexing her foil.

"Good to see you, Commander," she said, smiling like a predator smiles at its prey. "I was worried you weren't going to show."

I shrugged the barb off. "Good to see you as well, Commander Kierkopf." I swallowed a last shot of my hydrating drink, then motioned to the starting marks with a wave of my hand and an affected bow, hoping courtesy, no matter how disingenuous, would serve me well. She donned her mask without another word and took her mark with practiced ease. I stepped up slowly, dipped my leading foot in talc, secured my mask, and took my mark, left hand leading.

"I didn't know you were left-handed," she said, noting my stance with interest and stepping back from her mark while feigning an adjustment to her glove. No doubt this was merely a tactic to allow her to reassess her original strategy. I too stepped off my mark as a courtesy and circled briefly.

I was lucky in a way, having been born left-handed, but my parents, thinking it might be awkward, had converted me to a right-hander as a child. As I grew older I found that my natural left-handedness had come more to the fore and given me the advantage of being somewhat ambidextrous.

I replied to her inquiry nearly as casually as she had brought it up. "Well, we hardly got a chance to get to know each other last night, now did we?" I said. She nodded in reply.

"Quite right, Mr. Cochrane, quite right. Next time I won't be so casual," she said. I took my mark in response, sensing that I may have gained a slight advantage of surprise but still fully aware of my disadvantages in the match. She took her place again and said, "Mark!"

I touched her foil with mine, a small metal click as the blades connected. "Mark!" I said in reply. She tapped my foil.

"*En garde!*"

The next few seconds were a whirlwind of action, her foil flashing at me from every conceivable direction. I gave ground as fast as I could, trying to find space to set up a defense and hoping to avoid getting pinned. I circled left and tried to duck under her thrust to my open shoulder but she was too fast and caught the webbing of my tunic, sounding the scoring bell. One-nil. It had all taken mere seconds.

"Come on now, Cochrane, surely you can do better than that!" she taunted me. "What *do* they teach you at that Academy? Child's swordplay?" She went back to her mark. I took several deep breaths to buy myself time, then took my mark again, this time right-handed.

"Trickery doesn't suit you, Cochrane. I hope you're better right-handed," she said.

"Me too," I replied. This time I tapped her sword.

"*En garde*," I said.

I stepped back and this time she didn't charge, sizing up my right-handed skills, circling the mat furiously with her foil down at her side. I kept mine fully extended.

"You can't win if you never attack, you know," she said. Again this was obviously designed to distract me while she plotted her strategy. I said nothing in return, but dropped my foil in reply. She hesitated only a second before charging across the mat at me.

Our foils clashed again, hers whipping through the air with lightning precision, mine scattering from point to point, barely keeping her at bay. The thrust and parry went on nonstop. She pursued me from corner to corner, always attacking, with rarely a moment where we were not engaged. I judged we had been at it almost three minutes when she made her move.

She came in with her foil low, in a deep crouch as she flashed at me. My parry was relatively simple until I realized her true strategy. In two short lunges she was inside my right leg with her left and pushed me backward while our foils were locked, mine inside of hers. She drove her shoulder into my chest.

"Oomph!" I let out as the air escaped my lungs. I started to fall backward over her leg as she pushed me down to the mat with her free hand. Instinctively my arms spread out to cushion my fall and she released her foil, whipping it into my chest nearly the same moment as I hit the mat. The scoring bell sounded again. Two-nil.

I lay on my back, embarrassed and clearly outclassed again, or at least outsmarted. But I had learned one thing, I was good enough that I had frustrated her into making a move that was outside the rules of the game, at least the official rules. I sprang to my feet, whipping off my mask.

"Commander Kierkopf!" I shouted, more than a bit angry. "I didn't know that such tactics were allowed under the rules."

She turned back to me from her bench where she was taking a drink between games. "Formal fencing rules, yes. But we are engaged in sword fighting, my young man. We are in the military and this is no contest. It's training. So you'd better learn to fight as you would in real life. Real life conflict is not a game." I rolled my mask back down over my face to show my displeasure at her underhandedness. My mother had taught me to always respect a lady, but clearly this woman was no lady. "If you're not up to it, we can quit now," she said, taunting me again and challenging my pride.

I replied by taking my mark.

Seconds later we were engaged in battle. This time I didn't trifle with swordplay. She lunged at my left shoulder with her foil, missing the webbing and a third point—and the match—by mere millimeters. I stepped forward into the open space she had left by her attack and grappled with her, grabbing her firmly by the wrists with both hands. She resisted and I found her surprisingly strong, sinewy and difficult to move off her mark. Both our foils fell to the mat. In a match of pure physical strength I was always going to win. As she stepped in to gain leverage I put my left foot down on her right and pushed her to the mat. We landed with a thud and rolled. Again I was surprised by her strength and resiliency. After a few more moments of struggle I used my superior strength and size to roll her on her back, pin her arms under my knees, and then reached out to grab the nearest foil. It was hers. I drove it into the webbing of her tunic, right between her breasts. A killing stroke. The scoring bell sounded.

I stayed on top of her, holding her down.

"Let me up, goddamn you!" Then she cursed at me in German. I let her up, but only after gathering my own foil as well. When I stood the court erupted in cheers, whistles, and catcalls. It seemed that during our tête-à-tête we had drawn a bit of a crowd from among the other officers in the gym. There were now twenty or so ringing our court. I acknowledged the cheers from the crowd by bowing deeply from the waist and then holding up her foil as a prize.

"Give me back my foil!" she demanded under the cover of the cheering.

"Ask nicely," I said, loud enough for everyone to hear. She tapped her foot angrily, hands on hips, her mask still drawn down.

"Would you please return my foil, Commander," she said in an even tone.

"Why certainly, Commander Kierkopf," I said, making sure that everyone in the crowd, mostly Quantar officers, knew who I had just bested. I hesitated a second, then got a roundly evil idea. I took her foil and snapped it over my knee, then tossed the pieces over to her. The crowd roared in laughter and approval.

Dobrina Kierkopf looked down at her broken foil, then kicked the pieces off the mat. She went to the wall and grabbed the first foil off the rack, whipping it around as she came.

"Game time is over, Cochrane!" she said as she returned to the mat. This time she charged me without taking her mark. I scrambled to pick up my foil and scurry away from her, uncertain of my next strategy. One thing I couldn't do was repeat my assault tactics from the last game. She ran at me in full rage, an all-out attack.

"Yeee-ah!" she screeched as our swords clashed, metal glinting off metal in a fury of motion, point and counterpoint. She kicked me hard in the side, just below the ribs. It knocked the wind out of me, and I grasped her sword hand at the wrist to keep her from taking advantage. She did the same to me but I kept my body clear of her so that she couldn't repeat the kick. We danced around the mat in our struggle, arms locked and feet balancing us against each other. She dipped her right knee then and instantly I knew what she was up to. Faking her knee buckling to get me out of position; the tactics of mistake. With my body weight committed forward I had only one option, and that was to "agree" with her. I let my body fall toward her as she intended me to do, then instead of falling and allowing myself to be rolled over, I released her sword hand and grabbed her by the neck, placing my left knee under her thigh as support for her body. I rolled her over my knee as I swung her around, sending her flying forward with her back to me as I pivoted and brought my foil around in a flash, whipping across the webbing of her left buttocks as it flashed through the protective clothing. The bell sounded. Two-two.

The crowd had erupted in my favor again, and the cheering was wild as Dobrina checked her pants. Despite the shielding from the protection field the fabric was torn out at her buttocks. She looked at it for only a second before returning to her mark. I knew that it would leave a sizable welt, I'd had that kind of injury before, but not in that precise location.

Dobrina motioned me back to the marks, anxious to get on with the match.

"Very clever, young man," she said as we took our marks. "But now the match is on the line. No more games from me."

"Nor from me," I said, knowing full well I would do anything in my power to win. We clashed metal and the dance began again. We circled each other, testing, probing defenses. The crowd grew silent. Dobrina, as always, was the aggressor. I fended her off several times before opening my mouth.

"Come now, Commander! The crowd here wants a winner! You are so patient you're boring them!" They laughed.

"You could choose the attack, Mr. Cochrane," she taunted.

"I could, and be given away as a fool," I said back. She nodded.

"So we both grow weary of the chase. Very well then." She lunged forward with her foil lancing out at me, forcing me back as she came. I deflected a right-handed thrust with my backhand and in an instant I saw her foil in the air, floating free. I thought I had disarmed her and had only to deliver the point to win the match. But as I watched, almost in slow motion, I saw too late what she was really doing. Her left hand grasped the foil as it drifted through the air, closing down on it expertly as she changed hands, then whipping it into my exposed rib cage.

The scoring bell sounded.

The crowd let out a groan of disappointment. My hands went to my knees as I stood at midcourt, my lesson over for the day. I took off my helmet and looked to Dobrina, who was already packing her training bag with her back to me. She was out of her tunic in seconds and into lounging shells, wiping her sweat-beaded face.

I took congratulations from some of the officers who had watched the match and received more than one offer of a drink in the officer's lounge later than evening, which I intended to follow up on. Eventually I made it to my bench and unzipped my tunic.

Dobrina came across the mat. She looked down at me, her hair pulled harshly back, her face showing an outward expression of placidity. But I knew different. No doubt I had pushed her to her limits.

"Thank you for the match, Commander," she said as she walked past me to the women's locker room.

"Thank *you*, Commander," I said quietly to her back as she disappeared through the door.

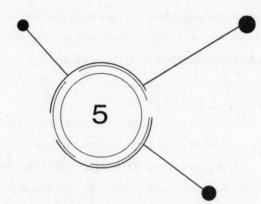

On High Station and Aboard the Outrigger Cordoba

Three hours later I was showered, packed, and out of my cabin, taking my gear to the shuttle port to stow it in advance of loading onto the outrigger for the trip to High Station Candle. I left a message for Commander Kierkopf on the station net, but the com relayed that she had already departed the station. For where, it didn't say.

I resolved to look her up the next time I came to High Station, and then decided to use my remaining hour before I left to make a last call home.

The longwave in the private call covey took unusually long to connect. No doubt military traffic was taking bandwidth priority over commercial calls with the launch of *Starbound* imminent. I got my father's office at the Admiralty after about ten seconds of blank screen. Madrey Margretson answered the call.

"Hello, Madrey," I said.

"I thought you might call today," she said, smiling warmly. "Your father's in a conference again, but I'll ring him. I'm sure he'll take your call."

"Thank you," I said, then waited as the Admiralty banner replaced Madrey's image on the screen. Scant seconds later it was gone and my father came on the channel from his office.

"Hello, son," he said. "Just an hour or so away now, I see." I couldn't really read him well, but he looked as if something was troubling him yet again. It was a look I'd seen on his face many times since I had joined the navy, if not so frequently when I was growing up. I supposed he had hidden the stress of his position to his family that whole time.

"Yes, sir," I said. "I'm off on an outrigger to Candle. Just thirty-two passengers and plenty of spare legroom. Should be more than enough time to read up on *Impulse*'s longscope and her specs," I said. It wasn't really what I wanted to talk about, but I was making polite conversation, as I believed an officer should do.

"Don't hit the books too hard, son. This may be your last real leisure time for at least six months," he said back, also making conversation before getting down to the point. Assuming there was one, this time.

"I'll probably take that advice," I said, trying to act like I wasn't concerned about my first deep-space mission, one that had gotten considerably more complicated in the last few days.

"Next time you're in range, be sure and call home, or to Government House," he said. "I'll be leaving this office in the next week, and Jonathon Wesley will be assuming the role of Grand Admiral of the Union Navy."

He was telling me in not so many words that he would be out of the military decision-making process shortly. I took this as an attempt to reassure me that he would still be running Quantar's civilian government as Commander in Chief. It didn't work. It was clear that the safety net I had relied on during my training days as a cadet was gone.

It was also clear that this is what the powers that be wanted. I had to grow up fast, and from now on I'd be dealing with Admiral Wesley.

"I'll be sure not to make that mistake, sir," I said. A long silence fell over us both then. I stood there staring at my father's image while he looked back at me. What went unspoken was our mutual fear that this could be the last time we saw each other. I could tell from his face that he was worried about me, his last son, heading off to parts unknown. The reality also sunk in for me that I was heading out on my first deep-space mission, directly into a battle zone. He finally broke the silence between us.

"Is this channel secure?" he asked. I verified my Union Navy security code.

"It is now," I said.

"Good. One other thing, son. Serosian sent a message directly to the Admiralty and Admiral Wesley was good enough to forward it to me," he said. "It seems the Historians have analyzed the telemetry from the *Impulse* incident and confirmed that the frequency of the Hoagland Wave that hit the ship couldn't be anything but artificial. In fact it's completely outside the natural spectrum, but it also didn't match with anything in the existing Imperial catalog. In short, it's a chimera."

I tried to appear confident, mostly to reassure him.

"So it's as we suspected," I said. "Any other good news?" I asked, trying to joke but getting no response. The awkward silence descended again and it seemed clear it was time to sign off.

"One last question, sir. When will the government be announcing news of the *Impulse* incident to the public?" I said.

"Not for a while, son. We have to see how this second mission to Levant turns out, and so much of that is about you," he replied. I had nothing to say to that, and again the silence fell.

"I've got to catch my shuttle, sir," I said. He looked at me for a long time, but as usual, I couldn't read his face or his emotions.

"Good luck, son," he finally said. I waved back at him.

"Thank you, sir. Goodbye," I said, then signed off the secure channel. Before I could cut the line completely I was switched back to Madrey's channel and her face reappeared on my display.

"Young man," she said to me. "You do us all proud out there, you hear me?"

"I hear you, madam," I said, even though I knew she had no idea what my father and Wesley were asking of me.

"Good luck, Peter."

I smiled back at her. "Thank you, Madrey," I replied. Then I cut the channel and hustled out of the covey to my waiting shuttle.

An hour later and I was on my way to Candle aboard the outrigger *Cordoba*. She was a new class of ship for interplanetary space travel and the fastest civilian ship in service. The outriggers were used mostly for transporting business passengers between High Station Quantar and Candle, which was the outlying station where most imports arrived first. Anything that got me to Candle quicker was fine with me, and *Cordoba* seemed like just the ticket.

I shared a double berth with George Layton. John Marker took up the double behind us all by himself. He had obviously continued his drinking from our previous adventure and was sound asleep and snoring inside of ten minutes after we detached from High Station.

It would be good to have friends I knew with me. Our relationships would obviously have to change due to the nature of our new mission, but even a familiar face or two in the Great Dark would be helpful.

I liked Layton. He was easy to talk to, with an outgoing personality. We chatted about various aspects of our new mission, about how things would change due to serving on *Impulse* instead of *Star-*

bound and the like. I pondered how much to tell him about my orders from Wesley, or about the *Impulse* incident, or even about my encounter with Dobrina Kierkopf. I decided that protecting him from my private complications was the honorable thing to do, for now. Inevitably though, the conversation turned to personal matters.

"So where did you grow up anyway?" I asked. We'd been working together for two years and I realized that I didn't know where he was from, a gap perhaps from being a bit too focused on my own training at the Academy.

"At KendalFalk, on the Northern Continent. Not far from your family's North Palace," Layton said.

"I know it, though I can't say I know it well," I replied. "Since my mother passed away we haven't spent much time at the North Palace. In fact I can't remember the last time we were there."

"When you were sixteen," said Layton matter-of-factly.

"What? How do you know?" He shrugged.

"You don't remember?" he said.

"Honestly, George, no," I said. He looked put off by that.

"We played against each other in a soccer match when you were in the juniors with New Briz Blues. I was with Shepperton Caledonian," he said.

"Really? I remember those matches! Summer of '72, right?"

"Right."

"What position did you play?" I asked.

"Left back," he said. That got me thinking.

"I was right wing in our starting eleven!" I said. "We must have played against each other!" Layton sighed.

"You don't even remember, do you?" he said.

I got defensive. "What, did I do something bad?" I was worried I had.

"Bad for me, yeah," he replied. Now he didn't seem to want to talk about it.

"What? Tell me!" I insisted. He sighed again and seemed to resign himself to telling me the story.

"You were sticking out on the right wing," he started, "and since I'm kind of stocky and all, I was able to keep pushing you farther and farther out, cutting off your crosses, that kind of stuff. I was walking back up on a goal kick and one of my mates complimented me, and I said, 'It's easy, he always goes outside.' Well, you must have heard me 'cause next time you got the ball you went inside and I was left holding my jock strap while you cut into the box and crossed to one of your strikers for the first goal. After that your confidence shot way up and I couldn't handle you. Your side won 4-1, I think, and you scored the third. Caledonian cut me the next day."

I looked at Layton, rather embarrassed.

"Oh. So that was you?" I said.

"Yeah, Peter. That was me."

"Sorry," I said. He elbowed me in mock anger.

"You finished my soccer career early and I joined the navy. The next spring you quit when everyone had you picked for a first team place with the Blues. Why'd you do it?" he asked.

"You mean quit soccer? Same as you. I wanted to join the navy and see the stars," I said.

"You gave up a pro soccer career."

"Yeah," I said, "I did. And I've never regretted it." And I meant that, too. I left out the part about wanting to follow in my brother's footsteps, about stepping up to my adult responsibilities. I wanted to change topics badly and get off my almost-soccer career.

"So tell me about your family," I said. He leaned back and folded his hands together.

"There's just my parents, me, and my little sister, Lynne," he said.

"You never told me you had a sister," I said casually.

He smiled at me. "Damn straight! She's only seventeen and she joins the navy next year—I wanted to keep her away from you."

I was surprised at his comment. "Really? Why?" I said.

"You have an influence on the ladies, Peter, whether you know it or not. And I'm her big brother and I need to protect her."

"From me?" He elbowed me playfully again.

"Yes, damn well from you! You really don't know the effect you have on women!"

I looked out the window. "Apparently I don't," I said, my thoughts drifting to Dobrina Kierkopf. "But I'll be sure and try out this mythical superpower on Lynne Layton when you introduce us."

"Fat chance of that ever happening!" he said. Again I changed the subject.

"So what's home like?" I asked.

"We live on a big ranch in the Caderlands. Two thousand head of cattle and five thousand pigs. My father exports beef and pork to the big southern cities, New Bournemouth, Q-City, New Briz, all of them," he said. "And off-planet as well, mostly to Candle."

"To Candle?" I asked, out of curiosity.

"Well not to Candle really. Candle is just the way port. To the new colonies, the High Stations, Carinthia, even the newly rediscovered First Empire worlds, when we find them. It's exciting times for my father. Exciting if you're a businessman, anyway."

I nodded and then things went silent between us. I thought again about Wesley's orders and what they might mean for my friends. Nothing good came to mind.

"They say she's cursed, you know," Layton said out of the blue. The statement caught me completely off guard.

"I'm sorry, did you say cursed? Are you talking about *Impulse*?" Layton nodded. "I didn't know that you knew about the attack." He shrugged again.

"That's been the scuttlebutt on the longwave nets for days. Apparently the Carinthians are a superstitious lot. As soon as they got in range of Candle the IM's started flying through the ansible network.

The story's been suppressed on the newsnets, but it's well enough known amongst the merchants. When they arrived at Candle the crew filled the bars. Said they'd never seen anything like it. Now they think she's cursed," Layton said.

"Great," I said, "that's just what we need. A superstitious lot of Germans onboard ready to flash their crosses and spell their hexes at the first sign of trouble." I was actually thinking about whether this development would make my assignment tougher or easier to carry out, if the need arose.

The conversation ended there and Layton talked me into playing some virtual games to kill the time. After I beat him on a tactical scenario game, a shoot-'em-up, and a soccer game, he gave up and decided to nap. I shut off my own light and crossed my arms, trying to sleep, fearing it wouldn't come.

The massive mitt of John Marker woke me up just a few minutes before we docked at Candle. To my surprise, I found I had finally drifted off.

"Didn't want you to miss your first glimpse of a Lightship, boys, cursed or not," he said to Layton and me.

"Thanks, John," I said, then activated my viewers to get my first look at *Impulse*. The outrigger had her longcams focused on the lee-ward wing of the station, "downwind" from the jump point. There were multiple merchant ships attached to the docking ports like puppies suckling their mothers. As we continued to circle the giant station just a bit faster than the spin of Candle herself, the outline of *Impulse* came into view, stern first, then creeping along her central axis, silver-and-chrome-colored splendor emerging into the distant light of Q-prime.

A few moments more and I could see the dark charcoal smears, no doubt where she had taken the hit from the Hoagland Wave, and the ragged rips in her side. I wondered about the crew that had lost their lives aboard her. I wondered what they had gone through, if they had suffered. It made me that much more resolved to complete my mission any way I could.

Otherwise, she looked as magnificent as our own *Starbound*, hanging like a glistening jewel against the black velvet of space. Marker squeezed his head in between Layton and me and broke my rapture at my new assignment, looking in at the view I had on my screen and smiling. Then he gripped me and Layton by the shoulders and gave us a friendly shake.

"Now that, my friends," he said, "is a Lightship."

I couldn't have agreed more.

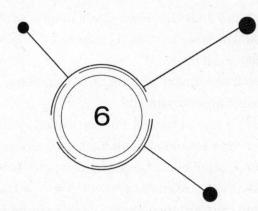

On High Station Candle

I stepped off the docking ramp of the outrigger and onto the deck of High Station Candle for the first time, Marker and Layton to either side of me. I was greeted by a young Carinthian staff ensign from *Impulse* herself, who snapped to attention and greeted me formally.

"Commander Cochrane, I'm Ensign Claus Poulsen, your assistant 'scopeman and attaché," he said in a moderate Teutonic accent. "Welcome to the Unified Space Navy."

"At ease, Poulsen," I said, offering my hand. He shook it with a smile. Poulsen was young, maybe nineteen, and didn't look like he shaved much. His skin was white with a firm pinkish tone, ginger hair stuck out from under his cap, and there was a bit of plumpness to his face. I guessed he wasn't of pure Germanic descent like most of the Carinthian officers. And he looked vaguely familiar.

Poulsen clicked his fingers and two ratings even younger than him quickly came up and gathered my bags from me.

"I'll keep my shoulder bag, Ensign. What's with all the attention?" I asked.

"Captain Zander has ordered you to meet with him at your first chance, sir. I'm to see to it," said Poulsen.

"What about my bags?"

"They'll be brought up directly to your suite," he said. I turned and smiled at my companions.

"Suite?" I said, surprised. Poulsen smiled again.

"I wouldn't get too excited, sir. You have your own bath, a bed with storage, some bookcases and a desk with two guest chairs. It's not exactly the LaandersPlatz in New Vee," he said. I smiled at the reference to the Carinthian capital city's finest hotel.

"Doesn't have to be, Ensign, doesn't have to be," I said. Frankly, I was excited just at the thought of something other than a standard junior officer's berth. Poulsen motioned for us to begin walking and I followed him down the access corridor and onto the promenade of Candle, Marker and Layton trailing.

"What about my men here?" I asked. Poulsen nodded.

"All taken care of, sir," he said. "Lieutenant Layton has a junior officer's berth one deck down from you. Corporal Marker is set up with the marine detachment on the hangar deck, sir."

I stopped. "No need to delay them on my account, Ensign," I said. He quickly waved another rating over and he came and got Layton's bag. Marker wouldn't have it.

"Just show me the way," he said in his gruff accent. The rating waved the two men off in a different direction. I nodded for them to follow.

"We'll catch up as soon as I have time," I said. With that they both popped off salutes and headed off down a long corridor.

"Service port," said Poulsen. "We'll be going down the Promenade. I think the captain wants to show off his ship to you, sir."

"Lead the way, Ensign." With that, we were off.

Candle had an abundance of viewing ports, and as we walked I had occasion to examine the asteroid that gave the station her name.

Candle was a yellow and orange sulfur-scarred rock, pockmarked with craters, with the station carved out of one end. It was efficient, no doubt, but also very ugly.

As we continued on, *Impulse* became visible, hanging in space at the end of a long crystal and metal spider-legged tunnel. She was enormous.

I stood and stared as I waited in line with repair crews and materiel vendors for my turn through security to get into the boarding tunnel. I went to the port window to take her in as much as I could. Crews were covering the scarring to her amidships with the same superconductive compound the Earthmen had provided for building her in the first place. The repair crews extruded new skin over the damaged areas, and the compound, a unique form of nanotechnology from Earth's science labs, raced to form itself perfectly into the wounds. It was an amazing sight.

There was a golden glow coming from *Impulse*'s window ports. The ports were aesthetically pleasing but would never have been possible without the protective Hoagland Field the ship generated from the twin gravimetric drives at her stern. The forward third of the ship was a long, oval-shaped tube with the conning tower on top and protective baffle shields covering her nose. The conning tower was another purely aesthetic touch, again made possible by the enveloping Hoagland Field, which let the cruiser glide through normal or hyper-dimensional space with equal grace. Since the field provided maximum protection equally to any part of the ship, the Lightship designers had exercised their dramatic license and chosen the conning tower for the bridge.

It was the baffles that had failed *Impulse* at Levant, but they could only do their job if they were properly engaged to catch the enveloping Hoagland Field. Clearly, for whatever reason, they had not been prepared at the time of the accident. The dark scarring present on her hull showed that plainly enough.

Impulse's amidships were wider and flatter than her forward tube, bulging nearly twice as wide but still managing to keep a sleek appearance. This section contained the major crew quarters, sickbay, science labs, and operational centers, as well as the landing bay for the onboard shuttles she kept as exploration vehicles.

To the aft she grew still wider, the gravimetric plasma drive generators pushed out away from the main hull of the ship, protected by the delta wings and winglets of the Hoagland HD drive generators. The final section was the stern, stacked between the Hoaglands and both serving as a rear defensive tower and holding *Impulse*'s drive regulators and sub-light impellers.

When I turned back from the window Poulsen had managed to get us clearance.

I rejoined Poulsen and we passed through security and into the tunnel. The views of *Impulse* from the tunnel gave me an even better view of the damage done to her. I looked through the glass to see a crew ripping out the longscope sensor array. Whoever had used it before me clearly would not be getting another chance. The longscope officer was the one who should have detected the rogue HD displacement wave before anyone else.

Finally we were at the main hatch. I saluted the lieutenant of the guard, who was wearing Carinthian green but with a USN crest and patches at the arms, and handed him my papers. I was surprised to see both him and Poulsen in their country's uniform. I had been under the impression that USN white was the standard dress aboard the Lightships. The lieutenant glanced at my papers and then compared me to my photo, asked me to validate my digital thumbprint, which I did, then waved me through. I took in a deep breath and let it out, stepping on to the deck of an in-service Lightship for the first time.

They said you couldn't notice the output of a functioning Hoagland Field, but I always did. A slight tingle of warmth at the back of my neck, an almost imperceptible flow of fluid down the spine. I supposed it would help if we knew how the field actually *worked*, or what it *was*, but the Earth Historians kept that information on a need-to-know basis. Somehow, though, I always knew when I was on board a ship with a functioning Hoagland Field.

Poulsen and I started down *Impulse*'s main galleria, what he had called the Promenade. It ran from stem to stern, cutting the ship into port and starboard, and served as the main makeway for everything from crew to cargo to parade grounds. As I looked down *Impulse*'s length the Promenade swept away into the distance, the deck curving up and out of sight a hundred meters behind me and nearly the same distance forward. *Impulse*, like her sister *Starbound*, was nearly three hundred meters long and a full sixteen decks deep, not counting the conning tower, making them easily the biggest vessels humans had built in a century or more.

I'd been aboard *Starbound* enough times to know that her main gallery was nothing compared to this. The Carinthians had spared no expense. What the QRN treated as a utility corridor the Carinthian Navy had converted into a grand presentation of their culture, quite literally a space-borne art museum cutting through the center of their greatest warship. I couldn't help but be impressed.

As we walked I noted full-size marble sculptures in classical styles dotting the hallway, with intricate woodwork and gilding around the coved ceiling a good fourteen feet up. Fanciful murals were painted on the blank canvas of the ceiling, like the pictures I'd seen of historical European palaces on Old Earth. Paintings of ancient battles so large they took up entire walls were hung between the sculpture alcoves. Doors leading to officer's quarters or any important room were made of dark hardwoods. One of these doors was open and revealed an actual library with hundreds of books and wooden bookcases.

"That's the Historian's quarters," noted Poulsen. "We don't go in there often."

"Can't wait to meet him," I said, with only a touch of sarcasm. It was true for more than one reason. I needed to size him up and see if he would be amenable to my secret orders, should they become necessary to carry out.

We passed a pair of portraits flanking the corridor on either side of a central rotunda. The portraits were lit by a dome that glowed with a reasonable facsimile of natural light. The subjects were the current Grand Duke of Carinthia, Henrik Feilberg, and the Lady Bertrude, his wife, no doubt from an earlier time in their lives. I paused to consider Henrik Feilberg's stern dark face, and wondered what the daughter of a man like that might look like. I was, after all, no doubt intended to eventually make the acquaintance of the Princess Karina Feilberg as part of my diplomatic duties. Thankfully an examination of the Lady Bertrude in her younger days revealed a gentle beauty with fair skin and hair and a pleasantly oval face. One could always hope.

Presently Ensign Poulsen ushered me along. "I need to get you to your cabin, sir," he said.

I eyed him. Something was up. "I thought you said the captain wanted to see me right away?" I asked.

"You're sure you don't want to examine your cabin first? Unload your bags, freshen up and get settled a bit?" he responded.

I stopped and looked around again at the luxurious surroundings of the galleria. No doubt my cabin would be of a similar class.

"Actually, Poulsen," I said, handing him my shoulder brief, "why don't you go on ahead and take care of things in my cabin for me. I'll be along after I meet with Captain Zander."

"But . . . sir . . . ." stumbled out Poulsen as I handed him the brief. "I've got a dress green uniform laid out for you in the cabin, sir. Your size was sent ahead. Proper attire and all that."

I looked down at my QRN uniform: dark blue with gold piping,

Cochrane family crest of three boars' heads, orange chevrons, and Southern Cross. I decided I'd make my first impression on the captain of *Impulse* wearing my own family's colors.

"I'm afraid that my Quantar blues will have to do for now, Ensign. Just point the way to the captain's cabin and take the rest to my suite. I'll be along after the meeting."

"But, sir, standard duty uniform aboard *Impulse* is Carinthian green. You don't want to meet the captain—"

"Actually, Ensign, I do want to meet him, just as I am. Now point the way, and carry on." The way I said it left no room for further discussion. Poulsen reluctantly obliged with directions and I headed off to a portside lifter as Poulsen made his way up to officer's country. He only paused once to look back and I waved in a friendly manner. No doubt part of his orders were to get me properly introduced to the Carinthian Navy way of doing things. I smiled a bit as the lifter doors closed. Captain Lucius Zander would just have to meet with me for the first time on my own terms.

I knocked firmly on the real wood door to Captain Zander's cabin. More precisely, I knocked on one of the *two* wood doors to his cabin. Again, it seemed the Carinthians had spared no expense. The door was opened from the inside by an ensign. I nodded at him as I proceeded through into the largest shipboard room I had ever seen.

It was a good twelve feet up to the ceilings, something that would have been regarded as a tremendous waste of space aboard a QRN ship. The walls were full of wooden bookcases stuffed with leatherbound editions. What wall space wasn't taken up by bookcases was filled with portraits, again of the Grand Duke and his wife, along with a hunting party scene and a portrait of an unidentified lady, possibly

Mrs. Zander, I surmised. A large cabinet full of naval souvenirs and brass sailing relics, complete with a large supply of liquor, took up nearly one whole wall.

An intricate and oversized map desk flanked by Carinthian and Union Navy flags filled the back third of the room. In front of me in the center of the room was a sitting area with a formal sofa, coffee table and two leather chairs on either side, all facing a simulated fireplace burning with a soft orange glow. The sitting space was pulled together by an exotic Persian rug full of muted greens, reds, and yellows, the colors of the Carinthian flag. I stood at the front of the room near the doors and snapped to attention, feeling as if I could have been naked, I felt so out of place.

The man seated in the center of the sofa put down his coffee cup on the table and stood slowly and with purpose, acknowledging me with a nod and then waving me forward in a welcoming manner.

"Come in, my boy. And at ease," said Captain Lucius Zander, all five and a half feet of him. He was wiry and slight, with exceptionally long blond-white hair. By looks I placed him in his mid-fifties, but I couldn't be sure. His gravel-sharp voice made him sound as if he were twice that age.

I stepped forward, tucking my navy cap under my arm as I came. Zander reached out to shake my hand and then clasped it with both of his when he took it. "Good to meet you, Lieutenant Commander Cochrane. Good to meet you," he said. His eyes were a steel gray and I could see from his demeanor how he had ascended to captaincy of his world's most important vessel. He may have been slight in stature but with that voice and those eyes I believed he could have withered grape vines in summer if he so chose.

Zander motioned me to one of the leather chairs and I sat down.

"I'm just finishing my morning coffee, Commander Cochrane, would you like some?" he asked.

"No, thank you, Captain," I said instinctively, and instantly regretted it. It was always impolite to refuse an offer of comfort from a superior officer, at least in the QRN. It made it seem as though you felt you were too good to be one of those types who liked to play on a captain's favor. My regret came from the fact that it was nearly midnight according to my QRN clock, not prime time for coffee, but here on *Impulse* it seemed as if the morning watch was just beginning. I glanced up at an ornate wood wall clock; it said 0645. After a moment Zander took another drink and then started right in with the formalities.

"I just wanted to offer my sincerest condolences on the loss of your countrymen. Your Admiral Wesley has informed me that you had a particular attachment to one of the young lieutenants aboard the First Contact shuttle. Lieutenant Decker was a fine officer, and a fine young lady, and I enjoyed having her aboard *Impulse*," said Zander, quietly and sincerely.

"Thank you, sir," I said. Natalie's death was the last thing I wanted to talk about. Every reminder of her struck a chord of pain in me, pain I was trying to get past to embrace my new duties. Perhaps proper grieving would come later.

Then Zander focused those eyes on me, took in a deep breath and said, "What happened at Levant was a tragedy, one I intend to set right. This crew has been through a lot. We all lost someone we cared about that day."

I didn't really know how to respond to that. They had all lost someone, a friend, a shipmate perhaps, but I had lost the girl who was my first love. I blurted out another "thank you, sir," for the offered condolences, then hoped the conversation would go anywhere away from this subject. Fortunately, it did.

"Well then, no doubt you have a great deal of unpacking to do, Mr. Cochrane," said Zander. "I want you to know that I won't be expecting you on bridge duty today until noon. We depart tomorrow for our return trip to Levant and you can report for full duty then. But I do run a tight ship. I expect my officers on the bridge most days by 0700. We take thirty minutes for lunch at noon and the day shift ends at five. I expect all my senior officers for dinner nightly at 1900 in the officer's lounge. The rest of your time is your own, except for Sundays when you are excused from morning duty to attend Church Worship, if you go in for that sort of thing."

"Yes, sir," I said, feeling weary already. The captain looked up at me.

"Yes, you understand, or yes, you attend Worship?" he asked.

"Yes to both, sir," I said back.

"Good," he said forcefully, "I like a man with morals. It's no fun putting your life on the line with atheists in space."

I nodded at this, again unsure how to respond. The fact was I wasn't really sure I wasn't an atheist. I just hadn't had much time to contemplate it, and I'd grown up going to Worship on Sundays.

"One other matter," said Zander. "I'd like you to meet with Tralfane, our Historian, before your first duty. What with the two of you working the 'scope together, I think it would be best if you got off on the right foot."

"He was on my list, sir," I said. Zander nodded.

"Good. Our previous 'scopeman never really had a good working relationship with him, and it cost us dearly at Levant." Then Zander looked away again. I could tell from the way he spoke that he took *Impulse*'s failure personally.

"I should also like to meet with your exec at the earliest opportunity," I offered. "Just to get more familiar with *Impulse*'s key personnel and my duties." Zander glanced at his watch.

"The new exec should be here any minute," he said.

"New exec, sir?" he nodded.

"We lost our XO at Levant, Commander. His replacement is an officer I have been grooming for several years. Capable, competent, and no-nonsense. You will be learning from one of my best," he said.

Just then I heard a knock at the door.

"Ah," said Zander, standing. "That would be her."

"Her?" I asked. He nodded.

"The commander and I have served together for quite a while, since she was an ensign, and it's her old job you'll be taking," he said. I stood automatically to greet my direct superior as the door opened. I was surprised that I already knew her.

"Lieutenant Commander Peter Cochrane, may I introduce my new Executive Officer, Commander Dobrina Kierkopf," said Zander.

I extended my hand in greeting and she took it. "Commander Cochrane," she said, shaking my hand. "So good to meet you." Her tone gave away nothing to indicate that we had met before.

I returned her handshake and tipped my head slightly in greeting.

"And so good to meet you as well, Commander Kierkopf," I replied, being equally coy. We all sat down, Zander and Dobrina on the sofa, I in the increasingly uncomfortable leather chair. The next few minutes were taken up with casual conversation about duties and protocol, though nothing was said of my uniform choice. Zander seemed satisfied at this exchange and then glanced at his watch at five minutes to seven, by the wall clock.

"More to come, Commander, but for now I have to make my appearance on the bridge or those rogues will start slacking. As I said, feel free to take until noon to report, and Commander Kierkopf here can continue to fill you in on the run of the ship." Then he stood and Dobrina and I followed suit.

"Thank you, sir," I said. "It's an honor to serve with you."

"Nonsense, my boy, the honor is mine. Here's to hoping we can resolve this Levant blockade and get back to doing what the Lightship fleet was designed to do, opening up new worlds once again." We exchanged handshakes and then he was off to the bridge, followed by his attending ensign. That left Dobrina and me alone. I stood for a second, hands on my hips, looking at the now-shut door and bobbing my head ever so slightly. I had been played by her again, and I didn't like it. I crossed my arms and turned back to Commander Dobrina Kierkopf.

"How—" I started, but she cut me off with a wave of her hand as she sat down on the sofa.

"How did I come to be here? Or how did I get aboard before you?" she said between bites of a croissant and sips of coffee.

"Yes! Both . . . I'm not sure. I just know I don't like it."

"You're not supposed to," she said. "You've got a lot to learn, Lieutenant Commander Cochrane, and I intend to be your teacher." That pissed me off.

"I don't need a teacher, I need a compatriot. You and Poulsen came to Candle to spy on me," I said, getting angrier at the thought of it. "I knew I recognized him from the bar."

"Nonsense," she replied. "I was assigned to *Impulse* by your Admiral Wesley, and I had to meet with him before he would approve me as Zander's XO. The trip to High Station was already planned."

"He sent you to check me out though, didn't he?"

She shrugged. "You're a very valuable asset to the USN and they don't want to lose you on your first mission."

"So you're my babysitter," I said. She stood to go.

"If you like. It doesn't really matter. I'm here and that's just the way of it. Now come on, let's get you to your cabin and get you properly dressed for duty aboard a Carinthian Lightship."

"This is a Union Lightship, madam," I said, just to be cross with her.

"Commanded by Carinthians. You'd be smart to remember that." Then she started for the door.

"Wait," I said, "I need to know—" she interrupted me.

"How I beat you here?" she finished. "It's very simple, young man." She paused, then said, "I just took a faster shuttle."

Again, I was mad, but I hit back fast. "Of course you did. Your travel here came without too much discomfort, I hope?" I asked, alluding to our fencing match and her wounded bottom.

"I am a bit sore," she admitted. "But I've had worse."

"Of course you have."

"Now, can we get on with things?" she said.

"Lead the way," I said. And with that, a new cycle of learning on the job began.

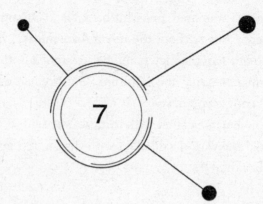

Aboard H.M.S Impulse

An hour later I was in my cabin, arguing with Claus Poulsen.

"But you have to wear it, sir. Captain Zander won't stand for anything but the regs being followed," he insisted, rather excitedly. Poulsen stood on the far side of my bed, which was big enough for two and had an elaborate wooden headboard. Commander Dobrina Kierkopf sat at the foot of the bed, admiring my unworn green Carinthian commander's uniform.

"You would be well advised to listen to him, Cochrane," she said. I turned away from my closet, where I had been busy hanging my clothes and filling my racks with my personal belongings. The stateroom I had been assigned was of course much larger and more elaborate than Poulsen had let on, but I decided he probably didn't know any better. He'd never seen a QRN ship and probably never would.

My stateroom had a separate sleeping area with the closet, bed, and a small chest of drawers built in to the wall. The working area had a workstation complete with a desk, a monitor, chairs, and a sofa facing the bed. I also had a private bath with sink, shower, and separate privy. Luxurious by Quantar standards, standard issue by Carinthian.

Though I wouldn't have asked for such accommodations, I wouldn't turn them down either. Rank hath its privileges.

I turned back to Poulsen and Kierkopf.

"I won't wear it," I said, "not as long as you two and Zander and all the rest insist on wearing your planetary colors. It would be wrong," I said. "And besides that, there's the issue of honoring my world and the sailors we lost."

"Those sailors knew how to follow protocol," said Kierkopf. I looked at her sharply.

"I doubt my countrymen paraded around the decks of *Impulse* in Carinthian green, Commander," I snapped at her.

I dropped the shirt I was folding onto the bed and looked to each of them in turn. "This is supposed to be the *Unified* Space Navy. If none of you wear USN whites, I won't either, and I won't wear the green. It's as simple as that," I said, then returned to my unpacking.

Commander Kierkopf stood and crossed her arms in front of her. "You're a stubborn young man," she said.

"It's a family trait," I replied. She took in a deep breath.

"Cochrane, I'm trying to help you out here," she said. "Zander will have you on his status report every day as a malcontent. His reports carry weight with the navy brass. You'll find your next promotion a lot more difficult to come by with him opposing you," she said. I stopped again and faced my two new compatriots.

"It's odds on my next promotion won't come on this vessel anyway," I said. "I don't think Zander is close to retiring and I doubt you'll be going anywhere soon, Commander, so what difference will it make? Navy brass will at least want us to *appear* to work together. Zander's insistence that we all wear Carinthian green on board goes against that unity, and I would not be honoring my family, my world, or the USN if I gave in."

"But we all wear the USN patches on our sleeves and chest. There's no planetary insignia or family crest anywhere," insisted

Poulsen. I looked at him again. I could see he took this issue seriously, but I wanted him to know that I did as well.

"Fine then," I said. I took my QRN-issue navy jacket from the closet and handed it to Poulsen, then picked up the Carinthian green jacket off the bed. "Have the USN patches and crest removed from the green jacket and attach them to my QRN jacket. Just make sure it's back here in time for my bridge duty, and please return my family crest to me here."

"But, sir!" Poulsen protested as I shoved the jackets into his hands.

"That's my final word, Poulsen, and that's an order. Now get!" I pointed to the door.

Poulsen took the two jackets in one hand and snapped to attention, but I could see he wasn't happy. "Aye, sir," he said, and then was gone through the cabin doors.

Commander Kierkopf eyed me with what I took as a mix of admiration and pity.

"I hope you know what you're doing," she said. I laughed.

"Oh, I don't. I've no idea actually. But I know who I am and why I was put here, and I intend to stand up for my kinsmen and my flag and my country if I have to. I just didn't think I would be put in this position by my captain."

"Zander's a tough man to work for," she said.

"So I've heard."

She smiled and stepped around to my side of the bed, placing her duty beret back on her head as she prepared to leave. It was a pleasant smile that lit up her face, if only for a brief moment. She was no beauty, but I could see what any man might see in her. She was lithe and athletic, with a very feminine body that provided a sharp contrast to her masculine demeanor, which I supposed was necessary in the navy. "I admire your dedication, Cochrane," she said. "I just hope it doesn't get you into too much trouble."

I nodded in agreement. "Me too."

"I'll let you finish," she said, turning to go, "but I'll be back later to discuss your first day on duty."

"I assume as third I'll have my share of long hours covering for both you and Zander."

She smiled again. "Oh, you will. Better take the time to get settled now."

I nodded as she went to the door, then something else came to mind. "Commander, before you leave, there is one more thing I'd like to discuss," I said. She stopped before opening the cabin door.

"Yes?" she said. I hesitated.

"You were in the Academy class of '74. So was my brother Derrick. I was wondering if you knew him." Her smile cracked just slightly at this, barely but noticeably nonetheless.

"That's nothing that I'm willing to discuss," she said, cutting me off. Then she went swiftly through the door, shutting it firmly behind her. I had an answer to my question, and I wasn't sure I liked it.

I called a late breakfast meeting of the QRN commissioned staff at 1030 hours. Commander Kierkopf had provided a small, separate space in the officers' dining room for me and my six Quantar Royal Navy reports. Marine Corporal John Marker sat next to me at the head of the table and across from *Impulse's* new chief helmsman, Lt. George Layton. Lieutenants Cort Drury from Propulsion, Brice Devlin from Engineering, Evangeline Goolagong, my intelligence officer, and of course Wesley's niece, Jenny Hogan of Astrogation, completed the team. Hogan looked incredibly young to me, but her navy bio said she was twenty and she had met the required minimum rating for early qualification, so Wesley had graduated her, and assigned me to watch over her, which I intended to do.

The noncommissioned officers, a warrant officer, two chiefs, and three specialist starmen, all of them the "experienced spacers" Wesley had promised me, had already been assigned and were busy with their new duties.

We'd been at lunch for nearly half an hour just getting to know each other better and going over our assignments. We had barely an hour left before they were due on duty, so I decided to wrap things up. I looked down the table at the faces before me, all of them except Hogan at least a year senior to me, Marker a good three.

"This is the only time we'll meet like this," I said.

"What? Why?" asked Layton. Layton was a likeable fellow, but he wasn't above challenging a superior within the boundaries of his duty. It was a quality I liked about him.

"Because, Mr. Layton, we should associate with the regular crew, not isolate ourselves," I said. "Commander Kierkopf only gave me this time so we could get to know each other better. I consider that task accomplished."

"I think you're right, Commander," said Marker. "Our officers should be seen about the ship, doing their duty, not hiding out together in a clique. I'm in a little bit of a different situation. I should be training with my new team full-time. It's the marine way."

I nodded in agreement. Marker was fit beyond belief, and in physical comparison I felt like a child sitting next to him. If he wanted to train with his marines full-time I wasn't going to stop him.

I looked down the table at the rest of them and started to ask for final reports before calling the meeting to a close. "Evangeline, any new intelligence that you can share?" She smiled, her beautiful white teeth flashing against deep brown skin.

"There's been some longwave chatter and newsnet postings, mostly from merchants operating on the edge of old Imperial space," she said.

"What kind of chatter?" I asked. She shrugged.

"Rumors, mostly. Some snippets about 'ghost ships' shadowing merchant vessels, usually when they jump into or out of the Union systems. Like they're being watched. One even swore he saw an Imperial dreadnought. It just seems the closer we get to the old battle lines from the civil war the more these reports crop up."

"That's a concern," I said. No doubt the closer we got to Imperial treaty space the more likely we would run into some kind of unidentified traffic. I wondered how many of the rumored "ghosts" were actually Imperial ships, or worse, pirates. I tried to smile confidently. "Well Levant was well on our side of the line, so hopefully things will go smoother there than the last time *Impulse* ventured in."

"Not worried about rogue hyperdimensional displacement waves, sir?" asked Marker.

"Always, John," I replied. "But that can't stop us from doing our jobs." There were nods all around and then I made my final point. "We all have to remember that although Quantar and Carinthia were on separate sides during the civil war that broke up the Corporate Empire, we're both part of the Union now along with Earth. As we explore new systems and rediscover others, old wounds from the conflict are likely to crop up. We have to deal with that, and we have to present a unified front, no matter what our personal feelings on the matter." Again there were nods. I asked Jenny Hogan, Drury, and Devlin to quickly give their reports and then we all broke up for our duty stations. On their way out I signaled Marker and Layton, my closest associates, to stay behind for a moment, then shut the door to make sure we had privacy, retaking my seat at the head of the table.

"Mr. Marker, please make sure the marines under your command are ready for Levant. I don't know what to expect, but I think Zander does, and it's not good," I said.

"Trouble ahead, sir?" he asked.

"Likely," I replied.

"What's the real story?" chimed in Layton. I debated not telling them about my orders from Wesley, then decided I had to give them some kind of warning.

"There may be some complications ahead, gentlemen, and I'm going to be needing your help," I said.

"What kind of complications?" asked Layton, pressing for more information.

"The kind none of us want," I said, then poured myself the last of the orange juice as I let that sink in. I looked at them both, and spoke in as serious a tone as I could muster. "I need you both to make a commitment to me personally that if you receive private orders from me during this mission, you will follow them unquestioningly. Do I have that?"

They exchanged looks of concern.

"Yes, sir," said Marker. Layton hesitated.

"It would help to know under what kind of circumstances we might be receiving these private orders, sir," he said.

"I can't tell you that, George," I said, "for your own good." Layton eyed me, reading my face, then looked to Marker, whose glare at him was intense, then nodded.

"I will, sir," he said. I reached out and shook both men's hands.

"Thank you," I said.

A tap at the door interrupted us and Commander Kierkopf came into the room.

"I was just leaving, Commander," said Layton, making a quick exit. Marker followed silently with barely a nod to *Impulse*'s exec. Passing behind her, he stopped at the door to turn and wink back at me before he left. I couldn't help smiling. Commander Kierkopf turned quickly but Marker was already gone.

"Did I just miss something?" she said.

"Nothing important," I replied. "What's up?"

"The Earth Historian is ready to meet with you," she said.

"Tralfane? Now? I was beginning to think this ship didn't have a Historian," I said.

Her smile returned quickly. "We should be so lucky."

I set my glass down on the table. "What about my shift at noon?"

"I'll cover for you with Zander," she offered, "He understands the situation, what with the longscope being Earth technology and all, and he did order you to meet with Tralfane."

I rubbed at my chin. "That he did," I said. She eyed me as I stayed put at the head of the table.

"Do I detect hesitancy in the brave young Quantar commander?" she asked.

"You do not, madam," I said. Her behavior toward me seemed very ambivalent, but despite our rough start I felt she was warming up to me. I started for the door.

"Walk with me, Commander?" I asked. She did as I requested, taking her place next to me as we made our way out of officer country and down the Promenade, heading toward the ship's library and the realm of the mysterious Historian Tralfane.

"I was close to Serosian, the Historian assigned to *Starbound*," I said.

"How close?" she asked.

"Close enough to know there are many secrets the Earthmen built into these vessels we know nothing about. It's technology we can't even comprehend. Usually the Historian and the 'scope officer work closely together, if not in tandem. I trained with Serosian for three years. I picked up on more than a few signals from him."

"Signals?" she asked. I nodded as we walked.

"Enough to know that the technological secrets within this ship are only a beginning. There are far greater secrets our new allies are keeping from us."

"I don't follow you," she said. I slowed my pace before making my next statement, thinking about how far I could go. I liked Commander Kierkopf, and trusted her to be a loyal officer, to Zander at least, and to the USN, if not to me personally. I felt she was a risk worth taking.

"Has it occurred to you, Commander Kierkopf, that perhaps we here on *Impulse* and the other Lightships are in reality not in command of these missions, but are in fact just pawns for the Earthmen?"

"Pawns?" she stopped me with her hand on my arm. "What do you mean?"

"I am a bit of a student of history," I said. "The war that caused the Great Regression, our war, Carinthia and the Corporate Empire versus Quantar and the Republics—was it in fact about republicanism versus empire, Union versus Royalist, or was it something more? The Church, perhaps, using the royal families of the realm to fight as surrogates in a much subtler conflict?"

She began walking again, more slowly, considering my words. I followed beside her.

"If such a conflict existed, and I'm not saying I believe that it did, what form would it take?" she asked.

"A war between the Holy Church and their true enemies."

"Who are?" I could see she was growing impatient with the conversation.

"Legion," I said. She narrowed her eyes at me, doubting now. "Have you ever heard of the Sri?" I asked.

"The Sri? A bit, I suppose. Weren't they priests of some kind in the Corporate Empire?" she asked.

I nodded. "Of a sort. They were founded many centuries ago by a group of research scientists on Old Earth, or at least that's what Serosian told me. They followed the first explorers out into space, as their kind always do. Apparently they were of some influence in the Dragon Court, especially in the latter days of the war. It seems as though they did a good job of wiping themselves from the history books after the war."

"All very interesting, but the civil war ended a century and a half ago. What does that have to do with us, today?" she asked. I had an answer.

"The old Holy Church of Earth banned certain activities, certain sciences, during the Conclave of 2284 C.E. Recombining DNA into bonding groups, human cloning, bio-nanotechnology, and certain mentallic arts. The Sri are said to be experts in all of them, and they use their knowledge—forbidden knowledge—to advance their cause."

She stopped again. "Which is?"

"That's harder to decipher," I said honestly. "Legends say they have tried to establish a group mind, that they want to turn mankind into a single entity. Ruled by them, of course."

"Of course," she said, walking slowly again. "The funny thing about legends is that they have a way of gathering strength simply through their retelling. All very interesting, Commander, but as yet unconvincing."

I had to agree with her. I leaned in close and spoke softly. "One more thing, Commander. Be aware that if it's a choice between our mission and the mission of the Historians, I have no doubt that they will act in their own best interests."

She looked at me with a frown on her face, but said nothing. We were approaching the library doors and I still had one more question to ask of her.

"There is another matter I have to ask you about," I said. She stopped now and stepped in my path, like a challenge.

"Are you sure you want to ask it?" she said. I shook my head.

"I don't want to ask it, but I need to know the answer," I said.

"Be careful, Cochrane," she warned. I didn't heed it.

"Did you know my brother?" I demanded. The suddenness of my confrontation surprised her. Her face flushed, I couldn't tell if it was with anger or embarrassment.

"What are you implying?"

"Nothing," I said, which was true, and it made me think perhaps I should have been implying something.

She straightened her spine, as if making a decision. "I was on the

Minerva when the accident occurred, Peter. I was a lieutenant and I was on damage control duty in Propulsion that day. When the impeller bulkhead blew I was one of the first ones down there to douse the fire. I personally pulled your brother's body out of the hold. He was one of nine we lost that day," she said. "Is that what you wanted to know?"

I shook my head. "I didn't realize—"

"I know," she said. "It is safe to say that I felt your brother's loss more acutely than most. Now, please, don't ask me any more questions about this. I won't answer," she said. I nodded, accepting her explanation for the moment.

She looked down the hallway toward Tralfane's quarters, just a few feet away. "And now, I believe you have a meeting with a Historian, Mr. Cochrane. Best get to it. That's an order."

Then she walked off without another word as I stepped up and knocked firmly on the library door.

I got no immediate response, so I waited a few more seconds and then tried the door handle, which, to my surprise, turned easily, and the door opened.

The library was fascinating. Four walls, two decks tall with a balcony, full of books in wooden shelves from floor to ceiling. There were two separate ladders for climbing to the highest level. I'd never seen so many printed books in one place in my life, not even in a museum. Chairs, research tables, and linked terminals were dispersed around the room in a comfortable manner. Our family had extensive volumes at home, but mostly for show. These days, like most navy personnel, I did most of my reading on a terminal or a plasma pad, or via a com.

Bound books, however, still retained their popularity. Nothing had ever replaced the experience of holding real paper and soft leather in your hands. Oh, you could read faster, you could read while you were asleep, or read via com download and have perfect, instant recall the next day. But no technology could replace the simple fact that human beings read for one primary reason more than any other: they enjoyed it.

I ran my fingers across the bindings of the volumes on the near wall, feeling the snap of the leather on my skin. It was pure tactile pleasure, like nothing I'd experienced since my early school days. A moment later I was scanning titles like *Aircraft Structures* by Perry, *History of the Imperium* by Wallace Shondar, and *Hoagland: The Man and His Vision* by S.D. Morton. My eyes settled on a beautiful brown leather-bound version of Melville's *Moby-Dick, or The Whale* in a case filled entirely with fiction. I'd read *Moby-Dick* in school, years ago, but this volume looked ancient. I couldn't resist and reached out to take it off the shelf. I got a jolt of static shock for my trouble.

"Ouch!" I said out loud, shaking my stinging finger at the sharp pain.

"That case is all virtual volumes," said a voice booming out from behind me, "and they're available on the terminal in your stateroom. The originals are stored back on Earth, in several different museums."

I turned to face the voice. The man who had entered the room was well over six feet tall, perhaps six-and-a-half. He had a full head of salt-and-pepper hair with a predominance of gray at the temples. His face was all sharp angles and craggy lines, worn by years of experiences I could only dream of, though appearance wasn't a useful factor when calculating a Historian's age. The Earthmen were well known for their anti-aging regimens. He wore the traditional garb of the Historians, a formfitting black suit with an insignia of open hands on the chest, signaling an openness to sharing knowledge. But he didn't look like the type to be trifled with, not at all.

"I'm Tralfane, ship's Historian. Lieutenant Commander Peter Cochrane, I presume?" he said.

"Yes, sir," I replied. The "sir" might not have been appropriate, as he technically had no rank, but he was an imposing figure and the honorific just came out of me. I moved to shake his hand, but something about his demeanor stopped me after taking only a few steps.

"How much time do you have on the longscope, Cochrane?" he asked. I found myself responding instantly.

"The requisite two terms at the Academy, three hundred twenty hours of in-service training, and I've spent the odd hour on the 'scope since as an Academy Instructor on *Starbound*."

He looked put out at my response. "That's not much, but it will have to do," he said. He motioned for me to join him at a large wooden reading table. We stood opposite each other with the table between us. He looked at me with an expression that implied not the slightest interest in me as a person, but only in what I could do to assist him in his tasks.

"I will be installing several new displays on the longscope, starting today," he said. "And I've informed Captain Zander of the need for the upgrades."

"Then he's approved them?" I asked.

"Captain Zander has no knowledge of what the upgrades do or why they're needed. I told him only as a courtesy," said Tralfane. That was certainly within his rights as *Impulse*'s Historian, but I found myself doubting that my friend Serosian would have behaved in the same way. Every impression of this man reminded me that he was *not* Serosian. "The upgrades will require you to stay clear of the apparatus for several hours during your shift on the bridge. Do you think you can manage that?" he said. I found the question demeaning in its tone but responded professionally.

"If you say you need the longscope, then certainly it's yours. I won't be disturbing you, or it, in any way during my time on the bridge, if that suits you."

He shook his head. "You don't understand. I will not be on the bridge. I will be in my sanctuary. All the work will be done remotely. I need you to not touch the equipment for security reasons. Do you understand?"

I nodded. "I do."

"Good," he said. "The process between us will go much smoother once we have established boundaries. I expect that you will have no problems taking orders from me?"

I hesitated. I already had enough people giving me orders that could cause conflicts. "As long as they're about the longscope or your other equipment, no problems," I said.

"Good," Tralfane said again, his face not changing expression in the slightest. "When you eventually log on to the longscope you will see displays that you cannot access. Ignore them. They will only be activated if I deem it necessary. Your part in that process will be to follow my instructions and carry them out precisely. Do you have any questions?"

I found myself frowning at him and his importunate manner. "Only one," I replied. "How will you let me know when the 'scope is clear to use again?"

He brought his hands together above the table. "I will inform you. That's all you need to know," he said. I just stared at him a moment, expecting more. When nothing was forthcoming, I asked another question.

"Are you expecting trouble when we get to Levant?" I said.

"That's two questions, Mr. Cochrane," he said. "And you already know the answer to the second one."

I looked at him but he remained completely impassive, like a stone monument standing across the table from me.

"You're still here, Mr. Cochrane," he said.

"I am," I replied, then I clasped my hands in front of me, matching his posture, and leaned forward. I wanted answers, at least as many as I could get.

"What happened at Levant?" I asked.

"Is this about the attack as a whole or about your girlfriend?" he said. I thought about that for a second.

"Both," I said.

"I'm under no obligation to tell you anything," he snapped. I was ready with a response.

"Consider it a courtesy that will help us to establish proper 'boundaries,'" I said. He looked at me with disdain. Clearly this was a man who didn't like being challenged. Nonetheless, he chose to reply.

"You saw your navy's report, did you not?" he said.

"I did."

"Then let me just say it was mostly accurate in its assessment," he said. I waited for him to continue. When he didn't I asked another question.

"So the displacement waves were generated by First Empire technology?"

"Undoubtedly," he responded. "And your government has good reason to be worried. This ship as it's currently trimmed will have difficulty defeating that kind of defense. Zander is on a fool's errand, and he may lose his ship in the process."

Now I wondered if I might have an ally after all. "If you were to intervene, or upgrade *Impulse*'s weapons and defensive capabilities—" I started. He quickly cut me off.

"There are limits, Commander, to what a Historian can do, let alone to what *I* am willing to do to save this ship. Now as to the matter of your secret orders—"

This time I interrupted. "You know about that?" I said. He looked at me like I was a child.

"We gave you longwave and Lightship technology. Do you suppose that we don't know how to use it in our own best interests?" he said. I had no answer to that. "It is possible, Mr. Cochrane, that your orders and my own *may* have some areas of overlapping interest. But don't count on me for support. Am I clear?"

"Perfectly," I replied.

"Good. One more thing to keep in mind." His eyes bore down on me now. "You may have to be prepared to lose a battle to prevent a war, for the greater good. Even if it means disobeying direct orders from your commanding officers. Are you prepared for that?"

It was the second time I'd been asked that question, and I didn't like it any better this time than the first.

"I'm prepared for that eventuality," I said. Tralfane smiled. It was cold and cheerless.

"Then I can see why your government picked you for this mission." With that, the room went silent and our conversation appeared to be over. I started for the library door without another word.

"Did you want to see the images of the attack on *Impulse*?" he said. That caught me by complete surprise. I half turned back to him and crossed my arms.

"Are you trying to hurt me?" I asked. The Historian shook his head.

"No. I just thought you had a right to see it," he said. I nodded and sat down at a reading terminal. After a few moments he brought up a video display. A chronometer ticked by in the lower right-hand corner. The video was grainy but detailed enough. It was undoubtedly from one of *Impulse*'s longscope cameras.

I watched as a white-hot energy wave smothered a tiny shuttle-craft. It twisted and burned, tumbling out of control, tossed around like a dried leaf in the winter wind. Inside, twelve of my countrymen, one of them Lt. Natalie Decker, burned with the flame of a thousand suns unleashed upon them. The shuttle rolled on through space, second after agonizing second, until the tracking camera lost sight of it.

Suddenly the visual display changed to show a camera view from the stern of *Impulse*, looking forward toward her baffle shields. Purple sprites rippled along the length of her body as her shielding kicked in, struggling to absorb the impact of the rogue wave. Ruptures opened along her leading edges and amidships, her Hoagland Field collapsing under the strain as bolts of energy streaked through to singe her shining hull. The camera view flickered for a few seconds but stayed on just long enough for me to see bodies flying out of *Impulse*'s belly and into the vacuum of open space. There, the image froze, leaving my navy comrades hanging in the cold abyss. A few moments passed as I held my breath, nauseated by what I had seen. Then, mercifully, the display went black.

"You're a brave young man for watching that," he said. I thought I detected the first bit of respect I had seen from him in his eyes, but it vanished quickly. "I wanted you to know what you were going to be up against."

I swallowed hard into a dry throat, then stood to leave as quickly as I could go.

"Mr. Cochrane," he called from across the room. I stopped. "I understand you had a close relationship with the Historian assigned to *Starbound*," he said.

"Serosian," I replied. He looked at me coldly.

"Understand, I am not him. There are different schools within the Church of the Latter Days. They have differing philosophies about how to best help your civilization return from barbarism. Not all of us believe this quaint little Union is in your best interests."

"So you're in favor of a return to Imperial rule? A second empire? After what you just showed me?"

Tralfane shook his head. "I never said that," he said. I contemplated this, not sure I could trust him, but certain I would probably never know.

"Fair enough," I responded.

"One last thing. I expect complete secrecy in these meetings. You are not to share the content of our conversations with anyone.

That includes Captain Zander or Commander Kierkopf," he said. I tilted my head at him, deliberately, to let him know he didn't intimidate me.

"I've sworn an oath to the service to always tell the truth," I said, "and I have no intention of breaking that oath for you or anyone else, sir. But I also have no intention of offering up sensitive information on a lark, either. Just don't make me choose between you and my oath and we should get along fine."

"Good," he replied, then turned and strode purposefully away to his inner chambers.

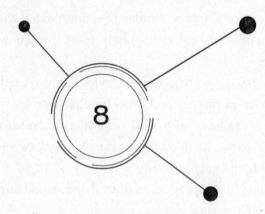

On the Bridge

An hour later I was freshly showered, shaved, dressed, and ready to take my station on the bridge at 1200 hours. With just a few minutes to go until my first duty shift aboard *Impulse*, I stepped into the empty lifter and pressed the button for the bridge. I felt a slight tug of motion as the lifter began ascending the conning tower, passing through the artificial gravity wells of several decks as it climbed. A ship with a functioning Hoagland Field provided equal protection to all areas of a space vessel, making the location of the bridge a style decision. When the Lightship designs had been drawn up they had debated placing the bridge somewhere more practical, perhaps even deep in the center of the ship, but in the end tradition had won out, and the builders of the Lightships had chosen to put the bridge "on top."

I took in a deep breath and closed my eyes, taking the last few moments to contemplate my situation and how far I had come. I'd dreamed of being a spacer since early childhood, then had given it up for a shot at professional soccer in my early teens before recommitting to a career in space when we had lost Derrick. Since that day I'd

worked almost nonstop to get to this moment, and although it hadn't
come aboard *Starbound* as I'd dreamed, I was still undeniably excited
by the step into the future I was about to take.

The doors slid open and I stepped off the lifter and onto the
bridge of *Impulse* at precisely one minute to noon, wearing my newly
pressed Quantar Navy jacket. The USN patches and crest were sewn
on at the arms and breast, as I'd requested, and I had Derrick's lieutenant commander's pins on my collar.

I took in the bridge, laid out in three levels, with the massive
main plasma display taking up the far wall. The microscopic com im-
planted in my inner ear provided me with a variety of possible over-
lays for the display; Tactical, Systems, Visual, and Infrared were
among my choices. Using the com with the visual options activated
was reserved for officers and necessary bridge personnel, and managing the different displays without being distracted was an acquired
skill, but one I'd been working on for almost two years. I was ready. I
decided to set the display setting on Systems so I could monitor shipboard activities, which would be my most likely function as third. The
display would stay centered to me as I walked about the bridge, tracking with me as I went until I changed my settings.

I acknowledged the bridge duty guard with a nod and then proceeded to the elevated captain's station. Lucius Zander sat with his
back to me, surveying the bridge and its myriad activities.

My eye was immediately drawn to the polished gold of the longscope, situated on the same level as the captain's chair next to the
Tactical station. I turned to observe the empty Historian's post behind me. It took up half the back wall with its various display panels
and workstations, all dark now. My curiosity at the goings-on there
would have to wait for another, less pressing, time.

Below, six crewmen, including Jenny Hogan wearing a green Carinthian Navy jacket, I noted, worked at the nav, helm, and con stations, which were recessed so their seats sat a few feet below the floor

of the captain's deck. Another level below them, a dozen or so junior officers occupied the daily duty stations: Environmental Controls, Engineering, Central Computing, Weapons, Propulsion, and the various and sundry operational activities of the ship. George Layton was absent, perhaps on a different shift than mine, and Commander Kierkopf was busy at the engineering station, no doubt monitoring final repairs.

I checked my watch one last time and then cleared my throat as I rounded the captain's chair.

"Lieutenant Commander Peter Cochrane reporting for duty, sir," I said, standing to attention.

Zander swiveled in his chair and looked up at me, coffee cup in hand. "Welcome, Commander," he said. Then he took a sip from his cup, never taking his eyes off me. He set the cup down and casually sat back in his chair. "I'm looking forward to having you aboard."

"As I'm looking forward to being here, sir," I replied. The next few minutes were taken up with general conversation about the layout of the bridge, duty stations, personnel, officer shifts, and the like. Then he got down to business.

"I understand you're fully certified on the longscope," he said. "Our previous 'scopeman wasn't up to the task at Levant. I'll be asking you to do better."

"Of course, sir. I am certified on the 'scope, sir, but Mr. Tralfane requested I stay off of it until his updates are complete," I said. He waved his hand dismissively.

"I've already spoken to the Historian. The 'scope is free for you to use. His updates can wait." This surprised me, as Tralfane had been quite insistent I stay off the apparatus. I wondered if he would take this opportunity to "look in" on me and monitor my session. Zander continued.

"As you may expect, my main concern now is getting this ship ready to go back to Levant. We still don't know what generated the rogue displacement waves. It wasn't us, and from the look of the surviving Levant system society it wasn't the natives either. It was something, or someone, else," Zander said. I mulled over his words in my mind, then came up with a question.

"So what's our next move?" I asked.

Zander eyed me very seriously. "I want to find out why my ship was blasted, Commander, and why twelve of your Quantar countrymen died in those shuttles. That's our first mission, and why I'll need an able longscopeman."

"I'll give you nothing but my best, sir," I said.

"I'm sure you will, Mr. Cochrane," he replied. I understood him better now, and I decided Lucius Zander was one tough little bastard. Still, my secret orders from Wesley about betraying him hung over me like a circling vulture.

"Sir, about this mission back to Levant," I started. He cut me off with a wave of his hand before I could voice my concerns.

"I know some of your people are against it, son, but Union Navy Command has approved the mission, and that's the last I'll hear of it," he snapped.

"Yes, sir," I said.

Zander motioned to the 'scope, at long last. "A demonstration of your skills, if you please, Commander," he said.

I stepped into the brass-railed 'scope covey, a circular extension of the captain's deck, then took off my duty cap and set it aside before closing the rails behind me. I placed my thumb over the thermal panel reader and the 'scope louvers descended down to my eye level from their stowed position. I placed my hands at the control rods on either side and leaned in under the hood. The hood closed behind me, enclosing me to the waist to keep distracting light from interfering with the displays. After a few minutes of calibrating the equipment to my preferences for contrast and brightness, the 'scope read my vision, which was 20/15, and adjusted itself accordingly to match my prescription.

"Ready, sir," I said via the com. I didn't know for sure, but I believed a man like Zander would have a test for me. I was right.

"Please scan section two-point four by four-eight, azimuth seventy, and tell me what you see," he said.

I took my hands from the calibration rods and engaged the infrared, keyed in the location, and then activated the wave beacon. The display went out of focus for several seconds as the 'scope adjusted for distance and time displacement. I fine-tuned the instruments as I waited for the display to firm up, trying to seem as professional as I could under the circumstances. This was my first full-duty shift on the longscope, and I hoped my inexperience wouldn't show.

After a few more moments the visual display painted in. I scanned the field in a series of interlocking triangles, as I'd been trained to do. In the lower left corner of the third triangle I spotted the first anomaly, an elongated black-gray dot. It could be metal, it could be natural, I wasn't sure. Wanting to stay ahead of the game I brought up the infrared display and then refocused on the anomaly while my sweep continued to run in the background. Infrared indicated it was artificial, so I bounced a low-density H-wave off of the object. The returned albedo clearly indicated a metal and crystal structure, the crystal probably from standard navy-issue carbonized glass. The Hoagland ping downloaded shape, size, and mass data into the 'scope and I ran an analysis by loading the object specs into the navy database. The result came back with a positive ten seconds later.

"Object number one is a Carinthian Navy bulwark shuttle, Werder class. Capacity of twelve when active, ten passengers, pilot, and copilot. Shuttle is currently powered down and on systems standby. Distance is one-three-point-four-five AUs from present location. Give me another minute and I'll have her registry information," I said confidently.

"Unnecessary," said Zander. "Send a longwave with the following code, encrypted: alpha, delta, one-five omega, seven-niner seven, tetragrammaton." I entered the code and sent the longwave communications packet. "That will start the shuttle up so she'll be ready to go when we get to her," said Zander. "Now, find me my other anomaly, Commander."

I returned to the 'scope and picked up my field search again. After several minutes of scanning I had found nothing. Except for the shuttle, the coordinates as given by Zander were clear of objects, anomalous or otherwise. Clearly, this was going to be the tough part of the test. I considered the possibility that there was no second object and Zander was merely trying to test my mettle. Would I stand up to him and stake my reputation on a clear field?

"The rest of the grid shows clear, Captain," I said, not taking my eyes from the 'scope as I continued to scan the various displays for something I'd missed.

"Correct, Commander. But I still want my second anomaly," said Zander. I looked at him on my bridge view display as he confidently took another sip of his coffee. "Improvise," he said. This was clearly the test he truly had in mind. Many could be trained to use the 'scope, but few had the intuition and logic skills to make it more than a tool, to make it an extension of their own personalities. I'd heard veteran 'scopemen call their instruments "she," or even use a proper name for it.

I ran through the navy catalog and my displays again and then found what I was looking for, an observation satellite in the same triangle area as the bulwark shuttle. Logic and intuition told me Zander was a man of intent, and with the rest of the grid clean the second anomaly must be in the same general area as the shuttle.

I bounced a longwave off the satellite, embedding a request for visual and infrared scans of the area around the shuttle. It returned my ping in approximately ten seconds with the second anomaly. Zander had said he wanted to recreate the incident at Levant exactly, and he meant it. The second object was tucked in behind the bulwark shuttle in the same plane relative to *Impulse*. A purely visual search wouldn't have found it.

"Second object is a light personnel carrier, Matilda class, complement of thirty-two with crew and passengers, sir."

"You feel no need to verify this finding?" asked Zander. I opened the hood and released the 'scope, stepping back and facing my commanding officer. Commander Kierkopf now stood beside his station.

"No, sir," I said. "Shuttle is the same class and displacement as the one lost at Levant, sir." Zander put down his coffee and stood up.

"Thank you for the demonstration, Commander," he said. "And well done."

"Thank you, sir," I replied.

"But there is something else we need to address, young man, something unsatisfactory," he said. I was at his station in a few short strides.

"Yes, sir?" I said. Zander motioned me closer and I joined him and Commander Kierkopf to make a closed rank of three.

"Mr. Cochrane, I've been meaning to discuss something with you, and I've been letting it slide, but I find I cannot ignore it anymore," he said. I cocked my head slightly at this, showing interest and, I hoped, respect.

"Sir?"

"It's the issue, Mr. Cochrane, of your uniform."

I swallowed hard, not wanting a confrontation but firm on my grounds for defending my country's honor. "Sir?" I said again.

Zander cleared his throat and then raised his voice loud enough for the entire bridge to hear. "On this vessel, Mr. Cochrane, we all wear the same uniform. It is a sign of our unity."

"Yes sir."

"And that unity is essential to a well-run ship, wouldn't you agree?"

"Yes, sir." Next to me, Commander Kierkopf shifted her weight, obviously uncomfortable with where this conversation was going.

"So why do I find you on my bridge not wearing the duty uniform I issued to you?" Zander demanded.

I looked him straight in the eye. I knew my answer would set my course permanently on this ship, either upward or downward. I decided to be brave.

"With all respect, Captain, to be asked to wear the uniform of another world is not a reasonable request. I swore an oath of service to my world long before I swore one to the Union Navy. Additionally, being asked to not wear my country's uniform would dishonor the memory of my countrymen from Quantar that were lost at Levant. And, at any rate sir, the uniform issued to me is not the USN standard. It is Carinthian."

At this Zander raised himself up, barely coming up to my chest. When he spoke his voice was even louder than before. "And so you refuse to honor this vessel and those who built and man her, those who toiled with your countrymen in a crisis, by wearing the uniform of *Impulse*?" That shook me up. I had expected a private conversation and now this seemed more a confrontation designed to embarrass me. I stiffened both physically and in my resolve.

"The uniform I wear honors those countrymen and their sacrifice, Captain. I do not wear it to dishonor you or Carinthia. I do it out of respect for my forebears, my brother, who was lost in Union Navy service, and my oath."

"That is unacceptable," said Zander flatly. "We must all wear the same uniform, Commander. If you do not comply your name will see the bottom of my report on a daily basis. You will accumulate enough fleet demerits that you will never see a promotion, or for that matter even shore leave."

This time I didn't hesitate in my response. "If you so choose, Captain, I cannot argue with you. But I cannot change a stand I have taken on principle." I was rigid as a bulkhead now, my whole body tense. Zander sighed and placed his hands behind his back.

"Is there no compromise in you, boy?" he said. I hesitated.

"There is, sir, I believe," I responded. Now Zander crossed his arms in front of him.

"Well go ahead, I can't wait to hear this," he said.

"We could all wear the standard issue Union Navy whites, sir. Then there would be uniformity among the crew, sir."

"Navy whites?" Zander boomed. "Navy whites?" He stepped forward to the deck rail and yelled out to the crew below. "Does anyone here want to wear those damnably ugly navy whites?"

"No, sir!" came the chorus from the bridge crew. I also noticed a good deal of snickering now and hushed conversations. I began to relax as it dawned on me: I'd been had. Again.

"No damnable whites!" Zander screeched in his gravel tones. This was greeted with cheers and clapping all around. Commander Kierkopf nudged me with her elbow.

Zander turned back to me. "The crew is having nothing of the damned whites, Mr. Cochrane," he said. "And since you won't wear the green of Carinthia, then I guess your current uniform will have to do." This was greeted with a smattering of cheers. "As has always been the policy of this vessel under my command!"

The crew roared with laughter and whooping in my direction, and I could feel the flush of my skin. Commander Kierkopf patted me on the back patronizingly.

"Well done, young lad! You've succeeded in maintaining standard ship's policy!" she said. I began to smile.

"Mr. Poulsen!" said Zander to Claus Poulsen, stationed at Propulsion. "We've had our fun, now I believe you owe me twenty crowns!" The crew broke into laughter again. Poulsen pulled the coin from his pocket and passed it to Zander, who held it up to me.

"He bet me he could get you into the greens," he said, laughing. "But I knew better! You're a stubborn one!" Now I laughed with the rest.

"Duly noted, Captain, Commander," I said, nodding to each in turn, then stepped forward to the rail myself and pointed at the rabble. "But the rest of you lot just remember, I'll have duty station on this deck often enough, and plenty of you will be serving shifts under me!" There were good-natured jeers at this. Zander waved the crew back to their duty stations.

"Commander Cochrane," he said, "the XO and I will be having lunch in the officers' lounge. In the meantime, Commander, you have the con. Don't break anything."

"Acknowledged, sir. I have the con, sir," I said. It was hard to contain my excitement. Less than an hour on duty and I'd already run my first longscope sequence and now was about to get the con. It was more than I could have hoped for. "Thank you, sir," I said as he departed with Commander Kierkopf.

I looked down on the nav and con stations, my hands on the rail of the captain's deck. The crew looked up at me expectantly.

"Let's look alive now!" I said, then barked out my first orders in command of a Lightship.

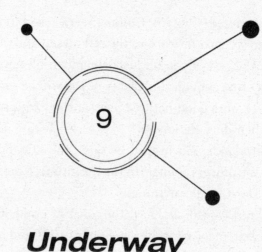

9

Underway

At 0700 the next morning I stood on the captain's deck next to Dobrina as Zander held court from the center seat. We were untethered from Candle and moving slowly away from the station on a general heading for Quantar's outer-system jump point for the crossing to Levant.

"Commander Kierkopf, please set our course for the shuttles and prepare to load them in the landing bay for the traverse to the jump point. And activate the Hoagland Field," said Zander to Dobrina, but loud enough for the entire bridge crew to hear. This was clearly a man who loved the pomp of command. Commander Kierkopf turned to me.

"Execute, Lieutenant Commander Cochrane," she said.

"Aye, XO," I responded. I was curious about the request to activate the Hoagland Field. Usually at sub-light speed in friendly territory the field was off. I stepped forward and put my hands on the railing, looking down to George Layton. "Helm officer, set course one-one-eight, mark four. Propulsion officer," I said, turning to see my adjutant Claus Poulsen on duty, "engage the impellers and charge the forward Hoagland Field. Take us out at zero-point zero-seven-five light."

"Zero-point zero-seven-five light, aye, sir!" snapped Poulsen. The sub-light impellers were useful for any travel under one-tenth light speed. Beyond that the Hoagland Drive was far more efficient, even if it did demand that we use the accompanying field to cut a swath through normal space.

I stood at the railing acting as if I expected my orders to be carried out swiftly and flawlessly. In reality I was as excited as any officer on his maiden voyage into deep space would be. I looked to the long-scope, wishing I could be under the hood, calculating time and distance to some forgotten First Empire world, or a relic like an Imperial Dreadnought, or some other fascinating discovery. But for now all I could do was watch and wait for my next opportunity.

"Main display forward," commanded Dobrina.

"Display forward, aye, sir," responded Layton. I sighed as the main plasma display switched on to show us nothing but dark space sprinkled with crystal stars ahead. Now the adventure truly began.

"Lieutenant Commander, may I have a word?" It was Zander, and it broke my momentary reverie. I was at his station in a few short strides and sat in my duty chair when I saw Dobrina do the same.

"Yes, sir?" I said. Zander shifted in his seat and put down his ever-present coffee cup. He spoke quietly, almost in a whisper.

"I'm calling the staff together at 1000 hours," he said. "I expect you and Commander Kierkopf to keep my bridge in suitable shape and get those shuttles stowed by then. From here on out I believe it's critical that we move with both pace and deliberate intent, without any advance notice of our next move. Do you understand?"

I looked to Commander Kierkopf. She was clearly already in the loop on these operating instructions. "I do, sir," I said. "Are we expecting trouble *before* we reach the jump point?" Zander looked put out at my question, but answered it nonetheless.

"I expect nothing, but I suspect everything, Commander. Now carry out my orders, and be on time for the staff." With that he was up in a flash and headed for the lifter. "I'll be in my cabin, XO. You have the con," he said loud enough for the whole bridge to hear.

"Acknowledged," said Kierkopf, "I have the con, sir." And with that, Zander was gone, Commander Kierkopf moved to the center seat, and I was left with more questions than answers.

A few minutes later, once things on the bridge had progressed to my satisfaction, I joined Kierkopf as she sat in the captain's chair.

"What did Zander mean about 'pace and deliberate intent'?" I asked while pretending to scan reports on my tablet display. "And what's with the Hoagland Field?"

"If he had wanted you to know that rather than just carry out his orders, don't you think he would have told you?" she said without taking her eyes from the main display.

"I'm just trying to get a handle on him," I said. "He's not the easiest man to understand."

"I will give you that," she replied. "But I also know he won't tell you anything until he's ready to."

"Obviously you trust him fully." I stated.

"I do," she said. "He recruited me from *Minerva* to *Impulse* based solely on the recommendation of my former captain. When I got here he tested me in multiple roles and kept advancing me. I owe him a great debt for my career, but I also respect him as military man. He knows what he's doing and he cares for everyone aboard *Impulse.*"

"I understand that. It's just I haven't learned his . . . idiosyncrasies yet."

"One thing I will say, Cochrane. If he didn't believe in you, you wouldn't be sitting here."

"I'll keep that in mind in the future," I replied, letting a smile of satisfaction touch the corner of my mouth. "Thank you, Commander."

Impulse's Historian stepped off the lifter. Commander Kierkopf rose to greet him.

"You aren't on my schedule today, Mr. Tralfane," she said. He stopped and looked at her distastefully.

"My station requires upgrades. I've already cleared them with the captain." He started toward his station again. Her voice stopped him a second time.

"Then you'll have no problem if I clear it with him?" she said. He looked at me, then continued to his station and started it up.

"I take it that's a yes?" she added after a few moments. He sat in his chair and swiveled to face her, his expression angry.

"*You* may do whatever you like, Miss Kierkopf. I don't need your clearance to proceed, only the captain's," he said. I stood and leaned in close to her.

"He did tell me yesterday that he had upgrades to install," I said, trying to assuage her. She seemed upset that he refused to use her rank when addressing her. She looked to me and then back at Tralfane.

"I assume you'll have no objections if Lieutenant Commander Cochrane here assists you, Mr. Tralfane? He could benefit from time on the 'scope," she said.

"I've no doubt of that," replied Tralfane without looking over at either of us. Now we were both insulted. With a nod from Commander Kierkopf I stood and took my position at the longscope station, going under the hood and activating the displays. I monitored his activities for a few minutes. It seemed as though he was installing new subroutines in the astrogation, propulsion, and weapons systems. I couldn't monitor what he was doing nor was he willing to communicate directly with me through the com. After about twenty minutes he rebooted the 'scope from his station, essentially kicking me out. I emerged from under the hood and went back to my duty station as he shut down his workstation and started for the lifter.

"Please don't interfere with the 'scope while it's loading the new routines, Lieutenant Commander," he said to me, then left without acknowledging Kierkopf again.

"What was he doing?" she asked me after he was gone. I shrugged.

"From what I could tell, adding new subroutines to some of the base systems. Does it concern you?" I asked. She looked away from me for a few seconds.

"Concern? Everything the Historians do concerns me, Cochrane. But ultimately it just comes down to one thing. I don't like him," she said.

I chuckled. "Me either." She crossed her arms. I was unsure what she was thinking.

"Let's get ready for the staff," she finally said, bringing the conversation to an end. I turned back to my plasma, running down the list of my duties one more time, unable to shake a growing sense of unease that had fallen over me.

Nothing could have prepared me for the shock I was in for at the command staff meeting.

I arrived ten minutes early and took my coffee to the third chair. A few minutes later the full staff was there, minus Zander. He entered two minutes after the hour, unusual for him, to make us a full twelve.

Zander looked to Kierkopf. "Report, Exec," he said. She cleared her throat before beginning.

"Both shuttles have been retrieved and stored in the landing bay. It's pretty cramped in there with the two of them and the Downship as well, sir."

"I'm sure we'll manage, XO. Mr. Cochrane, I understand there were to be upgrades to the longscope today," he said.

"Yes, sir. Mr. Tralfane began the installation this morning. Updates to some of the base systems as far as I could tell, sir," I replied.

"Well he'll not get the whole day. I've informed him he has until 1200 to verify his installations. We jump at 1400. No excuses," he said. Then he set down his coffee cup and sat forward, his hands clasped in front of him, an intense look in his eyes. I'd never seen him look like this before in my brief time with him, and it made me uncomfortable.

"Once we're in Levant space we will follow our game plan exactly, no deviations. I will remind everyone here we are trying to recreate the exact conditions at the time of the incident, but without the same results. The bulwark shuttle will launch first, at 1430 hours. It will be followed by the light shuttle fourteen minutes later. We will follow the exact course set out in the plan," he said. This set off alarms for me. I hadn't seen details on any sort of formal plan.

"Captain," I said, "I've seen no plan, nor been informed of one. As a senior officer—"

"Commander Kierkopf and I have discussed it at length," Zander said, cutting me off. "The rest of you are being informed of it now and a full composite has been downloaded to each of your workstations, personal plasmas, and coms," he said, glancing around the table for any sign of dissent. I chose to provide that myself.

"But, sir, we've had no time for a review," I protested.

"Noted, Mr. Cochrane," he snapped. "Now if you'll allow me to continue?" His tone indicated there was no compromise in the offing. I nodded my acknowledgment but said nothing. Zander continued.

"Commander Kierkopf will command the light shuttle with a single pilot. The bulwark shuttle will carry a complement of ten volunteer crew, plus one pilot and one commander. Mr. Cochrane, you will man the longscope and scan for unwanted activity of any kind, but most especially rogue hyperdimensional displacement waves, understood?"

"Aye, sir," I said. "Who will command the bulwark shuttle?"

"I will," Zander replied.

The staff exploded in protests, except for Commander Kierkopf. I noted this, even as I let the others calm down before speaking again.

"Captain, this is unacceptable. Our most experienced officer must remain on the bridge," I insisted emphatically. Zander waved me off.

"That's where I was last time while I watched my crew burn. I will *not* let that happen again." I noted the use of the words "my crew." Zander took the losses personally, even if they weren't his countrymen. I wondered if it was guilt about the last attack that made him want to take this irrational action. I thought about my orders from Wesley, then put those thoughts aside for the moment while Zander continued.

"Besides, Mr. Cochrane, if you do your job at the 'scope correctly, we will have plenty of time to activate our shielding," he said.

I protested again. "But, sir, you'll be leaving the ship—"

"In your capable hands, Commander. You're third now and you can handle it, otherwise Wesley wouldn't have selected you for this assignment and you wouldn't be here. This is not a debate, sir, it's an order," he finished emphatically. And that was that. He proceeded to explain logistics and other details. I was pleased to find that he had selected Claus Poulsen for his pilot, at least. A few more minutes and then he rose and left for his cabin. I lingered until Kierkopf and I were the only ones left in the room.

"This is insane!" I said. "The captain off the ship in the most exposed position! The XO right behind! And me? An over-promoted newbie officer fresh out of cadet school on my first tour, hell, my first few *days* in space, left in command? It's insane!" I repeated.

The commander shook her head. "You'll not convince him otherwise, Peter. He's made up his mind on this. And I've followed him long enough to know he's usually right in these situations. That's why I put my trust, and my respect, in him." I glared at her, my foot tapping impatiently on the floor.

"And that's what worries me," I said. "Inflexibility is a bad thing in a commanding officer."

"Perhaps you're mistaking inflexibility with loyalty to his command and crew," she responded.

"And perhaps he's acting out of emotion and pride rather than logic," I said, then sat back down at the expansive table and eyed her warily. "I know what this is about, Commander. He feels guilty about the men he lost, and so do you. He's leaving me on the ship to make sure I'm safe so that you can both put yourselves in danger to assuage your guilt. I'll not have it!" I slammed my fist on the table. She came at me aggressively and stared me down, her fingers flexed on the tabletop.

"Yes, you will, Commander," she seethed. "You'll follow your orders, because that is your duty. We don't get to choose what is wise or unwise. That's what they pay captains for, and they pay us to follow our captain's orders. So I'll ask you only one more question: will you follow your orders as given or will I have to replace you?" I stared hard into her eyes. I could tell she knew that I was right, but the order had been given. Still, I had a choice to make.

"I will follow my orders, XO," I said quietly.

"Good!" she snapped, then stormed from the room.

I headed down to the landing bay immediately and found Marker before reporting to my bridge station.

"John, I have a question," I said, taking him aside from his training and into a maintenance hallway.

"Sir?"

"Can the Downship be made ready before Mission Go?" I asked in a low voice. Marker looked over his shoulder.

"Aye, sir, it can," he said back, just as low. I nodded.

"Good, make her ready . . . quietly, Corporal. What's her crew capacity?"

"Up to twelve, sir, for diplomatic missions, less depending on how much storage you want for other scenarios. How many do you plan on taking out?" he asked. This time it was my turn to look around for eavesdroppers.

"Out, just you and I. Back . . . that's a different question. Pack her for search and rescue, Corporal." He eyed me like a man of experience questioning one of inexperience.

"Are you expecting trouble, sir?" he asked.

"Me? Hell yes! But the captain and the XO seem to be inviting it. Now get her ready and be prepared to go on my order."

"She'll be ready, sir," promised Marker.

I nodded. "And one last thing, pack some proximity charges, just in case. You never know what we might have to blow up, or through, out there."

"Aye, sir."

Our conversation over, I made for the lifter, stopping only for a moment to sweep my eyes across the landing bay to the two shuttles that would be protecting my commanding officer and my XO. I sighed and stepped off the deck, anxiety mounting in the pit of my stomach.

I was at my longscope station ready to go twenty minutes early. Tralfane sent a cryptic message at 1340 hours that said merely "Active." I powered up the 'scope and ran her through her regular calibrations, noting the addition of Tralfane's new displays, still blacked out to me, and placing them to one side of the icon grid so they wouldn't distract me.

Ten minutes later I withdrew from the 'scope station to give the captain my ready report. Zander nodded acknowledgment from the captain's chair as Kierkopf stood next to him, observing the preparations.

"All jump coordinates to Levant verified and passed on to the astrogation officer?" Zander asked me.

"Yes, sir," I replied, nodding toward Jenny Hogan at the astrogation station.

"Have we passed the outer marker beacon yet?" Zander asked Lt. Layton.

"Affirmative, Captain. Eight minutes ago," said Layton from the helm.

Zander stood abruptly. "Start the clock, XO. Five minutes from my mark." He raised a hand at this, then brought it down in a slashing motion.

"Mark!" he said.

Dobrina took to the shipwide com and made the call. "All stations, this is the XO. Five minutes to jump. I repeat, five minutes and counting," she said, then put the receiver down and sat back down at the XO's station, strapping herself in.

"Store the 'scope for the jump, Mr. Cochrane," she said to me. I shut down the 'scope as the jump alarms sounded throughout the ship. Readiness reports came pouring over the central com system and were acknowledged by the bridge crew. Once I had the longscope stored I made my way to the third station and activated my personal com before strapping myself in.

"We're going early, sir?" I dared to ask.

"Early being relative, Commander," Zander said. "Any time we're on mark and within two hours of a scheduled jump I demand my crew be ready at five minute's notice. Circumstances don't always happen by the clock, Mr. Cochrane."

"Understood, sir," I said. This was yet another of Zander's idiosyncrasies. I still didn't quite know what to make of him, fool or genius.

I took final reports from Jenny Hogan at the astrogation station and Layton at the helm as well as a final good-to-go from Marker and the marines stowed below decks. Dobrina reported her stations at the ready as well.

"Mr. Poulsen," said Zander to *Impulse*'s propulsion officer, "spool up the Hoaglands."

"Aye, sir!" said Poulsen. I watched as his hands ran over the heat-sensitive touch controls, setting marks and keying in spatial coordinates fed to him from Hogan at Astrogation. I switched over to my monitor to make sure our protective Hoagland Field and the hyperdimensional drives were nominal. Poulsen raised his left hand over his head to indicate *Impulse* was ready to jump.

"All systems green, XO?" asked Zander one final time as he sat down and strapped in, the last one to do so.

"All green, sir," responded Kierkopf, not taking her eyes from her board.

"Mr. Cochrane?"

"My board is green, sir," I said, indicating that the helm, navigation, and longscope systems were ready.

I watched as Zander leaned back in his chair, hands gripping the arms tightly. I did the same.

"Stand by all stations," he called. "On my mark." I watched the main bridge display as the forward baffles covering the nose of *Impulse* expanded like an umbrella, opening to catch the energy wave generated by the rear HD plasma drives. A purple glow enveloped the ship's exterior, caught by the forward baffles to create a closed energy field. Only one more act now, to engage the hyperdimensional drive and take our ship through the jump point to Levant.

"Three . . ." called Zander, "two . . . one . . ."

"Jump!" he commanded.

"Jumping!" said Poulsen, his voice echoing shipwide over the com as his free hand swept down his board from top to bottom.

What seemed like seconds passed. I was disoriented, as if pieces of me were missing and rushing to put themselves back into place before I noticed. The bridge looked blurry, and I felt an unpleasant vertigo that thankfully lasted only a moment. Unfortunately that sensation was then replaced by nausea. I heard a voice in my ear com, Commander Kierkopf, I guessed.

"Close your eyes," she said. I did, and the nausea slowly passed. Then I heard sounds of activity around me again, followed by a gentle tapping on my shoulder.

"Commander, are you with us yet?" I looked up into Commander Kierkopf's eyes. She had her hands on my shoulders and was looking intently at me. In my reverie I found the sight of her quite attractive. I reached up to touch her face, but she deflected my hand before I could go further. Then she stepped back from me.

"He's here, sir," she said, turning away from me to Captain Zander, who already had his coffee. She handed me a cup and added some fluid from a dropper.

"Helps clear the head," she said. I nodded, thinking about the theoretical physics classes that I'd had as a cadet. The instructors had stated that jumps were impossible according to physics as we knew it. The Earth Historians claimed only to know how to use the technology, not how it worked. I was just thankful that I'd passed through my first jump point and reassembled in a different part of the same universe in one piece.

Another minute passed and I regained my footing, picking up on the hum of activity around me. *Impulse* was already well underway in normal space and in full cry. I had made my first jump. We were in the Levant system.

"I'd like a report from the 'scope as soon as you're ready, Commander," said Zander.

"Ready now, sir," I responded.

"Nonsense, boy. Take another minute," he said. "First jump always takes it out of you. You're lucky. Many times I've seen the crew take advantage of a young man's first jump."

"Advantage, sir?" I asked, my head still clearing of fog.

He smiled. "Hand in warm water, that kind of thing. Academy pranks."

Automatically I looked down to check my pants. Thankfully, they were dry. I remembered reading that the jump disorientation weakened as you got more experience. Like your first drunk. Word was it killed about same number of brain cells. I took another sip of my coffee, hoping that was so.

Jump points were not exact locations in space, but rather areas of varying size that allowed a ship to jump into a region of space, usually close to a star, if you knew the Lagrange grid point references. Many First Empire system jump points were known, but many others were lost in antiquity. Levant was one of the closest major jump points to Quantar, and had been a bustling trading post in the old empire days. From the look of the astrogation display we had jumped pretty close to the center of the ingress point, an area bound by the marker beacons installed by the Unified Navy survey probes. I reminded myself to give Jenny Hogan a commendation when things calmed down.

"If you're ready, Mr. Cochrane, I'd like to get my longscope reading now," said Zander.

"Aye, sir, I'm ready," I said. I set my coffee down and made for my duty station. After a few minutes of scanning I had made my first pass through the displays, at least the ones I had access to. The Levant system consisted of four rocky major planets in the inner system, all within four masses of Q-standard, and eight outer gas giants. There were a wide array of minor planets and seventy-nine moons, including two orbiting Levant Prime. The jump point was located between the orbit of the fifth and sixth outer planets, both smaller gas giants, which would be a big advantage for future traders. No distorting gravity wells from the more massive outer planets would make traversing the Levant system a breeze. The only major obstacle was a cloud of asteroids between the orbits of L-5 and L-6. Levant Prime was the fourth planet outward from her F-type blue-white main sequence star.

I switched off the survey displays and proceeded through my regular protocols, scanning the path ahead to Levant Prime. There was minimal disruptive flak and no energy anomalies on the infrared. Stellar dust and debris was within acceptable ranges.

"First sweep complete. The path to Levant Prime is all clear, Captain," I called out, then began a second scan. After repeating the process I gave the clearance again and stepped back from the 'scope, waiting for Zander. He stood.

"I want a system-wide scan, Commander. Not just the path ahead, and not just the path we took before," he said.

"System-wide, sir?" I asked. That could take hours. Zander nodded affirmative.

"Start with the asteroid cloud between L-5 and L-6, Commander. Our longscope officer warned us of an energy anomaly there the last time we entered this system. I want to see if it's still there," he said.

"Aye, sir," I said, and dove back under the hood. Scanning the asteroid cloud would probably take me twenty minutes. Of course the whole crew would be waiting on me while I scanned.

Halfway through my scan I detected a pulsing energy signature. It was almost equally distant from the Levant star as our position at the jump point.

"I have your anomaly, Captain," I reported through my com.

"Let me guess," said Zander back to me. "Located at the opposite Lagrange point to our current position relative to L-Prime."

"Yes, sir," I acknowledged. "How did you know?"

"I didn't," said Zander. "But I guessed it would be there. Especially if this jump point we're sitting in is artificial. You'd need a hy-perdimensional generator at the opposing point to balance the solar system." I'd never heard of an artificial jump point before.

"Sir, are you implying—" I started.

"I'm implying nothing, Commander. I'm stating fact: if there is a hyperdimensional anomaly at Lagrange opposition to this jump point, then this jump point must be artificial," he said. I checked my scans again.

"Sir, although the energy point is anomalous, I'm not detecting anything that conclusively points to it being a hyperdimensional en-ergy source," I said.

"And you won't, Commander. Not unless you get much closer. Conference please, Commander," he said. I shut off the com and came out from under the 'scope hood. Zander and Kierkopf were already in close quarters.

"If I'm not mistaken, this is what set off the attack on our last encounter," Zander said once I had made us a threesome. "We made an unauthorized jump into an artificial jump point, probably setting off ancient automated defenses of some kind. They could have been around for centuries, from before the war even."

"So what do we do?" asked Kierkopf. Zander looked to me.

"Other than the anomaly, do I have your All Clear for ingress to Levant Prime, Lieutenant Commander?" he asked. I hesitated only a second.

"I haven't completed the system-wide scan, sir, but as for the path ahead to Levant, you have my All Clear, sir," I said. A part of me wished I could report otherwise.

Zander turned to Dobrina. "XO?"

"All systems are up and running, sir," she said. Zander stood and clasped his hands behind his back, then nodded to the communica-tions officer, who engaged the all-ship com.

"This is Captain Zander. We have entered the Levant system

right on the dot. We are proceeding to the rendezvous point of our last encounter. All stations, be on alert for displacement wave activity. They'll not catch us with our pants down this time," he said, then gave the signal to cut the line.

"EVA teams, man the shuttles. Prepare the docking bay for depressurization. All protocols in play for interplanetary excursion," he said. The bridge erupted in a flourish of activity. Our course was set for a minor planet in the asteroid cloud designated L-42, the location of the displacement wave incident that had killed my countrymen. It was thirty-four minutes away at our present course and speed.

"Mr. Cochrane," called out the captain as he made for the lifter, "congratulations, you have the con."

"I have the con, aye, sir," I said. Claus Poulsen disengaged from his station and followed Zander to the lifter.

"Commander Kierkopf," I called as she started for the lifter. She turned halfway back to me. "May I suggest that you take Lieutenant Layton here as your shuttle pilot. He's fully rated on the shuttle and I can vouch for his skills in the pilot's chair." She looked at me and smiled slightly from one corner of her mouth. I was trying to protect her and she knew it. She humored me.

"A fine suggestion, Commander. I'll have Ensign Kasdan report to take his station. Mr. Layton, you're with me," she ordered. She gave me the slightest of nods as Layton joined them in the lifter. He winked at me as the doors shut.

I looked to the center seat. Four short steps and I was there. I sat down in the chair and nodded once to Jenny Hogan at her post, pleased to see that she had reverted to a Quantar-blue duty uniform. She nodded so slightly in response that only I would likely have picked it up. We were both acknowledging the moment: a Quantar commander in charge of an in-service Carinthian Lightship. I clicked on the captain's chair com to initiate a direct link to John Marker and spoke softly.

"All ready, Corporal?" I asked.

Marker's voice came back fuzzy and crackling through the line. "Ready down here, sir. Looks like the captain and the XO will be out in just a few minutes, sir."

"Understood. Do they all have EVA suits?"

"Aye, sir. Zander insisted."

"Good," I said. The line became uncomfortably silent then. Finally Marker came through again.

"It will take us seven minutes to prep and follow them, sir, from the time you give the order," he said.

I took in a deep breath. "Consider the order given the moment the landing bay is inhabitable again, Corporal. Not a moment to wait. I want our only delay in leaving to be my transport in the lifter."

"Understood," said Marker, pausing before continuing. "Sir, if you don't mind me saying, you do have another option if you're so worried about this mission." I held a finger to my ear to suppress the sound coming through.

"Go," I said.

"You're officer of the deck. You can deny them liftoff clearance if you deem the conditions too hazardous." The earpiece crackled as I considered this.

"I have no basis for such a claim," I said. "And Zander would have my hide and find someone who would give him clearance to replace me. No. We have to follow the plan. Just be prepared with our backup."

"Aye, sir," Marker said a final time, and I cut the line. The time passed quickly until Zander and Kierkopf both called in requesting launching rights. Despite Marker's suggestion, I had no legitimate reason to deny them.

"Granted," I said, to each in turn, then watched on the main bridge display as they departed through the open landing bay doors, one after the other.

"Mr. Kasdan," I said, to the ensign who had replaced Layton at the helm position in the interim, "switch the main display to tactical. How long until the shuttles reach the exact coordinates of the incident?" Kasdan checked his panel.

"Thirteen minutes, sir," he said. I stood and made for the long-scope station, there to monitor the EVA.

Thirteen minutes. Time enough for disaster to strike.

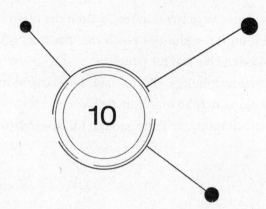

In the Levant System

Under the hood of the longscope, I watched anxiously as the clock ticked away the time to the shuttles reaching the rendezvous point. We had seven minutes. I flipped through my displays as rapidly as I could, then decided to focus on the infrared, the most likely display to indicate trouble from an HD displacement wave.

It worried me that Zander believed we were possibly facing a displacement wave weapon of some kind. Any weapon that could bend space and time would be formidable even for *Impulse* to handle. Displacement waves were the most potentially destructive force our technology knew of. Usually they only occurred when a jump-capable ship left our dimension for hyperdimensional space and then jumped back in again at its new location. They were also usually a localized phenomenon, but very destructive to anything in the general vicinity, especially if that thing was unprotected by a Hoagland Field. If the First Empire had a weapon that could project such a wave over long distances, that weapon would be the most dangerous force in the universe.

I watched the bulwark shuttle with Captain Zander and Claus

Poulsen aboard pass through a field of midsized asteroids, most less than a kilometer across, as it made its way toward L-5, the nearest gas giant to our entry jump point. Dobrina followed in the Search and Rescue shuttle on a slightly different vector, keeping station with Zander at a safe distance. I counted down the remaining minutes until the shuttles reached the X-point, where my countrymen had been burned alive.

"Five minutes," said Zander's crackling voice over the shipwide com. The tension on the bridge felt like oppressive air hanging over us all.

I gripped the longscope control rods ever tighter, but the displays were all clear. I heard the lifter doors open and checked my bridge display to see Tralfane striding on to the deck. I turned my focus back to the longscope display.

"Not a good time, Mr. Tralfane," I said out loud. I heard him walk behind me and activate his workstation. The ship shuddered slightly and I cued up my private com line to the Historian.

"What did you just do?" I demanded. I was acting captain of this ship and I wasn't letting anyone undermine me while I was on duty, even an Earth Historian.

Tralfane said nothing for a few moments, then: "You'll find your three new displays active, Mr. Cochrane. Use them."

I checked my display viewer and found that he was right. The three new active displays were available on the icon grid and I clicked on to each in turn. They were probes, launched by Tralfane moments ago from *Impulse*, the first two giving both visual feeds and telemetry on the shuttles, their location, course, speed, etc. I ordered Kasdan to track the telemetry for anything unusual while I kept a close monitor on the visuals the probes provided. They gave me a far clearer and closer view of the shuttles than what was normally available from the standard longscope displays. The third probe focused on the asteroid field ahead of the shuttles. If Tralfane was expecting an incoming displacement wave, clearly he wasn't expecting it to come from a natural source like the Levant star or the upper atmosphere of L-5.

Captain Zander was on the move. I watched my visual display as Zander came out of the dense asteroid field and into an area of clear space. "Five seconds . . . Mark!" came Zander's voice over the com. *Impulse* and the shuttles had reached their X-points.

As I observed the new probe displays I noticed three asteroids in the general vicinity of L-5 that were drifting in seeming sync with each other, in a circular orbit on a single plane. This sight in itself seemed highly suspicious, as they weren't large enough to generate a mutual gravity well that would keep them tidally locked together, drifting through space as one. I began scans of the first asteroid. Within seconds I realized something was wrong. The density was too light and the mass too small. I switched to another display and detected hints of alloy metals underneath the rocks and dust. This thing was a hollowed-out device of some kind.

The battle alarm claxon shocked me into action.

I switched displays again and saw the unmistakable energy signature of an HD displacement wave incoming. Each of the three asteroids had flared to life with the energy of a thousand suns, and each had fired at a different target. My first responsibility was to *Impulse*.

"Incoming displacement wave!" I shouted into the shipwide com as the alarm claxon blared. Then I switched to the bridge com channel. "Turn us to one-four-six, mark six, Mr. Kasdan, and fire up the baffle shields!"

"Aye, sir! Turning the ship! Baffles activated!" called out Kasdan. I felt *Impulse* strain under me to get into position to deflect the incoming wave as her gravimetric generators whined to life. With luck our Hoagland Field would deflect and dissipate the wave away from *Impulse*. If not . . .

"Countdown to impact!" I said.

"Thirty-six seconds!" replied Kasdan.

Suddenly one of the probe displays showed a back angle, toward *Impulse*. I could see the baffle shields rising over the nose, spreading their four wings to protect the ship while the gravimetric energy began sparking to life. But the ship was turning painfully slowly into position. If she didn't take the wave full on the nose we could be scorched again and severely damaged. I took one last look at the shuttles, to my horror.

The inbound displacement waves bore down on the small ships. The only advantage they had was the small footprint of their shielding compared to *Impulse*, but it was likely to make little difference. There was no doubt now that the triad of asteroids were all automated HD displacement wave weapons. This was not technology that the Union Navy possessed; it was far beyond us. Each weapon had targeted one of the ships and they had all fired simultaneously. That's why *Impulse* had taken such a hard hit the last time: she was felled by a different wave than the shuttles.

I watched on the infrared as the waves engulfed the bulwark shuttle and the Search and Rescue. The telltale purple signature of the Hoagland Field at work surrounded both of the small ships, but it was impossible to tell if they had survived the blast before the probes Tralfane had sent out winked out of existence, flung from our dimension to the next. The shuttles were so much closer to the weapons than *Impulse* . . .

"Report, Mr. Kasdan!" I shouted again.

"Twenty seconds to impact!" I shut the longscope down, lifted the hood, and ran to the captain's chair.

"Lock her down, Mr. Kasdan!" I ordered. Then I clicked on the shipwide com again. "All stations, prepare for imminent impact! I say again, prepare for impact! Radiation protocol Alpha One!" I strapped myself in as the seconds ticked away. I swiveled my chair to the side instinctively, away from the master display plasma, as if it could protect me from the golden-green mass bearing down on us. Layton began a countdown.

"Five . . . four . . . three . . . two . . . one . . . impac—" The shock of the energy wave hitting the Hoagland Field rocked the ship as our HD power curve rose to match and then disperse the wave's energy. The main power systems failed in the midst of the impact and the ship went to emergency lights. I was spun around like a child on a playground ride as the air inside the bridge crackled with kinetic energy. It was far more frightening than I'd imagined it could be, especially in the dim blue glow of the emergency lights.

A few seconds later the bridge returned to life at quarter power, essential stations only. I unbuckled and leaped from my chair toward my 'scope station.

"Mr. Kasdan! Priority power to the longscope, and reports from all decks!" I ordered.

"Aye, sir!" I stuck my head under the display hood. The probes had been annihilated by the waves, so the only display I had was the standard long-range visual. I furiously searched for energy signatures from the shuttles or any signs of environmental controls operating. Finally I spotted one of the shuttles on the visual display, still crackling with purple sprites and tumbling through space as waves of kinetic energy burned yellow-hot and dispersed off of her hull and shielding. It was the Search and Rescue.

"Mr. Kasdan!" I yelled out again, "Try and raise the Search and Rescue shuttle on the com, and move us toward her, vector one-four-four." I ran through my operating displays again; there was no sign of the bulwark shuttle. I pulled away from the 'scope to return to the captain's chair. Tralfane stood in my way.

"You have to destroy those asteroid weapons," he said flatly. I could hardly contain my fury. He was keeping me from launching a rescue party, from reporting those weapons back to the USN at Candle, from Zander and Dobrina . . .

"I'm aware of my duty, Mr. Tralfane," I said as evenly as I could in the chaos. The lights chose that moment to power back up to half. "Search and rescue teams—"

"Can wait, Mr. Cochrane! If those wave generators launch a second salvo there'll be nothing to rescue, and securing *Impulse* is your priority," he said, "Or it should be." I wanted to punch him, but I knew he was right. I turned to Kasdan.

"Belay that last, Kasdan. Do we have power to the impellers?"

"Yes, sir, but we can't reach—"

"Fire them up, Mr. Kasdan. Get us moving toward the Search and Rescue shuttle, now!" Tralfane grabbed me by the arm, and he wasn't gentle about it either.

"Commander—" he started. I shook free of him. I knew my duty, even if I hated it. Even if it cost me my friends' lives.

"And, Kasdan," I said, "keep the Search and Rescue shuttle between us and those displacement wave generators. Protecting *Impulse* is our top priority now," I said out loud. It hurt to say the words.

"But if we don't get ourselves between the shuttles and those displacement weapons they'll be finished," protested Kasdan. "Captain Zander and the XO—"

"They knew the risks, Lieutenant," I said, interrupting. "Now carry out my orders."

"Aye, sir!" said Kasdan, obviously disturbed but too good an officer to protest further. I turned back to Tralfane, looking up into his eyes.

"We're too close for atomics, and those weapons are too big and too well shielded for conventional missiles. Do we have any other weaponry options aboard?" I said, almost whispering to keep the bridge crew from hearing.

He looked down on me with contempt. "None that you are authorized to operate. No one aboard is, even Zander. They're only for extreme emergencies. Survival of the ship's data core and library," he said. "You'll just have to use the atomics."

"You know the shuttles won't survive an atomic blast! Not the way they're damaged," I said. I was calm outside, but inside I was seething at this man. Tralfane said nothing in response. Instead he crossed his arms and stared down at me, large and intimidating, as if he had spoken his final word. I wasn't willing to accept it. There had to be another option to both protect *Impulse* and rescue the shuttles. I had to make a decision; it was what Wesley and my father had warned me about.

I walked past Tralfane to the railing above Kasdan's nav station.

"Mr. Kasdan, your sidearm," I held out my hand while keeping my eyes focused on the Historian.

"Sir?"

"Now, Kasdan!" I ordered without looking at him. Kasdan unbuckled his coil pistol and put it in my hand. I released the safety and powered up a round, then stepped up to Tralfane with the gun trained on him.

"Is this an extreme enough emergency, Mr. Tralfane?" I said, loud enough now for everyone to hear. The bridge was dead silent and all eyes were on the standoff. Tralfane leaned in close to me.

"You don't want to do this, *young man*," he said, soft enough so that we were the only ones who could hear. I extended my arm so that the cold gun barrel rested firmly on his forehead.

"I think you're forgetting some of the people on those shuttles are my superior officers and my friends, people I admire," I said, equally softly. It was a bluff, but I was angry and inexperienced enough to try it anyway.

"I could take you out in seconds, Cochrane."

"Then do it before my finger slips on the trigger," I said. I was operating on pure adrenaline now.

"If you kill me you kill the knowledge of any weapon that might save your friends, and this ship," he said.

"My guess is you don't want to die any more than I do, Mr. Tralfane. But the longer we stand here the more time those displacement weapons have to regenerate and finish us all off," I said, as coolly as I could muster. My heart was pounding in my chest.

Tralfane's jaw clenched into a tight line as he considered the circumstances, then looked up to the gun barrel. He nodded almost imperceptibly. I immediately withdrew the pistol, powered it down, and handed it back to Kasdan.

"What the hell are you all staring at? You have your orders!" I bellowed at the crew. They scrambled back to their duty stations. Tralfane made for his workstation and I followed.

"We don't have much time," I reminded the Historian. He didn't look up from his station while responding.

"You could have saved some by not sticking that gun to my head," he said.

"I deemed it necessary," I replied, not willing to let him know I could never have pulled the trigger. Tralfane worked furiously over the controls, with no time to respond to me verbally. Finally he nodded to the longscope.

"Go! And use your com," he said. I went to the 'scope and fired her up again, clicking in the com while her displays came to life.

"Click on the new display icon and activate the controls," he said through the com. It was like he was standing next to me and whispering in my ear. Earth technology. I did as instructed, which he could no doubt track from his monitor station. The display came up with a green tactical target overlying a plain black screen.

"What am I looking for?" I said quietly.

"Be patient!" Tralfane snapped. He should have known it wasn't one of my better traits by now. Suddenly the screen painted with a hi-def display of one of the displacement wave weapons. It was still glowing red-hot from the first blast. I could see nearly into its maw, like I was just a few miles out.

"That's amazing—"

"Focus!" he hissed in my ear. I swallowed hard.

"What do you want me to do?"

"Get me the vector marks to the target," he said. I did as instructed. "Stand by," he said. A second later and the screen painted with the target hardened. A firing resolution showed in a column to the left of the display.

"Can you follow these instructions?" I nodded, then realized he couldn't see me behind the hood.

"Yes," I said quietly.

"Good. Give the orders and fire at will."

"What am I firing?" I asked. His voice came back after a second's delay.

"The forward coil cannon."

I jumped from behind the longscope and shouted orders to shut down our visual and tactical displays, along with communications.

"Lock her down! Go black, Mr. Kasdan. Those are my orders," I said. The bridge grew very quiet around me as I returned to the 'scope and my display. Coil weaponry was known on Quantar. It basically involved mixing chemicals in a chamber to produce and project high-amped laser energy. But we had never been able to use it for more than short-range pistols and rifles. I couldn't imagine what this one could do, but I figured I'd find out soon enough.

I peered in at my screen. The displacement wave weapon was changing color to amber, and its HD signature curve was climbing again. It was preparing to fire another salvo.

"We'd better do this quick, Mr. Tralfane," I said.

"Transferring firing control to you," he said, loud enough for the crew to hear.

My screen went all green as each of the items in the instruction list checked off. I targeted the asteroid and took the fire key in my right hand.

"Counting down!" I said loudly. "Three, two, one . . . firing!" I depressed the key, holding my breath. A beam of orange-white light shot across my view from right to left and struck the asteroid. The display exploded in a cascade of bright light, and I closed my eyes against the glare. When I opened them again, the screen was clear.

The asteroid had disintegrated in a second, and *Impulse* had felt nary a bump.

"Amazing!" I whispered, in awe of the power in my hands.

"Now you see why I wanted to keep this from you. Such power can destroy worlds if used improperly," said Tralfane. I shut down the longscope and came out from under the hood, looking at the Historian face-to-face.

"I've no doubt of that," I said.

I stood at the captain's chair, one hand on the arm, watching on the main bridge display as the remaining two displacement wave weapons propelled themselves away from the shuttles and toward the safety of L-6. I was amazed at how objects of such size and destructive power could move so fast.

"Do we pursue, sir?" asked Kasdan. I shook my head.

"Negative. Search and rescue is our priority now. Fire up the impellers and take us closer to the shuttles. I want you to calibrate the last known location of Captain Zander's shuttle and make for it at flank speed."

"But what about shielding, sir? Our Hoagland Field is inoperative. We could take a pounding from those asteroids if they come back and fire on us again," he said.

I looked down at Kasdan, a man just a few years older than me. Under normal circumstances we would probably be becoming friends and shipmates. Instead I found myself ordering a more experienced officer around.

"Par for the course, Mr. Kasdan," I said. "We have no choice. I want *Impulse* to find the captain's shuttle. I'll be taking the Downship out with Corporal Marker to assist in finding the Search and Rescue shuttle. As soon as you get the Hoagland Field back up and running I want you to extend the field around the captain's shuttle. *Impulse* will have to pull the heavy duty."

"Aye, sir, understood. But the Downship isn't prepped for S&R. She's made for atmospheric flight primarily, sir." I frowned down at Kasdan from my perch.

"I'm aware of her limitations, Mr. Kasdan, but we have no choice. We've got to find those shuttles and conduct a rescue before those displacement wave weapons decide to come back." *And while there's still a chance Dobrina and Zander might be alive*, I told myself.

"Is it wise for the commanding officer to leave the bridge in a crisis?" The words came from behind me, from Tralfane again. I turned to him.

"Wise?" I said. "This whole mission was unwise, Mr. Tralfane. But I intend to do what Captain Zander prevented me from doing in the first place, and that's being out *there* instead of locked into this chair." I took a few steps toward Tralfane's station.

"Which reminds me, I need an Officer of the Deck," I said. Tralfane shook his head.

"Not me. I'm not navy," he said calmly. I crossed my arms, emulating the Historian's favorite pose when he was being intransigent.

"But you serve at the pleasure of the captain of *Impulse*. Given the circumstances, that may end up being me for quite a while. And I think you'd find serving under me might be something you'd rather not do for the rest of your life," I said. Tralfane motioned me closer and I went.

"Cochrane, I'm not *navy!*" he seethed from between tight lips.

"I'm aware of that, Mr. Tralfane. But this ship is in crisis and it needs an experienced hand at the con. Now I'm asking you, will you take acting command?" I could see hesitation in his eyes, but also resignation. He knew it was the right thing to do.

"All right!" he finally said. "Go and rescue your friends! But keep in mind that once you relinquish command, I am under no obligation to return it to you." This last comment pushed me to the line again. I stepped close enough to the Historian to feel his breath on my face and spoke in hushed but intense tones.

"When I return, Mr. Tralfane, be assured that I will take you on in any physical challenge you so desire. In the meantime, I assume you have some natural human feelings for this ship and her crew. I'm asking you to take care of them, hopefully only until Captain Zander returns."

With that I stepped away, verbally gave the con to Tralfane, and was off the bridge in another second, sweat flowing inside my shirt as the lifter raced toward the landing bay.

"How long?" I asked Marker impatiently inside the Downship, watching as we approached the Search and Rescue shuttle in deep space. Marker checked his nav screen display, and then looked out the forward window for good measure. The shuttle grew ever larger.

"About four minutes, sir," he said. I nodded and unstrapped my braces to stand.

"Take us in as close as you can. The tether won't hold me over more than thirty meters," I said, "and I don't want to miss the hatch."

"Aye, sir. Still insisting on decompressing the airlock sir?" asked Marker.

"Yes, Corporal," I said as I prepped my EVA suit helmet. "I did it plenty of times in training. I'll just have to make sure I don't accelerate enough to punch a hole in the hull."

Marker looked at me, a quizzical expression on his face. "Accelerate? How do you intend to do that, sir?" I touched the small white plastic cones fastened at each hip.

"Compression jets. Used them extensively for space-borne jumps, mostly for maneuvering, but you can use them almost all the way to your target to decelerate as well, at least in zero-G." I didn't tell him that I'd never used them in such close quarters before, and that the last cadet I saw try ended up as a rather large stain on an exterior bulkhead of the shuttle he was trying to board. I figured, why worry him? It was my risk, and the commander and Layton were my friends.

"I still think we should use the umbilical," Marker said. The umbilical was a tube of clear plastic and aluminum that extruded from the Downship and similar sized vehicles as a means of moving anything from heavy cargo to people between ships in space. It was a luxury I didn't have time for.

I shook my head no as I donned my helmet and sealed the clamps, then activated the suit com. "We don't have time. They'll be out of air just a few minutes after we rendezvous, and the umbilical takes ten minutes. You know that."

I entered the airlock without another word and sealed the hatch behind me, then peered out the window just as the Search and Rescue shuttle came into view. Marker was indeed positioning the Downship perfectly, as promised. I made it less than twenty meters between the ships when he called full stop.

"Eighteen point six-five-four meters, sir," called his voice in my ear. *Smartass*, I thought. "You ready in there, sir?" Marker said.

"Affirmative," I responded. "Go on my mark." I positioned the cones to point at a reverse angle to the exterior shuttle hatch, then checked my tether one last time. I pulled myself down into a tight ball, like a sprinter in his set crouch, and held my breath, my attention fixed on the airlock door. With luck I would shoot out like a torpedo, the deceleration cones would fire, and I would come screeching to a halt before I smashed through the shuttle's hull. With luck.

"Three . . . two . . . one . . . mark!" I shouted into the com. The airlock door exploded open as the chamber decompressed. I became instantly disoriented—air rushing out around me, the shuttle above me, then the airlock door, then open space.

"You're stuck!" shouted Marker in my ear. "The tether's caught on something!" I believed what he told me but I had no way of knowing what to do about it. I was spinning wildly out of control and I felt nausea coming on strong.

"Which direction am I spinning?" I shouted out. If there was a touch of desperation in my voice it was because that's how I felt.

"Counterclockwise!"

I closed my eyes as I struggled to reach the firing mechanism for the cones on my inner left arm. I would have to shut one off and fire the other to slow myself down or I'd pass out before I could rescue anyone. I put my hands down to the firing controls. As disoriented as I was there was no way of knowing which one to fire, and there wasn't time. I had to fire one of them, but which? The sensation in my stomach was of falling from a great height and my ears were filling with the sound of rushing blood, my blood. Marker was yelling instructions at me but I couldn't recognize what he was saying anymore. I was passing out, and I had to do something.

I shut the valve on the firing control on one of the cones, I couldn't tell which, and then depressed the trigger on the other, praying for the best.

My universe went black.

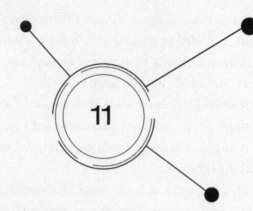

In Deep Space

The next thing I was conscious of was that someone was speaking. Whether to me or someone else I couldn't tell. The rushing in my ears was calming and I could feel weight again. Breathing in was difficult and my chest felt heavy, but after a few deep breaths I slowly felt the heaviness subside and opened my eyes. I recognized the lights of the cabin above me but my vision was blurry. I felt a warm hand on my face as the voice I was hearing became clear to me at last.

I looked up at Commander Dobrina Kierkopf. She was bending over me in her EVA suit, her helmet off, with a very concerned look on her face.

"Commannndddurrr," I mumbled out, my words slurring. There was a mask over my face feeding me oxygen, and it wasn't helping me speak any clearer. I tried to reach up to pull the mask off but my arms felt like lead.

"Stay put, Mr. Cochrane," she said to me, then tucked my arm back in to the safety seat I was strapped into. I nodded, then looked around the cabin of the Downship. Layton was at the pilot's station, with Marker at the copilot station. Dobrina and I were a few rows back and down, in the passenger cabin. She had me strapped in like a baby in a ground car. I felt her run a hand through my sopping wet hair.

"What happened?" I said more clearly, or so I hoped.

"Your tether caught on an explosive clip that malfunctioned. You were spinning like a top at a carnival," she said. I tried to smile.

"You needed help," I said.

"Like hell!" she responded. "Another half minute and we'd have been out there to greet you! We took the displacement wave straight on against our shields. It burned everything out, communications, propulsion, you name it. But thanks to Layton here we were as ready as we could be. When we saw you coming we were already kitted out for EVA. We figured we'd just pop the hatch ourselves and float on over. That was until I looked out and saw you spinning like a pinwheel. Oh, and by the way, you fired the wrong cone. Nearly sheared your tether off too. By the time we caught you, you were almost at escape velocity. Thank goodness you didn't puke in the suit." She smiled at me. I smiled back. The oxygen was quickly clearing my head.

"Did I have you worried?" I said. She squeezed my hand but said nothing, then turned to her pilot.

"Mr. Layton, ETA to Captain Zander?" Kierkopf asked.

"Eight minutes, sir," said Layton. She turned back to me.

"You have that long to get yourself ready," she said.

Captain Zander and his volunteer crew had less than ten minutes of air left when we rendezvoused with the bulwark shuttle. Marker had positioned us as close as he dared. Commander Kierkopf and I stood behind the airlock hatch watching the umbilical deploy foot-by-foot to the sealed main cargo hatch of the shuttle. It wasn't going fast enough.

"Status of the shuttle!" demanded Dobrina.

"Main cabin temperature 1140 degrees Celsius and rising. Cargo cabin is exposed and at space normal temperature," said Marker. "There must be a hole in the hull we can't see from here."

"If the pilot's nest is that hot then she must be burning hydrazine fuel," I said.

"There's a main fuel line running through the pilot's cabin on the Werder class shuttles," said Marker. "It must have burst."

"That's a great design. Who thought that up?" I was angry.

"It doesn't matter," said Kierkopf. "They can't survive much longer, even in the EVA suits. They're built primarily for space, not fire duty."

"If we can directly vent the main cabin, the decompression would burn the fire out," I suggested. She shook her head.

"Impossible. Blowing the cabin would send everything and everyone inside hurtling into space, including the captain. We'd never have enough time to rescue them all," she looked down at her watch. "If they were piped into the reserve air supply in the shuttle they should have seven minutes left. How much longer on the umbilical?" she shouted to Marker.

"Four minutes," he replied. Not enough time to get across, deal with the fire, and rescue the crew, not to mention we'd probably have to blow the service hatch with the charges I'd brought.

"We'll have to go now. Get your ass down here, Marker! Layton," she called to her Search and Rescue copilot, "you have the pilot's chair. Hold her steady and keep her ready to fly back to *Impulse* at a moment's notice." Layton nodded vigorously inside the helmet of his EVA suit.

"About *Impulse*," I started. "I ordered her close to extend the Hoagland Field around us." Kierkopf shook her head.

"She's taken a pounding from the displacement wave. I ordered her back out of range until we retrieve all personnel and return in the Downship," she said. I didn't take her countermanding my orders as a personal affront to my plan of action. Truth be told, I was glad to have someone else in charge. Marker joined us and we all donned our helmets and activated our coms.

"The umbilical isn't going to make it in time," said Kierkopf to both of us. "We'll have to go out through the maintenance hatch and propel over to the captain's shuttle."

"That's my job," jumped in Marker. "I'll go over, locate the damage hole in the hull from the attack, and set a tether for you to follow. Then I'll go in and cut open the crew cabin hatch from inside."

"Affirmative," said Kierkopf, nodding. Then we all made our way down the narrow spiral staircase to the maintenance deck. Marker hooked up a set of the cone jets to his belt and gave the thumbs-up.

"You'd better take a coil cutter with you, in case the bulkhead is sealed," said Dobrina. Marker took one from the shelf and Dobrina took another, then handed me a third. The cutting lasers were different from our pistols and rifles, using a highly concentrated beam of light to cut metal or rock. This one was a hand-sized tool, cylindrical and just long enough to fit in your palm with an emitter at the end.

"Will this be enough to get through the bulkhead?" I asked.

"It's all we have," said Kierkopf.

"We have proximity charges," I replied. "I had Marker pack them before we left. We can use them to blow the bulkhead door if we have to."

Kierkopf hesitated, then shook her head negative. "They're too dangerous. The explosion could kill them both, and us."

"And these will take too long," I said, raising the cutter. Kierkopf looked to Marker for an opinion.

"Wouldn't want to be inside when one went off, sir, but we may have no other choice," he said.

Kierkopf relented, raising a pair of fingers to me. "Two," she said. I went to the wall cabinet and unlatched it, then removed the charges as Marker sealed the deck and decompressed the cabin. We had six minutes when he popped the hatch.

Kierkopf and I watched from above as he dove through the small hatch headfirst, swimming into open space with the tether attached at his waist. I saw a small puff of air as he activated the cones and accelerated toward the shuttle. Dobrina followed next and I came out last, both of us holding on to EVA clamps and waiting while Marker crossed to the shuttle. By the time I got myself oriented Marker was almost on the scarred shuttle hull. It was black and mottled from the beating it had taken from the displacement wave. No doubt the collapse of her shielding under the pressure of the wave had caused a short in the shuttle electronics, and thus the fire.

I looked up to my left, toward the shuttle's pilot's nest. I saw a flash of deep orange reflecting out of the windows into space. "I've got visual confirmation of the cabin fire," I said. Neither Kierkopf nor Marker responded, focusing only on the job at hand.

"Five minutes," came Kasdan's voice in our helmets. I watched as Marker caught a handhold on the shuttle hull and pulled himself in, going hand over hand and quickly rounding the top of the shuttle, moving out of our sight. A second later he reported back.

"Tether secure, sir. There's a hole just big enough to get my shoulders through over here. Both of you should be able to make it in without a problem. I'm going in, one way or another."

"Acknowledged," said Kierkopf, then she started moving across open space, using a sweeping hand-over-hand technique on the tether. She was surprisingly fast. I gripped the line myself and tried to replicate her motion, but I was much slower than she was. One thing I was always told about open space EVA: don't look down. I reminded myself of this as I focused on Kierkopf ahead of me.

"Report, Marker," she said, her voice crackling through my helmet. She was breathing heavily but still pulling away from me. A moment of silence passed and I began to worry.

"Scan shows two survivors in the pilot's nest," Marker shouted. "Both in EVA suits. Low vitals but I can tell that they're breathing. Four dead in the main cabin, two survivors, both unconscious, four missing. Probably got sucked out when the hull ruptured."

"Four minutes left," came Kasdan's voice again.

"What about the captain?" said Dobrina.

"He's not among the crew here," replied Marker. "My guess is that it's him and Poulsen in the pilot's nest, behind the bulkhead."

Where the fire is, I thought, and immediately picked up my pace. My thoughts turned to Natalie, and I wondered if she had survived the initial wave attack, then been killed by a similar fire . . .

I shook my head to clear those awful thoughts from my mind and refocused on the task at hand. My shoulders and arms burned as I passed hand over hand in a frantic attempt to aid in the rescue. Kierkopf said nothing more as she reached the shuttle and gripped the handholds, propelling herself and vanishing over the curve of the hull and presumably into the cabin with Marker. It seemed an eternity until I was able to reach the shuttle and do the same, cresting the hull into darkness and then in through the jagged hole in the shuttle's side to the crew cabin.

Inside the cabin was dark and cold, colder when I saw the charred bodies of the dead volunteers. I switched on my helmet light. Marker was at the now open freight hatch attaching the clear plastic umbilical. Dobrina stood at the bulkhead wall cutting the metal around the door seal to the pilot's cabin with both of the cutters. It was taking too long. I joined her silently as Marker took the first of the survivors into the umbilical and pushed off with his feet. I watched his technique as he floated through the tunnel and into the open airlock hatch on the Downship, disappearing, then starting his return trip a moment later.

"Three minutes of oxygen left," said Layton in our ears.

The bulkhead metal was thick and difficult to cut through. I had started at the top right with Dobrina working the left side. She was almost to the bottom of the doorway but I was less than halfway down on my side. No air was escaping from the pilot's cabin. We weren't making it.

"Commander, this isn't working!" I said, putting down the laser. "We're running out of time!"

"I know!" she said angrily.

"We've got to use the charges," I said. I saw her shake her head inside her EVA helmet.

"Not until we get the other survivor off the ship. Keep cutting."

"Dobrina, there's no time! Zander and Poulsen will die if we don't blow the bulkhead!"

She put down her cutting laser, whipped her head around and slammed her helmet visor into mine. Her words came muffled through the visor but I could hear her clearly enough.

"Damn it, man, give me the charges then! I'll blow the bulkhead," she demanded.

"You don't know how to use them," I said, unwilling to let her put herself at risk. "It's my job. And with Zander incapacitated *you're* the acting captain!" I reminded her. She grabbed my arms while keeping her helmet pressed to mine so only the two of us could hear the conversation.

"*I* have to do this," she shouted. "Give me the goddamned charges!"

"You're too valuable to risk—"

She cut me off. "Goddamn it, Cochrane! This is *my* job! Now give me the goddamned charges and get that survivor out of here!" she ordered.

I looked to the hatch. Marker was only halfway back through the umbilical.

"Two minutes," updated Layton over the com.

"That was an order, Commander!" she held out her hands and I pressed the charges into them, then turned around to the other survivor.

"You'll need to set the charges for proximity zero!" I yelled back at her through the com as I picked up the injured man off the deck and headed for the umbilical tunnel. "Ten second delay to get to the umbilical or you'll risk being blown into space!"

"I know what I'm doing, Cochrane! Now get that man off the ship and clear the deck!"

I looked back at her as she was adjusting the charges, setting and resetting them, without success.

"You need to arm the media first!" I yelled. She waved me off. She clearly didn't know how to set the charges, but I did. I looked down the umbilical as Marker came toward me on his return, then back at the struggling Dobrina, and made my choice.

I tossed the survivor in my hands down the clear umbilical tunnel toward Marker as hard as I could.

The survivor hit Marker directly in his midsection and started both of them flying back toward the Downship hatch. Then I turned and flung myself toward Dobrina.

"What the hell?" she exclaimed as I grabbed her by the shoulders, pulling her away from the bulkhead and the two charges, both of which I could see were not set. One advantage of zero-G is that the body with the most momentum always has the upper hand.

"Goddamn you, Cochrane! Put me down! That's an order!" she screamed at me in protest. But my mind was made up.

"You don't know how to set the charges, Commander, but I do. There's no time to argue!" I spun her around with one hand and dragged her to the hatch opening as she flailed at me in vain. I began to cut away the umbilical plastic with the cutting laser in my free hand. Seconds later, I had her wrapped helplessly in the umbilical material, then cut it loose and shoved her back toward the Downship.

"Cochrane!" she howled in anger. I reached up and shut off my receiver, but kept my broadcast channel open. I watched as Marker began to retrieve Dobrina from the collapsing umbilical, bringing her inside the Downship, then turned back to the bulkhead.

"I'm setting the charges now!" I said into my com. "Armed, with a ten-second delay. Once I hit the fire key I'll secure myself and ride out the detonation. The door will blow and the fire should burn out in the first few seconds. As the cabin decompresses I'll try and grab the captain and Poulsen. With luck I'll be able to find the tether and direct us to the Downship hatch."

It seemed like a good plan. I had no idea if it would work.

I depressed the fire key using the detonator and then made for the far wall, picking up some scrap metal from a chair and then crouching next to the rear bulkhead, holding on to some safety straps and using the metal as a shield. Then I waited, watching the charges. The seconds ticked by, an eternity.

With a flash of bright yellow the charges went, the cabin door flying off in a silent ballet of metal, flame, and glass. Seeking escape from the pressurized cabin, the river of rapidly freezing fire went straight for the open freight hatch and out. Amongst the debris I saw an EVA-suited body rush out into vacant space. Then the bulkhead gave way, the metal turning to powder as it joined the flow of debris. I looked up as the exposed fire turned to silent gray mist, still rushing headlong to escape. Then I saw a second EVA suit, ripped free from a crash chair and moving rapidly toward the hatch. I let go of the straps and pushed off the way I had seen Marker do, plunging myself into the riptide. I felt stinging like thousands of needles poking me as I dove forward and then hit something with a *thump*.

I desperately tried to clear my visor of dust to see what I had captured. It felt like a man, but I couldn't be sure. An instant later I was through the hatch and floating free in space. I wiped the dust away and looked down at my captured prey.

It was Zander.

At least, it looked like him. I could see through his visor that he was unconscious. His face was charred black on the side, but his EVA monitor, still working, indicated respiration and heartbeat. He lived.

I had a moment of euphoria before I realized my new predicament. I was floating in open space and heading right for the metal hull of the Downship. At this speed I had no doubt that an impact could be fatal. I had only a few seconds, but I managed to duck my head and turn, protecting Zander from the impact by putting him beneath me, then fired my cone jets to slow us. I thudded hard against the metal skin and then we started skipping down the curved hull of the Downship in a painful, bumpy descent.

Shit! I thought. *If I can't stop we'll skid off the hull and into open space!* Rescue would be very difficult then, and Zander would almost surely die of oxygen deprivation. I bounced against the hull a second and a third time as we rolled down to the maintenance hatch, the tether there still in place. I had only a second to react and I reached out desperately, trying to grab a hold on the line.

"Ahhhgghh!" I shouted in frustration, grasping frantically at the tether. My hand slipped off and we started floating free, away from the Downship. I swallowed into a dry throat. I didn't want my first commanding officer to die in my arms.

The next second we were enveloped in a cargo net, shot out of the maintenance hatch. We came to a stop with a wrenching jar, then the net started retracting back toward the hatch.

As we were reeled back in I switched on my com again and called in to the Downship. No one answered. A few seconds later and we were inside the maintenance deck. Marker came down and together we transferred Zander up to Layton. Once that was done we shut the hatch and normal environment and gravity were restored. Marker came over and put a firm hand on my shoulder and said, "Welcome aboard, Commander."

I removed my helmet and nodded, taking in a deep breath of cabin air.

"Thanks, John. It's good to be here."

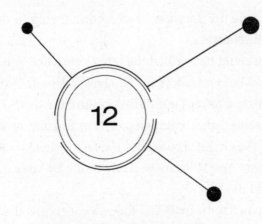

12

Stranded

"**Y**ou're going to stand for court-martial when we get back to High Station," yelled Commander Dobrina Kierkopf. She was standing over me and pointing her finger in my direction, flanked on either side by Marker and Layton. There was no doubt that no matter what friendship had developed between us, she was my commanding officer right now. In fact, she was more than that, she was acting captain of *Impulse*.

We had assembled in the crew cabin of the Downship after completing the rescue of the survivors from Captain Zander's shuttle. The chewing out was coming nearly an hour after I had been rescued at the last possible second by John Marker and his grappling net. We'd spent almost all of the time since then getting Zander and the other survivors stabilized and into the emergency medical docks where their vital signs had been reduced to absolute minimum as a means of preserving what little energy they had left. Zander was in a state of stasis, which at the moment seemed like a far better option than facing the fuming Commander Kierkopf.

"I'm prepared for that eventuality. Hell, I was prepared for it when I made my decision," I said back, trying to defend my actions aboard the shuttle.

"You could have killed the other survivors. You could have killed Corporal Marker. Hell, you could have killed me!" she seethed. "Your brother would never have pulled a stunt like that!"

I resented that comparison. "I'm not my brother, sir, and I'm aware of the chance I took. But the fact is that you weren't able to set the charges. You were more likely to die by your own hand than by anything I did."

"The hell with that! You follow orders or you end up in the brig! I'd put you there now if this ship had one!" I said nothing to that. I assumed that since we were still in hostile space and many thousands of clicks from *Impulse* that she would need me, at least for a while more. The discipline would certainly follow, but I was ready to face that on my own terms.

When I said nothing more she turned away from me and addressed the other two crewmen aboard. "Layton, get us underway back to *Impulse*," she said. The pilot departed for the cockpit while she swiveled to face Marker. "What's the report on our other survivors?" she asked. He looked dour.

"They're both in stasis and stable, just like Zander. But I'd have to say they're both in better shape than the captain. Mostly radiation burns and superficial debris wounds," said Marker.

"In other words, they were lucky," said Commander Kierkopf. Then she looked at me directly. "More than I can say for Claus Poulsen." That stung. I liked Poulsen, and it wasn't me who'd attacked the shuttle, it was the empire, or at least the remnants of their automated defense weapons. I wanted to say something back but a look from Marker told me not to. The commander sighed, put her hands on her hips, and stared down at me.

"Get down to the cargo deck and keep an eye on the medical readouts. If anything changes on any of them, call me. Otherwise stay out of the way and keep your mouth shut." With that she spun away from me and went up the three short steps to the pilot's nest to join Layton. Marker put a hand on my shoulder.

"I'm sorry, Peter. It's not for me to judge what you did or didn't do, but you made a decision and you saved the captain," he said.

"But Poulsen—" I started.

"Was probably already dead," cut in Marker. "There was nothing you could do for him. It wasn't your fault." I picked up my EVA helmet, resigned to my situation, and started for the cargo deck. "Peter," called Marker after me. "No matter what happens, remember Zander put you in charge for a reason. He trusted you to make the right decisions." I stopped at that, but didn't turn around. "You made good decisions today," Marker finished.

I said nothing to that. What could I say? I just started down to the medical deck, resigned to my fate.

An hour later I was still at my post, watching the monitors on the survivors in the medical docks. Zander's readings were very low, and I wasn't medically qualified to know whether he would survive or not. The stasis field had put him into a deep anesthesia mode, nearly suspended animation. Any lower and he would be officially "frozen," neither alive nor dead, waiting until he could be revived by the superior medical technology on board *Impulse*. *If* he could be revived. I checked my watch, noting that we should have docked with *Impulse* by now. I presumed there must have been some complication, but I was in the dark, literally and figuratively, and that's where Commander Kierkopf wanted me.

I was surprised a moment later when my com beeped in.

"What's your status?" it was Commander Kierkopf's voice.

"They're all stable. Captain Zander is in the deepest state of stasis. He barely registers on the readouts," I replied. For a moment there was no response, then:

"Lock them down in their current modes. We don't need anyone reviving right now. Then get up here." I was surprised by this but did as instructed, setting the docks so that all the survivors would be kept at their current level of stasis. They could go lower if it was required to keep them alive, but they couldn't be revived automatically by the system without changing the settings.

I hurried up the staircase from the cargo deck and through the crew cabin to the raised cockpit. When I came in, Dobrina was in the center seat with Layton at the nav station on her left and Marker piloting on her right, closest to me.

"Where was *Impulse*'s last location?" Commander Kierkopf demanded without looking back at me. I checked Marker's display for our current spatial coordinates.

"We should be right on top of her," I stated.

"Should," said Kierkopf. "But we aren't." I stepped up and ran my hands over the controls, verifying for myself. She seemed to tolerate this for the moment.

"These are the right coordinates. At least these are the coordinates she was at when we left her," I said.

"She's not here," said Dobrina. "We've scanned an area almost a full AU across. Nothing."

Marker turned to me. "She's not where we left her, Peter."

"Does this ship have any longscope capabilities?" Kierkopf asked. "We've got to get a better look, try and find her."

Without even thinking I pushed Marker aside and stepped in, accessing the limited longscope displays of the Downship. After a few quiet moments I had some answers—not many, but some.

"She wasn't destroyed, at least not by any weapons we know of, or there'd be debris and trace energy signatures," I said. I continued to scan. After a few moments Kierkopf was getting impatient.

"Have you got her, or not?" she snapped at me. I shook my head.

"The capabilities of these displays are so limited—"

"I'm sick of excuses, Cochrane."

"If you'll just give me another minute, Commander," I said, working swiftly through the displays, confirming my meager findings.

"Come on!" she insisted. I took another ten seconds before responding to her.

"What I can tell you is that she activated her impeller drives and left the area, apparently on her own. There are enough propulsion traces to indicate her direction, but locating her will be difficult," I said.

"Where did she go?" demanded Kierkopf. I turned away from my displays to face my new commanding officer directly.

"She was on a course for the inner system, Levant Prime, or possibly one of the satellites. And she was running full bore on the impellers, so much so that she'll run out of fuel reserves soon. She may be able to make it to Levant, but she won't be able to make it back out here without scooping more hydrazine," I said.

"She's not coming back out here," said Kierkopf. "She's on a one-way trip to Levant, for some reason. And I'm betting I know who's commanding her."

"Tralfane?" I said. "I left him in command during the rescue."

She nodded. "Remember when you told me the Historians had their own agenda? I didn't believe you. Well, now I do. Because the only explanation that makes any sense is that one of them just hijacked our Lightship."

"But the crew wouldn't just follow Tralfane's orders and abandon us," said Marker. "They'd fight."

"They may not have had a choice," said Kierkopf. "None of us really knows what a Historian is capable of, or what controls they have over the ship. The crew could merely be helpless passengers at this point." She turned to me and looked me directly in the eye. "Do whatever you can, but find *Impulse*," she said. Then she turned to Layton. "Plot us a course for Levant Prime, Mr. Layton. As fast as this bucket will go. And let's pray we can get there in time."

Nearly four hours later, we were nowhere close to finding *Impulse* or reaching the inner planets of Levant. To say the Downship was slow and not intended for long-term interplanetary runs was an understatement. Commander Kierkopf, for her part, had grown silent after riding me for the first half hour. Even she seemed to realize that the Downship was not made for pursuit and that her instruments, especially her longscope displays, weren't geared for the task assigned. We were all growing increasingly frustrated and quiet as we tried to do our jobs. It was Layton who broke the silence, unfortunately with bad news.

"Commander," he started, his voice jolting us all to attention. "According to the nav computer calculations we're quickly approaching a decision point. In less than thirty minutes we'll be at a point where we'll have to commit to going forward or turning back to the Search and Rescue shuttle."

"Explain," she said. Layton paused, considering his words.

"This ship was not meant for extensive interplanetary flight. We're still about 1.5 AUs from Levant Prime, a bit less from her moons, which might be habitable or have bases on them. We're still within range of a return to the Search and Rescue, at least for another thirty minutes or so. Once we pass that point though there'll be no turning back, and we'll run out of fuel less than halfway to L-Prime. Our life support will last a bit longer, but not much with the four of us on board and three more in stasis in the medical dock."

"I see," she said, then went silent for a moment. "So we can't catch

Impulse, can't track her," she looked at me then, "and we'll run out of fuel and energy before we reach Levant. Any other good news?"

"The Search and Rescue will buy us a day or possibly two if we drain all the power from this ship," said Layton. Dobrina nodded.

"Opinions. Mr. Marker?" she said.

"What about that HD anomaly we detected? It's a power source. Can we reach it?" he said. I shook my head.

"It's farther than L-Prime. 3.82 AUs distant," I replied. Dobrina looked to me.

"Any luck on locating *Impulse*?" she asked. I shook my head negative.

"Not really, sir. With this equipment, it's like finding a needle in haystack," I answered honestly. She considered all this for a moment. Then she made her decision.

"Turn us around, Mr. Marker. No point in delaying the inevitable. Mr. Layton, plot us a course back to the Search and Rescue shuttle." She paused before turning to me. "And you, Mr. Cochrane. Finding that needle would go a long way toward easing my anger at you." I nodded, then dove right back into my longscope scans.

The scans were fruitless. We were back to the S&R shuttle in due course and when we got to her, we did a damage survey and concluded our best chance was to actually drain the remaining resources from the S&R rather than transfer to her. We did a series of EVAs, connecting power transfer cables and running the Downship exclusively off of the S&R shuttle power supplies, which were lower than we anticipated. And now we had a clock: eighteen hours and eleven minutes until we exhausted both the S&R power and our own reserves. Then Captain Zander and the others would die, we would put on our EVA suits and live a few hours more, then join them. It was a bleak prospect.

Marker and Layton kept busy converting the rear of the passenger cabin to bunks so we could rest, though as tired as we were none of us were really able to sleep under the circumstances. No one wanted to spend their last few hours of life dozing as if they had no concerns.

I'd taken a rest shift after Layton and Marker, and I was halfway through my two-hour rest period when, unexpectedly, the commander parted the curtains and joined me, lying down in the second bunk across from me. We stayed that way in silence for several minutes, the cabin lights dim and the room quiet. Layton had my station at the longscope, but I felt useless lying there wide awake. So I sat up, ready to resume my duties.

"Please stay," came the commander's voice out of the darkness. I dutifully lay back down, waiting for her to continue. "It's hard for me to admit, but you did end up saving Zander, though I don't agree with your methods," she said. I pondered this a moment.

"I acted on impulse. Trying to save the captain was my only thought. I never thought about what I was doing, I just reacted . . . just did it," I said by way of explanation. She said nothing more for a moment, and I thought perhaps the conversation was done, then:

"I've decided your actions in rescuing Zander won't be in my official report."

"Thank you, Commander," I said. Then the silence between us resumed. I had hoped she and I would become friends on our mission. Now I doubted if that would ever happen. After a few more minutes of silence, I sat up.

"Request permission to return to duty, Commander, and resume my scans. I can't sleep anyway. If I find anything, I'll let you know right away," I said. She said nothing in response for a few moments, so I stood to go.

"You did good work in rescuing Zander. Carry on, Commander," she said from the dark. It was the best compliment she could give me.

Ninety minutes later I had something to report.

"Wake the commander," I said to Layton. "Tell her I've got an HD signal." What seemed like seconds later Dobrina was standing beside me in the pilot's cabin. Layton took the nav station again and Marker the con.

"Report," she said. I turned from my station to face her.

"About ten minutes ago I detected what looked like an HD signal," I said. "It was faint, and not coming from the direction that *Impulse* had gone, toward the inner planets. Rather, the signal seemed to be coming from the near jump point. I thought it might be a reflection of some sort of anomaly at the opposing Lagrange point, so I checked it further."

"And?" she said, impatient.

"The signal is powerful enough to be *Impulse*, but the mass displacement is far too small," I continued. "I can't know for certain with these primitive longscope instruments, but I'd have to say it's a new ship that has entered the system at the jump point."

"A *new* ship? Not *Impulse*, and not big enough to be a Lightship?" she asked for clarification. I nodded.

"Affirmative. It's much smaller, but every bit as powerful as *Impulse*, based on its HD signature. And it's heading our way," I said.

"To rescue us, or to finish us off?" she asked. I shook my head.

"Unknown," I replied. She contemplated this a moment, then:

"Everyone into your EVA helmets. Sidearms and weapons. If they're coming to finish this, we won't go down without a fight," she said.

There was a round of "yes, sir," and then we all got down to business.

The wait was excruciating. The HD signal was getting stronger, closing directly on our position. I used one of the 'scope displays to get a look at her—she was dark and shaped like a dagger. If I didn't know she was there from her HD signal I would never have seen her. I had to admit the shape of her looked menacing, and that wasn't very comforting.

"Is she close enough for radio contact?" asked Kierkopf.

"The ship-to-ship isn't strong enough for a signal from this distance, and this ship has no longwave," I said. "But we could try sending an IFF signal."

"And hope they're friend, not foe?" she asked. I nodded.

"The way they're closing on us, it will all be over one way or another in a matter of minutes anyway," I offered. She thought about this for a moment.

"Send the IFF ping," she ordered.

"Yes, sir," I said. I looked to Marker, who had control of the automated signal. He unlatched the key and typed in the code to send the signal. "At this distance we should get a reply within thirty—"

I was cut off by the positive beep from the return. Layton, Marker and I all smiled. Commander Kierkopf did not.

"So they say friend," she said. "We'll find out in a few more minutes."

At that, the radio com chimed for an incoming signal packet. Not a call, but a signal they were ready to receive a call from us. "Radio contact, sir," I said. Dobrina nodded.

"Let's reply." I hit the send button and she spoke. "This is Commander Dobrina Kierkopf of the Union Lightship *Impulse*. To whom am I speaking?" she said. There was a crackle of static as the line popped and blipped, but the response didn't come. "To whom am I speaking?" she repeated.

"This is Serosian," came the raspy reply, "Historian of *H.M.S. Starbound*, on a rescue mission. Do you need assistance?" Now I smiled broadly.

"Indeed we do," said Commander Kierkopf. "Indeed we do, sir. Can you lock on our coordinates?"

"Already done, Commander," came the deep and familiar baritone reply. "I will be alongside you in seven minutes. Prepare to transfer at that time."

"We have wounded here," she said. "Can you assist with them?"

"Affirmative," he replied. "I have full medical facilities on board. May I inquire as to the status of Captain Zander and *Impulse*?" he asked.

"Captain Zander is one of our injured. *Impulse* is . . . missing," Kierkopf replied.

"That's what I feared," came Serosian's voice back through the static. "One last inquiry. Is Peter Cochrane among you, or with *Impulse*?" he asked. Kierkopf looked at me and smiled.

"Oh, he's about two feet in front of me, Mr. Serosian. And I'll be glad when you arrive so that I can be rid of him," she said.

The chuckle on the other end of the line gave me hope for the first time in days.

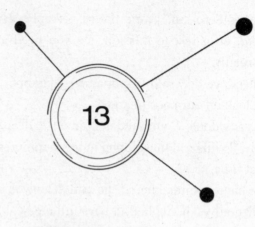

Rescue

erosian's ship, which he called a Historian's Yacht, pulled alongside us precisely seven minutes later and extended a sophisticated umbilical to the Downship's docking port. We had the injured
survivors, including Zander, out of their docks and transported to the
yacht within thirty minutes. The yacht contained a much more advanced automated medical facility than we had even aboard *Impulse*.
The automated system was contained in a crystalline chamber that
glowed and hummed with pulses of white light. I couldn't pretend to
understand its functioning, but Serosian assured me that Zander and
the others were already on their way to being healed and in no danger
of dying, once we had loaded them onto pallets and sealed them inside the chamber. Recovery could still take weeks though, he said.

The rest of the yacht was every bit as impressive as the medical
chamber. From the command deck, *Starbound*'s Historian oversaw
every function of the ship, monitoring from behind a central command console big enough for at least three people. He ran his hands
effortlessly over the console, his hands moving in and out of the display like he was dipping them in a smooth, black pond. The surface

rippled like water when he touched it, but his hands never came back wet from contact.

Behind the console was a pair of adjunct stations. The front of the command deck was entirely taken up with an impressive seamless visual display, which currently showed the way forward. Much like our displays on *Impulse*, there were a multitude of options: tactical, systems, star map, or "normal" visual view. The whole effect was like being in a high-tech, three-dimensional theater, only what you were watching was real. It was also of far higher quality than what we had available on *Impulse*, making it seem almost like you were looking out a window into space itself.

Once we were settled, Commander Kierkopf in the couch to Serosian's left at the main console and me to his right, with Layton and Marker at the rear stations, he put the yacht in motion on a course directly for Levant Prime, leaving the discarded shuttle and Downship behind.

"This vessel is not a standard navy ship," said Kierkopf, her comment half statement and half question. Serosian shook his head.

"No, Commander, it's not. But it is *part* of a standard navy ship," he said. Her brow furrowed at this answer.

"What do you mean?" she asked.

He nodded upward, not taking his attention from his tasks. "If you went one deck above you would find my library, office, and sleeping quarters as they appear on *Starbound*. In fact, when this ship is docked, it is part of *Starbound*," he said.

"Really?" I asked, fascinated by this. "You mean this yacht is the core of *Starbound*?" He nodded.

"In a sense, yes. Under normal circumstances the yacht is docked inside *Starbound*, with its own power source, of course, but I only activate it in an emergency or when the yacht needs to operate independently. I can control every aspect of the ship, any system, from here. It was designed as a failsafe, in case anything were to happen to the Lightship's own hyperdimensional drive."

"Wait," said the commander, "we were never told about this capability. Do you mean that at any moment a ship's Historian can take control of *any* Lightship?" Serosian nodded soberly in response.

"And this is what I fear has happened with *Impulse*. Tralfane is from a different school of thought than I am, a different sect of the Historian Order, if you will. Something must have happened to cause him to act, to take control of *Impulse*, for her own good."

"Or for his own purposes," I said. Commander Kierkopf waved me off.

"And the command crew of *Impulse*, or any other Lightship, are never told of this command override functionality that you Historians possess?" she asked. He looked at her sidelong for a moment.

"Since you are the acting captain of *Impulse*, I will answer that question, even though I am under no obligation to do so. Captain Zander knows of this, as does Captain Maclintock of *Starbound* and Captain Scott of *Valiant*. The idea was presented by us to the Unified Navy command during the design phase of the Lightship program, and signed off on by Admiral Wesley and your father, Peter," he said, turning to me. Then he turned back to Kierkopf. "And so now I am informing you because you are the acting captain of *Impulse*."

Acting Captain Kierkopf paused for a moment to let that sink in, which afforded me an opportunity to jump in with my own questions.

"I don't understand how *Starbound* is functioning without the yacht connected. And how did you know we were in trouble?" I asked.

He smiled at me, like he always did. "*Starbound* is perfectly fine. She has her own HD drives and can carry out her mission for months before the crystal will need any kind of maintenance. As for how I knew you were in trouble, I didn't. But I did have orders from Admiral Wesley to shadow your mission, in case you got in trouble. And you did, Peter," he said. "Though not in the way we anticipated."

"That's certain," said Captain Kierkopf. "And I don't want to break up your happy reunion, but I have a serious question: can we catch *Impulse*?"

Serosian's smile faded and he looked more pensive now. "Unlikely," he said. "We have the same impeller propulsion capabilities as she does, which means Tralfane can keep his distance as much as he wants to."

"But he's burning his impellers full bore. His fuel reserves must be nearly gone," I protested.

"The impellers are designed to channel energy from the Hoagland Drive if necessary. He may never run out of fuel," said Serosian.

"Something else that isn't in the specs," I stated. Things got quiet as Captain Kierkopf contemplated the situation.

"Where's he going with my ship?" she said. "Why Levant?"

"Because I suspect there is something there that he values, something he knows about, or suspects. Something he wants."

"To what end?"

"As I stated, his school has a different philosophy than mine. We are dedicated to the Union and to your well-being and protection, your nurturing, if you will. His school believes that the strongest should rule. It may be that he has decided that the empire represents the best chance for humankind's rejuvenation."

"Which makes him our enemy," said Kierkopf. At that a signal chime beeped in. Serosian checked his panels, which were a mystery to me, running his hands across the console. "What is it?" asked the captain.

"Bad news. I'm picking up signs of depleted hyperdimensional energy along our current path. That can mean only one thing."

"What?"

"He's bombarding *Impulse*'s primary HD drive crystals with anti-protons," said the Historian.

"Which means?" the Historian looked grim.

"He's destroying her hyperdimensional drive. If he's controlling *Impulse* from the yacht, it means he's crippling her."

Six hours later I was working at the yacht's impressive longscope station when our circumstances changed dramatically.

"I've got a signal," I called back to my companions. Serosian and Kierkopf were hovering over my shoulders in seconds.

"Report," demanded Dobrina.

"I'm not sure if it's *Impulse* yet, but the signal is strong and I'm detecting depleted duranium on the trail we've been tracking," I said. The two of them watched as I brought up the long-range tactical display on the main viewer.

"That's her," said Serosian, after only a second.

"What's she doing?" asked Dobrina.

"Maneuvering," said the Historian, pointing to a red path that displayed *Impulse's* track. "She slowed long enough to orbit the smaller satellite, here. It cost her nearly four hours of her lead on us. But now she's passed behind the satellite and is back on track for Levant Prime."

"But why would she stop? What could be on the satellite that would make Tralfane give up nearly four hours of his cushion against us? He must know we're coming," I said.

"He certainly does," said Serosian. "He needed something from the satellite, and felt it was important enough to risk going there and losing more than half his cushion. He'll need time to accelerate as well. What's our current distance?"

"Three point four light-hours," I replied after checking my display.

"Can we catch him?" Dobrina asked Serosian. The Historian nodded.

"At his current speed," he said. "we can get within firing distance before he reaches Levant. But it will be close. Very, very close. And we don't know for sure if Levant is even his objective. He could be aiming for some other target, something closer. Even the larger moon, perhaps."

Captain Kierkopf stood up and crossed her arms. "Is there something you're not telling us? Or something you suspect?" she said. "I insist that you share."

Now Serosian stood to his full height, facing the captain as I swiveled in my chair, looking up at both of them. Serosian was impressive in his tallness, his all-black Historian's garb making him seem even more imposing than normal. But Dobrina was strong in her own right, I'd seen it before, on the fencing court, and she wasn't going to back down from him. She believed herself to be in command of this mission, and she was going to fight for that command.

Serosian clasped his hands behind his back before speaking. "Commander Kierkopf—" he started.

"*Captain* Kierkopf," she interrupted, insisting that he acknowledge her acting rank. He nodded.

"Captain, I can only conclude that this maneuver had some intent. A Historian like Tralfane, so well trained and experienced, would not freely give as much ground to us as he did without some goal in mind. What that goal is I don't know," he said.

"But you suspect?" Again he gave that slight nod of acknowledgment. She eyed him warily. "Then I demand to know what it is that you suspect."

Serosian contemplated her, the two of them engaging in a standoff right above me.

"I would prefer to keep my suspicions private until I have more knowledge of the situation," he said.

"Not acceptable," she replied. "Not at all."

"Captain, please understand, there is certain knowledge that I possess that I have sworn an oath to my faith to protect. No orders from you or anyone else of any rank, or royal station," at this he glanced in my direction, "will be sufficient for me to reveal all that I know, or suspect."

Dobrina opened her mouth to protest again but he quickly held up his hand to her.

"However," he started again, lowering the hand, "I will promise you that at the proper time, if circumstances warrant, I will reveal to you and anyone else involved with this situation all that is necessary for you to know in order for you to act to protect your lives and this ship."

She nodded, not satisfied, I could see, but accepting, for the moment. "And what about *Impulse*?" Dobrina said.

Serosian got a pensive look before answering. "All I can tell you is that your ship and its crew are in grave danger, and that I will do everything in my power to save her and her crew."

"I will hold you to that, Mr. Serosian," said the captain, not breaking eye contact.

With that, Serosian started away, calling back to us. "I'll be in my private chambers. If anything changes, I will return. No need to keep me updated, I can monitor all stations from my personal console." And with that he was gone.

The captain dropped her arms down to her sides, hands clenched together in fists, clearly frustrated. Then she spun my chair back around to my station, leaned in close, and whispered fiercely in my ear.

"How well do you know this man?" she demanded of me. I hesitated, but only for a second.

"Well enough to know he would give his life for me or anyone else on board, sir," I said.

"Let's hope it doesn't come to that," she replied. "Your orders, Commander, are to keep your eyes open, your sidearm loaded, and your loyalty firmly rooted to the Union Navy. Do you understand me, Commander?"

"I do, sir," I said quickly. I felt her nod against me.

"Report any change to me immediately, not to him." Then she straightened up. "Carry on, Commander," she said in a casual voice, and then walked away from my station.

I turned back to my display board, wondering again what the hell I'd gotten myself into.

It took us six more hours at full propulsion, but we had halved Tralfane's lead in that time.

"What's he doing?" asked the captain rhetorically as we watched our former ship crawling toward the inner moon of Levant Prime. "It's almost like he's waiting for us."

"That's exactly what he's doing," said Serosian, surprising us both. The Historian's unexpected return to the yacht's nerve center had caught us off guard. We snapped around to see him standing over us after having emerged from his inner sanctum.

"Explain," said Dobrina. This time Serosian crossed his arms.

"I've analyzed both his power emissions and his projected course. I can only conclude that he is exactly where he wants to be. He could have accelerated a long time ago and put us out of range to even track him. I can only conclude that he is therefore waiting for us to arrive."

"Waiting for us?" asked Dobrina. "Waiting to do battle?"

Serosian shook his head. "I doubt that. He would know that this yacht and *Impulse* are an even match in any battle. He must have something else in mind. A display, perhaps."

"Display?" I said. "Of what?"

The Historian shrugged. "I could only speculate, which I am not going to do." Now Dobrina crossed her arms again as the two of them engaged in another standoff.

"You've been very unhelpful, Mr. Serosian," she said. He nodded.

"And yet, here we are, within barely a light-hour of our target. I suggest, Captain, that we adjust our course not to intercept *Impulse*, but to get us within firing range as soon as possible," he said. The captain looked to me.

"Can we do that?" she asked. I turned to my console.

"If we adjust our track, I can put us in a parabolic approach, which will shorten our distance to firing range by nearly twenty minutes," I said, turning back to my friend and my commanding officer in expectation. The captain hesitated only a second.

"Do it," she commanded, then walked away toward Marker and Layton, who were in their rest bunks. Serosian stepped up.

"Well done, Peter," he said. I shrugged.

"It is *your* ship," I said, plugging in the calculations as my fingers swept over the smooth console.

"Yes, but you have mastered the controls rather elegantly. You have great learning skills, Peter. And that may come in very handy in the next few hours."

"You suspect trouble from Tralfane?" I said without turning from my work.

"Suspect? No," he said. "I expect it."

I laid in our new course without another word. The yacht adjusted and moved at my commands, diving into the darkness between two moons and into a very uncertain future.

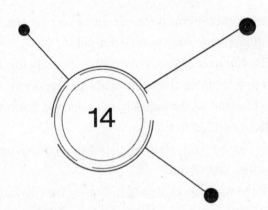

14

A Battle over Levant

Our track took us close to the outer moon of Levant Prime, the larger of the two. The inner moon was smaller and in a close orbit to the outer moon, only about fifty thousand kilometers distant. Both were tidally locked to the main planet however, and except for the occasional close approach we were witnessing now, the two seemed to rarely bother each other.

Impulse was between us and the inner moon. She'd slowed to nearly a crawl, in space terms, just ten thousand clicks between us. But we were starting to decelerate, hoping to gain a firing solution on her in the next few minutes as we curved under the larger outer moon and out of her shadow.

We were all at stations now: Dobrina and Serosian to my left, Layton and Marker at tactical stations behind us. I was responsible for helm and weapons, Marker for defense and Layton, propulsion. Captain Kierkopf sat nervously, obviously unhappy at being left out of both the decision making and the line duties. Her fingernails tapped on the console's metal edge.

"Status, Mr. Layton?" asked Serosian.

"Deceleration complete, sir. Impellers on standby at your command," he replied. The Historian nodded.

"Mr. Cochrane, you're flying her now. Bring us about to point seven-five-five above the solar ecliptic. Prepare to fire on my order," he said. I looked to the captain, who opened her mouth to say something, then nodded to me.

"Aye, sir," I said, then adjusted our course and speed to bring *Impulse* into our sights.

"Mr. Marker," said Serosian, "power the forward coil cannon and transfer firing command to Mr. Cochrane."

"Aye, sir," replied Marker. "Should I enhance the Hoagland Field forward to protect us from *Impulse's* reply?" he asked. It was a logical question, I thought. Serosian nearly bit his head off.

"*Negative*," boomed the Earthman. "Maintain full shield integrity in all directions equally. The field generators will adjust automatically as need be. We have to be prepared for an attack from *any* angle."

At this the captain leaned in to the Historian and spoke softly, but still loud enough for me to hear.

"What do you suspect?" she asked.

"Anything, Captain," said Serosian, equally quietly. "Anything."

I was momentarily distracted from my board. When I looked back at my tactical display it had gone red.

"Sir," I said loudly, "It's *Impulse*, she's—"

"Accelerating again. I see it," said Serosian. "Mr. Layton, impellers at half force, if you please. Mr. Cochrane, stay on your tactical display and continue to calculate a firing solution. I will handle the helm from here."

I acknowledged his order and went back to my board, recalculating every few seconds as *Impulse* maneuvered away from us, now tacking back toward the larger moon. I focused on her, tracking her every move as I scrambled for my firing solution.

I was unsure what happened next. I found myself on the floor, looking up at my console, disoriented and dizzy. I heard a voice in my ear, but it was muddy and distant. I closed my eyes again and rolled my head from side to side. Suddenly the sound of an impact alarm became clear in my mind, groaning loudly as I tried to sit up. I felt a firm hand lift me up by the arm and drop me back in my seat. I looked to Serosian, who was back at the control console, his hands moving desperately across the board.

"What happened?" I mumbled. My own voice sounded distorted inside my head, like I was hearing it through bad speakers.

"Displacement wave," said Serosian. "From the large moon. If we'd had our defensive field focused forward on *Impulse* we wouldn't be here now."

I looked to the captain. She was unconscious on her station couch, as were Marker and Layton. "How—" I started. Serosian cut me off.

"You were linked into the tactical system. It kept you from taking the full surge of the wave," he said. "Can you function, Peter? I need you to take the tactical again if you can. We have to take out those wave generators before they fire again or we're finished." I nodded yes and then turned back to my board, linking into the plasma and "feeling" the controls under my fingertips once again. My display came back online and I tried to track what we were aiming at. *Impulse* was long gone from my screen and I could see Serosian had turned us back toward the larger moon. As near as I could tell he was trying to track an energy tracer back to the origin point of the wave. I watched as he tacked the yacht, angling her away from the trace.

"Can you get a firing solution now, Peter?" he asked. "I've got my hands full with the helm." I nodded affirmative and took over the tracking, then activated the forward coil cannon. The tactical display gave me an almost instant firing solution.

"Got it," I said aloud.

"Fire when ready," Serosian responded. I hit the firing control and watched as the orange bolt of energy ripped through space instantaneously, lancing the surface of the rocky moon and causing a massive explosion of material, dust, and debris. Serosian scanned the site quickly as he turned the yacht back toward *Impulse*, which was accelerating away from us toward the inner moon on full impellers now. She'd apparently pivoted the instant we were hit by the displacement wave.

"Neutralized," said Serosian. "Good shooting."

At this Dobrina began to moan and opened her eyes. "What happened?" she asked.

"Displacement wave," I said to her. "From the outer moon. It's been neutralized." She nodded and then turned toward Marker and Layton, getting up and helping them back to their stations.

"What's our status?" she demanded of Serosian, ever the captain.

"We were hit by a displacement wave weapon from the surface of the large moon. This system seems riddled with them. The weapon has been taken out and I am now attempting to get us back in range of *Impulse*, but she's accelerating away from us again, toward the inner moon," he said.

"Why?"

"That I don't know, Captain. But flying this yacht is a difficult task, so if you don't mind?" His tone and his use of her formal rank indicated he was not about to be distracted or deterred in his quest for *Impulse*. She motioned to me and I went back to my board, alarmed at what I saw.

"Captain, I'm picking up another displacement wave," I warned, "Coming from the inner moon."

Serosian checked his board in alarm then hit the impeller controls, temporarily overriding our inertial dampers and sending us scrambling about the deck of the yacht once again. I regained my seat. "Sir, we're right in its path, and so is *Impulse*," I said.

"I know," both Kierkopf and Serosian answered at the same time. Kierkopf moved away from Serosian and back to her station couch, quickly strapping in. The rest of us did the same. I looked at my tactical display. It was as red as a holiday bauble, showing that the weapon on the inner moon had gone critical. From my station I could see Serosian was tacking us away from the line of fire as quickly as he could. Then I took a reading on *Impulse*.

"Sir, *Impulse* has dropped her Hoagland Field!" I warned. Captain Kierkopf checked her display.

"He's right. She's helpless!" she said. "Can we extend our field around *Impulse*, to protect her?"

Serosian shook his head. "Not at this distance."

"Is he trying to kill her?" I asked.

"Unknown," said Serosian. "But that weapon is at least a hundred times more powerful than the one on the outer moon. If Tralfane hopes to escape the destruction of *Impulse*, he's already too late."

We watched the primary display in silence as the wave shot out from the inner moon, a white-hot energy bolt cutting through space. I winced involuntarily, not wanting to see my ship and her crew incinerated.

The next instant changed everything.

The wave of energy terminated at a point in space, just a few hundred kilometers in front of *Impulse*. As we watched, the expended energy lit up a ring of satellites with a powerful white glow. The ring formed a perfect circle, kilometers across. The satellites pulsed into life, and a dark membrane of energy formed between them, blotting out the stars and the partial view of the inner moon's surface. We watched in astonishment as *Impulse* accelerated toward the membrane, impacted the event horizon, and then vanished completely as it crossed the plane.

Into the black.

We were investigating the now-silent inner moon, looking for the source of the wave. There was a large base on the moon, of unknown origin, and we were determined to find its secrets and figure out what had just happened to *Impulse* and its crew.

Unfortunately, we had other problems as well. The outburst of energy from the inner moon combined with the displacement wave we had taken dead-on from the outer moon had overloaded many of the yacht's principal systems. The damage was not permanent, but as Serosian explained, it would take time to repair.

"The yacht will heal itself, but that is not the issue at hand," he said.

"Then what is?" asked the captain.

"The issue is that the more use we make of the ship's systems, the longer time the ship will require to return to full function."

"So you're saying we should let the ship 'rest' while it repairs itself?" asked the captain. Serosian nodded.

"It would be best. And I have coordinates on that wave. It was fired from what appears to be a base on the surface of the inner moon." The captain looked concerned at this.

"A manned base?" she said. Serosian shrugged.

"Unknown. But I do think it might be in our best interests to find out," he said. Kierkopf nodded absently while she considered this tactic.

"If it's manned, we'll have to go in armed," I stated.

"Right now the base looks abandoned," said Serosian. "Barely half an hour since the wave was launched, and the base is as cold and quiet as the rocks it's embedded in. If you weren't looking for it, you'd never know it was there."

Captain Kierkopf ran her thumb across her lips, thinking. "What about backup? Can we contact *Starbound* with the longwave?" she asked.

"I already have," replied the Historian. "But a reply through all of the hyperdimensional scatter in this system is unlikely. If she received my coded pulse she will be on her way, but it could still be two or three days before she arrives in-system."

"So we're on our own. Very well. We go in then. Full shields and weapons, mind you," Kierkopf said.

"That will delay our repair," protested Serosian.

"I'm willing to risk that for the safety of my remaining command, Mr. Serosian," she said. She turned to me. "Mr. Cochrane, you will organize the recon team. We'll land within a click or two of the base and make our approach on foot. If there are no surprises along the way, we'll go in and find out what the hell just happened to our Lightship."

"Yes, sir," I said, unsure what was coming but excited about the opportunity ahead.

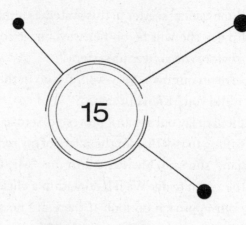

On L-4b

Serosian was guiding us down to the surface of the inner moon of Levant Prime, which we were now calling L-4b. The wave station remained silent and cold as we approached, but I kept my eye on the tactical 'scope all the way, looking for any sign of activity from the wave generator that had emitted the massive energy blast that had allowed *Impulse* to move through the gate. As Serosian had reported earlier, the base had returned to a state of stasis that for all intents and purposes made it indistinguishable from the rocks surrounding it. If we hadn't seen the wave itself we'd never have been able to find the weapon's location.

L-4b itself was a mostly colorless moon, with a dull gray surface and a narrow band of atmosphere that gave the sky a pinkish tone. The surface was mottled with craters and had no visible water, though the mineral scans showed likely underground water sources and carbon dioxide ice caps. It seemed like as good a choice as any for an outlying colony or base, and the main structures for said base were located near the middle latitudes of the satellite's northern hemisphere.

We all gathered in the main bridge area of the yacht to plan strategy. Captain Kierkopf cleared her throat and began.

"Marker and Cochrane will lead the investigation of the base," she said. "There's an isolated building near the main structure that could be a power station. I want you to go there first and check it out before approaching the main base in any way. Remember, your job is to observe first, make contact only if necessary, and then evaluate the status of the primary base, beginning with this station. All clear?"

"Yes, sir," Marker and I chorused.

"Mr. Layton will stay on board here to guard the yacht. Once you've scouted the outlying building Mr. Serosian and I will join you to investigate the main base. Got it, gentlemen?"

Again, we replied, "Yes, sir."

The captain nodded to us to go prepare for our EVA. Serosian said nothing, which I took as tacit acceptance of the plan. At least, I hoped that's what it was.

Fifteen minutes later Marker and I were ready in the yacht's airlock in our full EVA suits. Serosian's landing had been pinpoint perfect. "Looks all clear from here," I said over the com, looking out the airlock window to the surface of L-4b.

We had landed a click away from the nearest structure, a low-lying building set into the surrounding land and made of the same material as the rocks to disguise it. Another half click beyond was the main generator complex.

L-4b apparently got quite a bit of sun when she swung around her primary, with a slow but steady rotational day, and then the cold shoulder when she went behind Levant Prime or into her "night." Luckily, it was the satellite's day and she was in a warming cycle, and that meant air temperatures of just over five degrees Celsius at our landing site. I looked out of the shuttle window to see a gray sky with broken gray-pink clouds and about sixty-five percent sunlight compared to Quantar-standard. From the position of the sun I figured we had three hours of daylight left.

"All ready here," I reported.

"Proceed, Mr. Cochrane," came the captain's reply in my com.

I hit the airlock switch, the door panel slid open, and a drop-down ramp projected out to the surface. Marker went through first, taking a look around, and then signaled me the all clear. I stepped down the ramp and out onto the surface of an unknown world for the first time.

The ground was gritty with small rocks, pebbles, and ice, and my boots made a scraping sound as I walked out the rear hatch of the yacht. Marker turned to me, his voice cracking on the com.

"Reporting all clear, sir. Landing site is secure," he said.

"Understood," said the captain's voice in my com. Serosian may have been master of the yacht, but the captain was clearly in charge of any military mission we were engaged in.

I took a few steps. The gravity of L-4b seemed to be about one-third normal. I moved to secure my coil rifle and sidearm, and as I did my EVA suit made a loud crackling sound with my motion.

"What the hell?" I said.

"You're not going to be sneaking up on anyone," said Marker.

"Shit! What's the problem?" I started flexing to see if the sound would abate but I got the same result. In fact, it got worse.

"Probably a reaction to the change in air density and temperature. You'd better stay back and let me take the lead," Marker said.

"Won't you have the same problem?" I asked. Marker shook his head.

"Marine EVA suits are the latest Earth-issue. Exo-skin adapts almost instantly to environmental conditions," he said. "Yours is standard for shuttle duty, not for fighting in hostile atmospheric environments." I stood there, chagrined.

"Well, I'll just have to see about getting myself one of those new suits when we get back to High Station," I said. "Let's get going. Not getting any brighter here."

"I think that's wise, sir," said Marker, then he cut his end of the com line. In the low light and with a slight shadow across his visor I couldn't tell if he was laughing at me or not.

We started a stealth approach to the base building, Marker stopping every ten meters or so to wave me forward once he deemed things to be safe. It was embarrassing, hopping from rock to rock, then huddling down as my suit crunched loudly in the cold air. I longed to be at the front, but that job belonged to Marker for the moment.

After several minutes of reconnoitering we arrived at the closest building. It looked simple enough: hexagonal, one level, featureless concrete with a flat roof. Marker went around the corner of the building and out of my sight as I huddled next to a rock. Waiting for him to report from the other side was almost unbearable. After a few seconds I prompted him.

"Marker, any sign of an entrance?" I called impatiently into my com. His reply came back quickly.

"Yes, sir. North side seems to have a man-sized metal door of some kind," crackled Marker's voice in my receiver. I looked to the gray-pink sky.

"Which way is north?" I said. The com stayed silent for a few moments.

"Offset your compass to .626 degrees from Q-normal magnetic north. That should do it," came back Marker. I did so in the tactical heads-up display in my suit, using an attached panel embedded in my EVA suit's left arm to key in the changes.

"Set," I said. "I think I should—"

"I'm at the door," cut in Marker. "If all goes well I'll be inside in two minutes."

"Hold," I said instinctively, then I left the line silent to let Marker know of my disapproval. It was bad enough to be stuck in a crunching EVA suit, but to be babied like a child was humiliating. I felt I should be leading us in. After all, I was the commanding officer.

I came around the building and found Marker standing casually in front of the entrance to the building.

"Report," I snapped. He kept his cool despite my tone.

"My scan indicates a simple airlock sequence of three. The interior registers sufficient oxygen and heat for human life," he said.

I simply nodded and walked toward the door, crunching all the way. Marker caught up to me at the first airlock door and scanned the environment beyond us. The airlock was of a simple and utilitarian design, with a magnetic locking system that was easily breached.

The first room was just big enough for the two of us. We shut and locked the door behind us and proceeded to the second gate. Beyond that was a room big enough for five or six men, I guessed. The last barrier had a window that was obscured by dust and grime from the inside. None of these areas looked like they had been occupied in a very long time.

"So let's do it," I said, facing the last airlock. To be honest, I was excited about the prospect of discovering some long-hidden secret of the First Empire.

I was disappointed when Marker opened the door to a simple holding room with a concrete floor and metal superstructure. I stepped inside and began to investigate. Marker resealed the door behind us. I noticed then that my suit had stopped crunching with every step. Likely the atmosphere was more stabilized, or closer to what we considered normal.

"We've lost contact with the yacht," said Marker. I looked to him.

"Our orders were to investigate this building, Mr. Marker. Let's proceed," I said. He nodded, and we started going farther into the room.

Ambient light seemed to emanate from the ceiling, but there was no one particular light source I could identify. I noticed that the light was roughly equivalent to the outside of the building in daylight. At the far end of the room, which was big enough to hold perhaps ten people, there was a dusty staircase leading down into the dark.

"Most of the complex must be underground," said Marker. "It would make sense. Use the natural terrain as an insulator." I looked around the room.

"What do you make of the technology we've seen so far?" I asked. Marker spun in a circle illuminating the room, his flashlight scanning through gray dust kicked up by our entrance.

"Rudimentary," he said. "Minimum required to maintain operations. What I suppose you'd expect from a military base."

I nodded. "Yeah, just what you'd expect. I just don't know if that should worry us or not."

"Don't worry, sir, I'll protect you," said Marker, hefting his coil rifle. I smiled at that.

"Comforting."

I switched on my suit light and Marker did the same. Then we proceeded down the metal steps into the darkness with Marker taking the lead. Neither of us said a thing until we reached the bottom, where there was a small landing.

From there we walked down a long, wide tunnel of blank concrete with no doors or openings of any kind. After a hundred meters the long tunnel split into three. Straight ahead was more of the same, and to either side were curving hallways with deep-set door coveys at equal distances on either side of the hall. Marker flashed his light to the right; I illuminated left. The halls seemed identical.

"Circular design, possibly laboratories or living quarters," I suggested.

"More likely maintenance areas," said Marker. "This main hall is clearly for moving large items from one location to another, maybe even from building to building. The rooms on the outer rim would be for receiving and maintenance, most likely."

"Let's find out," I said. We began to explore the rooms. Marker and I went left to the first door. It opened simply enough with Marker's magnetic lock breaker.

Inside we found very little. Empty metal racks, hanging electrical wires with nothing attached to them, and consoles with large square holes where it looked like control panels had been stripped out.

"Whoever left here took anything of value, anything they could carry, with them," said Marker. I grunted my agreement.

"And it looks like they left a long time ago." I said. This time it was Marker who had no answer.

We moved on, but going from room to room the situation was the same. Anything of value, anything that would have left a clue as to the colony's former inhabitants or their technology, was stripped away. We found what could only be a loading dock with lifters, now immobilized, a galley, and even a vehicle maintenance bay, but nothing of any significance left behind. Eventually we came to a large, seamless door on the far side from where we had come in.

"Freight lifter," commented Marker. He attached the magnetic lock breaker to what looked like the lock, offset to the left of the doors. After a few seconds the key lock turned and the doors split along an invisible seam, opening to a wide and tall lifter.

Marker and I went in and examined the door mechanism. It was the first one we'd found that was electronically active. There were three buttons, glowing with a white LED light source. The characters on the buttons were unreadable.

"Not Imperial Standard lettering, that's for sure. I'm guessing we have a choice of three levels," I said.

"So we go to two?" asked Marker. "Shouldn't we report back to the captain and Serosian?"

I looked at my chronometer display. "We're down to less than two hours of daylight up top, and our suits won't keep us forever," I said to Marker. "If we go back to make a report our time will be nearly up. I think we should press on, explore the second and third levels, priority on the third."

"Why the third? Is that where all the interesting stuff's likely to be?" Marker asked.

I shrugged. "Usually so, I guess. The upper levels are most likely to be maintenance, like you said. Anything interesting should be on the third level. But we'll check two just in case." I pressed the button for two and the doors resealed, the lifter moving so smoothly it was hardly noticeable. The doors opened again on two, which looked remarkably like one. We randomly reconnoitered a few rooms, which were completely uninteresting, then returned to the lifter. I resealed the lifter door and then we made our way down to three. Both Marker and I noted a difference this time.

"We're going a long way down," he said. I nodded.

"Hopefully not so deep we can't get back," I said, my anxiety growing.

Finally the doors opened onto three and we stepped out into total darkness.

"Hold!" I ordered. I held up my arm and ran my light down the length of the hallway. Any part of the wall not directly illuminated seemed to fade away against pure black.

"What is it?" asked Marker.

"Unknown," I said, then made my way slowly out into the hallway.

"Sir, perhaps I should take the lead—"

"Just hold your position, Corporal," I said. I extended my arm out into the black. I felt a slight resistance just a few feet in front of me, my arm vanishing into a black event horizon. Then I seemed to punch through. The area around my arm itched with the buzz of a static current. "Some sort of energy field, like a membrane," I said. My hand and arm on the other side of the event horizon seemed fine, I could bring it back out of the black or flex it at my leisure on the other side. I made a decision.

"Wait five seconds, then follow me in," I said to Marker. He started to protest, but before he could finish I slid my arm back into the black and then passed through the event horizon, static energy buzzing around me as I went through.

Marker must have been surprised when he came through behind me. I hadn't moved, too awed by what I saw.

I was standing on a vast glassed-in deck, looking down on a carved-out cavern that had to be miles across. A giant cylinder, wider at the back end farthest away from me to my left, lay horizontally across the center of the cavern. It pulsated with a vibrant blue glow, as if simply waiting for instructions to act again as it had many times before. The floor beneath us seemed to hum from the power of it. The end of the cylinder closest to us was capped by a copper-colored nose cone, illuminated at the end by a glowing orange light. For all the world it looked like a cannon just waiting to be fired. Above the cylinder on the ceiling of the cavern was an enormous, flat, circular membrane, like the one we had just passed through, black as could be in the center but rimmed with pulsating white lights and rippling with energy. I didn't even notice Marker come up beside me as I stared at the marvel of it all.

"Looks like somebody left the lights on," he said. He was right, the entire cavern was lit up and the focus seemed to be on this one object.

"This entire base must have been built to support this device," I said, regaining my bearings.

"But we've been getting no power readouts at all," Marker said, pulling out a handheld scanner and checking it. "How do they mask it?" Then he started rattling off statistics while I watched the awesome device glow in front of me. I felt like a child encountering a mountain or a skyscraper for the first time, overwhelmed by the enormity of it.

"Nearly a hundred terawatts of power being generated, though I don't know how or from where," Marker said. "Temperature inside is twenty-one Celsius. Oxygen levels near standard. Bio filters read normal. Definitely designed to support human life in a comfortable setting. It's almost inviting."

"Almost," I said, "But not recommended."

"You're nervous about this?" said Marker. I nodded.

"Aren't you? This whole base is just sitting here, abandoned but operational, like it's just *waiting* to be found. And the lack of security is also a concern. If you had something this big wouldn't you keep it a bit more tightly wrapped?"

"I would, sir. But I'm not from the First Empire. Who's to know what their motivation was?" I nodded at that. In front of us was a display board, the first one we'd seen with functioning controls. It was lit up in a myriad of colored lights.

"Let's have a look at that board, shall we?" I said. We studied the controls together in silence for a few moments. Again, the characters were not Imperial Standard, far from it. In my mind they looked not just foreign, but like they were in code.

"It would make sense," I said, thinking out loud.

"What?" asked Marker. I motioned to the board.

"These characters seem like some sort of code to me. If they're encoded they're also likely to be booby-trapped, to prevent unwanted tampering with the system. I highly recommend we don't mess with this."

"Agreed," said Marker.

I looked at my watch. Forty-seven minutes of oxygen left. I had a decision to make.

"We're getting short on time if we're going to make our assigned rendezvous. Let's take digital records of everything in here—panels, input ports, output ports—and see if we can make sense of it back on the yacht. I don't want to keep the captain waiting on my first EVA mission," I said.

We proceeded to record everything of note in the control room and all we could photograph of the cavern, the cannon, and the membrane shield. With that we began our egress to the yacht, ending up outside in the twilight of L-4b, and beat a quick retreat to our ship.

An hour later, we were standing next to Serosian and the captain as they scanned through our recordings.

"Can you identify those characters?" Captain Kierkopf asked the Historian. He shook his head.

"Not with enough certainty to attempt to operate the machine, if that's what you're asking."

She pushed a curl out of her face, hands on hips. "If what *you're* asking is do I plan on making an attempt to rescue my shipmates aboard *Impulse*, Mr. Serosian, the answer is yes. Whether or not you recommend such an action is not my concern. So I only have two questions. Is this the device that activated that gate and allowed Tralfane to take *Impulse* through it, and can you operate that device if I request it?"

Serosian turned away from the displays and faced the captain again. I could see that theirs would never be a trusting relationship, at least not like the kind that Serosian and I had. I signaled to Marker and he stepped away from the conversation, going to the rear stations to make busy with Layton.

"The answers to your question, Captain, are most likely yes to the first and no to the second," he said. "This script is some sort of code. Some of the characters I recognize as being of Sri origin. Others, I am unsure of. One thing is certain though: attempting to operate this device without knowledge of that code would most likely be suicidal. The Sri were not ones to give up their secrets easily."

"So you say," she replied. "Yet Tralfane operated this device just a few short hours ago and made off with a Lightship, the most sophisticated weapon in our arsenal. How did he do it?"

Serosian pondered this a moment before replying. "I think most likely, Captain, he had knowledge of the code and he came down here in his yacht, like we did, and activated it, probably setting a remote timer of some kind. Then when he knew we would be close enough to observe him, he activated it and took *Impulse* through."

"Through what? To *where*?" demanded the captain. "If you have answers, Mr. Serosian, or even educated guesses, I want to hear them."

"Most likely it's an artificial jump gate generator," I heard myself saying, then regretted it. Now the captain's attention was squarely on me.

"Explain," she said plainly. I hesitated a second before answering.

"There is a theory," I said. "During the Imperial Civil War, Corant was effectively sealed off from the rest of the empire. The natural jump points simply weren't there." I looked to Serosian. He and I had had this conversation many times.

I continued. "Jump points are essentially wormholes that balance out the dark matter of a system with the light of a primary sun. They're a part of the natural topography of space. If you were trying to defend an embattled capital planet in a time of war, you would most likely do it by collapsing the natural jump points, especially if you had a way of generating one of your own."

"The ultimate defense," said the captain, apparently engaged with my theory. "But the power curve would be off the charts. Something like that would have to be the size of a small planet."

I shrugged. "Or a large moon."

"Or a large moon," Kierkopf agreed. "With enough power to generate an artificial jump point—"

"By using a massive Hoagland Wave," I finished. I looked at her for a few moments, gathering my thoughts. She seemed skeptical.

"It would take the power of a full sun gone nova. How could a small station like this generate that much energy?" she demanded of Serosian.

"By pulling it in from higher dimensions," he said. "Torsion energy—the spin rotation of objects in normal space—combined with the energy of counterbalanced objects in higher dimensions would provide more than enough power." He pointed out one of the pictures we had taken of the cannon. "What this device likely does is open a singularity to that dimension or dimensions, then channel the power through the cylinder and up to the membrane on the cavern ceiling—likely some kind of conduit—then onto the gate itself, opening an artificial singularity on this side and likely connecting to a similar device, or possibly a natural jump point, on the other side, allowing a ship to pass through unimpeded."

"But just where is the other side?" asked Kierkopf. "And where is *Impulse*?"

He shook his head. "Unknown. Possibly Corant, or perhaps some other world."

"It would make sense for there to be a series of gateways, to act as a buffer between the Imperial home world and any potential enemies," I said, and instantly regretted it again. The captain was now fully focused on me once more.

"So we don't know where *Impulse* went, but we think we know how she got there. So tell me, Mr. Cochrane," the captain said, "What would you do next?"

"Well," I said hesitantly, "If I couldn't activate that device from this location, I suppose I would go to the gate itself and see if I could activate it from there."

The captain nodded. "Precisely," she said. "Mr. Serosian, is your yacht sufficiently rested for a trip to the gate?"

He nodded. "Sufficiently," he replied.

"Then let's set a course for the gate. No time to waste," she said.

"Captain, there could be a problem with that strategy," Serosian said. "If we approach the gate, we could make ourselves a target of this technology, and its origin is still unknown." She pondered this a moment, but just for a moment.

"Then I suggest you redouble your efforts to decode that control panel, Mr. Serosian. You are the expert, after all." She turned to me. "Take us up as soon as she's ready, Mr. Cochrane." Then she marched off to Marker and Layton's stations to give them instructions.

I turned to my mentor. "Can you decipher the code?" I asked.

"I hope so, Peter. Before your captain here gets us all killed." And then he was back off to his private chambers.

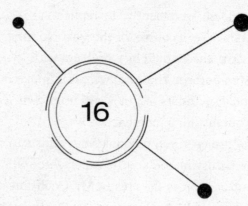

16

We approached the gate structure with extreme caution. It was basically a ring of connected satellites nearly a kilometer in circumference, big enough to move a ship, or a fleet for that matter, in a single maneuver. That would give the users of this device a distinct advantage over the Union Navy, which could scarcely move a single ship in and out of a natural jump point at one time. Fleet maneuvers were slow when gathering large groups of ships, which was why the new Lightships were so important. They were designed to be as autonomous, and as powerful, as a strategic battleship or a trio of cruisers with half the displacement. The key was hyperdimensional power, provided by the Historians of Earth, driven by the minute singularities stored inside HD crystals. Without that nearly unlimited power source, the Lightships would be about as powerful as small destroyers and just as vulnerable.

I watched my display board, looking for visible light fluctuations or power curve signatures in infrared coming from the gate. None were forthcoming. The ring was as dead as it had been before being activated by Tralfane and powered by the HD energy cannon. We crept along the circumference of the ring, illuminating it with our running lights. The technology was exotic, to say the least, and counterintuitive in its design.

"It's like we're looking at solid blocks of metal," said Marker from his station.

"Not metal," I said. "More like a cast or molded material, like a ceramic. It shows no sign of metallic properties."

"I'm not interested in *what* it is," came the captain's voice from behind us. "I want to know how to get it working again so that we can use it to rescue *Impulse*."

"Understood, sir," I said, then cleared my throat nervously before continuing. "The power curve is nil. Scans for energy signatures or residual radiation are nil. The material resists all my attempts to do an internal scan, sir. It may as well be made out of rock."

"Is there a control complex of any kind?"

"Not that I can detect," I said.

"That's not good enough!" she said, her voice rising in frustration.

"Perhaps," said Serosian, joining the conversation. "But it is all we have. We already know where the device is activated from. Our time would likely be far better spent exploring that option than putting ourselves out here in the line of fire."

Though Dobrina was standing ramrod-straight to assert her position, she was barely five foot seven. Serosian towered over her.

"And are you any closer to deciphering that control code?" she asked the Historian.

"Yes," he said, to my surprise, and the captain's. "Enough to know that it is *not* a code. It's a language. Complex, perhaps as much as sixteen hundred characters, but a language nonetheless."

"Alien?" she asked. He shook his head.

"Human. Likely Sri, but human."

"So we have some hope of cracking it?" she asked. He nodded.

"With time, if we don't suffer any more setbacks," he replied.

"Mr. Serosian," she started. "I know you would like us to hunker down on that moon and play it safe, take our time and get things right, but nearly three hundred and sixty of my shipmates are out there somewhere, presumably in grave danger. Every moment we wait here trying to solve a riddle, we are getting further and further away from rescuing any of them safely. I can't have that. We need to find a way to follow them."

"And has it occurred to you, Captain Kierkopf, that that strategy is exactly what Tralfane wants?" snapped Serosian. I could see from his expression that he was truly angry now. "Did you notice how he purposely slowed his approach to this station, allowing us to catch him, allowing us to see what mechanism he used to take *Impulse* to unknown space? Has it occurred to you that perhaps he's waiting for us on the other side, and it is part of his plan to capture not one Lightship, but two? Or at least this yacht and her HD drive, which would make him even more powerful? What better way to cripple the Lightship program than to take out two-thirds of the fleet with one blow? If he captures *Starbound*, or this yacht as well as *Impulse*, the Union Navy could be crippled."

Dobrina was furious at him for showing her up in front of her men. "It has occurred to me, yes," she said, measuring her response to control her anger. "But it doesn't in any way dilute my desire to rescue *Impulse* and her crew, most of whom are not only my comrades but my friends. Maybe you Historians are trained to be loners, to keep your personal feelings in check, but that isn't the navy way. A captain must consider all possibilities, and sometimes use emotion and intuition, not just cold facts and technology, to make his or her decisions."

"I care greatly about your crew, Captain, and want nothing more than to see them rescued," he responded. "And I too have friends in the navy service." He tilted his head slightly at me here, but I couldn't tell if she noticed. "But I want them *all* to be safe. *Impulse*, this crew, and *Starbound*, in fact the entire Union Navy and the people of both your worlds. So you will pardon me if I also consider their well-being in my recommendations to you."

This seemed to have a calming effect on her. "Understood," she said. "But we do seem to be at an impasse about what to do next."

As if on cue, we all heard a warning beep coming from the navigation board.

"Sir!" said Layton from his station, alarm in his voice. "I have a power flux coming from Levant Prime on my board!" Everyone turned their attention to their stations.

"Can you get a fix, Peter?" asked Serosian. I was at my longscope display in a second.

"Confirmed," I said. "It looks to be three vehicles rising toward our position from the planet's surface. By their mass I would estimate they are cruiser class ships. At the rate they're moving, they will likely intercept us in . . . forty-one minutes." I turned to look to the captain for orders.

"It appears the Levantines have solved the dilemma of what we do next for us," said Serosian to Dobrina. She looked at my board, then to me.

"Take us away from the gate, Mr. Cochrane, but do it deliberately. Don't let them believe we are trying to escape. Let them catch us," she said.

"First Contact protocol?" asked Serosian. She nodded. I turned to my board to execute my orders.

"And let's hope the natives are in a friendly mood," she said, as I maneuvered us away from the jump gate, uncertain what the next move would be in this increasingly complex game.

"You are ordered to stand down and heave to," said the voice on the com in heavily accented Imperial Standard. The message repeated in

several other languages as well, none of which I, or apparently anyone else onboard, was familiar with.

"What's their position?" demanded the captain.

"Thirty clicks and closing, sir," said Marker from his station.

"Full stop, Mr. Layton," she ordered, then came and stood over my tactical station. "Can you scan them, Cochrane? What kind of weapons have they got?"

"Judging from their design and energy signatures, I would say at least six coil cannon batteries each and multiple torpedo launchers, perhaps four each," I said, delivering the bad news. "Cruiser displacement, I estimate."

"Analysis, Mr. Serosian?" she asked of our host, firmly ensconced at his central station, his hands flying smoothly over the liquid-like console.

"They have nearly equivalent weapons to our own, less sophisticated perhaps, but still formidable. We can withstand a lengthy attack and give as good as we get, but even an HD crystal can run low on power," he said.

"So ultimately, we're vulnerable," the captain said.

"Ultimately, after taking the blows we already have, it would be wise to avoid a fight," said Serosian. The message demanding our acquiescence continued unabated through the com, obviously a recording. The captain paced for a second, then made her decision.

"Mr. Cochrane, stand down on all our weapons and defensive systems. Let them know we don't want a fight. If they wanted one they'd have likely fired on us by now," she said.

"Aye, sir," I replied, and carried out my orders.

"Mr. Serosian," she said, "Reply on their com frequency, please." He opened the channel silently, then nodded to the captain.

"This is Captain Dobrina Kierkopf of the Unified Navy ship *Impulse*, We are on a rescue mission and request your assistance. Please identify yourselves and reply," she stated. The line stayed quiet for a few seconds. The reply came again in a heavy accent, but we could still make it out.

"Captain Kierkopf, this is the Royal Levant Naval Command, Captain Salibi speaking. Your vessel will be boarded and impounded. If you resist, we will destroy you. Do you understand?" said the voice. The captain left the line open for a second before replying.

"As I stated, Captain Salibi, we are on a rescue mission and request your—"

"You will stand *down*, Commander," the voice shouted. "Open your airlock and prepare to receive Royal Navy personnel. Any other action will result in your destruction!"

The captain signaled for Serosian to cut the line. "Still think this is a good idea?" she asked him. He shrugged.

"As opposed to fighting, yes," he replied.

"I'd sure like to show him what an HD-powered ship can do," she said, then signaled for the com line again.

"Understood, Captain Salibi. And welcome aboard. We come as friends," she said.

"That will be determined," came the quick reply, then the line was severed from the other side. The captain looked at me and let out an exasperated sigh.

"Mr. Cochrane, open the outer airlock. Everyone into EVA suits, full helmets. I don't want to lose anyone to space if they come in shooting," she said.

"Sidearms?" Marker asked. She shook her head.

"Stand down means stand down, Mr. Marker. No matter how crazy I might think it is." Then she sat down heavily. I kept my eyes pinned to my board, hoping we could get out of this in one piece.

Six armed men had boarded, carrying rifles that seemed roughly equivalent to recent-issue Union coil tech. My guess in eyeing the guns was that they would probably have to recharge after three or four volleys, whereas a proper Union rifle, or even a pistol, could fire ten times as many shots before a recharge would be required.

We all sat in our safety couches while Serosian guided the yacht to a docking bay on a low-orbit space station, escorted closely by the Levant cruisers. The station itself seemed fairly modern in design but was less than half the size of High Station Quantar. After landing, we were escorted by an unnecessarily large coterie of guards into pressurized cabins where our EVA suits were confiscated and we were, I assumed, interrogated individually for a short time by intelligence officers who spoke poor Standard. After being left alone for a while, I was escorted into what looked to be a command ready-room and sat at a single table with the captain and Serosian on one end, me in the middle, and Marker and Layton to my right. We were seated by presumed rank, I noted. After a few minutes of silence with swarthy guards staring at us, a man in a scarlet and black uniform with a large number of medals on his chest came through the door. He was dark-complexioned with a thick mustache that twisted upward at the ends. He was accompanied by a young attaché, clean-shaven and with hardly any rank insignia.

"I am Captain Salibi," he stated. "This interrogation is now my responsibility. Whether you live or whether you die may now depend on your answers to my questions. I suggest you hold nothing back and tell me the truth." I found this odd, as their initial questions had to do with our mission, and I assumed that each of us had answered truthfully already. If the interrogators had conferred at all then Captain Salibi must know our situation was as we stated. Although I was nervous, I didn't take the captain's threat of death seriously. He just didn't seem the type.

Salibi sat down at a table facing us, his attaché standing respectfully behind him, a plasma in his hand that I assumed was for notes. "Captain Kierkopf," he started. "Please recount to me how your ship came to be in the Levant star system."

"I've already told your questioners this five times," said the captain evenly. Salibi smiled thinly and with a bit of menace.

"Nonetheless, please indulge me," he replied.

"We came here in our vessel, the Union Lightship *Impulse*, on a mission of contact and friendship to Levant," she said. "And then—"

"And then you encountered our gatekeepers," said Salibi, interrupting her.

"I don't understand what you mean."

"The Imperial weapons," he said, offering nothing more. The captain looked nonplussed, then continued.

"We encountered those weapons once before, on our first foray into your space," she said.

"Yes, I know. We watched with interest. Even more so when we saw you were not destroyed, and that you came back," said Salibi.

"Of course we came back. As I said, we are on a mission of peaceful contact."

"That has yet to be determined," said Salibi. At this, the attaché leaned in and whispered something to Salibi. I began to wonder if some hidden observer was asking the questions through the attaché. "When you again ran afoul of the gatekeepers, your ship left you for dead and proceeded into our home space," he continued.

"That was a rogue Historian, Tralfane. He took control of our vessel and brought it here, to your world," said Dobrina.

"Not to our world, but to Tyre," he corrected, meaning the moon with the HD cannon. "Where your vessel activated a device that is more a legend on our world than anything we believed could exist in our system, then vanished. And then we see your tiny vessel approaching, landing on Tyre, attempting, no doubt, to repeat the same action: activating an Imperial gateway."

"We were trying to rescue our vessel, as I stated already," said Dobrina. Salibi looked away from her to Serosian.

"And you, sir, you have no rank uniform, and say your name is Serosian, a Historian from Earth, of all places. Speaking of legends."

"It is no legend," said Serosian, "I assure you."

"Your captain here—"

"She is not my captain," said Serosian, interrupting. "My ship is from another vessel, like the first one. Which should, incidentally, be arriving here soon."

Salibi eyed Serosian with annoyance. The attaché leaned in again. I could see a small earpiece in his left ear.

"Tell me what an Earth Historian does aboard one of these ships," asked Salibi.

"I monitor, record, and transmit all our mission logs to Earth to store the data. I monitor ship's systems, make sure they are in optimal condition," said Serosian.

"And?"

"Engage in First Contact missions, like this one, to establish friendly relations between emerging worlds and the Union."

Salibi shifted in his chair. "Tell me about this Union."

I sensed Serosian tense ever so slightly next to me. Nonetheless, he was ready with an answer. "The Union was established by treaty a decade ago between Carinthia, Quantar, and Earth as an exchange of culture, technology, and trade. The goal is to establish a peaceful and democratic interstellar government as a balance to any remnants of the old empire and its corrupt government. By choosing two well-established worlds on the verge of acquiring interstellar capability again as the core of our Union, we hoped to promote cooperation, as each world was on opposite sides during the Imperial Civil War. And as Captain Kierkopf stated, we came here hoping to explore the possibility of inviting Levant into the Union as well," he said.

"So you claim you are not Imperial agents?" Salibi asked. I sensed this was the key question, but which side would the Levantines come down on?

"We are not," said Serosian.

"But you came here seeking to use Imperial technology."

"Which we failed at, whereas our enemy succeeded. That alone should be evidence enough of our intentions," interjected the captain.

"But we have only your word to go on. This Historian has locked out your ship's computers. We can't break the code, which would verify your story. Perhaps you are agents of the empire and your other vessel was attempting escape," said Salibi.

"We aren't from the empire," I burst out, angry and frustrated at the questions. "I came here to stop the empire. The *empire* left those displacement wave weapons here in your system. The *empire* used them to surprise *Impulse*, killing an entire crew of my countrymen. The *empire* killed my friends. I hate the empire!" I said, half-standing from my chair.

"Sit *down*, Mr. Cochrane," said the captain, furious with my outburst. Serosian's hand on my arm and her withering stare made me sit back down again, but I was fuming that we were here wasting time with this man and his interrogation.

Once more the attaché came and whispered in Salibi's ear. At that moment Salibi stood to attention and the door behind him opened. I wasn't the only one surprised at who came through.

She was as tall as me, wearing a black one-piece formal suit with a white blouse underneath. Her skin was a soft caramel color and her eyes were a deep olive green and slightly almond in shape. Her hair was dark and hung well past her shoulders. I guessed she was about my age. She was stunningly beautiful.

Salibi and the attaché both bowed when she came in, indicating she clearly held a position of high authority. But her demeanor was not that of a military commander; she carried an aura of both power and privilege. She ignored Kierkopf and Serosian and looked straight at me, pointing.

"You, stand up," she said to me in perfect, uninflected Standard. I did as commanded—there was really no other word for it. "State your name."

I cleared my throat. "I'm Lieutenant Commander Peter Cochrane, of the Union Navy ship *Impulse*. Serial number—"

"I'm not interested in your military rank," she said. "I demand to know if you are from the Cochrane family of Quantar."

I swallowed. "Yes."

"The ruling family of Quantar?"

"Yes."

"Your title?"

There was no hiding it from her now. "Viscount of Queensland, heir to the Director's Chair, soon to be occupied by my father, Nathan Cochrane," I said. Her hands went to her hips and she contemplated me a moment. Without breaking eye contact with me she said:

"Captain Salibi, escort our *guests* down to Levant, to the palace at New Sydon. You will give them all the honors afforded to invited guests of Prince Sunil Katara of Levant, and of his sister, the Princess Janaan," she said. "Do you understand?"

"Yes, madam," Salibi said, then bowed again as she left in a rush.

"What was that?" I asked, turning to my companions. Serosian smiled.

"I'd say we just passed the smell test," he said, then laughed in his deep baritone.

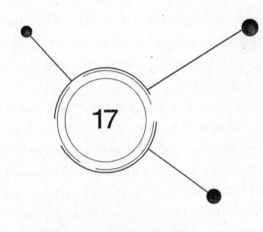

On Levant

We left the yacht at the station, which Salibi informed us was called Artemis, and flew down to Levant Prime in Salibi's own cruiser. He was apologetic and went out of his way to explain his actions toward us. It seemed that the Imperial technology left in this system had been keeping the Levant Navy from leaving their own star system for nearly a decade, since before the Union had been formed. Every ship that had tried to venture to Levant's natural jump points had been destroyed, as had ships approaching too close to the HD cannon on Tyre. It seemed Levantine culture and technology were nearly equal to our own, absent a few decades of Historian assistance. I could see now why Imperial forces would want to keep us apart. Levant would make the Union even stronger. And they hated the old empire as much as we did.

We landed at an empty airbase in the dark of night and were escorted to a pair of military vertical-lift vehicles, there to take us on the nearly thirty-minute ride to the Royal Palace. Levant medical teams took our injured, including Captain Zander, to the base medical facility. I felt relieved that they would be getting proper care now, even if Levant medicine was likely a decade behind ours.

We arrived in New Sydon at 0400 local time, which was fine with me. We had all been running on minimal rest for what seemed like days and, truth be known, I was exhausted. I hoped Prince Katara wasn't an early riser.

We were ushered in to a grand foyer by Captain Salibi's men, who addressed him as "General." He admitted as much to us, apologizing for being deceptive. It seemed he wouldn't dare risk leaving First Contact with an advanced potential enemy to some lowly navy ship captain.

I sunk into a large embroidered chair as we waited, feeling in my bones just how tired I was. Salibi said his goodbyes to the others and then bowed to me as he departed. I could barely lift my arm in response.

I must have dozed off immediately, as I was gently awakened by a military adjutant a few minutes later and we were escorted up an ornate, swept double staircase to the second floor. One by one each of my companions was given a room and an adjutant to see to their needs. Captain Kierkopf inquired about our forthcoming meeting with Prince Katara, and she was politely informed that we were scheduled to see him at lunch and would be allowed several hours of rest before the meeting. This seemed satisfactory and before I knew it I was at my room at the far end of the hallway. Wooden double doors swung open to reveal a large apartment with a sitting area in the middle and two large bedroom suites, one to each side. The adjutant asked which I preferred and I lamely pointed to the one on my right.

He was gamely explaining about how proper clothing would be brought up and asking if I needed anything like tea or toiletries. I said no and trundled off to the ridiculously large bed, pulling off my boots and crawling in. After a few moments, he said his goodbyes and was gone. I closed my eyes and was just about to drift off when I heard an unmistakable and unexpected sound.

Giggling.

I sat up and looked toward my bath where two young girls in

exotic-colored garb, like that of belly dancers I had seen in trivids, were standing with a gold plate full of bottles and small cups. I was so tired I didn't really register the implications of this. One of the girls stepped forward and offered me a massage in broken Standard.

"Later. Sleep," was all I could mumble out. They giggled again and the near one kissed me on the forehead and set my head gently down on the pillow. I heard them leave the room and quietly shut the door, then I drifted off into sweet oblivion.

I was awakened at 1000 hours by the sound of bathwater running and the girls giggling again. I was escorted into the bathroom, which was also enormous, quickly disengaged from my clothes and then sank into a massive tub full of hot, bubbly water. The girls sat on the edge of the tub, still thankfully fully clothed, chattering to each other in their native language, which I had no way of understanding. One of the girls washed my hair for me while the other took to rubbing my arms and shoulders, giggling and chattering the whole time. I had to admit that after the last few days, this was heaven.

After a while, they left me alone, and I didn't really miss them as I sat soaking my sore muscles for a few precious minutes. The next thing I heard jolted me back to reality.

"You seem to have settled in well," came a deep female voice from behind me. I opened my eyes and whipped my head around to see the woman from the Levant High Station interrogation sitting in a boudoir chair observing me.

"How long have you been there?" I said, more forcefully than I would have liked. She laughed.

"Long enough, Sire Cochrane. Are our accommodations to your liking?" she asked. I noted she had changed into a less formal but still businesslike body suit. And she was still stunning.

"They are," I said, swishing the bubbles as I tried to obtain a more dignified position. It was impossible. I was, after all, in a bubble bath.

"Good. I hope you had a chance to indulge in some of our . . . other offerings," she said. I sat up in the tub as best I could.

"I am a gentleman, madam, and would do no such thing," I replied. She laughed again, and I enjoyed watching every second of it.

"So you say," she sat forward now. "I have come here on a bit of business, Sire. I wish to inform you of some helpful protocol before your meeting with the prince."

"I'm in the bathtub, and you want to talk to me about protocol?" I deadpanned.

She smiled impishly at me. "What better place? I have a captive audience," she replied.

"That you do, madam," I said.

"First, I want you to know that this meeting is an informal one to welcome you and your people. There will be no serious exchanges made at this time. Tonight, however, will be a state dinner, and both the prince and princess will be there. This will be a formal occasion and you will be expected to talk business. Don't be surprised if the prince offers his most serious proposals after dinner in some informal setting, over an after-dinner drink or even during a walk in the royal gardens," she said.

"Understood," I replied. "About the prince—"

"He is only twenty-one years old," she continued, "but don't mistake his youth for innocence. He was well trained by his father in preparation for leading our people."

"And where is his father?"

She grew somber. "Both parents are dead. The mother from complications after the multiple birth, the father just a few years ago from heart disease," she said.

"I'm sorry," I said sincerely. "We have many treatments for heart disease that our Earth friends have given us. We would be glad to share them with you." She was still smiling, but I could see there was pain behind it.

"That is something you can discuss with the prince," she said.

"You mentioned a multiple birth. Are the prince and princess twins?" I asked.

"Yes," she said. "Fraternal, obviously. They are joint regents, but tradition dictates that the male heir controls most of the decision making."

I nodded. "Traditions are difficult things to break," I said. She replied only with a wry smile, then:

"And one more thing, Sire Cochrane. At some point the prince may propose an alliance, not between our world and your Union, but between his family and yours. It is critical to proper protocol that you do not refuse this proposal," she said.

"You mean I have to say yes?" I said. "Tell me you're not talking about marriage?" She looked at me very seriously.

"You may conditionally accept," she said, "Without refusing. This will be acceptable and likely create a strong bond between you and the prince. His family thrives on strong personal connections. Do you understand?"

"I think so," I said. "And what of the princess?" At this she stood to go.

"Treat her with dignity and respect, and you cannot go wrong," she said. Then she started out the door.

"Madam," I called after her. "I don't even know your name. Will you be at dinner?" She turned halfway back to me.

"I will," she said. "And you may know my name then." At that, she was gone, and I was left alone with my tub of bubbles.

A few minutes later, I finished bathing, then dressed in one of the formal suits left for me, which fit perfectly, and headed out of the bedroom suite to the living area. I was surprised to find Serosian and Dobrina waiting for me, Serosian in his traditional Historian's garb and Dobrina in one of the formal female business suits. My two attendant girls giggled again when I entered the room. I quickly shooed them off so we could talk.

"I see your accommodations were a bit more *personal* than ours," said the captain. I shrugged, refusing to take the bait, then sat down on a sofa.

"They seem to value royalty," I said dryly. Serosian smiled.

"They do indeed. Which brings up some interesting questions," he said.

"Such as?"

"Levant was once a republic, back in the old days before the civil war. They seem to have regressed back to a class structure here that favors the monarchy in decision making. That puts them much more closely in line with the old form of Imperial government than with the Union's system," said the Historian.

"Which brings into question how good a match for us they would be," said the captain. Out of uniform, in her business suit, the captain, no, Dobrina, seemed suddenly much more at ease to me, and much more feminine. It was a development I noted before returning my attention to the conversation.

"It would certainly be a better situation for Levant to come into the Union than to fall back under Imperial influence," said Serosian. "Hopefully they can be persuaded to adopt a more open form of government, perhaps even a parliamentary system, as a condition of entry into the Union. Still, a constitutional monarchy is not the worst form of government possible after a century and a half of isolation."

"It would be in their favor if they were to adopt more modern practices, both socially and politically," said Dobrina.

"They do seem to favor males in most social customs," I noted.

"Really, and how have you discovered that?" asked Dobrina, clearly annoyed at the concept.

"The woman from the station paid me a visit. She explained how things work here in some detail," I said.

"How much detail?" she asked. I sensed the slightest bit of jealousy in her, which intrigued me. I ignored the implications and went on.

"It seems that the prince will likely wish to deal directly with me," I said. Serosian nodded at this.

"Your diplomatic skills will undoubtedly be called into play. Prince Katara will likely only negotiate with you because of your royal lineage," he said.

"I am no diplomat," I said. "I'm trained for the navy."

"That is a failing of your rather egalitarian upbringing," commented Serosian. "One we will have to adapt to. You were trained early in your life as to the protocols of royalty, weren't you?"

"Only as a necessity," I stated. "I was the second son, not destined to be burdened with the problems of governance and protocol. So I avoided them as much as I could get away with. My experience in these matters is minimal."

"Perhaps it would be better, as mission commanding officer, if I took the lead," said Dobrina. Serosian shook his head.

"With apologies, Captain, that seems unlikely," said Serosian. "Not only does it appear that women carry less authority here, but so does the military. You saw how General Salibi was treated. I think our best bet here is to let Peter take the lead, with me as his attaché, and you as military commander."

"That seems to be the structure they favor," I added. Dobrina shifted in her chair, clearly uncomfortable with this arrangement.

"Are you absolutely sure this is the preferred protocol?" she asked.

"That's how it was explained to me," I replied. She crossed her arms.

"By that woman, whose role is completely unclear and whose standing is completely unclear," she said.

"She certainly carried weight with the general," said Serosian. He paused for a second, eyeing Dobrina, who finally gave in.

"Very well," she said. "For the sake of protocol and diplomacy we'll proceed as you've outlined. But I *am* in military command of this mission, gentlemen, and I *will* make any military decisions as I see fit."

"As you wish, Captain," said Serosian with a deferential nod of his head.

At that, a military guard appeared at our door, and we were ushered in to meet Prince Sunil Katara.

He stood to greet me as I came through the door into a sunny dining room, the table set for six. His handshake was warm and sincere, as was his smile. I found myself taking a liking to him instantly.

He was indeed young, with the dark skin and features of his countrymen. We were quickly seated at the table, with Katara at the head and me to his right, followed by Serosian and the captain in descending order. To his left was a diplomatic attaché named Kemal, a silver-haired man who had the look of a lifelong adviser about him, and lastly General Salibi, seated directly across from Dobrina with an empty space in between them. It was clear that the military personnel were to be separate from the rest of the discussion.

When we were seated, Prince Katara immediately started in with questions as we were served hot tea, cold fish sandwiches, and assorted pastries.

"Tell me, Sire Cochrane, what is your formal title?" he asked. I gave him my full peerage, with details as to the length of the family line, and so on. He seemed satisfied that I carried sufficient royal linkages, and once these formalities were out of the way he started asking questions that any young man would ask of another.

"So tell me of your travels! What new worlds have you seen?" he asked. I was embarrassed to relate that Levant was my first stop in interstellar space, and that I hadn't even been to Carinthia. He asked me about my shipboard duties, and I related them as best I could without giving away too much. I told the story of how we had entered Levant space and confronted the hyperdimensional displacement weapons left by the empire. This seemed to intrigue him the most.

"We have been trying to leave our system since before I was born. My father used to tell me about the failed missions. He grieved for every man we lost," said the prince.

"Without the help of our Historian friends from Earth I fear we would be in the same situation," I said. This turned the conversation to more practical matters as the prince addressed Serosian.

"So I gather your mission to our world then was originally First Contact, and got sidetracked by your encounter with our 'gatekeepers,'" he said.

Serosian nodded and smiled. "That was our goal. We came here to offer our friendship, trade, and advice, and hopefully to ask you to consider membership in our Union," he said. I noted that Dobrina and Salibi had been making small talk that had now ended, their attention focused on our conversation.

"That is certainly something we are considering," said Prince Katara. "The benefits of an alliance with your Union could be enormous to us, Mr. Serosian. Perhaps you and Kemal could meet to discuss what form such an agreement would take and we can discuss a formal framework tonight at dinner."

After the food was taken away, Prince Katara and I went to some side chairs to talk again while the others continued at the table, working out a framework of cooperation. I was surprised at the light air of the conversation.

"I was a soccer player at university," I related in response to the prince's questions. "Some said good enough to be a full-time professional. But I gave up my apprenticeship after two years to enter the Lightship program the first chance I got. Soccer was my passion, but space was in my blood, and my family's blood."

"My game is polo," said Katara. "The biggest problem I have is getting a fair game. No one wants to beat the prince's team." We both laughed at that.

After an hour, the prince rose to take his leave and the lunch was over, with a formal invitation to the state dinner at eight o'clock. I of course accepted for all of us, and we departed for my suite, there to debrief.

Serosian related the diplomatic conversation, Dobrina the military.

"They want a Lightship if they join," she said. "I tried to explain to Salibi that we only had three and we were trying to rescue one, but he wasn't hearing it."

"It's a reasonable request," said Serosian, "as were most of their diplomatic inquiries. I'll be receiving a packet from Kemal this afternoon. I'll know more before dinner."

Dobrina nodded. Serosian left then to continue his work as I sank into a large stuffed chair, my eyes barely able to stay open.

"Sleeping on the job, Lieutenant Commander?" Dobrina said.

"The Lieutenant Commander is ready any time, Captain. Sire Cochrane, however, is in serious need of another nap." She sat across from me, her legs crossed, one foot gently bobbing in my direction. For the first time since our battle on the fencing court I saw her again as more than just my commanding officer. She was a woman to me in that moment, one I was finding myself drawn to more and more. Her

combination of competence, accomplishment, and physical attrac-
tiveness was having an effect on me.

"And how is it the good captain has so much energy in reserve?"
I asked, one eye open and on her. She smiled.

"Perhaps it's because I didn't waste any of my rest time on giggling schoolgirls," she said back. I took that comment as her fishing
for information. I readily acceded to her subtle inquiry.

"Neither did I, Captain," I said, looking at her sincerely, with
both eyes open. "I'm saving myself for someone special." This got a
rise out of her as her cheeks flushed red, but she had a quick retort.

"Someone like a princess, perhaps? Or your unnamed bathing
assistant?" She seemed perturbed.

"Captain," I started in mock protest, "surely you don't think me
so vain and venal?"

She kept smiling, but then surprised me. "Please, Peter, you may
call me Dobrina in social situations."

"Is this a social situation?"

"Well, a state dinner certainly isn't a military one."

"All right then, Dobrina, I have to say that I'm not comfortable
with what my social duties may require of me with tonight's festivities, but I will do all I can to ensure that we complete an alliance with
Levant. It seems that we need the allies," I said.

"It seems we do," she agreed, while committing to nothing else.

"I need allies too. I'm asking you if you will be one with me in
these circumstances," I said. She frowned just a bit at this.

"I'm not sure I understand," she said.

I sat up. "Socially, the young duke may be required to do things
that the man in me is not comfortable with. I'm asking for your understanding, and I'm trying to assure you that I've made no decisions
about where my heart lies."

Again her face flushed, more broadly this time. She looked at me
from across the room for a moment, then answered.

"Thank you for clarifying things, Peter. But these are matters that are best left to be discussed at a more appropriate time. We're still in a crisis, and we cannot afford to dawdle here long. I expect you to do whatever is necessary to secure these people's assistance, nothing more, nothing less, as soon as possible, so we can be on our way and rescue *Impulse*," she said. "Everything else will have to wait for another time."

"I understand," I said. She stood to leave.

"I will leave the young Viscount of Queensland to his rest, and his giggling servant girls. I do suggest, however, that you *do* rest. You never know, the princess might just be a beauty," she said, "and that may require all your strength." She started out the door, stopping only once to turn back and smile at me before closing the door behind her.

I sighed, then lay back down on the sofa, drifting quickly off to sleep again.

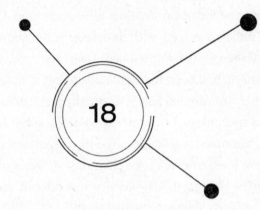

After a restful nap I repeated the bathing routine, this time by myself, and dressed in the formal dinner wear provided by the palace. The attention to detail by the royal attendants was apparent. All my clothes fit perfectly, even though they had never taken my measurements, and my dinner jacket even featured a version of the Cochrane family crest: Southern Cross of white stars on blue background, vertical chevron of orange, and three boars' heads on a white standard. The style was out of date but probably accurate for the last time Levant and Quantar had shared diplomatic relations. I had to admit, I was flattered by the effort.

I met the others, including Marker and Layton this time, in my suite area at 1945. Dobrina was busy checking the enlisted men to make sure they were presentable. Serosian was dignified in his usual all-black and cloak. But it was Dobrina who impressed me the most.

Her dress was a bright orange-red with gold brocade patterns woven through it. It wrapped around her body in a very flattering, feminine style, and was complemented by a shawl that flowed from her bare shoulders to drape over one arm. She turned to me once she had completed her examination of Marker and Layton. They had done her makeup as well, with dark lines accentuating her eyes in the style I had seen all the women here wear. Her hair, although still regulation length, had been manipulated so that it looked very flattering, framing her fine, angled face with small, dark curls.

I was speechless. I tried to say something but I could only croak out a few mumbled words. I cleared my throat and tried again. "Captain . . . you look, um . . ." Then they all laughed at me.

Dobrina shrugged. "The service was offered, and I accepted. See what you miss by sleeping the day away?"

"I do indeed," I said, smiling my approval. At that Serosian offered his arm to her and we started out of my stateroom.

Our attendants led us down a long hallway to the rear of the palace, where we had not yet been. The hallway opened up over an enormous ballroom, and we found ourselves looking down on a grand scene.

The dinner table must have been set for a hundred, adorned with gold and crystal, fine linens, and massive candelabras. It was finery that exceeded anything we had on Quantar. The room was filled with regal dignitaries and their escorts, the men dressed in formal suits, the women in a startling variety of colored gowns in the style worn by Dobrina. There was a buzz of conversation and the gentle clinking of glasses as the guests shared drinks and hors d'oeuvres.

As we were escorted to the main staircase and down the stairs, an orchestra started up playing music and the crowd broke out in applause. As the leader of our entourage I acknowledged the greeting with a polite wave of the hand, trying to remember my mother's lessons on royal protocol.

"You seem far more well versed in this than you let on," said Dobrina in my ear as she waved to the crowd, still on Serosian's arm.

"It must be in the blood," I deadpanned as we walked down to the table and were seated. This was the signal for the rest of the guests to be seated as well. I sat to the right of the prince's ornately carved wood chair, with Serosian, Dobrina, and the enlisted men in descending order of rank. We were greeted by Kemal, the prince's adviser, and his wife, as well as General Salibi and his wife. Both women were pretty, but not overly so, and both worked to make the acquaintance of *Impulse's* captain, no doubt another cultural norm on Levant.

We were served drinks and made simple conversation while we awaited the prince and princess, whom I was anxious to meet. At precisely eight o'clock the orchestra stopped the dinner music and began what I could only assume was the royal anthem. All the guests stood and we followed suit.

From underneath the balcony at the far end of the room the prince came in dressed in full royal regalia, his crimson military uniform adorned with numerous medals and what I assumed was the family crest, which to my surprise contained a symbol of a green tree. He hesitated for a moment at the door, then extended his arm. Out of the shadows came the princess, her dress in the same style as the other ladies, but in pure white with only a few gold adornments, her hair topped by a sparkling tiara. The crowd started applauding as they approached and we joined in. It took only a few steps for me to recognize the princess as the woman from the interrogation room on the station, the same woman who had visited me in my bath. I looked to Serosian and Dobrina. He smiled at me and tipped his head as if to say, "What did you expect?" Despite her best efforts, Dobrina couldn't quite conceal her displeasure.

The princess was seated directly opposite me, ahead of Kemal and his wife, while Prince Katara waited for the glasses of everyone at the table to be filled with sparkling gold champagne. When the task was complete the prince rose and raised his glass.

"A toast," he said in Standard, "to our newfound friends of the Union, and to Sire Peter Cochrane, of Quantar." He tipped his glass to me and I rose and touched mine to his, then we all drank and the table erupted in applause.

The band started in again with background music as we began our dinner, avoiding any formal discussion for the time being. I did note that Serosian was fully engaged with Kemal over some sort of proposal, while Dobrina was clearly unhappy at swapping conversation with General Salibi and his wife, stealing looks in my direction as often as she could.

The prince's hand on my arm brought my attention back to the matter at hand.

"May I introduce you to my sister, Sire Cochrane," he said with a sweep of his arm. "The Princess Janaan." I stood and bowed my head to her, and she extended her lace-gloved hand, which I kissed.

"A pleasure to see you again, Princess," I said as I sat down. "And it seems I do finally know your name." Prince Katara looked back and forth at us.

"You've met before?" he asked of me. I nodded.

"Yes, on your space station," I said, tasting an hors d'oeuvre. The princess smiled narrowly. "And again later, in my bath." At this her face went blank. I couldn't tell if she was angry or embarrassed.

"She came into your *bath*?" he said under his breath, clearly agitated. He turned to her "Janaan . . ." he started, shaking his head, but she cut him off.

"Do not lecture me, Sunil. I do what I have to do, you know that," she said tightly, then returned a happy smile to her face for the benefit of the guests.

"I know, Janaan, but the bath—"

"He was available and so was I. We did nothing but talk, you can ask Sire Cochrane yourself," she said, smiling all the while as if we were making small talk. Prince Katara turned to me.

"She's practically uncontrollable. Still, she is my most valuable asset," he said, loud enough for her to overhear.

"Of that I'm certain," I said, smiling back at her. I admired her forwardness, obviously a tough task in light of Levant's customs. She eyed the two of us, assessing our conversation, but was then forced to return to her social duties as a pair of court ladies came up to greet her.

As the princess was engaged in small talk with other guests, Prince Katara leaned in close to me.

"So what do you think of the princess?" he asked. I wiped my mouth with a napkin to buy myself some time to formulate a response.

"Honestly, I'm not sure what I think," I said. "First I met her as an interrogator on your space station, then in my bath as a protocol adviser, and now as a princess. I'm not sure which is the real one."

"Sometimes, neither am I," he admitted.

"The role of women on your world is limiting, isn't it, Prince Katara?" I observed. He said nothing for a moment and I feared I had insulted him, but then he leaned in close to me again.

"It is something I'm desirous of changing, yet these things move slowly. After the war, once we were cut off from the more progressive Imperial culture, our society regressed to more conservative norms. Religious institutions gained more sway over our morals and society. Thankfully, my father instituted reforms, but when he died it was left up to Janaan and me. In some ways it's an advantage for her, being co-regent, which would have been unheard of in my grandfather's time. She can move about without much question of her motivations. Other times it is more of a burden, and I find myself having to make excuses for including her in major policy decisions. The military sees her as an asset, and that's good enough for now. Still, perhaps these negotiations could be used as means of liberalizing more of our customs?" he said. I nodded.

"This may be a good time to bring in our chief negotiators," I commented. "These things have a way of being worked out to the advantage of everyone involved." Prince Katara agreed and waved Kemal and Serosian into the conversation. Princess Janaan and Dobrina both gave us annoyed looks, occupied as they were with court ladies.

"And what progress have you made, gentlemen?" asked the prince. It was Kemal who spoke first.

"We have a framework agreement, Your Highness. Trade and cultural reforms, technology, establishing forward bases for the Union Navy near the jump point, and such," he said. At this Katara looked right at Serosian.

"And our request for full Union membership immediately, complete with, shall I say, appropriate military considerations?" said the prince. Serosian smiled.

"He means a Lightship of their own," he said to me. "This is acceptable, as long as the prince understands it will take time to train even your best naval officers to the demands of such a vessel."

"I am sure our spacers can make the transition. How soon until we receive our new vessel?" asked Katara.

Serosian contemplated this. "Optimally, we would require two years of training. That can probably be condensed down to one, after the signing of the Union Concord agreements," he said. Katara looked from the Historian to Kemal, then to me.

"Six months," he said to Serosian, "after we sign the accords. Not a day longer."

The Historian's eyes narrowed just a bit at this, but then he smiled and laughed. "You drive a hard bargain, Prince Katara," he said.

Katara smiled back and then gestured for more champagne. "Let's drink to our newfound friendship," he said. And we did.

By this time both Princess Janaan and Dobrina were looking quite put out, so we resumed our dinner courses and kept the conversation light and friendly.

After dinner the crowd took to the dance floor, swaying to the delightful music provided by the orchestra. I found myself in a receiving line the with prince and princess, Dobrina, and Serosian, shaking hands with well-wishers and court hangers-on. The handsome Marker had more than enough attention from the ladies, and even Layton had an impressive array. This went on for a while until the prince broke from the line, bringing his sister with him by the hand. The orchestra changed quickly into a classic waltz and the two of them began dancing to the applause of the crowd.

I never got more than a few feet without someone putting a glass of champagne in my hand, and I was beginning to feel the effects as I watched the two siblings dance elegantly. The waltz concluded and the prince bowed formally to his lady, who replied in kind. The crowd thundered again and then the dance floor filled with many couples. I was about to turn to Dobrina and ask for a dance, feeling my oats, when General Salibi stepped up and beat me to it. Dobrina gave her assent to the general but still managed to glare at me with a put-out look.

"Careful," came Serosian's voice in my ear. "A lady's heart, even a Lightship captain's, can be a delicate thing." I turned to him.

"I appreciate the advice. Captain Kierkopf and I are friends, for the moment. Probably best we keep it that way," I said before draining another champagne flute. Before I could even put it down it was gone and another took its place.

"Are you sure she feels the same?" he said.

"You're not serious?" I said, then took another drink. "In all the years I've known you, for all the advice you have ever given me, this is a first."

"What do you mean?"

"The great and knowledgeable Serosian, Earth Historian, Man of Mystery, giving his young charge advice on the one subject he knows nothing about: women," I said, taunting my friend.

He laughed. "Just because you've never seen me with a woman doesn't mean I have no knowledge of them."

"Pray tell then, what is your expertise in this matter?" I asked, pressing him.

"I have been married for thirty-five years," he stated. I scoffed.

"You're lying, man! To look at you you're barely that age now!" He smiled but revealed nothing. "So what is your advice?" I finally asked.

"Treat her as your commander when you're both on duty. But treat her as a woman in all other things," he said.

I nodded agreement. "Sound advice in any situation," I said. Then there was a hand on my arm. I looked up to find the prince and princess standing in front of me.

"Sire Cochrane, I would be honored if you would share this dance with the princess," the prince said. I looked into her dark, sultry eyes. It was not a difficult decision.

"The honor is mine," I said. Serosian made as if to say something to me, then shut his lips again as I took the princess by the arm to the dance floor. The crowd parted for us and the orchestra broke off the song they were playing to start a new waltz.

"I fear both my experience and my dancing skills are lacking, Highness," I said to her. She smiled.

"It's no matter. I will pick you up if you miss a step and fall," she said confidently. Now I smiled.

"I believe you would." We swung out to the center of the dance floor as the crowd began to applaud. On the third turn I spotted Dobrina in the crowd, just in time to see her turn and stalk determinedly away from the festivities. I felt a lump form in my throat.

Big mistake, I thought.

Just as my concern for Dobrina came to the fore, the princess engaged me on another line of battle.

"If Levant joins your Union, will you be willing to support feminine equality and religious freedom?" she asked, no, more like *demanded* of me.

I was startled. "I haven't really thought about these things, Princess, except in passing conversation with the prince. My position is—"

"You are the highest ranking member of your contact party. Are you telling me you don't have the power to negotiate such things?" she said.

I stumbled a bit but quickly recovered as we spun around again.

"Princess, this is a *military* mission. By rank I am third in command. My royal standing gives me no special dispensation to negotiate such matters," I said.

"So you cannot include these terms in our agreement? Do I have to tell my brother that you are a powerless puppet?" She was growing angry with me now, but still we spun to the music.

"Diplomatically I hold the senior rank. But any agreements I make would have to be cleared with my compatriots—"

"Sire Cochrane, my people, especially the women, look to me as the cultural leader of our world. My standing allows me to negotiate these issues for all of Levant. If you are not empowered to act, just tell me now and I will find another dance partner," she said.

I was stuck between my roles as a navy officer and as royalty, but I had to make a decision or risk blowing the entire mission, at least the diplomatic part. I made my decision.

"I will take your requests to my contact party, if we can reach an agreement on terms," I said firmly. This now put the negotiating onus back on her and seemed to quell her anger a bit. The Levantines were serious about their haggling.

"You would support language in our agreement that encourages the promotion of women's roles on Levant if we join the Union?" she asked. That was simple enough.

"I would."

"What about religion?" she asked. "We have a mixed population: a Maronite majority and a small Muslim minority. Would they all be welcomed by the Holy Church?"

That was more difficult. I seemed to remember reading *something* about this once in the Union Concord. I decided to take a risk. "Serosian speaks to all matters regarding the Church, but to my read-

ing of the Union Concord Agreement, as long as the Levant government pledges loyalty to the Union and secular law is obeyed, then
religious pluralism is acceptable, if not preferred," I said.

We spun around the dance floor one last time as the music concluded. It was easily the most important and eventful dance of my
life.

"Then I believe, Sire Cochrane," she said to me as the crowd applauded, "that we have an agreement." I bowed to her then as I had
seen Prince Katara do, and she returned the gesture. I took an extra
step then, pulling her hand to my lips and kissing it again.

"I believe we do, Princess," I said, then escorted her back to the
table, there to resume our social duties for the evening.

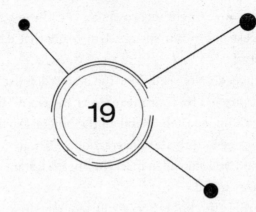

19

Dobrina was noticeably absent for most of the next hour. Only when the prince insisted we take a walk in the royal gardens did she return, and even then she avoided eye contact with me at all times.

We walked in pairs, Katara and I together, trailing the ladies, with Serosian, Kemal, and the others following behind us. Katara had a cigar and offered me one, which I lit, even though I had no idea how to smoke it. I sensed we were nearing the conclusion of our negotiations and our mission on Levant. If *Starbound* had received Serosian's signal, then they should be entering Levant space soon, and I would be able to return to my more natural duty as a navy officer.

The women were in pairs as well, and I noted that Dobrina and the princess were together.

"So tell me, Cochrane, now that you've met my sister, what's your opinion of her?" the prince asked.

"Very impressive," I complimented her. "In many ways."

"I agree. So tell me, what are your intentions toward her?"

"Intentions?" I thought about that a second. "Actually," I said, "I was wondering what her intentions were toward me."

"Come now, Cochrane, a woman can't have intentions toward a man, at least not in our society. Is it really that different in yours?" Katara asked.

I shrugged. "Not really, no. The man still must be the suitor. But I am a bit puzzled by your meaning of the word 'intentions,'" I said. The prince stopped then, as did all the others, leaving us with a considerable space for private conversation.

"Would you consider marrying her?" Katara asked out of the blue. I was stunned.

"I hardly even know her!" I blurted out. He waved his cigar, like he was discarding bad business advice.

"As if that matters. This is about politics, my good man," he said and started walking again. I followed.

"I think I hate that word."

"I understand your reticence," Katara said. "But our culture is different, Cochrane. We seek to bond ourselves to our allies by more than just financial and military means, and the strongest bonds are family bonds. Surely you agree with this?"

The mention of family turned my thoughts toward to my brother. If Derrick were here, he would be dealing with these issues, but he wasn't. I had to step up and make the decisions now.

"I do agree, Prince. Family makes the strongest of bonds," I said.

"Then you can see the wisdom of joining our two families?" This time I stopped our walk.

My thoughts turned to Janaan's earlier warning about accepting any proposal that was offered, even if only under unlikely conditions. I rushed through the scenarios in my mind.

"With respect, Prince, you must realize I am still a young man. If I should marry now, what if the next world demands the same of me? And the next? And the next? There is only one of me to go around," I said.

We started walking again.

"So your answer is no?" he said.

"I did not say that. Your sister is a fine and capable woman, and quite attractive. Would you have her married to a man who spends years in space? Returning home only briefly for short leaves? Or would you have her come with me, and lose her to Levant for those many years?"

"That would not be my first choice," admitted the prince.

"So let us reach a compromise," I said. Katara eyed me.

"I'm listening."

"I will agree to marry your sister, on the condition of my *not* being married to another woman of royal standing before the end of my navy service. That way I am free to make political alliances for the benefit of the Union, you retain the companionship of the princess, and if things work out, I can return to Levant in the future and our two families can be joined," I offered.

"How long?" said the prince.

"I'm twenty-three now, so say, seven years?"

"Five," he said. I nodded agreement.

"Five it is."

"And we can announce the engagement before your departure?" Katara asked.

"If the princess will agree to marry me," I replied.

"Oh, she will, I guarantee it." Then the prince took a long puff on his cigar and held out his hand to me.

"I'd say our negotiations are concluded," he said. I took his hand and shook it.

"I agree. Thank you, Prince Katara," I said. With that, the prince went over to the women, his arms spread wide.

"Ladies! Back to the palace! Our negotiations are completed, and we have much to celebrate!" The court ladies all erupted in cheers and then the prince whispered in Janaan's ear. She stopped and looked back at me, her smile revealing her pleasure at the news. Then she turned and said something to Dobrina. The look of shock that crossed the captain's face was obvious, but Janaan was already off with the group, running back to the palace. Dobrina turned and glared at me, then went off on her own in a different direction.

I hardly noticed as Serosian came up and stood beside me.

"I hope you know what you're doing," he said. I thought about that for a moment, then took a slow puff of my cigar.

"Actually, my friend, I have no idea," I said.

We were celebrating in a private two-story drawing room filled with books from floor to ceiling, a fire burning in a huge fireplace at one end, a billiards table occupying the other. There were about two dozen revelers celebrating with us. Janaan was in a corner with the ladies, taking congratulations, while the prince, Serosian, Kemal, Salibi, and I took up another corner. We'd been at it for an hour, and the buzz of our "good news" had made its way around the court in a flash. Dobrina, I noted, had gone to her room immediately upon reentering the palace, and I doubted I'd see her again tonight.

I had taken congratulations from many a courtier I didn't know, most telling me I had made a wise choice in choosing a Levantine bride. I smiled through it all. Though I'd never thought I'd be involved in any kind of arranged marriage, especially one with political overtones, I had to admit the *idea* of the Princess Janaan as my future bride, even if conditionally, wasn't something I was entirely resistant to. She was beautiful and certainly quite capable in many capacities, both in political qualities and no doubt domestic ones. She would make a fine wife for a young viscount or duke. But just now I was still a commander in the Union Navy, and my heart's desire was to explore the universe. And, quite frankly, between Janaan and Dobrina, I was unsure where my true romantic feelings lay.

After another half hour of making small talk and drinking, I was starting to yawn. The prince graciously allowed me to withdraw and I did, leaving Serosian to tend to completing business matters. The Historian never seemed to require sleep.

I went over to my prospective bride and bid her goodnight with another kiss of the hand, but the court ladies were having none of it.

"We must have a proper kiss!" said one of the courtiers. I smiled at Janaan, who looked up at me expectantly through her dark and alluring eyes. She stood and I drew her to me, our lips meeting pleasantly for a moment, then lingering a bit longer than expected. This drew "ahhs" from the ladies and applause. I bowed to them all, then made my way out the door and up to my room.

I hesitated a moment at Dobrina's door, but decided against knocking. What I had done was what was required of me, as she had asked me to do, and I hoped when this was over she would see that. I remembered Serosian's advice to treat her as a woman when we were "off duty." Right now I suspected that the woman in her would be hurt and angry.

A few minutes later I dismissed the servants and crawled into my own bed, tired and wondering what the day ahead would bring after such a busy night. I found, however, that sleep eluded me, and after nearly an hour of tossing and turning I called down for some tea to be brought up.

I was out of bed and sitting in a side chair when the knock came at my door.

"Come in," I said. A female servant in a dark cloak, with a hood covering her face, came in and set the tea tray down on a table near the only light in the room. I noticed it wasn't one of my regular servant girls, but I couldn't see her face in the dim light. No matter. I rubbed at my eyes as she poured a cup for me and then added a bit of cream, just as I liked it. I wondered if the staff had been observing my habits during our stay. She handed me the cup and saucer and then said, "Is there anything else, Lord?" so faintly I could hardly hear her.

"No, thank you," I replied, then took a sip. The tea was sweet and the warmth relaxing. I watched in the dim light of the lamp as the servant girl withdrew to the door and shut it, then locked it from the inside. She walked toward me then, pulling back her hood.

It was Janaan.

She dropped the cloak onto the floor, revealing an elegant silk nightgown underneath, then came and sat next to me on the floor, wrapping her arms around my legs in a gesture of submission.

"Janaan—" I started.

"Please wait," she said. I looked down into her eyes. God, she was *beautiful*.

"I cannot come to you as your wife," she continued. "I don't know if I will ever be able to. So I come to you now as a servant girl. Command me, and I will obey."

I set the tea down and reached out to her. She pulled my hand to her face. "I have no wish to command you, Janaan. Only to please you, but . . ." I trailed off.

She looked at me expectantly, then her expression turned sad. "But you cannot marry me, can you? It is because of her, isn't it? Do you love her?" she asked.

That question evoked a swirl of emotions in me. Thoughts of Dobrina and the beautiful and alluring woman before me crossed paths through my mind. Finally, I made my decision.

"I think so," I said. Her face fell, the disappointment hard to contain.

"Then you should be with her," she said. "She is a very lucky woman." At this she stood to leave, and I stood with her and took her hands.

"Don't misunderstand me, Janaan," I said. "Were the circumstances different I would gladly marry you this instant. I still have work to do, but the promise I made to you is real. If I am unmarried in five years to this very *day*, I will return to Levant and marry you without a moment's hesitation. If you would still have me, that is."

She smiled bravely, then said: "Would you grant a princess one request?"

"Yes," I replied.

"Take me in your arms and kiss me, as you would if we were husband and wife," she said.

There were all kinds of implications to her request, but I couldn't deny her, nor did I want to. I took her in my arms and our lips mixed sensually for a long moment. It was pure pleasure, and I lost myself in the moment.

The knock at the door startled both of us, and broke our embrace. The guard at the door didn't hesitate to open it and come in, disregarding our privacy. "Apologies Sire, Highness," he said. "There is an urgent matter. You are both required in the prince's military command center, immediately."

Janaan grabbed her cloak, and I put on the nearest set of clothes from my closet. Then we rushed out the door, our moment of passion forgotten in the face of the unknown.

We were taken down the stairs and rushed into a narrow hallway, through several doors, and then into a reinforced military-style lifter. We said nothing as the lifter seemed to go down very deep in the ground. Instinctively I reached out for the princess's hand to comfort her, and she took it, but when I looked in her eyes she had a serious look on her face, all business. I had forgotten she was not just the emotionally frail young woman of the evening's events, but also a valuable military adviser to the prince.

She parted hands with me as the doors opened, and she pushed past the guards into a short hallway connected to a central, brightly lit room. I followed her in and found the prince, Salibi, Serosian,

Dobrina, Marker, and Layton already inside along with technicians at various stations.

The prince's command center was more of a bunker, with a large main plasma display on the center wall. Currently it showed a tactical breakdown of the Levant solar system.

"What's this?" demanded Janaan. I looked behind us as the doors to the room were shut and locked from the outside.

"A hyperdimensional anomaly has appeared, near the artificial jump gate," said the prince.

"We noticed it about fifteen minutes ago," added General Salibi. "We haven't identified it as yet, but it is moving away from Levant at a high rate of speed."

We watched as the object accelerated away from Levant Prime and toward the outer solar system. With their primitive tactical computers it was impossible to determine the size or displacement of the unidentified vessel. I looked to Serosian; concern was etched across his face. Dobrina was all business.

"If it came through the jump gate, then it must have come from the same place they took our vessel, and it must be Imperial in design," she said, turning to Serosian. "We have to go after it."

"We can't guarantee it came from the same location, Captain. For all we know these portals are programmable with multiple locations as possible destinations," said Serosian.

"I'm guessing it came from the same place, Mr. Serosian, which makes it a priority to intercept. Do you have an alternative to offer or are you merely speculating?" said Dobrina, an edge to her voice.

"At this point, speculating. But until we can monitor it with our instruments on the yacht, we can't be sure of anything," he replied.

Dobrina considered this, then turned to the prince. "He's right, Prince Katara. We must return to our ship and intercept this vehicle, whatever it is. Lives could be at risk over this."

The prince considered this, then turned to Salibi. "General, can our ships catch this intruder?" Salibi reluctantly shook his head.

"No, Highness, it is too fast and likely too advanced for our ships to catch. The Historian's yacht seems the most likely choice for pursuit," he said. Prince Katara considered this for a moment, then turned to Serosian.

"Mr. Serosian, my government formally requests under our new alliance with your Union that you pursue and, if possible, detain this intruder into our space. If you are unable to detain it, we request that you destroy it," said the prince.

"Those actions will be at my discretion," interrupted Dobrina. "I am the military commander of this mission."

Prince Katara turned to her. "Then I make the same request of you, Captain Kierkopf," he said.

"I accept your proposal on behalf of the Union, Prince Katara," replied Dobrina. "I suggest General Salibi here get your fleet into a defensive position around Levant. This ship is an unknown, and as such, could be very dangerous."

"See to it," said the prince to Salibi, who nodded and went to a nearby station, giving orders in the Levantine language. The prince turned back to us. "Now, when do we leave?"

We all looked at each other. "We?" asked Dobrina. "You're not thinking—"

"Of going with you? As a matter of fact, I insist," he said. Dobrina looked astonished at this.

"Prince Katara," she protested. "A ship going into an unknown situation, possibly even battle, is no place for the Head of State of Levant."

He shrugged. "Perhaps so, but I am also Commander in Chief of our military, and in that role I insist on being aboard your vessel for this mission."

At this Janaan stepped up. "As do I," she said.

"No," I replied without thinking. "It's too dangerous."

"I agree," said the prince. "Your place is here—"

"In case you don't return?" she finished for him.

"Janaan, this is not the time—"

"For women to get involved. I understand you clearly, Sunil. It is my duty to stay here and tend the house," she said, fuming.

"We are co-regents, Janaan. One of us must stay here . . . in case something were to happen to the other. Logically, it must be you. Don't you understand?" the prince asked. She crossed her arms, looking back and forth between the prince and I.

"I understand," she said finally, "but I don't like it."

"Your Highness," said Serosian with urgency, "we must be moving soon. That vessel is not getting any closer to us. And if I may offer another solution?"

"I'm listening," said the prince.

"Command your defense fleet here. Levant will need to be protected, and you can do that better from your command ship than from our vessel. And, quite bluntly, you would simply be in the way on board our ship," he said. The prince reddened at this, but after a few seconds he gave in to logic.

"Very well," he said, and motioned for Salibi to join us. "We will head for the spaceport. Janaan will run the government from here. She is not to go up to the surface for any reason until this crisis is past," he said. There were acknowledgments all around and then we made for the lifter again. Janaan grabbed my arm just as the group exited the bunker.

"Make sure my brother stays safe," she said to me. I nodded to her.

"I will do my best," I said. Then she rushed in and gave me a brief kiss before turning away. I hurried out the door and into the waiting lifter.

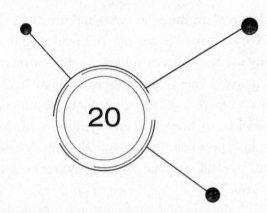

20

In Levant Space

We were powered up and airborne in the yacht in less than thirty minutes. It seemed like a short time, but when you're chasing an object at hyperdimensional speeds, it's valuable time lost. The yacht had taken the down time to do additional self-repairs and all systems were now at one hundred percent after our encounters with the HD weapons. It took me another seven minutes to get a bead on our bogey.

"She's moving away from us at point-two light," I reported. "Bearing is still a bit unclear, but if we can match her course and speed, I think we can close the gap."

"We can do better than that," said Serosian from his command console. "Her drive is hyperdimensional, but it's not as efficient as ours. That indicates an older design."

"Design of what?" asked Dobrina, hovering over him. The Historian may have been in command of the yacht but it was clear *Impulse*'s acting captain was unwilling to take second seat on the mission.

"I'll have it identified in a second. There it is," said Serosian as the image of an ancient Imperial vessel appeared on the forward plasma display. We all turned to see the 3-D rendering of the bogey. It was essentially a series of three connected cylinders interlocking together, with a fourth cylinder rotating about the main body on a strut. I was no weapons expert, but I recognized a coil cannon array when I saw one. "Vessel is an Imperial Hunter-Killer, sixth generation design. Use was most prevalent in the last half century before the Civil War broke out. I would estimate its age at approximately three and one-half centuries."

"What's the crew complement?" asked Dobrina.

"This generation of HuK was designed to be automated and operate on autonomous missions for long periods. Mission-critical updates were likely sent via the Imperial ansible network before it was destroyed. No crew. It made for an efficient weapon of mass destruction, though each would likely be a single-use weapon," said the Historian.

"Automated for attack?" Dobrina asked. Serosian nodded.

"On missions with low survivability outcomes," he said, not looking away from his board.

"A suicide mission," I said. They all looked at me.

"Technically there would have to be a living crew aboard for it to be a suicide mission, Peter, but your analogy is essentially accurate. This ship was built to execute a mission with little or no chance of returning intact," said Serosian.

"You mentioned the ansible network was destroyed during the Civil War," said Dobrina. "What would happen to a vessel like this in that event?"

Serosian shrugged.

"It's likely many of these devices simply shut down or went offline, awaiting new orders that never came," he said.

"Which makes them convenient for an adversary to locate and reassign," said Dobrina. Serosian tilted his head to one side before responding.

"Or, it could be that an event like *Impulse* coming through the gate led to the HuK's programming being reactivated. It could be merely carrying out a mission it was programmed for centuries ago and was never able to fulfill," speculated the Historian.

"Have you got a better read on its course yet, Mr. Cochrane?" asked the captain. I stopped listening and turned back to my board.

"I do, ma'am," I said. "It's on a course that will take it to the Trojan point asteroid we detected upon entering Levant space. The one with the HD anomaly," I said.

Serosian's eyebrows popped up at this. "Then it's got only one mission in mind," he said to Dobrina.

"Which is?" she asked, stepping up to Serosian's console.

"I can only speculate, but if there is an HD energy source at the asteroid, then the HuK wants that power for something."

Dobrina looked grave. "Attacking Levant?"

"Possibly." At this, Dobrina turned to us at our stations.

"Mr. Marker, get us something extra from those impellers, I want to catch this thing before it reaches the asteroid. Mr. Layton, keep us on course, and if that thing deviates one ten-thousandth from its course I want to know about it," she said, then swiveled to me. "Mr. Cochrane, a word in private, if you please."

I did as I was ordered, following my commander and Serosian into his private chambers. The Historian's inner lair was, to my surprise, very simple. On the left, an altar dominated the near wall, the only appointment being a padded knee rest I assumed was for prayer and communion. Serosian stepped behind a large, black console to my right. Behind him was a wall-sized plasma display. I was baffled as to what it was, and thought it could be artwork. I watched as colors swam across the wall, some in waves, some angles, and still others as sparkles of brilliant light. In a room beyond the main chamber I could see a simple pallet for resting, though I could never recall seeing the Historian sleep.

Serosian sat down and waved his hands across the console, his fingers dipping slightly into the surface like at the main console on the command deck. After a second or two of these motions he nodded to Dobrina.

"Raise your right hand," she said to me. I was surprised but did as instructed.

"Do you swear on your oath to the Union Navy to never disclose that which I and Historian Serosian are about to reveal to you, under penalty of imprisonment and discharge from the navy?" she said.

Again, I was surprised, but curious. "I do," I said. She nodded and dropped her hand. I did the same. We both turned to Serosian.

"This HuK has a hyperdimensional drive, but it is ancient technology. We can close on them, but we can't catch them before they reach the asteroid. We'll have to fight them off when we get there," he said.

"Why are they going to the asteroid? What's so important about this anomaly?" I asked. "Isn't it possible it could be nothing more than an abandoned Imperial power station from the last war?"

"I'm sorry, Peter, but it's not that simple," replied Serosian. He looked up to me, crossing his arms and leaning back in his chair. "This could be a Founder Relic," he said plainly.

I was surprised by the statement, and I had no idea what he meant by it. "What's a Founder Relic?" I asked.

Serosian looked to Dobrina, who nodded a final time. I felt as if something very important was about to be revealed to me.

"A Founder Relic is a device or mechanism created by a group we call the Founders, usually left in a time capsule," he said.

"The Founders?" I said, my curiosity piqued. He continued in a matter-of-fact tone, as if he were giving one of his Lightship Academy lectures.

"The Founders are what we call the original interstellar human civilization that thrived in this part of the galaxy between approximately two hundred thousand and eight hundred thousand years ago," he said, then let the words sink in. I looked at him for a moment, forming my thoughts.

"*Original* human civilization? You mean, originating somewhere other than Earth?" I said. The Historian nodded.

"We believe their civilization was based near the binary star Beta Lyrae. It's a long way from our space, eight hundred eighty-four light-years, but Founder Relics have been found all over the Sol system and in many other systems nearby. Some were thought to be left as 'gifts' to us as a successor human civilization. Others are more complex, and their intent is less clear. They may have been stored for safekeeping, or even hidden away during an ancient interstellar war," he said.

"We, the Historian Order that is, believe Earth was founded and possibly even terraformed as a 'cradle of life' in case the parent Founder civilization ever collapsed, which it did. The Union Navy has standing secret orders to investigate any potential Founder Relic discovered in any system. This anomaly certainly qualifies, as does the HD cannon in the cavern on the Levant moon," he concluded.

"I assumed the weapons we found there were left over from the First Empire," I said. Serosian shook his head.

"Unlikely. The sophistication evident, the level of precision, is beyond the capabilities of the First Empire. Remember, Peter, we Historians preserved as much of the scientific knowledge of the First Empire as could be gathered before the war ended, preserved it so that it could be reintroduced at the proper time. Believe me, I have seen the best First Empire technology and I've seen Founder Relics. That cavern was built by the Founders," he said.

"But there are records indicating those weapons were active during the Imperial civil war. Salibi told me," I said. "How could First Empire soldiers have the expertise to operate them?"

"Likely they had help from someone with ancient knowledge," Serosian said.

"Someone like the Sri?" I asked. He nodded.

"Someone like the Sri," he agreed. "You learned your lessons well, Peter. Remember, operating machinery is not the same thing as designing and building it. Whatever the case, finding a working Relic outside the Sol system is a rare occurrence. They are highly prized, as they usually contain some form of ancient high technology of the Founders. The Relics are designed to activate like this when they detect a hyperdimensional drive, to attract attention to themselves," said Serosian.

I was stunned. "So they *want* to be found? And you're telling me that this Relic was activated by our entry into the Levant system, and now this HuK has come here to what, collect it?" I said.

Serosian nodded. "Essentially, yes." Now Dobrina cut in.

"Every command-level officer is trained in the knowledge of Founder Relics and their known history. And every ship captain and XO in the Lightship program was given this training along with standing orders to locate and obtain any Founder Relic discovered in the course of our mission, at any cost," she said.

"There is more," said Serosian. "The Historian Order keeps this information understandably close, with only a select few given full knowledge. Your standing, Peter, as both a command officer aboard *Impulse* and as a potential future leader within the Union demands that you have this knowledge one day."

"Today is that day," said Dobrina. "Our mission, above all else, is to obtain that Relic. Do you understand, Commander?" she asked.

"I do," I replied. "And what of Levant? This places them in great danger, doesn't it?"

"We will do everything we can to protect Levant, but I make no promises," said Dobrina. "Our priority is securing the Relic and neutralizing that HuK, in that order."

"So this Relic is more important than a planet with thirty million people on it?" I asked. Dobrina crossed her arms determinedly.

"I have my orders," she said, then quickly departed for the command deck. I turned to Serosian.

"One day, soon," I said, "this will change, and we will protect our friends first, above all else."

"I hope so, Peter," said Serosian. It was little comfort.

After half a day of acceleration at HD speeds, we were closing on the HuK. It was clear now we would catch it before it reached the Trojan point asteroid and the Relic. The question was, what would it do? Turn and attack us? Destroy the Relic at all costs? Or something else?

Everyone on the yacht was tense as we all stayed glued to our stations: Serosian at the command console, Marker and Layton at propulsion and navigation respectively, and me at the 'scope station, weapons at the ready. Dobrina hovered over Serosian, who in turn was watching my tactical display on the yacht's main monitor.

"Three minutes until we reach firing range," I reported.

"I see it," replied Serosian, his attention fixed on his console. I wondered what Dobrina could see there as his display was a complete mystery to me, a jumbled mess of lines and dots, colors and textures, like a fluid, moving schematic that never settled on any one configuration. "Power the forward coil cannon, and prep the tactical torpedoes for launch," he said to me.

"We have torpedoes?" I blurted out, not thinking before I spoke. This got the Historian to glance away from his console to focus on me.

"Check the icon menu on the left," he said. I did. Sure enough there was an icon for the torpedoes that I could swear wasn't there before. I gave my mentor a look but said nothing and then quickly brought the system online. I couldn't make out all the details, but it looked like the torpedoes carried a significant atomic payload.

"What's the tactical scenario under which we'd use these?" I asked. "The yield seems pretty high."

"The torpedoes are for long-distance pursuit and disabling of an enemy, not for close tactical exchanges," explained Serosian, who I could tell was trying hard not to look annoyed at my questions. "I want to have them online in case we need to use them."

"How close can we get to the asteroid and still use them safely?" asked Dobrina.

"That's debatable in this circumstance, Captain. We may have already passed the safe-use range, but I want them available for any eventuality," Serosian replied.

"Then I take it we'll be using the coil cannon as our main weapon in this engagement?" I said. He looked up to me again before responding.

"Affirmative. However, we may find ourselves outgunned in that department," he said. That gave me no comfort.

"I thought you said the yacht was more advanced than the HuK?" I said.

"It *is* more advanced, Peter. However that doesn't mean we have superior weaponry. These two vessels were built for very different purposes." I turned back to my board.

"One minute," I said as we edged ever closer to attack range. We didn't have to wait nearly that long for the action to begin. "Enemy vessel is breaking course, decelerating and turning to attack," I reported seconds later.

"Confirmed," said Serosian. He nodded to Dobrina and she strapped herself into the sole remaining safety couch. "Coil cannon?"

"Ready," I replied.

"Torpedoes?" I checked my board.

"Armed and hot."

"Cut the drive, Mr. Marker, switch us to impellers," he commanded.

"Aye, sir, switching to impellers," said Marker.

"Mr. Layton, change our vector by point-oh-oh-three-three positive to the ecliptic."

"Aye, sir, point-oh-oh-three-three positive," said Layton, then quickly carried out his commands.

"We'll fly right past her at this speed," stated Dobrina. "Aren't we going to change course and try to engage her?"

"No," said Serosian flatly. "Once we complete our maneuver we'll have the asteroid to our back."

"But we'll be vulnerable to her weapons fire as we pass," she said. I turned to look at my commander and saw the concern on her face. We exchanged worried glances.

"The Hoagland Field should be enough to protect us from any attack from the HuK," said the Historian.

"*Should*?" said Marker from his station.

"*Should*. Now if all of you don't mind, I have a battle to fight. I suggest we all check our straps again, get ready, and debate tactics later," replied Serosian. It was the first time I'd ever detected annoyance in his voice.

"Ten seconds to firing range," I said.

"And the enemy ship's firing range?" asked Dobrina.

"Unkno—" I was cut off by the yacht rocking from a coil cannon barrage, knocking the wind from me in midsentence. When I got my breath back the tactical display showed the HuK closing on us, the coil cannon array spinning rapidly about the center cylinder of the craft, looking for all the world like a metallic whirling dervish spewing out green-tinted lances of energy at us. "Inertial dampers are compensating, but we're taking direct hits to our defense field," I said, anxiously waiting for the command to strike back. When it didn't come I grew concerned. The HuK was closing, and pelting us with coil cannon fire as it came. "Sir!" I blurted out in between hits on the field. I could tell the dampeners were weakening. It felt like we were being shaken apart.

"Target the forward cannon!" commanded Dobrina from her safety couch.

"Belay that!" replied Serosian over the din of coil fire erupting off the shields. "Stay the course, and hold your fire. I don't have time to argue with you, Captain!" he yelled at Dobrina. I watched her clamp her jaw shut and she nodded at me reluctantly as we shook and bounced through the enemy fire. We went on like that for what seemed an eternity, the yacht absorbing volley after volley from the HuK. Sweat was running down my forehead as I looked back to Serosian at the command console, waiting for the order to fight back.

It didn't come.

Just when it felt like we'd fly apart from the strength of the barrage and our rapid deceleration maneuver we passed by the HuK and the volleys stopped. The enemy would have to recalculate our position and rotate its cannon to get a new fix on us. I watched the tactical as Serosian executed a perfect maneuver, rotating us on a dime, so smooth that I didn't feel a thing.

"Cut the impellers Mr. Marker!" he demanded. Marker did. Suddenly our forward cannons were in firing position on the HuK and the asteroid was behind us as we hurtled toward it, our momentum carrying us into its minute gravity well.

"Lock the cannons and fire, Mr. Cochrane!" he ordered.

"Aye, sir!" I replied. It took me barely a second to carry out his command. I targeted the stanchion supporting the enemy's coil cannon array and fired all four of our batteries. Orange fire launched from our triple cannon ports and converged on the enemy, cutting through her weaker rear shields as she tried to turn away from us and recalibrate her attacking vector to place her stronger forward shielding between us. It was a vain attempt. My cannon fire seared a long scrape up the stanchion, slicing across the support and then severing it with a satisfying explosion as displaced energy flowed out into the vacuum of space. The wounded HuK spun like a fish on a hook trying to break free, then quickly accelerated out of our firing range before I could get another fix on her.

"Good shooting, Commander," said Dobrina.

"I agree," chimed in Serosian. I wiped the sweat off my forehead with my sleeve.

"I did have ample time to calculate a firing solution," I deadpanned. Serosian shrugged.

"It was necessary in order to maximize our strategic position, which we have now achieved," he said.

"Won't the HuK come back?" I asked.

"Very possibly," said Serosian. "But she's been badly hurt. Likely she has some reserve cannon ports on her, and possibly torpedoes. But if she intended to destroy the asteroid she could have used them at any time. My guess is it will watch and wait for another opportunity to attack us. This is not over. However, we are now between the asteroid and the HuK, and that was essential if we are to retrieve the relic," he said.

"Then let's get on with it," Dobrina said, unstrapping from her couch and standing to give instructions, taking over the mission command again. "Mr. Marker, reengage the impellers. Mr. Layton, take us in to the asteroid. Mr. Cochrane, try and pinpoint the location of the . . ." She hesitated. ". . . object. Mr. Serosian, I hope you don't mind, but I need to have a word with you. Alone." Serosian nodded agreement. "Carry on," she finished to the rest of us, then stalked off toward the Historian's quarters. He reluctantly got up and followed her down the short hall, shutting the door behind him as he entered.

"Wouldn't want to be in his shoes," said Layton. I laughed.

"Neither would I." Then I turned my attention back to my board.

The asteroid itself was a mystery. It had a shape to it almost like a cut diamond, the kind you'd see on an engagement ring, which seemed unnatural. As I scanned it, the mystery only deepened.

The object reflected all of my attempts to probe it right back at me. Frustrated, I switched to a visual display using the yacht's high-resolution 'scope and adjusted the display to show the asteroid in a north-south orientation. To my great surprise, true "north" on it was in the exact center of the diamond shape's table, or top. It still looked like an asteroid at this distance, complete with a mottled surface and impact craters, but some of them were in disturbingly geometric patterns. The ratio of the thing—I hesitated now to call it an asteroid, even in my own mind—was almost a perfect three miles tall by one mile across. This confused me, as miles were an old Earth measuring system and not considered as accurate as metrics. If it was artificial, and I was beginning to believe it was, why would an ancient culture of humans use a seemingly arbitrary and archaic system of measurements?

I bounced a low-density radio wave off the object and got back another surprising result. There was a delay in the return, indicating that the object was scattering the wave before bouncing the signal back. But that would indicate—

"What have you found, Commander?"

It was Dobrina's voice and it startled me. She and Serosian had emerged from his cabin, having apparently concluded their discussion, and I'd been so engrossed in my explorations I'd failed to notice their return. I turned to them as she sent Marker and Layton to check on their stations for battle damage, putting them out of hearing range.

"All of my scans appear to be reflecting back, except the radio wave, which seems to indicate—"

"That the object is hollow," finished Serosian, speaking quietly, leaning forward and looking over my data. "This is common with Founder Relics. They were often disguised within an asteroid-type body by a covering of natural material, rock and dust, to both protect the Relic and act as a shield in case of attack."

"Attack?" I asked. "Was that common?"

"From what we know of the Founders they had many rivals, and war was as standard for them as it is for modern humans, unfortunately," Serosian said. He ran his hands over my display, checking the radio wave data. "This object is completely artificial, look at the radio return." He put the display up on the yacht's main monitor. It showed highly reflective surfaces, facets and . . . what appeared to be innumerable rooms and connecting corridors.

"This technology is far beyond us, and yet they fell," I said as I watched the signals echo about the object.

"But they left the Relic for us, their children, to find," replied Serosian.

"Wait, I'm unclear," said Dobrina. "Is this asteroid the Relic, or are we searching for something more?"

"The asteroid, or rather the artificial object masquerading as an asteroid, is merely the housing, the protection for the Relic itself, which is no doubt secured inside. The Relics we have found in the past tend to be small in size, so as to be more usable, or rather more accessible to interfacing with our technology," Serosian said. Dobrina looked back at the display and the cascading radio signals.

"And how will we find it, inside that maze?" she asked.

"We can track the hyperdimensional emissions to a certain extent, but the faceting will make communication difficult, especially if the interior is crystal, which is likely. The best way will be to simply explore the rooms," said the Historian. She looked up at the display again. It was painting in a myriad of pathways and rooms as our signals bounced around inside.

"That could take months," she said.

"Then we'd best get started. Mr. Cochrane and I can do the EVA together. Likely we'd work most efficiently that way."

"If you think I'm staying here while you go on a walkabout—"

"I'm not willing to risk more than the two of us on this mission," said Serosian, interrupting the captain. "Peter and I have trained together for many years and I know that I can trust the commander to follow my instructions. Can you say the same?" Dobrina crossed her arms in frustration but that seemed to settle the issue for the moment.

"Very well," she said, raising her voice. "Mr. Layton," she called, "get back here and take us in, slowly. Mr. Marker, one-hundredth speed on the impellers, no faster. And Mr. Cochrane," she said, turning to me. "Your job is to find us the way in."

It took me nearly an hour to find it. We had set our course to a series of passes from pole to pole on the object, searching in the dark the old-fashioned way, running lights across her surface. We did manage to blend in some radar mapping so we could make judgments on the most likely locations, but in the end it was just good old eyeballing that produced the result we were looking for.

"There!" said Dobrina, pointing to the main display. "It's almost a perfect hexagon."

"Confirming," I said, running my hands over my 'scope display. "Odds of artificiality are over ninety-nine percent. It's also aligned at the energy epicenter, nineteen point five degrees north latitude. I'd wager a week's pay that's our way in."

Serosian nodded. "I agree," he said.

"Mr. Cochrane, calibrate your run and then take us in. Slowly," commanded Dobrina.

I was very conservative with our approach, taking nearly thirty minutes to descend to a distance of five hundred meters, then I rolled the yacht so that her airlock was facing the black hexagon.

"Can we confirm that there's an opening?" asked Dobrina. Layton responded.

"Negative, sir," he said. "Navigation light beams terminate at the event horizon, at what would be the surface if it were natural. Nothing goes inside or reflects back to us. We have to make our own call, sir."

"I wish I had a rock," said Dobrina.

"What, sir?" I asked, not understanding the analogy.

"Just an expression from back home. Wish I had a rock to drop down the well so we could tell how deep the water is," she said.

"I would say the only way to tell how deep the water is, Captain Kierkopf, is to let Commander Cochrane and me get on with our EVA," chimed in Serosian.

"I wish I had an argument against that, but I don't," said Dobrina. "Proceed."

It took us fifteen minutes to don and check our EVA suits before heading to the airlock and depressurizing.

"Take us down to one hundred meters," ordered Serosian.

"Why so close?" came Dobrina's scratchy response in our coms.

"Because we only have twice that much in EVA tether," replied the Historian. There was no reply but the yacht started moving closer to the black field. It was eerie. The field was exactly like the one Marker and I had encountered at the colony base, but the circumstances gave me a serious case of the willies. I shook off my anxiety as the yacht slowly ground to a halt. I watched Serosian attach his tether and then open the airlock's outer door. He wasted no time in proceeding out, using a short burst from his cone jets. I attached my tether and followed suit, just a few meters behind him.

"How do you intend to proceed?" asked Dobrina on our private com line.

"I'll go in first," said Serosian. "When I am clear on the other side I will yank on my tether three times. That will be Peter's signal to proceed. Once he is clear on the other side he will also signal you. From there, communication will depend on what the environment beyond the event horizon allows us to do."

"I don't like it," said Dobrina.

"Do you have an alternative?" asked Serosian. Her line stayed silent for a moment as I listened in while my superiors debated.

"No," she finally admitted. "Make communication your top priority, if possible. I want to know what's going on at all times. And remember that HuK is still out there."

"Understood," replied Serosian.

"You have two hours and fifty-two minutes of environment to complete your dive, gentlemen. I suggest you get on with it," she finished.

"Activating my suit camera," said Serosian. I did the same. At least until we crossed the unknown barrier the yacht would be able to receive our camera images.

I watched as Serosian used a burst from his jets and accelerated toward the blackness. The dark field was all-enveloping now, extending to either side of us in every direction. I was anxious and looked around to get my bearings but could scarcely make out distant details of the object's surface. I turned my attention back to Serosian just in time to see him vanish suddenly and completely beyond the event horizon.

My heart pounded in my chest.

"Are you all right, Cochrane?" came Dobrina's voice in my ear.

"Affirmative," I croaked out, my mouth dry and stale. I watched for anxious seconds as Serosian's tether extended to its full length. For a moment I worried the three tugs wouldn't come.

And then they did. I sighed, fogging my visor.

"Note that we've lost Serosian's camera and com," said Dobrina. "You'll be on your own on the other side."

"Acknowledged," I said, then tapped my cone jets to life, moving toward the abyss.

It seemed to take hours as I closed on the blackness, extending my arms in front of me, my breathing becoming harsh and jagged.

The surface of the void rippled as my hands penetrated the barrier, like dark water disturbed by a tiny pebble. The material swished and formed around my arms, then they simply disappeared into the void. The blackness penetrated my visor plate and I tried in vain to scream, but couldn't.

Darkness filled my mouth.

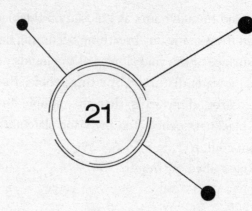

21

I wanted to vomit, but I managed to hold off. It was like the darkness had been *inside* of me, as if I could still feel it in my body. I shuddered and held my stomach, fighting the urge to retch again.

"Are you all right, Peter?" It was Serosian's voice, clear and jolting in my ears.

"I think so," I said between coughing fits.

"The experience is unpleasant, I have to admit," he shared. "I think it likely this type of null-energy field is used as a filter to keep anything unwanted out. Apparently, humans are allowed to pass through. I doubt it would feel the same if we came through with an active Hoagland Field protecting us, though."

"That's some comfort, I guess," I said as I fought for and regained my bearings. We were free-floating inside an empty chamber many hundreds of meters in circumference and multiple times as deep. It was awesome in scale, if not in its decor. The chamber was filled with what I could only describe as trash and debris, and it looked for all the world like a loading dock for spacecraft. I glanced around. There were no spacecraft now, just the detritus of a long-abandoned outpost floating past us on all sides. I reached down to unhook the tether at my waist and join Serosian, who was some fifty meters "down" from me. I spun as I took hold of the hook and looked out into space. Beyond the event horizon I could see the yacht holding her position, her image clouded by waves of energy, like ripples on a pond. My tether distorted as it passed through the surface of the membrane and into normal space.

"We can see out," I commented as I unhooked and gave the tether three tugs, indicating to my captain that I had arrived safely on the other side.

"Yes," commented the Historian. He said nothing more as I engaged a short burst from my jets and joined him. We were looking down on a flat metal landing bay, empty now and devoid of any spacecraft. There were bridges leading off of the platform in multiple directions like the threads of a spiderweb, with large gantry towers attached to the perimeter. We continued our dive with short bursts, taking us down to the platform surface. Once there, Serosian engaged his gravity assist at one-tenth weight and I followed suit. Our orientation now shifted to the plane of the platform surface. It was huge.

"How far did we come in?" I asked. Serosian checked his distance calculator.

"Five hundred meters or so. And this deck is at least three times that size in circumference," he said.

"We could stack a dozen Lightships here."

"More like dozens," he replied. "But that's not why we're here." In my curiosity I couldn't help but take in the view while Serosian began tracking the hyperdimensional signal from the Relic. The supporting gantries, now long abandoned, loomed over the platform. Their control rooms towered stories above us; their function had obviously been to monitor activity here at the landing deck. This had once been a bustling station, that was certain, but how long ago?

"I have a signal," said the Historian. "The exact direction is unclear, but I would say . . . that way." He pointed to one of a half-dozen spider-legged bridges leading off the platform.

"You're not certain?" I asked. "I thought the Relic *wanted* to be found?"

"It does, but not by just *anyone*," said the Historian. I thought I detected a slight tone of annoyance in his voice. "This way." He started off and I followed, our boots gripping just enough to allow us the motion of natural walking without much effort, keeping us stuck to the metal deck.

"I'm having difficulty getting an exact fix on the chamber we're looking for," he said as we walked. "Much of this superstructure is metal, but there are also high concentrations of crystal in the walls and the inner rooms. It's making the signal bounce around like a loud voice in an echo chamber." As he said this, we walked across a bridge with no rails. Beneath us the hollow center of the "diamond" dropped off for what seemed like miles. The Historian was completely unfazed by it all.

"How deep is this . . . object?" I asked, steering myself away from the edge while I looked down at the endless series of rooms and compartments below us, dropping off into a mist of infinity, some of them clearly shattered open by violence of some sort.

"This is a station," Serosian said. "It has been disguised to look like a natural asteroid in the Levant solar system. We've seen this level of construction before, on the same scale."

I took time to digest that information as we explored, eventually coming to a landing that led off to innumerable corridors. Again the Historian pointed, this time down the central corridor of a nearby group of three. "That way," he said.

"You're certain?" I asked. He shook his head.

"The instruments that I would need to be certain probably do not exist. But the signal leads us here," he said, then started down the corridor. I followed, and after a few twists and turns I was certain we were descending.

"This path is slightly inclined," I said.

"Yes, likely this will go on for some time," he replied.

"Is that a guess?" He shook his head inside his visor.

"A supposition," he said. Now it was my turn to make one.

"You've been on one of these stations before," I stated. He looked at me as we walked side-by-side down the corridor.

"This is one of the smaller ones," he said. I shivered a bit at that thought, then looked down at my suit readouts to distract myself.

"Two hours and fourteen minutes of environment left," I said.

"Noted," he replied. Then we walked on in silence, every step taking us deeper and deeper into the unknown.

The last four levels were pure crystal. Our helmet lights reflected off literally millions of faceted surfaces. It was confusing as hell to me, but Serosian soldiered on, never taking his eyes from his peculiar detection instruments and never wavering in his determination. Suddenly he took a surprising hard right turn and we were there, standing in front of a crystallized covey just big enough for us both, our lights reflecting rainbows off prisms in a thousand directions.

"Is this it?" I asked. Serosian bent down.

"What we seek is beyond this wall," he replied as he ran his instruments over dozens of pointed crystalline surfaces. They looked to me like they were growing out of the wall.

"What are you doing?" I asked as he passed a glowing wand over the crystals, emitting a pure white light from its tip.

"Trying to match frequencies with the crystals," he said, not breaking his pace. I looked down at my watch. One hour thirty-eight minutes. We were getting close to a point-of-no-return decision.

"The crystals have a frequency?" I asked casually, taking my mind off of our time predicament.

"All living things have a vibrational frequency," he replied, apparently implying that the station was "living." "The crystals act as energy transducers, converting one form of energy to another. If I can match their inductive frequency, I can likely crack the code."

"Crack the code?" I said. I heard him let out a chuckle.

"Then we'll have to pass the test," he said.

"Test?" But he said nothing more. I stood dutifully by as he continued his work, unsure whether to be terrified or encouraged. After several minutes of this the wand glowed gold in his gloved hand.

"I've matched the vibrational wave," he said. "Now as to the test . . ." he trailed off, his eyes searching as the crystals began to glow in a slow sequential pattern.

"Is this the test?" I asked.

"Quiet!" he snapped. I watched as his eyes followed the sequence of lights emanating from the crystals. It seemed to me that it was repeating, with a very small pause between the sequences. I counted them all the third time through. Then the lights all went dark.

"Is . . . is that it?"

"Yes," he responded. "It's a riddle, or more precisely a mathematical sequence. Usually some form of universal constant, but I don't know if I follow this one . . ." He trailed off. I could see he was struggling with the code. I looked down at my timer. One-hour twenty-two minutes to go. We were cutting our point-of-no-return time tight.

"There were fourteen lights in the sequence, if that helps," I said as precious seconds clicked by, unable to contain myself.

"What?"

"Fourteen flashes. I counted them. And they moved right to left across the panel," I said. He looked at me and smiled.

"*Adonai eloheinu adonai,*" he said, then started working feverishly.

"Is that the code?" I asked. He shook his head inside his helmet as he adjusted the instrument.

"No. It's the fourteen-letter name of God in ancient Hebrew. It also happens to be a mathematical constant, which are used often by the Founders. Each of the letters has a corresponding numerical value that can be related into any written language. It's like a universal code, which, with your timely insight, we are about to crack." He pointed the light wand at the now dark crystals and activated it. Light projected from the wand in a series of pulses, reflecting off of the crystal wall. After the sequence completed, we waited for what seemed an eternity before the crystals once more repeated the sequence back to us.

Then the crystal wall dissolved away.

We walked through the opening. Inside, the room was shaped like a sphere made of crystals, with the walls completely covered in geometrical patterns: triangles and hexagons, interspaced and woven together in a seamless pattern and glowing red. It was two decks high to the top of the sphere and perhaps half a deck down from the door. The only flat surface inside was another narrow bridge that led from the opening to the center of the room. The center was occupied by a round pedestal, and above the pedestal floated an opaque turquoise star with six sides to it. It looked like it was made of a ceramic material rather than the crystal we saw everywhere else.

I followed Serosian across the bridge, not looking down as we approached. The Historian took the star in his hands, and I was happy to let him stay in the lead. I'd had quite enough ancient-human creepiness for one day. He pulled the star from its protective suspensor field and then rotated it, looking for an opening or lever of some kind.

"There's no obvious means of opening the Relic," he said. I looked at my timer again.

"We should take it with us," I suggested. "We're getting close on time." He looked perturbed but nodded.

We were down to the red line, thirty minutes to go, by the time we got back to the platform. From there we disengaged our gravity boots and jetted up to our waiting tether lines. This time I didn't hesitate—I flew through the membrane as fast as I dared, getting the unpleasant experience over with as quickly as possible. Fractions of a second later my com burst to life.

". . . calling. Can you hear me? Emergency situation. Repeat, emergency situation." It was Layton's voice.

"Cochrane here. We've got the Relic," I reported. Immediately Dobrina jumped on the line.

"Then get your asses back over here! That damned HuK is on the move again!" she said.

"Acknowledged," I replied. I looked to Serosian as he emerged from the membrane, the Relic in tow. "We'll be inside in five minutes."

"Make it three," said the captain, "Or we may just leave without you."

Ten minutes later, we were back on the yacht. Serosian stored the Relic in his chambers while we began a retreat from the station using the impellers. The HuK had a good start on us though, and was making her attack run at us at flank speed.

"Take us away from the station, Mr. Cochrane," ordered the captain. "But try and keep it between us and the HuK." She turned to Marker. "Full-on with the impellers, Mr. Marker. Mr. Layton, plot us an evasive course out of here and back to Levant, and prepare to use the HD drive on a moment's notice." Switching to the HD drive and running off of its plasma rather than the chemical impellers when we were outside of jump point space would allow us to accelerate our way out of any potential losing confrontation with the HuK, but it would leave the station defenseless. To me it seemed as though the station was a potential treasure trove of technology, but now that we had the Relic, it wasn't clear whether or not the captain still cared about saving the station.

"It's still using chemical impellers," reported Serosian from his central console. "No sign of an HD signature, but I am picking up some other energy pulses that I can't identify yet."

"Keep working," said the captain, her tone indicating she was totally in charge. "I want to know what we're up against. What's our status, Cochrane?"

I perused my board. "We're maintaining distance, although it doesn't look like the HuK is targeting us. It's bearing almost directly for the station," I said.

"Do we defend the station?" asked Serosian of the captain. Dobrina debated this a second.

"No doubt any Founder station will have invaluable secrets to reveal. But my orders are clear in this matter, Mr. Serosian: protect the Relic at all costs. Keep our distance, Mr. Cochrane. Close enough to stay engaged, but not close enough to put us in danger," she said.

"Close being relative to what we know of their weapons. This vessel could have something very nasty up its sleeve," said Serosian.

"But I took its arm off already," I chimed in. The Historian chuckled.

"I think we both know there's more to it than that," he said. "They could have any number of dangerous weapons systems aboard."

"Which is why we'll stay cautious. What's the range, Mr. Cochrane?" said the captain.

"We're ten thousand clicks out, Captain. The HuK is closing to within the same distance from the station."

"Then we should know soon what she's planning," said Dobrina.

"Detecting an energy surge from the HuK," said Serosian in a hauntingly calm voice. "It's an unusual pattern, not one I'm familiar with. I suggest—"

"Power up the HD drive, Mr. Marker, and set our course for

Levant, Mr. Layton," said the captain, interrupting. "Engage the Hoagland Field, Mr. Cochrane."

I did as ordered then turned to the captain, who started to speak.

"I don't want to take any chances—"

She never finished the sentence. I couldn't tell what had happened or where I was for many seconds. My thinking was fuzzy and my eyes were blurred. I struggled to move any part of my body but could feel nothing, and everything was dark. I wondered, just for a moment, if I might be dead.

Then the pain started. At first it was cold and numbing, then it turned to a stinging that fired from every nerve ending in my body. Finally, after what seemed an eternity of timeless suffering, the pain began to subside. I opened my eyes. I was on the floor of the yacht, emergency lights glowing blue above me. I tried to roll over onto my stomach. That was a mistake, as I quickly became nauseated and vomited onto the floor. I tried to regain my bearings, crawling up to all fours and making my way about the deck. I found Dobrina on the floor, twisted in an awkward pile where she had fallen. I rolled her on to her back and tapped her face gently, trying to rouse her. She coughed and choked, not opening her eyes, then suddenly grabbed me by the shoulders and tried to pull herself up.

"Station," she croaked out. I took it as an order to get back to my 'scope, not as one to determine the status of the Founder station. I laid her back down on the floor and then crawled to my chair, pulling myself up to my display, my head pounding. Behind me Serosian was starting to rise, as was Marker. Layton was retching beneath his nav station. My board was a mass of red lights, with one or two amber and one green: the Hoagland Field. I watched the board begin to turn from red to amber, then slowly to all green, system by system.

"Ship's systems are recovering, we're still operational," I blurted out. As my head spun less and less and my vision and balance steadied I went back to the captain and raised her to her seat, where she rewarded me by vomiting onto my boots.

"Sorry," she said in a heavy voice, wiping her mouth. I wiped my boots on the deck carpet and watched as it got absorbed instantly. I looked to the spot where I had lost it and saw that it was also clear.

"Effective cleaning crew," I said, then returned to my station. The yacht's systems were still in the process of rebooting and repairing from whatever had attacked us. "Systems at forty-three percent and rising rapidly," I reported.

"What hit us?" asked Dobrina, collapsing back into her chair.

"Unknown," said Serosian from his console. I turned as Marker helped Layton back into his seat.

"Think I can get a visual," I said, manipulating my 'scope as the main display flickered several times and then came back on. What we saw stunned us.

Half the Founder station was gone, perhaps more than half. It spun in space at a rate much faster than normal around a gravitational nexus that was no longer there. Her orbit was also changing rapidly due to more than half her mass having been disintegrated.

"What the hell . . ." was all I could muster. The captain was at my shoulder in a second.

"Explain," she demanded of our Historian.

"I can't. More analysis is needed," he said flatly. She turned to me.

"Where's our bogey?" I scanned my board, whipping through my displays as fast as I could.

"Not in our visual or tactical scanning range. They must have activated their HD drive," I said.

"Marker, how long until *our* HD drive is operational?" she demanded.

"Twenty minutes," he replied.

"Make it ten." She turned her attention back to me.

"Play back the visual record on the main display. Back it up to the attack," she said. I did, speeding through the record until the last few moments before the attack.

"According to this reading we were out for almost eleven minutes," I reported. Dobrina motioned for Serosian to come forward.

"I'd like your observations, Historian," she said. He came up just as I activated the playback. We watched as the HuK, a distant dot ten thousand clicks out, unleashed some sort of enveloping plasma. It closed on the station at a rapid pace, so fast that I had to slow the playback down. When the glowing silver plasma hit the station it turned the rock, metal, and crystal infrastructure to glittering dust instantaneously. I played it back several times just to be sure of what I was seeing. The recording continued on to the point where the plasma enveloped our ship, then stopped for several seconds before returning.

"The Hoagland Field saved us," said the captain.

"Yes," agreed Serosian.

"But from what?"

"Only one thing possible, Captain. An anti-graviton field."

"Anti-*graviton?*" I said. "You mean—"

Serosian cut me off before I could ask my next question. "Theoretically, a weapon of this type nullifies the effects of gravity within the field's range, separating matter at the subatomic level."

"Effectively, instantaneous disintegration, in the purest sense of the word," said the captain. Serosian continued.

"We have to assume the range is at least twenty thousand kilometers since it took us out. Activating our Hoagland Field, as we did just seconds before the attack, quite by chance I might add, dispersed the energy just enough to save us," he said.

"That weapon was pretty effective for being theoretical," said the captain.

"Historian research theorizes that such weapons are possible.

We had no idea that the First Empire could have had them centuries ago," Serosian said.

"If indeed the HuK is in fact that old. Could it be that it was captured and modified for use by a present-day enemy, not one from the ancient past?" she asked him. He nodded reluctantly.

"I have to admit that's a possibility," he said. She crossed her arms and went back to her chair.

"Get that HD drive running, Mr. Marker. Your next promotion depends on it."

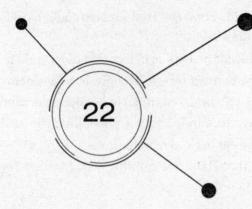

22

We were thirty light-minutes behind the HuK all the way, less than two hours now from the inner Levant system of Levant Prime and its two moons. Thirty million souls were at risk. We watched as the Levant Navy rose to meet the aggressor, a mission that was suicide for them and for Prince Katara aboard their flagship. We tried several times to make contact with the Levant fleet to no avail, the HuK blocking our longscope transmissions with heavy electronic interference.

Serosian stayed in his chambers for most of the voyage, working on the Relic. Dobrina and I met with him there as we closed on the scene, Levant and its two moons hanging in space on our main display.

"No change in the HuK's track," I reported. "Still on course for Levant Prime."

"But why are they going there?" the captain asked. "*We* have the Relic."

"Likely the HuK's assigned mission included varying parame-ters, changeable as conditions warranted," Serosian said. "It knows the Relic is safe for now behind our Hoagland Field, thus it has moved on to a different priority."

"Which would be?"

"Destroy the base," I interjected. I'd spent much of my time while tracking the HuK going over different tactical scenarios in my mind. "Close the gate behind them. If they destroy the jump gate generator on Levant B then we can't follow *Impulse*, can't find our way directly into Imperial space. Then it will turn and attack us again, to try and get the Relic."

"A very interesting tactical analysis. And most likely correct. Well done, Peter," said the Historian.

"Can we survive another attack of that plasma weapon?" asked the captain.

"Our ship can survive it. Whether *we* can is another question. You saw what it did to us, even through the Hoagland Field. I would think another assault could cripple the yacht, shut off our environmental systems. Taking the Relic would be easy then. The bigger question is Levant," he said.

"I'm listening," said Dobrina.

"If they use the anti-graviton plasma on Levant B, it could endanger the entire planet," he said.

"I calculated the effective range of the plasma weapon while you were working on the Relic," I said. "It's at least one hundred thousand kilometers for any unshielded natural object. I tracked that much residual energy from the plasma that hit us. The Hoagland Field will protect us unless we get inside ten thousand kilometers. Inside that range, all bets are off."

"And B is only sixty thousand kilometers from Levant," said Dobrina. "There's thirty million people living there."

"The planet would be devastated," I said. Serosian said nothing. I thought of Janaan. "We have to stop it."

Serosian looked thoughtful. "Perhaps it's time you see what I've discovered in my chambers," he said, looking to Marker and Layton.

Dobrina nodded. "Perhaps it is."

We walked back to his chambers, Dobrina leaving Layton in charge. When we entered, I could see the Relic casing on the floor, disassembled, with a small device sitting on a table. It looked like metal, but I decided it could be some kind of artificial material. It had a rough-hewn trapezoidal base of a deep black material, with a central raised area of silver metallic ridges, almost like pewter, that curved into and out of the base.

"That's it?" I commented. "That's our Relic?" Serosian nodded.

"That's it," he said.

"What is it?" asked the captain. Serosian crossed his arms.

"As near as I can tell, based on the specification, it's an artificial jump point generator," he said.

"Wait, did you say there was a spec?" I asked. He nodded again.

"Relics usually contain a data crystal with some sort of guide in them. This one came with a star map."

"A star map?" asked the captain. "Seriously?"

"Affirmative. It shows the locations of several local stars within about a twenty-light-year radius of Levant. My assumption is that these systems are the ones within range of the device. Now, adjusting for the motion of stars over the millennia, my analysis indicates this object was placed here approximately two hundred forty thousand years ago. That would put it in what we call the 'Late Period' of the Founder civilization, when we believe they were fighting for survival against forces unknown."

"So this is a weapon?" the captain asked. Serosian looked pensive.

"Its intent is unclear. But it can be used to move objects from one star system to another without the necessity of navigating to a natural jump point," he said.

"Objects? You mean like a ship?" the captain asked. He nodded again.

"Or, quite possibly, something like the station we found it on," he said. I looked at the small box.

"You mean this thing could move that asteroid from star system to star system?" I said. His eyes bore down on me.

"With a properly functioning HD power source, I would say clearly, yes, that was what it was designed to do," he said.

"If only it was working," I commented.

"It is," said Serosian. Dobrina looked to me and then back to the Historian.

"You activated it without my approval?" she said.

"I don't need your approval on my own vessel, Commander," he said, slipping back to her formal rank rather than her active rank, by intent, I presumed. "But the question is irrelevant. The device was active when I opened it, and I suspect it has been so for the entire duration of its existence. I've already integrated it into my console. Just by tapping into even a small hyperdimensional power source it adapted instantaneously to our systems."

"You mean we can use it?" she asked.

"Affirmative," he said again.

"But for what?" I asked. "To escape? So we can fight the HuK up until the last second and then before they use their anti-graviton field we jump out, leaving Levant to her fate?"

"That," said Serosian, "may be our only option."

"Unacceptable," said the captain. "We'll just have to find another option. In fact, I demand we do." And with that she left the room, heading for the command console.

Back on the command deck, just twenty light-minutes out from firing range on Levant B, or Tyre as the natives called it, I watched as the HuK slowed in a maneuver that seemed designed to maximize its potential for destruction with the anti-graviton plasma weapon. From what I could calculate it was taking a vector that would place it squarely between the two moons and Levant Prime, with enough range to completely envelop B, clip A, and cause massive destruction on Levant itself. And that's if I was correct on the range being close to one hundred thousand kilometers. If it was more, the devastation would likely be total.

For my part I'd been trying to punch through the flak the HuK was sending out to block our longwave signal. As we all watched the main display helplessly, I turned to my commander, finally with some good news to report.

"I've bored a longwave tunnel through hyperdimensional space and managed to raise the Levant fleet, Captain," I said simply. "But I don't know how long it will last." Dobrina sprang immediately into action, activating the com link to the Levant fleet.

"General Salibi, this is Captain Kierkopf, can you hear me?" she said, raising her voice as if that would help clear the line.

"Prince Katara here, Captain," came the voice over the com. It was scratchy and slightly distorted, but since it was traveling through multiple unknown higher dimensions to make the connection, I thought it sounded pretty good. "Glad to finally hear from you."

"I wish we had better news, Prince Katara," said the captain. "I don't know how long this connection will last, so I'll cut straight to the chase. Your world is in grave danger. The HuK has a weapon we weren't prepared for, a weapon that puts your entire world in imminent danger. They used it on us at the Relic station, caught us off guard and nearly destroyed us."

"What's the nature of this weapon?" came the prince's reply. The captain looked to Serosian, who stepped up to the com.

"The weapon is an anti-graviton plasma field, Prince. Basically, it separates matter at the subatomic level, breaking down any matter it encounters to microscopic dust. We saw it used at the Relic station. It disintegrated half the asteroid. Fortunately we were able to recover the Relic before the station was destroyed," he said.

"Well, I'm glad for that," said the prince, I couldn't tell if he was being sarcastic or not. "What can we do to stop it?"

"There's very little we can do, Prince Katara," said Dobrina. "If the HuK activates this weapon, and we think it will soon, your world will be in grave peril. We're asking you to take your fleet and retreat to the far side of Levant, and order an evacuation of your world, to whatever extent possible," she said. The line stayed quiet, the silence hanging on for long enough that the captain gave me a hand signal to ask if we still had a connection. I nodded yes.

"You're talking about saving a few thousand people, out of more than thirty million," came his response finally.

"I'm aware of that, Prince Katara," she said. Again the silence. I thought I could hear conversations in the background, but it could have been interference.

"Evacuation ordered, Captain. But it will be a tiny drop in the vast ocean if this weapon is as powerful as you say that it is. And I'm not prepared to abandon defense of my world. Our fleet is accelerating toward the HuK," he said.

"Prince Katara, your ships cannot help us with the HuK, and they certainly can't survive the anti-graviton weapon without a working Hoagland Field. It's suicide," said the captain.

"Then suicide it will be," the prince replied. Dobrina moved away from the com and Serosian stepped up, not looking hopeful.

"Prince Katara, if this weapon is activated, it will devastate your world and its people, a people that will be left leaderless if you sacrifice yourself," he said.

"I'm aware of my responsibilities, Historian," the prince replied. The line went silent again. Serosian tried one last time.

"Prince Katara, please, if you are in range when this weapon goes off, it will not matter that you died a hero . . ." he trailed off at this, then continued. "Half your world will disintegrate, Prince Katara, as if it were never there." The line crackled and popped in silence for several seconds and I feared I had lost the longwave. Then another voice came on.

"This is General Salibi. The prince has put me in military command of this mission. I am ordering our flagship to be withdrawn to the far side of Levant, to rendezvous with the evacuation fleet. Two ships will accompany us. The remaining vessels and their commanders insist on defending their world. They will not withdraw."

Dobrina stepped up to the com again. "Good luck, General. And Godspeed to your ships." At that, the signal was cut from the other end of the line. We watched as the Levant flagship and its escorts withdrew from the main body of the fleet. The other ships pressed on, their impellers on full burn.

"I'm not sure the general will be in command of the Levant Navy tomorrow, but he made the right decision today," said Dobrina.

"Agreed," said Serosian.

"Tactical report, Mr. Cochrane?" said the captain. I went back to my board and scanned the readouts.

"The HuK is slowing even more than anticipated," I reported. "I don't understand. There's no tactical reason for them to do this."

"They're trying to draw us into the range of the weapon," said Dobrina. She turned to Serosian. "They want the Relic."

"I agree. And in my opinion we have no choice but to put it at risk," he said.

"What do you mean?"

"The only card we have to play is the Relic. The HuK is programmed to recover it. If we risk going inside the plasma weapon's firing range, it's possible we might delay activation of the weapon if it perceives that it can recover the Relic as well. Remember, it was much closer than its full range when it fired on the station," he said.

"How close did you say it was when it fired?" the captain asked me.

"Ten thousand kilometers," I replied.

"That's almost torpedo range."

"Exactly," said the Historian. "If we can get off a torpedo against an unshielded ship, we *might* have a chance at disabling it. That's *if* we can present the Relic as enough of a temptation."

The captain contemplated this, then made her decision. "Take us in, Mr. Cochrane. Match the vector of the HuK. Keep our Hoagland Field at max. And if you detect any hint that it's about to fire that weapon, unload everything we've got, regardless of the range."

"Aye, sir," I said, then set course to match the HuK and engaged the impellers, uncertain whether any of us would live through the next few minutes.

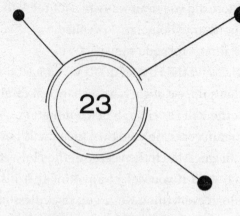

A Sacrifice

We followed the HuK's track to the centimeter, staying on course and using our HD drive to substantially close the gap. Nonetheless, we were still eight minutes behind her and a good twenty thousand kilometers distant. Not close enough to even try a torpedo. And the ten-thousand-kilometer effective range of the HuK's anti-graviton weapon against our Hoagland Field was looming.

"She could fire any time now," warned Serosian. "She's still six minutes from her optimal firing point between Tyre and Levant."

"But once we cross inside ten thousand clicks it will know we can be disabled, temporarily at least, even through the Hoagland Field," said Dobrina. "We need another option."

"What about the Levant ships?" I asked. "They're closer than we are."

"They're no match for the HuK," said Dobrina.

"Perhaps they don't need to be," said Serosian. Dobrina crossed her arms and stared at him.

"Explain."

The Historian thought for a moment. "If one of the Levant vessels could activate an atomic burst, send out an electromagnetic pulse, it could damage the HuK's systems enough to take the weapon offline for a brief time and allow us to get close enough to engage it again," he said.

"It's likely the HuK is hardened against EMP," said Dobrina. "What about one of your torpedoes, Mr. Serosian?"

"It would have to get close enough for a full-yield detonation, say fifty kilometers or less. But the HuK would likely fire the anti-graviton weapon as soon as we fired the torpedo. At least that's what I'd do."

The captain contemplated this for a brief moment, then came to a decision.

"Mr. Cochrane, can you still bore your longwave tunnel to those Levant ships?"

"Yes," I replied, "In fact, the HuK is now putting out a lot less interference."

"Likely conserving power, preparing to use her weapons," said Serosian.

"Get on the line to those ships, Mr. Cochrane," she said. "Tell them we need a volunteer to save their world, and we need it fast."

"Aye, Captain," I said, then did as instructed. I got a coded message back two minutes later. All it said was, "Understood." We watched as the Levant fleet closed on the HuK. The HuK began a barrage of coil cannon fire from its remaining batteries at the flotilla. The Levant ships responded in kind, but with little effect. They were seriously overmatched. We watched as the seconds ticked by to the ten-thousand-kilometer mark we knew was effective even against our Hoagland Field.

"Full stop, Mr. Marker," ordered Dobrina. "Station keeping, Mr. Layton." They both responded with "Aye, sir," as we watched the unfolding battle on our main display. Both Marker and Layton had inquired about what a "Relic" was, but I had told them it was need-to-know.

"The Levant fleet is inflicting little damage on the HuK, Captain," I said.

"As expected," she replied. "Hopefully they're planning to evacuate the crew from the sacrificial ship. Mr. Marker, when I give the signal, fire the sub-light HD drive back to full. Mr. Layton, plot our intercept course. Mr. Cochrane will take us straight in at the HuK. We may have seconds. We may have minutes. But we'll have to fire our torpedoes and hope for the best."

"The coil cannon has a greater effective range," I noted.

"Yes, but can you identify the plasma weapon on the body of the HuK? Pinpoint its location exactly? If you can't guarantee an exact shot, then we can't take the chance," she said. I went back to my board as the captain started pacing around the cabin. No one liked our options now.

"I'm not seeing any evacuation activity, Captain, All those ships are holding steady, closing on the HuK," I reported. Dobrina's head snapped up at this news.

"Raise them again, they're not following the plan," she said excitedly. "We only need one ship for the EMP." I sent my coded signal through the longwave. There was no reply.

"I don't understand, they're not responding," I said.

"Repeat, Commander," she demanded.

"They're still holding steady and not responding to my hails, Captain." Dobrina's eyes went wide.

"They're all going to self-destruct!" she said. "Marker! Take us in now, sub-light HD drive on full! Cochrane, raise them on the longwave again! Tell them to stop!"

It was too late. In the next instant the Levant fleet, all nine ships, exploded in a series of fireballs that lit up our main plasma to a blinding level before the compensators took over and lowered the light. When the display cleared and readjusted, the HuK was drifting and sparking, damaged heavily. The Levant fleet and all of their crews were gone from the universe forever.

I looked to my captain. Her eyes turned red, her face flushed with anger at the devastation and loss of life she had just witnessed. "Commander Cochrane, take us in on Mr. Layton's course, as fast as she'll go." She wiped at her eyes. "They've given us our opening, let's not blow it."

She turned to Serosian. "Can we destroy that thing with one of your torpedoes?" she asked.

"I don't recommend it, Captain," said the Historian. "The HuK is drifting but its internal systems are still operational. From what I can tell it's in a rebooting sequence and the plasma weapon appears to still be active. Anti-graviton levels are off the charts. A direct hit by an atomic detonation would likely result in the anti-gravitons being dispersed all over the inner Levant system, with much the same effect as the HuK firing the weapon itself."

Dobrina let out a grunt of exasperation. "Do we have any other options? I don't want their sacrifice to be in vain," she said.

"Can't we go closer and EVA over to the HuK? Disable it somehow?" I posited. Serosian shook his head.

"Not enough time by my readings. Its power curve is coming back up. We may only have minutes," he said.

"We can't just stand here and watch it detonate!" said Dobrina.

I chimed in at this, just shooting my mouth off in frustration. "I wish we could attach that damned Relic to the HuK and send it back to whatever hell it came from." Dobrina and Serosian exchanged looks of recognition, then Dobrina said:

"Mr. Cochrane, you may have just earned your tactical commendation for this mission." I looked at them, confused, and then wondered what the hell I might have just gotten us into.

We were on the lower deck of the yacht, working quickly on a torpedo. I was holding the Founder Relic, our local jump point generator, while Serosian was busy removing a tactical nuclear warhead from the torpedo's "brain."

"You really think this thing will work after two hundred thousand years?" I asked nervously, the Relic humming with power and warmth as I held it with both hands. Serosian didn't look up from his work to answer.

"Theoretically, yes," he said as his hands moved swiftly over the warhead casing, disconnecting it from the torpedo. "Replacing the warhead with the jump point generator should allow the Relic to access the torpedo's hyperdimensional drive. Although it's got minimal power, it should be enough to keep the Relic active until it reaches its destination."

"And you're sure you've programmed it properly?" I asked.

"When dealing with Founder technology, one can never be sure. But it does appear I was able to set both a timer and a destination properly within the unit."

"What destination?" He let go of the warhead with one hand and picked up a tool.

"I set it for Tarchus, a system with no habitable planets. It was mostly used as a refueling base back in the First Empire days. It has some valuable mineral deposits," he said. Then I watched as he pulled the warhead out slowly and set it aside. He gestured to me. "Hand me the Relic."

I was glad to do so. I watched again as he set the Relic in place, securing it with an inertial damping field and then connecting it to the torpedo's power source. The device accepted the torpedo's power plug and I watched as the plug melted seamlessly into the Relic. "And we're still here," Serosian said, holding his hands clear, then resealing the torpedo with his tools.

"Was that a joke?" I asked. He smiled grimly.

"Dark humor, Peter. There was a tiny possibility connecting the

Relic to the torpedo's power source would have activated it, but we seem to have avoided that predicament."

I helped him finish the seal and then we both scrambled up to the main deck, retaking our positions.

"We're ready to fire, Captain," I said. Dobrina nodded, then turned to Serosian.

"You have this timed correctly?" she asked him.

"It will be very, very close, but the torpedo should arrive before the HuK can detonate the weapon, and the Relic should activate in time to send them both away to Tarchus," he said.

"That's a lot of 'shoulds,'" she said.

He nodded. "It's our best shot."

"Time to detonation?"

"Three minutes, by my estimate," Serosian said. The captain turned to me.

"Mr. Cochrane, fire our torpedo," she ordered.

"Aye, sir," I said, and launched the torpedo. "On course, Captain." She turned to Marker and Layton.

"Mr. Marker, activate the HD drive again and give us some distance. Mr. Layton, set us on a course away from Levant." I could tell she hated giving that order. Retreat was not in her makeup, but it was the wise thing for the mission.

The next few moments passed in impatient silence for us all. Eventually I overheard Dobrina speaking to Serosian as we watched the clock tick down.

"Navy brass is going to be upset about losing their Relic, Mr. Serosian," I heard her say under her breath.

"As will the priesthood. They will both get over it," he replied, just as quietly.

"Tracking the torpedo. On course for the HuK," I said so that everyone could hear. Serosian's alarmed voice behind me caught my attention.

"Power levels have jumped on the HuK," he said. "It's spooling up the weapon ahead of schedule. Its systems must have recovered enough to detect the HD signature from the torpedo's drive and assess it as a threat. It could fire anytime now."

"Time and distance, Mr. Cochrane?" the captain demanded.

"One minute forty-three seconds to the HuK. Seventeen thousand kilometer range," I reported.

"Can we detonate that device remotely?" asked the captain.

"From Peter's board we can," replied Serosian. He came up and pushed me aside, pulling up the torpedo display on my board, then retreated back to his station. "Transferring firing control to your console, Peter."

"Why me?" I responded.

"Because I have to monitor the Hoagland Field," he said. "If the weapon goes off prematurely the Field has to be optimal."

"What's the range on the Relic?" asked Dobrina out loud. Both Marker and Layton looked up from their stations at the reference, then quickly returned their attention to their boards.

"Nineteen thousand," replied Serosian. "Maximum range for the Relic activation signal is probably twenty thousand clicks."

"How much time left on the plasma weapon?" asked Dobrina.

"Fifteen seconds until its able to fire," replied Serosian.

"Mr. Cochrane, prepare to activate the Relic remotely," ordered Dobrina. "How close is the torpedo?"

"Three thousand kilometers," I said.

"Is that close enough?" she asked Serosian.

"It doesn't matter," he said, "It's our only chance, and Levant's."

"Ten seconds," I counted down.

"Range?"

"Two thousand," I said.

My hand hovered over the activation control. The captain

gripped the sides of the console so hard that the fluid surface bubbled around her fingers.

"Five. Hoagland Field at maximum," called Serosian.

"Range twelve hundred!" I said.

"Mr. Cochrane . . ." said Dobrina.

"Two . . ." called Serosian.

"Activate the Relic!"

I pressed down on the button. On the main display the torpedo glittered with the light of a hundred stars. The HuK detonated with anti-graviton plasma at nearly the same instant. We watched in awe as the starlight from the Relic burst out into space, covering the distance between itself and the HuK, enveloping the plasma, and then exploding in a sparkle of pure white fire.

The next instant, the space where the HuK had been was empty.

"A small ejection of anti-graviton plasma escaped the Relic activation, but it won't be in sufficient mass or at sufficient speed to impact anything before it dissipates. In short: we did it," Serosian said.

I slumped over my console.

"Mr. Layton," said the captain's voice from behind me. "Take us back to Levant. I think we'll have some celebrating to do."

Celebrating was the last thing I felt like doing.

Two days later, I attended a memorial ceremony for the fallen Levant Navy sailors who had given their lives. It was a somber occasion, and I attended not as a Union Navy officer, but as a royal diplomat. Prince Katara sat on his official throne, Janaan next to him on hers. I was first on the dais of dignitaries, and although I had been asked to speak I chose not to. I did join both of Levant's regents in laying a memorial wreath near the cedar coffin symbolizing the navy sailors lost defending their world. As I set the wreath down, Janaan reached out a lace-gloved hand and gripped mine, if ever so briefly. The funeral music brought me close to tears even though I didn't recognize the tune.

That evening I attended a wake at the palace, once again as the honored guest of the prince and princess. We were all there, and the talk turned to the imminently arriving *Starbound*. I was anxious to get aboard her and get on with the *Impulse* rescue mission that I assumed would follow in short order. But I had to confess I was enjoying playing the role of royal and diplomat more and more. Janaan's presence had more to do with that than I would probably have liked to admit.

Dobrina was with the prince's group, which included General Salibi and Serosian, with her back to me, out of disdain or respect, I couldn't tell which. I felt bad for the general. He looked as if he hadn't slept a wink since the sacrifice of his navy commanders, and I didn't blame him. His guilt at surviving must have been tremendous. But he still had his job, which I had taken great care to inform the prince that I thought was appropriate under the circumstances. He had done the right thing in taking the prince to safety.

An hour into the reception, Janaan cornered me in one of the anterooms over a cup of tea.

"May I join you?" she asked, gesturing to a pair of chairs.

"I would be honored, Princess," I said, and sat with her. The servants abruptly scattered, and we found ourselves alone with as much privacy as one could get in a royal palace.

"So I assume you're anxious to leave the luxury of our world and join your compatriots in space again?" she said.

"The palace is not without its charms, my lady," I said. She smiled.

"It will be a lonelier place without you," she said.

"I'm sorry," was all the awkward response I could muster. Then there was silence between us as our tea got cold. Finally I took her hand. "I wish I could stay," I said.

"I know. But your heart is elsewhere," she replied.

"My heart is with the stars, Janaan, nowhere else. I hope you know that."

"I wish I could believe it. Still, you know I will wait for you, until you either return to make me your wife or send me a message from some distant world that you belong to another."

I thought on that for a moment. "My promise was sincere. I will gladly come back here, to you, when my days of adventuring are over."

"I will hold you to that," she said, then she rose and started to walk away. I followed and stopped her with a gentle hand on her arm. Pulling her to me, I kissed her softly. It was sweet and pleasant, and I thought it truly could keep me warm through the long months in space. She parted with a last squeeze of my hand then headed back out to the reception, there to play the princess once again.

Prince Katara closed the formal portion of the evening with a public pronouncement that Levant had signed the agreement to join the Union, and that in return they would be getting a new Lightship, to be named *Resolution* both in honor of the official documents being signed and to reflect the character of those who had given their lives to save their world.

We walked back to our palace apartments as a group, losing Marker and Layton first and then Serosian. Dobrina and I found ourselves alone in the hallway. We walked the last few steps in silence until we reached the doors to our respective rooms, across the hallway from each other. I turned and faced my captain, who in her formal evening gown once again looked much more a woman than a soldier.

"So, *Starbound* arrives tomorrow," she said. I thought about how to reply. She wasn't nearly as beautiful as Janaan, but I still found myself drawn to her like a magnet.

"It does," I said. "And I have to stop playing the young royal and go back to being a lowly lieutenant commander."

"And I am now an officer without a commission," she said. "And you're no longer under my command." I sensed the foreboding in her, the worry over her crewmates somewhere in deep space, in danger, but I couldn't help but notice the reference she made to her no longer being in command. I was for all practical purposes a civilian at the moment. She took a step closer to me.

"Did you get all you needed tonight, Peter?"

I shook my head. "I'm not sure I even know what that means," I said.

She looked down the hallway at the distant guards, our only companions, then back to me. "I think it means that sometimes we can accept what we can have, even if our hearts long for something more," she said.

"I understand," I said. The thought of being with her was extremely attractive, no question. But something inside was stopping me. "But . . . I think we should wait. There is the *Impulse* rescue mission—"

"There is always another mission, Peter. Perhaps when you're a bit older you'll recognize that," she said. Then she abruptly turned away from me and walked to her apartment doors, stepping through without looking back and shutting them firmly behind her.

I sighed, then entered my own empty room. Truth was, I couldn't wait to take my diplomatic costume off and get back to being a Union Navy officer once again.

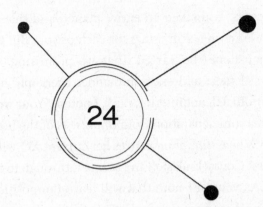

On High Station Artemis in the Levant System

The next day when I left the palace Dobrina was already gone and Serosian was in conference with dignitaries from the Levant government about the new alliance, so I took a shuttle up to Artemis Station with Marker and Layton.

Upon our arrival Levant soldiers escorted us to a communications center. We were told on the walk that a communications packet would soon be arriving from *Starbound*. Dobrina was in the communications room when we arrived. I stood next to her but said nothing as we waited for the packet to download.

After a few minutes of technical translations, the visage of Grand Admiral Jonathon Wesley appeared much larger than life, looking down on the four of us. We all snapped to attention and the admiral said, "At ease, gentlemen," to us, which was strange since the message was recorded. I felt like a fool for reacting out of instinct but nonetheless maintained a professional attitude as Wesley started speaking.

"Word of your mission at Levant has reached us here at the Admiralty from Mr. Serosian, and I just want to congratulate you all on your success. You saved an entire planet, and that in and of itself is worth at least one of my stars for each of you. But for now, our work is only half-done," he started. That was promising.

"First I must address Commander Kierkopf," he had resorted to using her official, not interim, rank, I noted. "Your work in leading this team after your separation from *Impulse* is of the highest order, Commander. When *Starbound* arrives her current XO will be put in charge of the First Contact mission and seeing it through to a satisfactory conclusion. As you may note that will leave the position of *Starbound*'s executive officer open. I am assigning that position to you on a temporary basis. Once we recover *Impulse*, and we *will* recover *Impulse*, I expect you to guide her safely home." At that, he changed his tone.

"Now, Lieutenant Commander Cochrane," he began again. "Your actions as reported to me, especially in the rescue of Captain Zander aboard the shuttle, seem on the surface reckless and not becoming of an officer." He paused here and I tried to swallow, uncertain of what was coming next, but my throat was bone dry.

"However, your actions since that time, and indeed even your success in rescuing Captain Zander, show an outstanding quality of valor and care for your fellow officers. Because of these actions, your disobedience during the shuttle incident will be noted in your file, but no demerits will appear on your record so long as you maintain a one hundred percent performance record for a period of no less than twelve months," he said. That was a relief.

"You are further reassigned to *Starbound* to serve at the convenience of Captain Maclintock and Commander Kierkopf. They will determine your new assignments and I urge you to emulate both of them in your future actions." I wanted to say "thank you" here but I reminded myself that I was indeed watching a recording. "In addition, your new duties on *Starbound* will involve integration of the marine teams aboard ship. I urge you to give this work your highest priority." I looked over at Marker and he winked at me.

Can't wait, I thought.

Both he and Layton received promotions, Marker to sergeant, plus commendations and pay raises, which made them smile. At the end, Wesley saluted us and we found ourselves automatically saluting back.

As the screen went black I turned to Dobrina, but she was already on her way out of the room, not looking at me. I decided at that point that my best course of action was probably just to let her go. I knew she was upset about the events on Levant, and I didn't blame her. Everyone, including her, had told me I should do what I had to in order to secure the alliance. It would seem however, that the feelings of a woman ran a lot deeper than those of a navy officer.

Marker, Layton, and I made our way out into the station. *Starbound* was due in port in just over three hours and I was excited that I would finally get to serve aboard her as I had originally trained to do.

We passed the time with some good-natured chess matches in the officers' mess, all of which I won. About an hour ahead of the docking, we stopped the games to go over their coming duty assignments on *Starbound* as conveyed by Wesley.

As we sat around waiting, a new question came to mind, so I asked it of my two closest friends in the navy.

"Why did you two follow me?" I said. "I mean, we trained for so long to serve on *Starbound*, then when the *Impulse* mission came up, with the chance to join me, you could have said no." They both said nothing for a moment, then Marker shifted in his chair to face me directly.

"Not sure I understand you, sir," said Marker. Layton followed by also shifting in his chair and then leaned in toward me across the table we three shared.

"It's because you're the best, sir," Layton said.

"What?" I said, thinking he was joking with me. "Don't be ridiculous!" I finished.

"No, sir," insisted Layton. "It's true. Really."

"Bollocks!" I said. Marker laughed, but Layton jumped right back in.

"Sir, I watched you train for two years, and I played against you on the soccer pitch," he said. "The same talent I saw on that field I saw in our training. From the first week of cadet school I knew I wanted to be on your squad, and I did everything I could to make that happen."

"Gods, really?" I was taken aback. "Didn't think I was that good," I muttered. Now Marker spoke up.

"No, it's true," he said. "I saw it too. You have something special, and not just because you're the grand admiral's son. I knew I wanted to work with you, sir, and that's why I'm not afraid to follow you through thick and thin. That's why when our probationary year is up I'm going to ask to attach my billet to yours, sir."

Now I was truly flattered, and surprised into silence.

"I'll make that request as well," chimed in Layton. "If you'll have me."

I looked at my two friends, impressed by their enthusiasm and humbled by their belief in me. I stood and they stood with me.

"Gentlemen," I said, "I am honored by your trust in me, and I hope and pray to be worthy of it, and of you." Then I extended my hand to each of my friends in turn, and we shook hands as gentlemen do, resolved in our new, now formalized, bond.

Then the claxon sounded, signaling the arrival of *Starbound*.

We made our way to the docking arm and used our military passes to gain access to the debarkation area. We mingled with excited Levantine officers, all trying to get a glimpse of the grand lady as she arrived. I was stuck to the window, watching as the pointed nose of *Starbound's* forward baffles moved slowly past me. I looked up the height of her, past the Hoagland Field generators to the brilliantly lit conning tower, soon to be my new home. Lights shone out into space from officer's cabins and operations stations on the main decks. The name *"H.M.S. Starbound"* was illuminated on her hull. I felt my heart jump with excitement. I would finally get to serve aboard the ship I'd trained on for two years! I felt like a first-year cadet again.

The station's umbilical stretched the final few yards to *Starbound* and then locked and sealed around her holding doors. Once completed, the doors began to part as a loudspeaker announced her arrival.

"Attention on the station. Attention on the station," said the announcer in both Levantine and Standard. "Her Majesty's Ship *Starbound* now docking at port six. Please refrain from boarding her until all moorings are secure and all arriving crew have debarked." The message repeated several more times as we waited.

I stood with my hands behind my back with Marker and Layton to either side of me and watched the process begin. Passengers and crew began filing out, milling around and greeting friends, others making professional connections. I watched as Marker and Layton shook hands with Academy friends.

When the deck cleared of debarking passengers I approached the hold entrance. A Quantar ensign acknowledged me with a crisp salute and then held out his hand for my ID card. He cleared me with a nod, checked Marker and Layton's orders as well, then waved us through.

"Welcome aboard *Starbound*, gentlemen," he said. "The Officer of the Deck will greet you at the Purser's station."

"Thank you," I said, tapping my cap as I went. We weaved our way through a forest of officers and enlisted men, some coming, some going, some packing equipment or moving cargo on large racks. The air was crackling with the excitement of an arrival at Artemis Station for those who had been aboard her, and just as much excitement for those of us joining her crew.

We passed through the busy crowd and finally made our way to the Purser's station. I could see the arms of an officer through a rack of crates motioning vigorously to a pair of noncoms. It was hard to hear the conversation over the din of activity, but clearly someone was being chewed out. I leaned over the Purser's desk and raised my voice.

"Lieutenant," I called. One of the noncoms looked at me but didn't say anything as the conversation, or the chewing out, continued. "Lieutenant!" I called again, a bit louder this time. Still the conversation persisted outside of my hearing range, accompanied by furious arm movements and pointing from the unseen officer. I looked to Layton, who shrugged with a bemused smile, and then glanced at Marker before I took a deep breath and cupped my hands to my mouth, shouting.

"Lieutenant! Attention on the deck!" I yelled. This time the noncom cut into their one-way conversation and pointed at me. The deck officer came whirling around the crates and slapped his clipboard down on the desk before verbally snapping at me.

"What's so goddamned important that you have to interrupt—" he stopped in midsentence as he looked up at me, recognition in his eyes.

"Commander Cochrane!" he said aloud, then caught himself and saluted. "Sorry to keep you waiting, sir!" I smiled and returned the salute.

"At ease, Lieutenant . . ." I checked his ID badge. "Ensign Daniel. I was just anxious to get your attention. No harm done," I said.

"Yes, sir!" he snapped his salute hand down to his side and then stood at attention, almost frozen. Daniel was a slight kid with wavy blond hair and looked barely old enough to be serving in the navy. He had obviously been flustered to meet the grand admiral's son, so I decided to help the kid out.

"Perhaps you should finish your business with your crewmen and then see to our needs," I said.

"Of course, sir," he said, regaining his composure and then turning back to his crew, quickly snapping off orders and giving them the "Go" sign with a pointed finger. They left in a hurry. I watched him take a deep breath and then turn back to me at the desk.

"How can I help you today, sir?" he said. I pointed to Layton and Marker.

"These two men need berths. Sergeant Marker here with the marines, and Lieutenant Layton with me in junior officer country."

"Of course, sir. Let me see what I've got," he said formally. I watched him work his terminal. After scanning his manifest for a few seconds he came out with assignments. Marker seemed satisfied but I made an issue of Layton's location. It was a deck down from where I'd be.

"He's going to be my adjutant and I would like him close by," I said. Daniel went back to the manifest.

"There's really nothing else open except . . . I can make a single stateroom available three doors down from you, sir."

I nodded. "That will do. I hope we won't be inconveniencing anybody?"

"It's no inconvenience, sir. I was planning on moving out anyway," he said.

I bristled at this. *"You're* giving your own cabin up? That's not necessary, Ensign," I said, trying to wave him off. He clicked a couple of keys while I protested and then handed the men their pass cards.

"Already done, sir. Welcome aboard *Starbound*, gentlemen. Lieutenant Layton, I'll have my things packed and out of your way by 1800 tonight. Is that adequate?"

"It is," said Layton. I nodded them both off to see to their berths.

"Thank you, Ensign," I said, as he coded in my pass card and handed it to me. I took it, then turned and bent over to pick up my bags just as a loud voice boomed into the conversation from behind me.

"There you are, Daniel! I've been looking all over for you." I whipped around, dropped my bags, and saluted. Captain Jonas Maclintock of

Starbound saluted back without really looking at me and continued his approach to Daniel. I recognized the captain from his navy profile. Maclintock was thirty-five, rail thin, but not much taller than me, if at all. He had a slightly receding hairline of close-cropped black hair with a rock-set chin and rugged face. I stood frozen in place.

"I wanted to let you know in advance that a certain Commander Peter Cochrane will be boarding here at Artemis. Please make sure he gets a senior officer's cabin with full accoutrements," said Maclintock.

"Already done, sir," Daniel said. Maclintock nodded and continued.

"And Commander Kierkopf will be taking over Devin Tannace's quarters as the new XO," Maclintock added, rubbing his forehead in a sign of fatigue. "I don't know why I've been chosen to wet-nurse some damned Director's son, Ensign, but it's my lot. Cochrane's probably used to pampering so I want you to give him anything he wants. Quite frankly I don't expect much out of the kid but it's always possible he has some potential."

"Sir—" interrupted Daniel.

"Hold on, Ensign," he replied with a wave of the hand. "I guess this kid's been through training on the longscope but I don't want to let him near ours until we've had a chance to observe him in action. Could you arrange for him to have a 'tour' of the ship before we leave and have Chief Arnold check out his skills? Hopefully without him knowing?"

"Sir!" said Daniel again, this time nodding ever so slightly in my direction. Maclintock turned to look at me. I was still at attention. He crossed his arms and sighed.

"And I suppose . . ." he trailed off and I picked up the conversation.

"Lieutenant Commander Peter Cochrane reporting for duty, Captain," I said. He rubbed his hands on his face again and sighed, looked straight at me, and then extended his hand.

"Welcome aboard, Commander," he said. I shook his hand for a moment and then he broke off and walked away without another word. I picked up my bag, cabin pass in hand, then looked back at Daniel once more. He seemed as embarrassed as I was. I shook my head.

"Thanks for your help," I said, then wandered off alone.

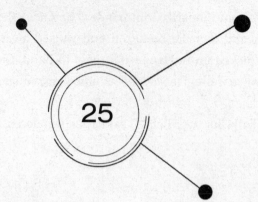

25

Aboard H.M.S. Starbound

Four hours later I was ensconced in my cabin, still too embarrassed by my first meeting with Captain Maclintock to walk the deck alone. I could have paged Layton and done a tour of duty stations but he deserved the rest after all we'd been through. Besides, I didn't assume my duties for a day yet so there was no real reason for me to be prowling the decks. Most of the crew would be on liberty anyway.

I had glanced through the manifest to see how many of my old friends were still aboard and found it was a lean list. There was just Duane Longer, who I didn't really like, and a handful of others I didn't know too well. Serosian, it seemed, was still on Levant finalizing negotiations on implementation of Church doctrines and wouldn't be returning until *Starbound* had a scheduled departure.

Maclintock had called his staff together for the morning but I hadn't really looked at the note. I figured it would be typical welcome type stuff for Dobrina and me. I was happy that they had transferred her commission to *Starbound*, if only temporarily, until *Impulse* was rescued. No doubt Navy Command was still formulating that rescue plan based on our reports of the actions in the Levant system. The way these bureaucracies usually worked I figured that it would take at least a couple of days for them to get us our new orders.

My com buzzed at 2030 and I was surprised to see it was Layton, prompting me to join him for some recreation and a pub crawl. I wanted to refuse but I really didn't have a good excuse, so I prepped myself and by 2100 we were off the ship and heading for the undiscovered pleasures of Artemis Station.

"I hear there's a restaurant here that has belly dancers!" said Layton, far more excited by the prospect than I was.

"I've heard that myself. I take it you're wanting to indulge?" I said.

"Well, unless you've got a better idea?" I shook my head no. I liked Layton a lot, and I felt some responsibility toward him as his superior officer. I was flattered he had chosen to follow me from assignment to assignment as a career path. I didn't question his choice. He was a good man, smart and versatile, and I was happy to have him in my employ.

"I think we need to go one level down from here," said Layton, pointing to an escalator. We went down from the main military level and soon found ourselves in a world very different from the one we had just left.

Rather than the rich Mediterranean luxury of the upper decks of Artemis, we had entered the seedy underbelly of the station. No view windows or com-ports needed here. This was a cash-only market with every kind of exotic pleasure a man or woman could desire available for a price.

We passed kiosks filling the main hall so thickly that you could hardly walk between them. Spices and perfumes tugged at our senses from every angle. The sound of lilting music, exotic and foreign, wafted through the air. The buzz of the crowd, the sound of glass breaking, a merchant and customer haggling over the price of some trinket, colonnades of blinking lights on every support post. It was indeed what the Levantines called a *bazaar*, and it was delightful.

The outer walls of the broad deck housed restaurants serving local fair. Goods and services from every corner of Levant were proffered at small storefronts, while female merchants of human pleasure offered their wares in small-windowed rooms no bigger than an ensign's berth.

Within a few minutes the sensations began to feel overwhelming. Layton pointed to a side "street" in the open market, a small corner away from the mayhem. We made our way there and I was happy to follow him. We stopped in front of a place lit up with the name "Mamouna."

"I heard about this place from the midshipmen who got liberty," said Layton. "Dinner, good drinking, and the most beautiful women in the Known Worlds!"

"If you say so," I said. I was trying to match Layton's enthusiasm, but I was skeptical. And if I had to admit it to myself, I was somewhat depressed about the day's events with Maclintock.

Once inside, my mood was soon lifted by the ambiance of the place. We were asked for our preference, dinner or the bar, and we chose dinner. It turned out to be a wise choice. An older woman in traditional Levantine dress with gray hair and a wizened face showed us through a "door" of colorful hanging fabrics and beads and into a room full of low-set tables. Huge pillows for reclining surrounded the tables and the area was lit with candles and hanging oil lamps. Fabrics reached from all corners of the room to a canopy high above us, giving the impression we were in a desert tent. The room was crowded with patrons—some businessmen, some military, and a good number of them Quantar sailors on liberty. Exotic music played in the background.

A stunning, caramel-skinned girl with huge brown eyes and a bare midriff came up to us, wearing a glittering traditional beaded headdress above an orange and black gown. She had a dangling jewel in her pierced belly button and streams of colored fabric flowed from her hips. She bowed ceremonially, hands in front of her, and then went to her knees facing us. She reminded me more than a bit of the Princess Janaan.

"I am Gimona," she said.

"I'm Peter, and this is George," I said, motioning to Layton. Gimona bowed slightly and smiled at Layton before returning her attention to me.

"If you like, I will be your hostess for the evening. If you would each like a hostess, I can arrange for another girl to join us," she said. Her voice was sweet and her accent was alluring, combined with an amazing smile and beautiful white teeth. I cut to the chase.

"How much?"

"My services are free. If you choose to have a second dinner companion join us, the price is twenty crowns for each of you." I exchanged glances with Layton. I could tell what he wanted to do, but I wasn't willing to concede just yet.

"So what do we get for our twenty crowns?" I said. Gimona smiled broadly.

"I shall be your servant, bring you your dishes, serve you, and entertain you," she said. Layton couldn't contain himself.

"Sounds like a great deal to me!" he blurted out. Our negotiating position was now ruined and I conceded the point.

"Let's see your friend," I said. Gimona rose and bowed again, then departed behind a curtain. As I looked around the room I saw that most tables had companions, excepting those where business was obviously being done. Gimona came back with a petite girl in tow, just as beautiful as she but several shades darker in skin tone and dressed in a blue gown.

"This is Channa," she said. Channa smiled at Layton. Layton smiled back and extended his hand, clearly pleased.

"Welcome, Channa. I'm George," he said. It was strange, but yet here it was again—Gimona had clearly brought out a younger companion for Layton, even though he was older than me. I guessed my duty rank had something to do with it. Channa sat next to Layton while Gimona departed to see to our service. She returned in a few moments with a tea set but only two glasses.

"You're not joining us?" I asked. Gimona smiled that stunning smile as she poured for me, then passed the pot over to Channa. She shook her head.

"Our service is our trade," she said. "We are here to serve you, not the other way around."

We proceeded this way for more than an hour, the girls alternating bringing us different parts of our meal. Bread and hummus, a kind of spiced lamb or beef with flatbread, yogurt to cool the spices, and fresh vegetables that I was unfamiliar with. Gimona dutifully poured my tea, and then later pomegranate wine and ale. She wiped my mouth with a soft napkin when I had food on it, gave me fresh mint leaves to chew on between courses, and dipped her finger in rose-scented "blessing water" to douse me each time she served me something. Her attention to me was total, and I felt like a king. She was always close enough for me to feel the warmth of her body, and I wondered how much I had actually bought with my twenty crowns.

As we drank our after-dinner ales the entertainment started. We reclined back on our pillows, each of us with a woman at our side, and watched as the room filled with loud music, fire pots, and belly dancers in thin veils swaying to the beat of the music. Gimona gently rubbed my temples while the performance went on and made sure my ale cup was never empty.

The show lasted for almost an hour. The veils came off, of course, and the dancers came to our table to entertain us, shaking their hips in amazing ways to receive well-earned tips, with which we were happy to oblige. Then the dancers bowed and were gone. The live music continued, however, and in a flash both Gimona and Channa were up and dancing for us. I looked once at Layton, and saw his face was covered in a smile, oblivious to anything but his dancing companion. I turned my attention to Gimona, who rewarded me with a slow, sensual dance. She drew me in with her eyes first, never taking them from mine, then her hands went to her voluptuous body, enticing me with swaying arms running over her gown and exposed skin. As the music picked up faster and faster she spun into a whirlwind, coming to a stop above me just as the drums, cymbals, and horns crashed for a final time.

I applauded her enthusiastically and then the music resumed in a much softer tone. She went to one knee and bowed to me, a glow of sweat covering her body, her chest gently heaving as she breathed deeply from her dance. I took her by the hand and lay her down beside me and we faced each other on the pillows, her dark flowing hair framing her face. The drink and heady atmosphere of the evening had had its desired effect on me.

"I want to kiss you," I said quietly. She smiled and laughed a bit and bowed her head before looking back up at me.

"You might have kissed me anytime you wanted," she said.

"Is that part of what I paid for?" I asked. She looked at me very seriously.

"No. When I do that, I do it for love."

"I see," I said, then felt embarrassed for asking. "I need to apologize—" She cut me off by putting a finger to my mouth.

"Quiet," she said, "no need for that." Then she pulled her hand away and kissed me sweetly. I looked over at Layton, who was similarly engaged with Channa. I leaned in, resting my head on her softness while she gently stroked my hair. It was absolute bliss.

I woke up on the pillows, Gimona snuggled next to me, still glowing from my evening's entertainment. Layton was already gone. I disengaged myself from Gimona's arms, being careful not to wake her, then slipped out and made my way back to *Starbound* in the quiet of the early morning. My blissful recollections of the evening, however, were broken when I turned the last corner to my cabin and found Commander Dobrina Kierkopf waiting in the hall for me, arms crossed in a very serious pose.

"There you are!" she said, obviously agitated. I looked at my watch. Twenty minutes after five in the morning.

"I'm sorry, did I miss the staff meeting already?" I said sarcastically, then wobbled a bit and put out a hand to the wall to support myself.

"No," she said back, "it starts in ten minutes. And you're drunk."

"What?" I said, not sure if I'd heard her correctly.

"Maclintock's staff is at 0530 every morning, or didn't you know that?"

"I sure as hell didn't!" I ripped past her and keyed in the entry code to my cabin. She followed me in as I rifled through my clothes, searching for a clean shirt and jacket. The ones I was wearing smelled of blessing water and spices.

"You need to read your status reports. The outgoing XO sent them out last night at 2100," Dobrina said, leaning against the doorframe and watching me scramble about.

"I was out by then," I said.

"So you were," she watched me for a few more seconds as I stumbled helplessly about the cabin, trying to shave, wash, and find fresh clothes all at the same time.

"Oh, for God's sake!" she finally said, starting the shower for me and pushing me into my small bathroom. "Get those clothes off and I'll see what I can do with your uniform," she called from behind the door. I peeled off my clothes and tossed them to her as I jumped into the shower, turning it cold to try and wake myself up while I cleaned. She handed me my shaver over the shower stall and I started in on my beard. Another second and she gave me a hangover pill, which I took and washed down with the shower water. There would be no napping today; the pill contained a twelve-hour stimulant.

I heard her spraying freshener on my clothes, the kind of thing only a woman would think to do, and then shaking them out. "These are pretty randy," she said from the cabin. "I hope she was worth it." I said nothing to that, but it was easy to pick up the tinge of resentment in her voice.

I was out and dressed in a few minutes, or so it seemed to me, and we were on our way to the captain's briefing room at 0528. We stood together in silence as the lifter took us up five decks to the conning tower and the nerve center of *Starbound*.

"How do I—" I started.

"You smell like roses and paprika," she said. I let that sink in for a second, then started to laugh. She resisted for a few seconds, then joined me. I lost it at that point, giggling as if I were still drunk, which I supposed I still was despite the hangover pill. She elbowed me to get me to stop. When that didn't work she slugged me hard in the upper arm.

"Oww! Goddamn it, that hurt!" I cried in mock pain, still laughing. She cocked her arm to hit me again, but this time I was having none of it.

I grabbed her arm as she swung and pulled her in to me, pressing her close with a hand in the small of her back, all the giggling gone in a second. We stayed that way for several seconds, feelings present that had stayed unspoken between us. Then I kissed her.

It was long and passionate, and she matched my inappropriate advance with plenty of enthusiasm of her own. After a few long moments of this, she pulled away from me, looking up into my eyes.

"You're still drunk," she said softly.

"Perhaps I am," I said, refusing to release her. She tried to step back then, but I held on.

"Goddamn you, let me go!" she said as she shrugged free of me, untangling herself from my grip. We both took a moment to straighten up our uniforms at the last second as the lifter slowed to a halt and then opened onto Starbound's Command Deck.

There were three rooms on the deck: the bridge, Captain's Office, and here at the rear of the deck, the Command Briefing Room. I looked down the hall toward the bridge with longing, then stepped off the lifter and went left into the Briefing Room. I snapped to attention and saluted upon entering, and at the head of the table Captain Jonas Maclintock saluted back to me without getting up. It was 0532.

"I was beginning to wonder if you were going to make it, Commander," Maclintock said, then motioned to the chair next to him on his left. "Have a seat." I did and tea was passed around promptly, which I took as I looked about the room at the other officers. There were six, all men, none of whom I recognized. There were three lieutenant commanders, one of whom was a chaplain, and three first lieutenants. Serosian, I noted, was still absent. Dobrina took the seat next to Maclintock on his right as he introduced me around the table, showing no indication that he disapproved of my scent, and then he started in with the briefing.

"Our orders, gentlemen," began Maclintock, "are clear. We are to activate the jump gate on Levant B and proceed via the jump point to determine the status of H.M.S. Impulse. There, we will perform a rescue if possible, and destroy her if she cannot be salvaged." The last part hit me hard, like a blow to the chest. I had never considered that we might not recover Impulse. I was also surprised navy brass had been so decisive and so quick to respond. Perhaps I'd underestimated Admiral Wesley.

"Both Commander Kierkopf and Mr. Cochrane here have experience serving on Impulse, plus Mr. Cochrane trained here aboard Starbound as a cadet. They will both be vital to our success. The Admiralty has seen fit to name Commander Kierkopf as XO for this mission, and though I know you all have some misgivings about losing Commander Tannace to the First Contact mission on Levant, I have full confidence in our new XO," he said, nodding to Dobrina. It was what he had to say, whether he believed it or not, and I suspected similar words of false praise were coming my way.

"Lieutenant Commander Cochrane will serve as our longscope officer, and I believe he will do a fine job in that capacity. Historian Serosian has assured me he's more than up to the task." He nodded my way while I wondered what about my behavior so far had given him that impression. The faces around the table all eyed me, but their expressions gave away nothing. These were experienced spacers and to them I must have come off as a child, the overprivileged son of a royal family that they didn't even officially recognize yet, though they all knew it was likely the monarchy would be reestablished soon.

The door buzzed and then opened and a striking red-haired woman in a green Carinthian Marine Corps uniform with the rank of colonel entered. She saluted Maclintock and then took the seat directly opposite me, which had been left open.

"Commander Cochrane, may I introduce Colonel Lena Babayan, commander of our Carinthian Marine detachment here on *Starbound*," said Maclintock. I stood and stuck out a hand and she took it, looking at me with sharp, piercing green eyes.

"A pleasure," she said in a husky voice. Her grip on my hand was as firm as any man's.

"I've asked Colonel Babayan here to review the status of our marine detachment," said Maclintock. "Colonel, if you please." Colonel Babayan stood and faced the other officers, a plasma pad with notes on it in her hand.

"We're staffed with sixty marines for this mission, in four squads of fifteen each, half Carinthian and half Quantar The Quantar teams are commanded by your man, Sergeant Marker," she said, nodding to me. "But I retain overall command of the detachment. Each of these units is equipped with upgraded heavy weapons: double-barrel coil rifles, shoulder mounted RPGs, heavy grenades, and the latest EVA suits. We've swapped out our Downship and light shuttle for two heavy bulwark shuttles, which means we've also had to discard the individual dropships. This means we will carry a higher risk by putting all our marines in just two ships, but the bulwarks are much better suited for this type of scenario than the dropships. Based on your experience with the HD displacement wave weapons, Commander Cochrane, would you agree with my assessment?" I looked up, surprised to be asked a question, but recovered quickly. Dobrina shifted in her seat as I started to speak.

"The bulwark shuttles are more durable at close range against any conventional weapon, no question," I said, then continued. "Their ablative plating makes them less vulnerable to energy weapons and concussion mines. But nothing will stand up well to a hyperdimensional displacement wave or the anti-graviton plasma we faced, especially without a Hoagland Field at least as large as *Starbound*'s. And quite frankly, sir," I said, turning to Maclintock, "those are the weapons of choice we saw in both incidents here at Levant."

Colonel Babayan pondered this a bit. I used this pause as an opening to get more information. "Colonel, under what scenarios are we planning on deploying the marines?" Babayan looked around the table, and others returned her look of surprise.

"I thought you had been briefed?" she said.

"No," I said, embarrassed. But I wasn't about to admit I'd been out drinking and hadn't read my reports. She frowned and then continued.

"Three scenarios. One is a rescue aboard *Impulse*. Second, a defense of *Starbound*, and third," she paused at this, "an attack on an Imperial ship, Cruiser class or higher."

"With marines? Is this something we're expecting?" I asked. "Has anyone here besides Commander Kierkopf and I actually seen an Imperial ship in the last hundred and fifty years? Do we even know if they're still functional?"

"No one knows," cut in Maclintock. "But based on your encounter with the unmanned HuK, we have to be prepared for any eventuality."

"I'll forward you the scenarios again," said Colonel Babayan, pressing commands on the pad with a stylus.

"One last thing before we move on, Mr. Cochrane," said Maclintock, "I'm making you responsible for the marine teams, specifically for their integration and joint training. I expect any two marines, Quantar and Carinthian, to be able to operate as a unit with no breakdowns in communication or performance. Colonel Babayan will be your go-to for how to get this done, but I'm making you responsible for the outcome."

"Yes, sir," I said. He was giving me a bone to prove I belonged, but he couldn't have failed to notice my lack of preparation. My first staff meeting and already I was showing the command crew of *Starbound* that I wasn't ready.

The rest of the meeting was taken up by general orders about staffing, shifts, and the like. He told us all to be prepared for departure from Artemis on one hour's notice.

"Thank you all," he said, "Dismissed." Then he turned to Dobrina and me as the staff filed out. "Please stay, Commanders," he said. We sat back down. When the room had cleared he swiveled in his chair to face me.

"I wanted to apologize for our introduction yesterday, Mr. Cochrane. It was inappropriate of me and insulting to you," said Maclintock.

"Understood, sir," I said. He nodded and then looked to Dobrina.

"I also want to apologize for the circumstances you've been put in, Commander Kierkopf. The crew aboard *Starbound* have had the same XO for the last two years, and most of them feel losing Devin

Tannace to the First Contact mission is just navy brass playing politics to make an opening for you. I don't agree. I've checked your record with the Carinthian Navy and it's a damned fine one."

"Thank you, sir," she said.

"And don't grieve for Commander Tannace," continued Maclintock. "He's up for command of one of the new Lightships launching next year."

"I'm sure he'll make a great captain," I said, not really knowing if he would or not. Maclintock nodded again and moved on.

"That being said, neither of you can expect to be accepted here until you've earned it. The *Impulse* rescue mission should give you both plenty of opportunity to do so. Specifically, Admiral Wesley has given me personal orders to get that jump gate above Levant B operating. Mr. Cochrane, I understand you have some experience with this thing?"

"I've been in the control room, yes, sir, but I've never operated the machine," I said honestly.

"So my question to you both is this, then," said Maclintock, "can you get this thing operational?" I looked to Dobrina and she answered for us both.

"We damn well can, sir," she said. Maclintock nodded.

"Then I'll issue the formal orders putting Commander Kierkopf in charge, along with a requisition for any equipment or personnel you need," Maclintock said. "You'll be her Number Two on this, Mr. Cochrane. The marine teams will escort you down to B. Anyone else you think you'll be needing?"

Dobrina opened her mouth, about to say no, I suspected, so I piped up with, "Just access to Historian Serosian." Maclintock nodded.

"He'll be available to you as time permits," said the captain. Now I nodded. "I'll give you until tomorrow to assemble your team, Commander," he said to Dobrina. "Then I expect to see you on the surface of B. And remember, much of your reputation on this ship will rest on your success or failure on this mission."

"Understood, Captain," said Dobrina.

"Now if you'll excuse us, Commander, I have some personal business to discuss with Mr. Cochrane," he said. I tensed at this, expecting a chewing out about my preparation, or lack thereof. Dobrina saluted and left, off to plan the mission. I turned to my new commanding officer.

"Now, son, as to expectations," he started. "You're new here. You're very young, and you're also the likely heir of the would-be Director of Quantar. None of that is lost on me. But we all take our chances equally out here. You'll have to prove yourself to me and to those men you just met, all of whom are experienced spacers."

"Yes, sir."

"And it would help if you didn't come to the morning staff smelling of brothels and the bazaar," he said.

I nodded without making eye contact. "Understood, sir. It won't happen again."

"Good," he replied in a matter-of-fact tone. "So we've both made one mistake already. Let's make sure we don't repeat them."

"Aye, sir," I said, stiffening in my resolve.

"Now, onto more serious matters. I reviewed your training record aboard *Starbound* before I took command, and it's a good one. Top five overall, number one on the longscope in the entire service, and your friend Serosian raves about your potential. But this is not about potential, son. This is about performance." He stopped there to let his words sink in.

"You've been given the rank of senior lieutenant commander aboard. Whether that's deserved or not isn't my problem. I expect you to act the part. Keep this ship running, carry out my orders, rely on your experience from this Levant incident. Hell, that experience is something you have over all of us. I'll be relying on you to provide leadership. Don't hesitate, or you will lose the confidence of those men who just left the room."

"Also understood, sir," I said. He pushed back from the table, as if to get up and leave, but stopped and turned toward me instead.

"There is one more thing," he said. I shifted uncomfortably in my chair. "It's been brought to my attention that you lost a very close personal friend in the first attack on *Impulse*."

I didn't hesitate. "I did, sir."

"I want you to know that all the senior staff are aware of that fact, and you have their sincerest condolences, and mine."

"Yes, sir."

Maclintock eyed me with his steel blue eyes, taking my measure. His next question surprised me.

"Was she your first?"

"My first?" I stumbled. What the hell was he asking?

"Your first love, Commander?"

My mind whirled with how to answer that one. I decided to go with honesty. Maclintock seemed like the no-nonsense type anyway.

"Yes, sir, but . . . we hadn't had an ongoing relationship since she'd gotten her assignment to *Impulse* a few months back," I said. Maclintock contemplated me, hands tapping gently on the table.

"Son," he finally said, "I just want to make you aware, most of us in the service have lost someone we cared about, friend, family, even more than that. I just wanted to warn you, she won't be the last one you lose out here."

I nodded acknowledgment. "Thank you for the insight, sir," I said. Maclintock nodded back.

"You're welcome, Commander," he said. "You're dismissed."

And with that I stood and saluted and made for the door, my head spinning from more than just the previous night's drinking.

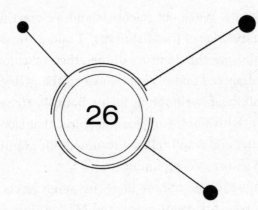

26

Dobrina came by my cabin at 1800 for dinner and a mission planning session. We needed to talk, since we had no real idea what we were going to do to try and activate the jump gate on B. We reviewed the digital records that Marker and I had taken from our trip down to the control room, looking for clues. After forty-five minutes of review I set my plasma tablet down on the table in frustration.

"What?" she asked. "You're not giving up already?" I sat back in my chair, the table between us. My mind was on other things, and it showed.

"Without Serosian to help us we'll never crack this code," I said. "It's pointless."

"I've already checked with Maclintock. Serosian won't be available until sometime tomorrow. He's pulling double duty with the First Contact team and working for the Church."

"Which reiterates my point. Anything we do here could be rendered completely irrelevant in the first fifteen minutes that he looks at this. Trying to figure out how to activate this thing is way beyond our pay grade. We're not scientists and we don't have access to the private knowledge of the Historians," I said. Now she sat back.

"I think we should order dinner, then take another crack at it," she said. I agreed and ordered down to the galley, choosing an old Earth dish, beef Wellington, for us both. It arrived a few minutes later, along with a bottle of Quantar shiraz that Dobrina had ordered. After eating and small talk we resumed our planning with just our glasses of shiraz as companions.

"Longwave scans show there are seven levels to the base," she said. "On your first venture you and Marker only explored one, two, and seven through the freight lifter. Seven is the level with the cavern and the cannon in it. I suggest we take our full detachment of marines down in the bulwark shuttles, give them some practice at deploying out of them, then have them do a full reconnoiter of all the levels while our technical team proceeds down to the control room via the freight lifter."

"That makes sense, but what do we do when we get there?" I said. "Knock on the windows? That console is not likely to let us mess around with it. And if I owned that valuable a piece of equipment I wouldn't allow just anybody to go strolling around the cavern."

"So you're presuming there will be some kind of defensive mechanisms in place?" she asked.

"That's what I'd do," I replied. She picked up her wineglass, sniffing and swirling the liquid before taking a drink. She was getting low so I refilled her glass, then topped off mine.

"The bottle's empty," she said. I took a drink of my wine, then looked at her over the top of my glass. "Should I order another?" She smiled.

"That's very tempting," she said, then drank again. "I think we have a solid plan for now. I'll tell Marker and Colonel Babayan to have their marines ready at 0800. We'll drop in, do the reconnoiter, then set up in the control room and wait for Serosian. There's really nothing much else to do."

"Agreed," I said. She eyed me, as if wanting to ask a question, which she presently did.

"Are you worried about the marine teams? How they'll work together, react under pressure? Maclintock did make you responsible for their performance, you know," she said. I shook my head.

"I'm not worried. Marker is a professional and from what I've seen of Colonel Babayan she doesn't seem the type to allow much leeway. I expect they'll all do their jobs properly."

"You seem very confident," she said.

"I usually am," I replied. I looked at my watch. It was 2130 hours, and we were basically done, but she was lingering in my cabin. I looked up at Dobrina. She seemed to be waiting for something, so I prompted her.

"Dobrina, is there something you want to say?" I asked.

She looked away and stayed silent for a moment, then volunteered, "There's something that's been on my mind, yes." She had another drink while I waited patiently.

"We won't get anywhere if you don't talk," I said. She gave me an annoyed glance, then stared at the bulkhead of my cabin, wineglass in hand, as if making a decision. She took a deep breath and exhaled.

"When I told you about the fire that killed your brother, Derrick, I wasn't entirely forthcoming about all the pertinent details," she finally said. This jolted me.

"What . . . details?" I asked. She took in another deep breath before continuing, still staring at my bulkhead wall.

"There was a report on the incident that stated that it was an accident. That was the official report. There was also an unofficial report," she said.

I was surprised by this. "Which said what?" I asked.

She shifted on the couch before continuing, then turned to me. "It said that there was a forty percent probability of sabotage."

"Sabotage?" I said. I was shocked. "You mean—"

"It wasn't conclusive, Peter. Nothing in the report was. No smoking gun. But yes, there is a possibility your brother was killed intentionally."

I was stunned. "By whom? For what purpose?" I asked. She shook her head.

"All unknown, and the report does not speculate. I'm telling you all of this to give you a warning, Peter. There may be forces out there that could be targeting you as well. Be careful."

"Always," I replied. This news had shaken me and I wanted time to digest it. "If that's all—"

"There's more," she said, interrupting. "On a personal note, when I told you that I was on fire control, I wasn't actually telling the truth. I was officer of the deck that day. When the accident happened I went rushing down to the Propulsion room, because . . . you see . . ." she trailed off.

"Dobrina—"

"Just let me get this out!" she snapped. I shut up. She had turned back to the bulkhead now as though to avoid looking at me. "I went down there because I had . . . more than a casual relationship with your brother."

It wasn't like I hadn't expected that, I realized. Something had been wrong about her story, and now I knew what it was.

"So, you're saying you and my brother were lovers?" I said as gently as I could. She had another drink from her wineglass.

"Yes, in violation of the navy's policy on fraternization—"

"Which has never been enforced on long-duration space missions," I said. "Don't punish yourself, Dobrina. It happens all the time and it's something we all accept in the navy. Deep-space missions are difficult, at best. We all know that. We're only human. It's hard to keep our emotions bottled up for months at a time. To be honest, I for one am happy to know that someone like you gave him comfort, even in his last moments."

At this she started to openly cry, and I automatically went to the couch to comfort her, putting my arms around her and pulling her in close. She cried for a few seconds, then stopped herself. "Damn wine," she muttered. I pushed back a lock of hair from her face. "I thought those feelings were behind me. And then you show up, and you look so much like him, so proud, so strong in defending your country's honor. Those were so many of the traits that I loved about Derrick. And now I see them in you," she said.

"And I can see what he saw in you too," I said. "Honor, duty to your friends, facing danger with such bravery. I can see why he fell for you."

"Stop it," she said, waving me off with a hand and smiling a bit. "You're just being nice. I'm the homely girl who never gets to dance with the prince, I know that."

"Dobrina . . ." I said, and then words escaped me. I leaned in and kissed her, and immediately realized I'd been wanting to do it for a very long time. She didn't hesitate. Her lips met mine and it was a warm and inviting kiss, full of promise and affection. She started to pull back but I kept her close for a minute longer as we exchanged small kisses. Then I released her, but stayed close, our foreheads touching.

"Peter, for the sake of the mission—"

"You're the one who said 'there's always another mission,'" I reminded her. Then I took her hand and our fingers intertwined. "There is never a good time, Dobrina."

"I did say that," she said. "But that was back on Levant. Tomorrow is the most important day of our lives, Peter, and rescuing *Impulse* is the most important thing to me, at least for right now."

I just nodded. I had nothing to say to that, so I leaned in once more and kissed her again, passionately.

"The only promise I can make," I said to her as I pulled back, "is that next time you'll get the first dance with the prince."

She smiled hesitantly at me, then took my face in her hands and pulled me in for a final kiss.

"I'd better go. See you in the morning," she said.

"See you in the morning," I agreed, then watched her go. I sighed deeply, staring across the room at my lonely, empty bunk. I took one last drink of my wine, then headed straight for my bed.

I was awakened a few hours later by an alert buzzer on my com. It was the night duty officer on the bridge, a lieutenant named Cox. "There's some sort of disturbance down on the hangar deck, sir. Sergeant Marker called up asking for you," he said.

I looked at my clock. Half past one. "How urgent is this?" I asked. Cox cleared his throat.

"There seemed to be a lot of commotion in the background, sir, and the sergeant was insistent on my calling you," Lt. Cox said.

"I'm sure he was," I said. I sat up in bed and started putting on my socks and underwear. "Couldn't he just call in some of his marines?"

"I think that was the source of the commotion, sir," said Cox.

"What?"

"Um, I think the marines were fighting each other, sir," said Cox.

"The marines? Shit!" I cut the line and scrambled to pull on my shirt and pants, then grabbed my jacket and shoes on my way out the door.

The lifter took me down fourteen decks and then laterally to the hangar deck. I tucked in my shirt but my jacket was still unbuttoned as I tied my shoelaces. As the lifter doors opened I stood quickly and stepped out onto the hangar deck.

Into a riot.

I ducked at the last second as a metal dinner tray came flying at my head and smacked against the lifter's back wall, leaving a trail of food that looked like spaghetti or lasagna as it fell. I swung low and rolled to my right, ending in a defensive crouch a few feet away from the lifter. It looked as though all sixty marines, Carinthian versus Quantar, were engaged in a knock-down, drag-out brawl across the deck. I looked for Marker but had no luck locating him, though I could hear someone shouting cease and desist orders to no avail.

I took the risk of standing and turned back toward the lifter, coming face-to-chest with a green-clad Carinthian marine the size of a truck. I looked up just as he sent a haymaker my way, with no chance to stop it. A strong hand gripped my collar and pulled me back out the line of fire an instant before my face would have become oatmeal mush.

"Stay down!" yelled a voice in my ear. I looked up to see Colonel Lena Babayan step over me and zap her countryman with a fifty-thousand-volt stun gun. The man stopped for only a second, then brushed the barbs from his arm and returned to the fray with a guttural shout.

"That's impressive," I said from the ground. "What do you feed them, anyway?"

The colonel looked annoyed and then helped me to my feet. "Do you have a better idea?" she said. I looked around the room as fists flew and battle cries filled the air. It was mayhem. Then I noticed the door to the hangar deck control room was wide open.

"As a matter of fact I do!" I yelled over the din. I grabbed her by the hand and we made for the control room, dodging flying bodies, furniture, and food as we went. We got to the door and I yanked her inside, then slammed the door shut against the chaos.

"What are you going to do?" she said, her face flushed with frustration and anger. I wondered if I had angered her by tossing her in here so roughly, then decided that in the current situation niceness counted for nothing. I looked up and saw the red emergency decompression handle under glass on the wall behind her.

"I'm going to finish this, now!" I said, and ran across the control room. I slammed the glass with my elbow and it shattered to the floor, then I reached in and yanked down on the handle as hard as I could. The lights on the deck flickered out and a red flash replaced them, accompanied by a blaring alert claxon.

"Warning! Emergency decompression in thirty seconds! Warning! Emergency decompression in twenty-eight seconds! Warning . . ." the emergency voice droned on.

"Let's see if that gets their attention!" I said. Colonel Babayan looked worried.

"You're not serious!" she said. I glared at her.

"I am if they are!"

By the twenty-second mark all the fighting had stopped and the men began banging on the control room door and windows, cursing at me. I stood with my hands on my hips staring each one of them down. At the ten-second mark the cursing had turned to fearful pleading. At five seconds I slammed the lever back into place and the alarm shut off, the normal room lights coming back on. Babayan looked at me with what I fancied was admiration on her face.

"Nice work," she said.

"We're not finished yet," I said, nodding to the mob. "Let's go tame the apes." I went to the door and unlocked it, stepping back out onto the hangar deck, pushing marines aside as I went.

"Form lines by home world and rank!" I barked at the marines. I let them shuffle around dejectedly for a few seconds before I took the Quantar marines to one side of the bay while Colonel Babayan gathered hers on the other side. Marker emerged from the pile and stood next to me, a rising shiner on his face.

"You were supposed to prevent this," I whispered as he took up his station, "not get involved in it!"

"What could I do?" Marker said stiffly. "The old rivalries run deep. Plus, they insulted the queen." I waved him off and turned to the marines.

The deck was littered with empty beer cans, garbage, food, and traces of blood from the brawl. Nearly every man in the corps had a mark of some kind on him. I walked up and down the lines, saying nothing for several minutes. Colonel Babayan did the same, but deferred to me as senior officer to mete out punishment. I couldn't decide what to do, but I knew I didn't want to look weak in front of the men, so I acted.

I went to the open space halfway between both lines of marines—no man's land.

"This, gentlemen, is a disgrace," I said to both sides of the deck, pacing now back and forth between them. I used a quiet, direct tone of voice, then raised it with my next command.

"Each one of you are to pair off with a counterpart, one Quantar, one Carinthian, preferably the man or woman you were fighting with. I want this deck cleaned in five minutes or I'll pick five of you from each side and throw you in the brig on C rations for a week! Now move!" I shouted.

Move they did. C rations were minimal water and only oatmeal gruel to eat once a day, enough to scare any man, especially the cuisine-loving Carinthians. The deck was rapidly cleared of debris and put back together with minimal incident. One of the Carinthians even found a mop and took it to the floor. They were back into ranks in four and a half minutes.

I looked around the deck, standing between the two units, unsure what to do next. I was keenly aware that not only they but also Captain Maclintock would be judging me based on my next move. I looked over to the lounge area, hastily constructed out of bunk foam, chairs, and packing pads. It was supposed to be a common area for the men to play cards or backgammon or chess. Instead it had doubled as a beer hall.

There was a large round table in the center of the lounge, low set with closed sides. It was rather solid looking, and it gave me an idea.

"At ease, gentlemen. We're going to gather in the lounge. I want you to pair off again, one Carinthian and one Quantar marine, then sit around the table. Now!" I yelled. The marines shuffled into order and sat as instructed. Marker and Babayan gave me peculiar looks but said nothing and stood together outside the ring. I went to a wall console and shut down most of the deck lights, then parted a pair of marines with my boot as I made my way to the table. I stepped up on top and tucked in my shirt, buttoning my jacket before I addressed the crowd.

"Punishing you in any conventional way would be pointless," I said. "I think you understand that, if you understand nothing else. Tomorrow we drop to Levant B, and from there beyond the gate, to Corant or Altos, to see what's left of the First Empire and find out if they've harmed our comrades aboard *Impulse*." I paused to let that sink in. Very few eyes met mine.

"So you have to be ready, and I have the godforsaken job of making you ready," I crossed my arms and stepped around the table, addressing every part of the crowd as I went. "I said any conventional punishment would be pointless. So now you will get an unconventional one. Your punishment, ladies and gentlemen, will be to listen to what I have to say."

I looked at the faces around me. They were curious now, at least.

"There is a story in our family history, the Cochrane family history, a story of the final battle of the old war." This seemed to raise their interest.

"Have any of you ever heard the story of MacEachern's Run?" I said. There were a handful of nods and raised hands, all of them from Quantar marines. "Good, then this will be educational for most of you." I cleared my throat once and then started in, pacing in circles with my hands on my hips for dramatic emphasis.

"MacEachern was a Quantar Navy speedwing pilot at the Battle of Carinthia." Now I had their full attention.

"Vat's a speed-*ving*?" asked one of the Carinthian marines in a heavy Teutonic accent.

"A speedwing is a tri-winged, single-seat fighter, the kind of ship made obsolete by coil flak cannons and ship-to-ship missiles," I said.

"Now, MacEachern was so obscure that no one even knows what his first name was or where he came from, but we do know he was a Union pilot. His ship was damaged during the battle. He took a hit and it knocked his inertial dampers out. His flight controls and navigation were gone. He couldn't turn or maneuver. He couldn't land. He couldn't eject or go in reverse. All he could do was fly a straight line. He struggled and fought with his controls, trying with all his might to turn his fighter back into the battle." All eyes in the room were on me now. I felt like a schoolteacher at story time.

"Eventually, MacEachern got some control of his ship and he managed to turn it back toward the battle. But when he did, he saw the truth: the Union Navy was losing. He had no chance of making it through the flak, the coil cannon fire, the Carinthian heavy fighter wings, the cannon of the frigates and the destroyers and the dreadnoughts. So he did the only thing he could do, he pointed his tiny ship toward *Imperious*, the Carinthian Navy flagship, and fired his impeller engines to full, turning himself into a missile."

I went down to my haunches, getting closer to my audience. I had them in my grasp now.

"Now, normally using impellers on full in close combat would get you killed very fast, simply by running into something at high speed. But MacEachern shot through the first line of heavy fighters,"

"The Carinthians gave chase, but MacEachern was too fast for them to catch. Then the picket line of coil fire, crossing beams of orange and green, flared across his path. He lost his vertical stabilizer, he lost part of his wing; but he kept going. It was suicide, but then he'd known that when he fired up his engines,"

"Now, he was being picked up by *Imperious* and her defenders. Frigates moved to fire at him, and missed. Missiles came in a nonstop barrage from defensive platforms. *Imperious* herself tried to move, to escape, firing cannon and flak charges at will. But still MacEachern came on,"

"There were voices in his earpiece: shouts of encouragement, prayers of hope, and only prayer could help the Union Navy now. He sped on, frantically looking at his unused missiles, praying they would stay attached to his wings. MacEachern was a rocketing bomb, an uncontrolled missile with a man inside. But he held the stick steady and true." I paused again, then started pacing out my circle again, but in the reverse direction.

"MacEachern looked up one last time. *Imperious* filled his vision. Through his burned-out canopy he could see the great lady trying to escape, but she was too late. MacEachern screamed his last, a war cry of rage and pain and glory and sorrow that they say echoed through the ansibles from the far reaches of the empire to the royal palace itself!"

Every eye was on me now.

"MacEachern slammed his fighter into the base of *Imperious'* conning tower. His missiles exploded, and his hydrazine fuel, what was left of it, ignited. The tower burst as the fuel from his fighter mixed with oxygen and hydrogen tanks aboard *Imperious*, and then twisted and split in half."

"*Imperious* fell out of control, colliding with the *Emperor's Galley*," I smacked a fist into my open palm for emphasis, "destroying them both in a blaze of white fire. Frigates and support ships by the dozens were destroyed. Their loss was a shock to the defending Carinthians. It's said the grand duke himself fled at this sight, that he left his home world for the safe haven of Corant."

I put my hands to my hips. "We'll probably never know the truth of it. But what we do know is that the destruction of *Imperious* and the *Emperor's Galley* stunned the Royalist Navy, so much so that they scattered, allowing the Union fleet to escape to Quantar and Minara, Sorel and Pendax. Five days later the Feilberg family, negotiating for the emperor, concluded a cease-fire agreement via ansible, and the Constitution Wars were over. Neither side talked to the other for a hundred and fifty years, until a decade ago, when the Earthmen landed on Quantar and Carinthia on Reunion Day."

I looked over the crowd. You could hear a pin drop on the deck. I sighed heavily and spoke softly.

"That can never be allowed to happen again," I said. I put out my hand to the crowd. "Now gather 'round." They did as instructed, placing their hands over mine or on the shoulders of their neighbors. I bowed my head and closed my eyes.

"Dear God, hear our prayer. Tomorrow these brave young men and women go into a dangerous situation, against forces unknown. Make them ready. Keep them safe. Guard these marines, and give them a spirit of unity as they fight. And deliver our comrades aboard *Impulse* back to us safe and sound," then I opened my eyes. "Amen."

The marines softly echoed my last word. I stepped down from the platform and broke through the circle, not looking back nor glancing at Marker or Babayan, making straight for the lifter.

Behind me, all was quiet on the hangar deck.

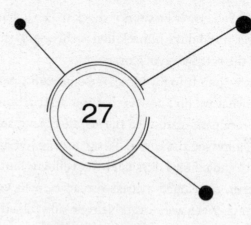

To L-4b

By 0730 Dobrina, Layton, and I were on the flight deck of one of *Starbound*'s bulwark shuttles, programming in our flight path and prepping the cabin for our drop to the surface of L-4b. Marker and his marine troop of mixed Carinthian and Quantar marines arrived fifteen minutes later in full EVA suits, decked out as if they expected trouble. I was pleased that the two sides seemed to have made peace after the previous night's escapade. Colonel Babayan called at 0755 to confirm that her shuttle was ready as well.

I decided to take a stroll through the cabin before the launch. The marines themselves were impressive, in a size-is-everything-and-I-can-kill-you-with-my-dog-tags kind of way. Most of them said nothing and none of them would meet my gaze as I passed them in the personnel bay. All of them were sporting cuts, bruises, or black eyes from the previous night's festivities. I hoped their lack of acknowledgment of me was due to a sense of shame about their behavior, but I couldn't be sure. I stood in the bay, arms behind my back and watching them, saying nothing but not moving to leave until they were all strapped in like little tin soldiers in their toy box. Marker completed his lockdown and then gave me a thumbs-up. I took that as my signal to head back up to the flight deck, don my EVA suit helmet, and strap myself in.

After the final flight checks we were away at low speed, dropping out of *Starbound*'s landing bay and running as silently as possible toward B and the cannon complex. Dobrina was all business as we made quick progress toward the surface. She seemed anxious to get on with the mission. I switched my com over to a private channel with Marker as we made our descent.

"Your marines are certainly impressive," I said. Marker chuckled in response.

"After last night how could they fail to impress you?" he said. I laughed.

"I hope I made some impression on them," I said.

"Oh, you did, sir," replied Marker. "They probably won't follow you to the gates of hell but I think they'll provide cover while you make a run at it." I laughed again.

"Look, Commander, we need to face some facts here," Marker continued. "These men don't trust each other. We'll have to instill that in them. Missions like this can only help."

"I hear you, Sergeant," I said. "Just make sure they're ready when we need them."

"Will do, Commander." I cut the com line and switched to Dobrina's channel.

"Sixteen minutes to landing," I said. "Any last-minute thoughts?"

"None that don't involve a marine brawl on my hangar deck," she said.

"That's been handled," I quickly replied.

"Has it?" she questioned without taking her eyes from her board. I shifted a bit in my chair.

"You have my guarantee, Commander Kierkopf," I said.

"Good," she replied. "I'll hold you to that." With that, the conversation seemed over. We were clearly back to a military standing between us and I didn't want to ruffle her feathers with inquiries about where our relationship was going, even if I did have questions. I checked my vector display again. We were making good time. I switched back to Marker's channel.

"We'll be on the ground in ten minutes, Mr. Marker. Tell your men I want them deployed on the surface with a full perimeter no less than one minute after we land," I said.

"That I can do, sir," he said over the com, then switched channels and started sending preparation orders to his men.

Layton brought us down a good kilometer away from the nearest structures, low-lying buildings set into the surrounding land. I unbuckled and stepped down into the personnel bay. "Secure the dock and unload the cargo, Sergeant. Get your men out there!" I ordered. Marker may have been in charge of the marines, but I was in charge of Marker.

Marker started barking orders, then the back hatch flopped open and the marines bounded out as I holstered a coil pistol. I waited my turn at the back of the line. When Marker signaled me the all clear, I stepped down the ramp and out onto the surface of L-4b again.

"Reporting all clear, sir. Landing site is secure," he informed me. I nodded and put my gloved hands to my hips.

"Deploy your men. Keep a guard here at the shuttle and the rest of us will proceed as planned. I'll stay in the back."

"I think that's wise, sir," said Marker, then he cut his end of the com line. With that, we started a stealth approach to the complex buildings, marines waving me forward when things were deemed safe. After several minutes of reconnoitering we arrived at the entrance building Marker and I had encountered in our previous visit.

"All set for entrance here," I reported back to Dobrina.

"Proceed," she replied. "Layton and I will be right behind you with the analysis equipment."

"Acknowledged," I replied, then gave orders to Marker for his troops to begin the search of the inner building. A minute later Colonel Babayan and her troops were at the door as well. I gave them their marching orders as Dobrina and Layton came up with two escort marines hauling their equipment.

"Marine teams engaged in reconnoiter of the unexplored levels, Commander," I said. "We're ready to head down to the freight lifter and proceed to the control room."

"Then let's do it," she said.

The control room in the cavern was just as we had left it, all lights and humming power and the warm glow of the cannon. Layton directed the marines in the setup of the testing equipment, though I doubted much of anything could be gleaned from what he'd brought with him. I looked down at the control board. It was still a mystery. I racked my brain to try and access the knowledge of the Sri I had been given in my instruction, both publicly in the Academy and privately by Serosian. I looked down at the symbols on the illuminated plates, all of them either closed equilateral triangles or pieces of triangles in primary colors. In the center was a color display that looked like the historical Star of David, with sections of yellow, red, green, blue, purple, and orange on the outside and a perfectly formed triangle in the center in white, overlaid by a hexagon. It made no sense to me apart from its obvious familiarity of form.

Colonel Babayan called in to report that her troops had encountered a gangway on the sixth level that led down to the cavern floor where the cannon resided. Dobrina ordered them to explore and report. Layton finished his equipment setup and began working behind his odd-shaped tools, which were attached to what was essentially a steel rack with a portable plasma display.

"What do you hope to discover with all that?" I asked.

"We should be able to read electromagnetic pulses and fields, see if there is anything we should be aware of before we start poking around on that thing," Layton said. He took some readings with his instruments, then frowned.

"There's nothing that I can detect with this equipment," he said. "No stealth fields, no EM fields, no pulses, nothing. But the console is powered and ready to be activated, from what I can determine."

"So it's not booby-trapped?" asked Dobrina.

"Not as far as I can tell."

"So once again, we need Serosian," I stated. Dobrina called up to the nearest marine and asked about the status of our setup of a daisy-chain communications wire so that we could talk to the Historian on *Starbound*. They reported we were ready five minutes later, but when we called up to *Starbound* Serosian still "wasn't available." So we waited.

After half an hour of frustration I got up and went to the board, taxing my memory again on what I knew of the Sri and of encryption codes.

"Are you planning on trying that board yourself?" asked Dobrina.

"I don't know about you, but I'm getting tired of waiting," I said. "And Layton says it's not booby-trapped."

"As far as I can *tell*," interjected Layton. Dobrina thought about this for a moment.

"It could simply be that the code is the security. You don't get it right, we all get fried," she said.

"Nothing ventured, nothing gained," I replied. She looked down at the innocuous looking control board and then nodded for me to proceed while Layton monitored from his display.

I touched the display board with no apparent effect. No displays lit up, no combination of keys seemed to give any reaction. Still the board continued to hum with power. After a couple of minutes I gave up. Seconds later Colonel Babayan called in from the cavern floor, her voice frantic.

"Are you doing something up there, Commander?" she demanded.

"Mr. Cochrane is attempting to hack the control board, why?" Dobrina replied.

"Well he's got to stop! I couldn't report in before due to a dampening field down here!"

"So what's the problem?"

"The problem, Commander, is that there's a massive atomic power plant down here, and it just became active," Babayan said. "And if I didn't know better, I'd say it was building toward some kind of self-destruct." We all looked at each other.

"Call up to *Starbound*," said Dobrina to me. "Tell them we have to talk with Serosian. *Now*."

Starbound's Historian was on our com channel two minutes later.

"You shouldn't have tried to access the console. I have the best minds back on Earth looking at this," he said. I could tell he was angry.

"We were tired of waiting," I said right back.

"No matter now," he said. "From what we're reading up here you seem to have activated the main power system, only in the wrong sequence. It's quite like the Founders really to allow full access to their secrets, just as long as you know the proper methods."

"And if we don't?" asked Dobrina. Serosian didn't answer her.

"Captain Maclintock has ordered the marines to be evacuated, on my recommendation," he said. "Fixing this will require a volunteer to remain behind."

"I'll do it," I said instantly.

"You will not," cut in Dobrina. "At least not alone."

"You'll both be at risk. Both shuttles will need to be withdrawn to a safe distance. Return and rescue, should we succeed in shutting the destruct sequence off, will be problematic under any circumstance," said Serosian.

"Understood," replied Dobrina for us both. Colonel Babayan came in and left us an extra set of oxygen canisters and power packs for our EVA suits. It wasn't much, perhaps two extra hours, but it would have to do. We made Layton go with her, and then Maclintock came on the line and ordered Dobrina out as well.

"I can't lose two of my senior officers on this, and Serosian has informed me that Mr. Cochrane is the best option to solve this crisis," Maclintock said. Dobrina was angry and argued with him, but to no avail. Colonel Babayan had to practically drag Dobrina out, but eventually she went, steaming mad, and I was alone in the control room. I got back on the line with Serosian.

"Why didn't we detect this power plant before?" I asked.

"Some kind of advanced stealth shielding, powerful enough to warp our longwave scans and mask the power plant," said Serosian. "And that plant, if I'm reading this right, is almost half the size of B herself. It's like they hollowed her out and built the plant right inside."

"Founder technology," I said.

"Certainly not First Empire," said Serosian. "And as such it is likely to have multiple access methods. You're going to have to try and interface with the console."

"Interface? You mean touch it?"

"With your hands, yes, that's the most likely way in."

Reluctantly I reached up with my right hand and unlocked the seal on the glove at my left wrist. I felt the glove depressurize and a damp cold crept up my fingers. My EVA suit repressurized and made a seal just below my wrist, as it was designed to do in an emergency. I pulled the glove off. The room was well below freezing and my hand began to numb almost immediately. I repeated the process, removing my right glove as well.

"Beginning interface," I said. I looked down at the glossy black panel, then slowly touched the controls with my fingertips.

Images burst into my mind: flashes of color and shape, indiscriminate sensations of light and sound, then a burning pain crawling up my arm. I withdrew my hand and went to one knee. The images were overwhelming, and my head pounded from the interface. I couldn't see in front of my visor more than a few inches, my eyes tinged with a blinding yellow blaze and shadows of the unseen images in my head.

A wave of nausea overcame me and I fell to all fours. Hunched over and gasping for breath, I unlocked my helmet in a fit of anxiety, popping it off my head, then retched twice and vomited. After a few moments of deep breathing I regained my equilibrium, both physically and emotionally. The air inside the control room was stale but breathable. I pulled myself up to the console once again.

"Peter, are you still with me?" crackled Serosian's voice in my ear.

"I am," I replied. "I think the console just tried to kill me."

"I've interfaced with Founder technology before," Serosian said. "It's not pleasant."

"Thanks for the timely insight." There would be pain, I knew that now, but if I was to complete my mission, it couldn't be avoided. I drew a deep breath, taking in the cold and bitter air of the control room once more, then looked down at the projector. It still hummed with its blue and amber glow, and nothing about it gave me any comfort that I could shut it off. This, I decided, was an *alien* device.

I reattached the helmet to my EVA suit and locked it. I wouldn't allow myself any more moments of panic. It was now or never.

"I'm ready," I said.

"If the console is open to your control, it will be disorienting at first. You will likely have to solve some sort of test. If you fail—"

"I don't want to know," I said. I looked down at the board once more.

"So be it," I said aloud, and pushed both my hands into the console, all the way up to my wrists. Colors and images, symbols and numbers, mathematical equations beyond my understanding, and strange structures of sight and sound filled my senses. The impression of pain ran up my arm, inexorably moving toward my head. Upon reaching my brain the pain abruptly stopped and was replaced by a sensation of warmth. I wondered if there were nanites, micromachines, pouring through my bloodstream and into my brain. It felt like I was being drained of *me*, of my consciousness, as if the machine was reading my every memory, all my thoughts and intents. Just as I felt I was about to lose myself to the machine I suddenly flashed to full awareness of the system I had now merged with.

It was as if I instinctively knew what the systems were for, what the symbols meant, how all the interfaces worked, like being one with the Gods.

I was in control.

I freed my right hand and it flashed over the control board, activating systems, checking others for preparation, dispensing codes for boot sequences. I was in an altered state of consciousness, but it was like I was merely a linked part, an automaton with a mission to complete.

I could understand and react to the language of the machine, but I couldn't retain it. Like I was speaking in tongues without knowledge of what I was saying.

Suddenly, with a loud crack inside my mind and a flash of white light I found myself free of the console and sitting on my backside, hands behind me. I had no idea how long the process had taken, but my intuition told me it was measured in seconds, or fractions of seconds.

The nausea returned abruptly and I peeled away the helmet just in time to vomit again. As a chalky white fluid passed out of me I

realized what was happening: the nanites were eliminating themselves from my body. Apparently I didn't rank high enough on the
divine scale to retain the knowledge of the Gods, or at least of the
Founders, and I was in many ways thankful for that.

I reattached my helmet and gloves, resealing my suit against the
elements of the station. I looked to the cavern. The projector was
glowing with an intense orange light.

As I watched, the deck beneath me began to vibrate and I held on
to the console for support. The power in this unknown device was
building beyond anything I had ever seen. I watched as the gun rotated and raised itself, pointed toward the deep black membrane in
the cavern's ceiling. An amber beam lanced out of the cone of the
projector and into the membrane, where it seemed to vanish. I could
only assume it was projecting its energy somewhere into space.

"What's happening down there?" came Serosian's voice over my
com.

I took a deep breath before answering. "Apparently I've shut
down the self-destruct sequence and activated the jump gate. Can
you confirm?" I said. It took a few seconds before Serosian answered.

"Confirmed Peter. The jump gate is active. Sending down the recovery shuttle. Good job. You did it."

"Thank you. I just wish I knew *how* I did it."

"The important thing is that the gate is open. The *Impulse* rescue
mission is on."

I looked down at the console, an alien device that had for some
reason chosen to help me and not destroy me.

"On my way," I said, heading out of the control room, on my way
back to *Starbound*.

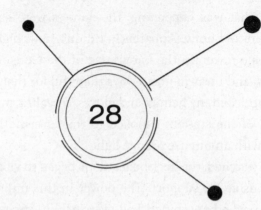

28

Departing Levant

Maclintock had us locked down and ready to go in less than two hours. We said our goodbyes to the First Contact team on Levant, and I even managed to get a goodbye note to Janaan loaded in the packet. By the time we returned here, *if* we returned, the Union Navy would have half a dozen support ships in the system, and word was the Lightship *Valiant* and its captain, Wynn Scott of Earth, were on their way as well.

We still had no way of knowing where we were going, what star system or what part of the galaxy we would end up at, or if it would even be the same location as the one *Impulse* had jumped to. It was a massive risk to the Union Navy to send *Starbound* through the jump gate and risk losing her, but it would be an even bigger loss if we let *Impulse* disappear without a rescue mission.

I took my station on the bridge at 1300. *Starbound* was set up slightly differently than *Impulse* had been, but in most respects the bridge was identical. I checked out my longscope and ran her through a series of initial display checks under the watchful eye of Commander Kierkopf. She hadn't said much since my return from L-4b, but she didn't have to. I knew she was pissed about being excluded from the crisis, but we both knew Maclintock had made the right call. She paced the bridge like an impatient panther waiting for her prey to arrive on the scene.

Colonel Babayan rang in from the hangar deck as I was preparing for my second systems check.

"Have you decided what you're going to tell Maclintock about last night?" she asked. I held the com receiver to my ear silently for a few seconds, then:

"I have no idea what you're talking about, Colonel," I said.

"I think that's a wise course," she said.

"Mmm. And how are things down in the monkey pit today?"

"We're all packed and ready for jump stations. Just waiting for the call," she said. I paused again before responding.

"Let's hope there is no need for a call, Colonel," I said.

"Amen to that," she replied, then hung up the line.

Maclintock took the deck promptly at 1400.

"Anything to report, Mr. Cochrane?" he asked as he took the center seat.

"I report all is go for jump. All systems nominal, all personnel at stations."

"Anything to report from overnight?" he said casually, looking down at his afternoon log. Lt. Cox had no doubt mentioned the incident on the hangar deck in his report.

"Absolutely nothing, sir," I said, keeping my eyes riveted to the streaming systems reports on the tactical screen.

"Are you sure, Commander?" Maclintock asked, pressing me. I turned and looked him in the eye.

"Dead sure, sir," I said. He flipped through the pages of the report, scanning them one more time, then handed it to an ensign who took it away. Then he turned his attention to the tactical stream.

"Carry on then, Mr. Cochrane," he said.

"Aye, sir!" I snapped, then stepped forward and yelled down at Layton when his nav stream dipped below minimums. Maclintock called me back to join him and Dobrina.

"Incidentally, good job down on B today Mr. Cochrane," he said as we huddled around the captain's chair.

"Thank you, sir," I replied. Dobrina stiffened at the praise sent my way. Maclintock didn't fail to notice.

"Commander Kierkopf, even though I placed you in charge of the mission to activate the cannon and the jump gate, I want you to know that my decision to withdraw you was strictly by the book. You're the higher-ranking officer and thus less expendable. It was a simple decision."

"Yes, sir," she responded, clearly not happy at being left out.

"I'll make the same decision in the future," he continued, "so I think it best if you look at Lieutenant Commander Cochrane as an extension of yourself on these types of missions. An extension that is expendable, at least more so than you are. Are we clear?"

"Yes, sir," she said again. Maclintock looked to me.

"Aye, sir," I said.

"Good," the captain said. "Now get on the horn to your friend, Mr. Cochrane. This ship needs its Historian on the bridge to make the jump."

"Aye, sir," I said again, then went to the com and made the call.

Serosian arrived on the bridge at 1430. Maclintock gave the order to spool the Hoaglands at 1445 as we closed on the jump gate.

"Status of the Hoaglands?" called out Maclintock.

"Spooling, warm, and ready," I replied so all the bridge could hear.

"Gravimetric shielding?"

"One hundred percent, sir!" called Dobrina.

"Personnel status?"

"All stations report green, Captain," I said.

"Astrogation?" I nodded down to Layton on the second tier, a silent acknowledgment that he could report his own status.

"Plotted and locked, sir," he said. "On course to the jump gate event horizon in seven minutes."

Maclintock turned to *Starbound*'s Historian. "Mr. Serosian?"

"My board is all green, Captain," he said in his deep and confident voice. Then he caught my eye and winked at me.

The next few minutes involved the swapping of instructions and preparation for the final traverse of the jump gate membrane. When this was complete, Maclintock leaned forward in his chair.

"Mr. Cochrane, you've been through one of these fields before. I want you to get on the intraship com and explain it to the crew, such as you can," he ordered. I acknowledged his order and stepped up to the com at his station, opening the channel that would allow me to address the entire ship.

"This is Lieutenant Commander Peter Cochrane, reporting from the bridge. The captain has instructed me to inform you what you might expect in the next few minutes, so I will do my best to describe the experience," I said.

"When we pass through the membrane at the jump gate, you are likely to experience an unpleasant sensation, almost like you're drowning. Don't let this panic you. It passes in an instant, almost as fast as it comes on. When we come back out into normal space you may feel strange and disassociated from yourself, almost as if you are in a new body, but let me assure you this is not the case," I said.

"Once we get through the event the best course of action will be for you to resume your duties immediately and report your station status. By the time you finish these tasks, any unpleasant feelings will surely have passed," I lied. They'd probably all puke, but it was my duty to reassure them. I signed off then.

"Are we ready, XO?" asked Maclintock, apparently satisfied at my performance.

"I say yes, sir," Dobrina replied. Maclintock opened the intraship com himself then.

"Stations!" called out Maclintock. "Prepare for jump! I say again, all hands prepare for jump in two minutes." Layton switched the main display from tactical for forward view as we closed on the membrane ring. It was illuminated with energy and pulsed every few seconds as we approached.

"Shut down the impellers, Mr. Layton. Forward momentum only," said the captain.

"Impellers off, sir," called out Layton from his station at the thirty-second mark in our count. This time there would be no jump key. Layton would take an active Union Navy vessel through the membrane and into unknown space by himself. I felt a knot in my stomach tighten with anxiety.

"Take us in, Lieutenant," ordered Maclintock. I held my breath.

Ten seconds later I was drowning in black.

I fought the desire to vomit again. I'd had enough of that for one day in the control room, thank you very much. But this traverse was unlike any other, and quite different from what I had told the crew to expect. I felt like I was carrying a rock in my belly and I huddled over my longscope display, head down. With each breath the effect seemed to wear off a bit and I felt more and more normal.

"Tactical situation, Mr. Cochrane!" called Maclintock. I looked down at my plasma display.

"All clear, sir," I said. I could hear the rough edge to my voice.

"What's our status, Historian?" he asked Serosian.

"We appear to have jumped into stable jump space, Captain.

We're at station keeping, no forward momentum carried over from the jump. The area of jump space we're in is tiny and highly irregular in shape compared to a normal jump point. I would say this jump point was literally *carved* right out of normal space by some artificial means. If we weren't right on top of it I doubt our instruments could even find it," Serosian said.

"Helm, can we retrace our steps back here if we need to exit in a hurry?" Maclintock asked Layton.

"My confidence is high in that, sir," said *Starbound*'s helmsman. Maclintock stepped up to the rail and leaned over to Layton's station.

"I don't need your confidence, Lieutenant, I need your certainty," he said directly. "We've just jumped into unknown space which could contain numerous enemies. I need to know, can we navigate our way back to this jump space? Yes or no?" Layton looked to me and then back to Maclintock.

"We can, sir," he finally said.

"Good," replied the captain. He returned to his seat and then addressed me directly.

"Longscope scans if you please, Mr. Cochrane," he said.

"Activating the longscope, sir," I replied, then took up my station. The familiar voice of Serosian filled my ear com.

"This is very odd," he said. "There is no hyperdimensional resonance wave . . . that's not possible, unless . . ." he trailed off. I waited several moments before speaking, growing more anxious with each passing second.

"Unless what?" I finally asked in a hushed tone, placing my head farther under the hood of the 'scope to avoid being overheard.

"Unless *Impulse* is not generating any hyperdimensional energy at all," he said, only loud enough for me to hear. "She should have left some sort of trace signature, unless her HD power core has been removed."

"Removed? I didn't think that was possible," I said, trying to cover my growing uneasiness.

"It's not, Peter," replied Serosian, "Not by any member of a Light-ship crew," then he paused. "Except the Historian."

"Tralfane," I said. The line was quiet for a few seconds.

"Begin spectral scans on this vector," he finally said, feeding me display coordinates. "We've got to find that ship."

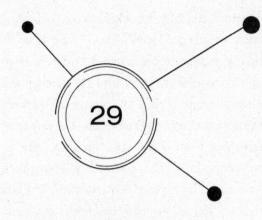

The Search

An hour later our search had proved fruitless. No disaster beacon. No radio signal or IFF transponder. No residual hyperdimensional signature. Nothing.

Maclintock called the staff into the Command Briefing room. I left Layton in charge of the search and joined Dobrina, Colonel Babayan, Serosian, and Maclintock. Dobrina, Babayan, and I sat around one end of the table while Maclintock occupied the other. Serosian, as always, placed himself in the middle.

"So what you're saying," said Maclintock, collecting his thoughts, "is that *Impulse* has gone dark in a very significant way. If we're to find her, it will be by pure luck."

"I don't believe in luck," retorted Serosian, more pointedly than I had ever heard him sound before. "And neither does the Church. It's true that there is no hyperdimensional resonance signature. If we assume that we've jumped to the same star system as Impulse, then that leaves us with one of two possibilities: either *Impulse* has been destroyed so completely, down to the molecular level in fact, that she has virtually disintegrated, or her hyperdimensional drive has been removed."

"Removed?" said Maclintock, his voice revealing his alarm at this potential turn of events. "From what you've told me of the HD drive it's an unlimited power source. No one outside the Historian community has the ability to disengage it, and the energy source itself is self-perpetuating. Anyone trying to 'remove' it without the proper tools would be exposing themselves to what—the power of a sun?"

"Much more than that," said Serosian. "The power of an entire dimension, potentially. That's why I believe the hyperdimensional drive was removed by a qualified Historian. Tralfane, to be exact."

Maclintock looked around the table, then back to Serosian.

"So let's get answers to the simple questions first," he started. "Where are we?"

Serosian folded his hands in front of him, thumbs twitching together.

"I've analyzed the local stars, done a calibration to the galactic core, run our position through a series of complex algorithms. I'll spare you the details, but there can be no doubt. *Starbound* is in the Altos system," he said.

"Altos is the legendary home system of the Sri," said Dobrina. "Do you think they're behind this?"

Serosian shook his head. "It's impossible to know. There are fourteen major planets in this system. But only Altos, which was planet two, and a moon of planet six were habitable in the First Empire days. And even in that time Altos was a very secretive world."

"Didn't the Church bombard Altos during the Secession Wars?" asked Colonel Babayan.

"I thought that was a myth," said Dobrina. Serosian shook his head.

"It's no myth. It's not something the Church is proud of today, but one of the inciting incidents in the First Secession War was our bombardment of Altos with multiple atomic weapons," he said.

"Why?" asked Maclintock. Serosian shifted in his chair at this. It was clear from his manner that he was reluctant to discuss it. He spoke anyway.

"The Sri are an order with no spiritual beliefs. They were dedicated to the pure pursuit of science and the exploitation of the material universe. This put them at odds with Church hierarchy. It was an uneasy truce held together by the empire, which had interest in both sides being in opposition to each other. The Sri were masters of technology. The Church saw themselves as the moral regulators of the excesses of that technology. When the Sri began to work actively toward an evolution of man, a conscious blending of man and machine through nanotechnology, the Church believed it had crossed a moral line from man's domain into God's domain. When Emperor Vilius IV publically declared himself to be a user of the Sri implants, it placed the Church in an untenable position."

"Vilius was declared a 'non-human' by the Church," said Dobrina. Serosian nodded.

"Exactly. What had been a deteriorating situation with an empire-wide economic and political crisis suddenly became a religious one as well," he said.

"The perfect cauldron for war," said Maclintock.

"And they fought for half a century," added Dobrina.

"But what about the bombardment of Altos?" I asked. This was information I had never before heard from my mentor.

"The Church ordered it when it became apparent that the empire would win the conflict, using Sri technology. You got a taste of that technology today, Peter. The merging of a man's mind with a machine. We believe that path was also the downfall of the Founder civilization. For the Church, at that time of the war, they believed the attack was justified," Serosian said.

"Extermination of an entire world," stated Dobrina, her distaste obvious.

"I cannot justify the actions of the past, Commander," said Serosian. "The fact remains that we are in the Altos system. No one knows whether the Sri survived the war or not. All we know is that a Historian apparently loyal to forces of the former empire or the Sri themselves has hijacked a Lightship and brought it here. Our presence in this system must now undoubtedly be having the same effect on those forces as kicking a hornet's nest on a summer day. We need to be prepared for whatever comes next."

"And thank the Church of the Latter Days for rolling out the welcome mat," said Dobrina.

"All of that was two centuries ago, Commander," cut in Maclintock. "Our job today is to rescue *Impulse*." He turned to Serosian. "What's our location relative to the major planets? Where do you recommend we concentrate our search efforts?" he asked.

"Currently we are in the cloud rim of the Altos system, far away from even the most distant of the major planets, so we've little chance to explore the system from here. I suggest that we begin our search in a standard sweep pattern, perhaps using the shuttles to broaden our range," said Serosian.

"That's not much to go on," said Dobrina. Serosian turned to her.

"Well, unless Tralfane, or the Sri, or the remnants of the old empire have the temerity to come and find us, Commander, it's the only real option we have right now," he said.

At that moment my earpiece com buzzed in. It was Layton. I linked him into the room line so we all could hear his report.

"Sir, we've discovered an object in the area, a ship, we think," he said.

"Is it *Impulse*?" Maclintock asked. The line stayed silent for a second.

"I would say no, sir. The object we're tracking is ten times the size of a Lightship, sir. And one other thing . . ."

Maclintock raised an eyebrow as Layton's pause grew longer.

"Yes, Lieutenant?" he prompted.

"It . . . it appears to be drifting, sir," said Layton. Maclintock shot from his seat.

"Hold stations, Lieutenant," he said, making for the door.

"We're on our way."

We rushed onto the bridge, *Starbound*'s main plasma display filled by the image of a dark, pyramid-shaped hulk floating in space. Each of the four base points of the pyramid held a pillar, most likely coil cannon arrays that looked to be about as big as *Starbound* herself. In other words, it dwarfed us.

"Analysis, Mr. Serosian," said the captain, taking his seat. I went quickly to my longscope station and started my scanning protocol.

"Very low level of energy detected, Captain, almost equal to background radiation from the Altos star. I would say for all practical purposes this is a derelict, probably abandoned for several centuries," Serosian said. My scans told a different story. I stuck my head out from under the longscope hood.

"With due respect, Captain, I'm getting something on the bioscanner," I said. I looked to Serosian. His face was impassive, showing no emotion at my report one way or the other. I switched the main plasma to a display showing the biosigns. They were faint, but they were there.

"Can you explain that, Historian?" asked Maclintock. From his tone I could tell he was annoyed that his 'scopeman had delivered information he had expected to get from his Historian.

Serosian didn't miss a beat. "With their demonstrated ability to disguise energy signatures behind stealth fields I suggest we proceed with extreme caution. This could be a lure to get our troops over to the dreadnought," he said. "They've already taken one Lightship from the Union Navy. Capturing or destroying a second would certainly advance their agenda, whatever that might be." The captain turned at this.

"So you've identified the vessel as an Imperial dreadnought?" Maclintock said.

"Given its size, displacement, and apparent weaponry, what else could it be?" Serosian said. "Though stories of their use at the end of the war to destroy entire planets was part of the propaganda designed to intimidate enemies into quick surrender, this vessel appears to fit the description rather accurately."

"I'd like to take a marine team over, Captain," said Dobrina. "The biosigns we're detecting could be anything, including the crew of *Impulse*. If so, we have a duty to try and rescue them. And before you object to having your two most senior officers off the ship at the same time again, I would remind you that myself and Lieutenant Commander Cochrane are the only officers aboard with experience dealing with Imperial technology."

"I won't argue with your logic, Commander, just your wisdom," said Maclintock. Colonel Babayan stepped up then.

"I insist on going as well, sir," she said. "A mix of thirty marines in a single shuttle should be sufficient to determine the conditions aboard."

"I disagree," I said, crossing my arms firmly. "We came here with sixty marines and two heavy shuttles for a reason. This dreadnought is that reason. I say we go over in full force or we don't go at all. And I insist that we go, sir," I said the last directly to the captain.

Maclintock turned to Dobrina, his decision made. "Request denied, Commander. I need my XO here on the bridge, commanding the teams. We'll go in full force, both shuttles, all weapons. Mr. Cochrane will lead the Quantar marines in one shuttle, Colonel Babayan will lead the second shuttle with the Carinthians." Babayan's hands went to her hips at this and anger burned in her eyes.

"We've worked hard to get these detachments integrated! Why are you splitting us up now?" she asked Maclintock.

"Colonel, this is a critical operation. I don't want someone to mess up an assignment because of language differences or a cultural misunderstanding. Let's just keep to our own, and do our jobs." The firm set of the colonel's jaw indicated she didn't agree, but she didn't make any further protest.

Dobrina fumed in silence as Maclintock turned to Serosian.

"Thoughts?" The Historian shook his head.

"Nothing more than I've already stated. Proceed with extreme caution. I'll continue scanning for *Impulse* on the longscope," he said, then turned to me. "Keep your personal channel open, Peter. Things may end up moving much faster than we expect."

"I'll keep that in mind," I replied.

We were fully loaded and both shuttles were clear of the landing bay when Colonel Babayan's signal buzzed in my ear. I turned control of the shuttle over to Marker to take her call.

"I hate to admit it," she said over the com, "but the captain may have been right. My marines have that look about them, no one doubts the man sitting next to them. It's something we haven't achieved with a mixed crew yet."

"I agree. Perhaps now isn't the time for diversity just for diversity's sake," I said.

"One more thing, Cochrane," she said. "I had my doubts about you when you first came aboard. But since the brawl, well, I just wanted to say I appreciate your talents more now."

"Thank you," I replied. I was uncomfortable taking praise from a junior officer, especially one with so much more real space experience than I had.

"What's your plan?" she said, jumping quickly to the subject at hand.

"It's very direct," I said. "Serosian has identified a landing bay. We take the shuttles in; we land and deploy. There are sporadic bio-signs aboard, and we'll be landing fairly close to them. We will recon-noiter to those biosigns, identify them, then determine what our next course of action will be, always with an eye on our egress."

I looked up at the looming hulk of the dreadnought on our plasma, lit up now by our searchlights. It was as imposing as could be. The hull was pitted and marred, with streaks of seared metal, indicat-ing she'd been in a battle, though from all indications it could have been centuries ago. The stuff of myth and legend.

"Do you think *Impulse* did this?" asked Babayan, her voice break-ing up with static. It was almost as if she read my mind. I shook my head, then realized she couldn't see me and spoke up.

"I doubt it. Those battle scars look like they've been there for a long time," I said. I checked my watch. "Five minutes to the landing bay, Colonel. Get your men ready."

"Aye, sir," came the reply. Then I switched her off. Dobrina called in moments later.

"Remember, Peter," she said, "If these are our compatriots from *Impulse*, save as many as you can."

"And if they aren't?" I asked. There was a pause on her end of the line.

"Then destroy as many as you can," she finally said.

"Understood," I replied. Then I cut the channel. The massive landing bay of the dreadnought loomed over the shuttle as we made our final approach.

"And God help us."

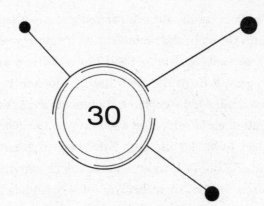

Aboard the Dreadnought

The landing bay of the dreadnought was empty and huge compared to the one on *Starbound*. Our shuttles seemed like tiny toys parked low and heavy on the metal decking. We hadn't needed to open the bay doors ourselves, they'd been blown off in a battle untold decades ago.

The QRN marines stormed out of the shuttle and onto the deck, looking for cover but finding none, so they went to their bellies instead. Marker and I charged our coil rifles and came out last. I hit the deck with a thud that was even stronger than the one you'd get with gravity-activated boots. It was clear I'd landed on a deck that maintained a full G. I looked around at the men sprawled out on the deck, then tapped my wrist display. My grav boots hadn't activated. They were designed to do so automatically in a near-zero- or zero-G environment.

"This ship has artificial gravity," I said from my defensive crouch. "There was no indication of that coming in. What do you make of it, Colonel?" Babayan stepped freely about the deck, then came up to me, just she and I and Marker on the command channel.

"There's certainly no central generator creating a gravity wave throughout the ship, and no indication from my readings of an artificial well emanating from a focal point. I'd say we're dealing with something built in to the deck itself." I looked to her and Marker through our shielded faceplates, then made a decision.

"Gentlemen," I said, after switching to the general marine band. "We appear to be dealing with a deck-based gravity system. Disengage your grav boots. If we encounter a deck with no artificial gravity be prepared to turn them back on at a moment's notice. Now let's clear this deck! Advance!" Then I turned to my colleagues, switching back to the command band.

"Let's hope there's no more surprises," I said as we departed the landing bay. I tried to report back to Dobrina, but the signal was blocked.

The passageway outside the landing deck split in two directions, curving away from us. I took out my hand scanner and swept the deck in front of us. "These two passages connect again about two hundred meters forward," I said. I linked my scanner to Babayan and Marker so they could see the same display and then gave out orders.

"Colonel Babayan, take your unit to the right," I said via the command channel. "Sergeant Marker, we'll go left. We'll converge at the intersection. Be cautious, but ignore any reconnoitering of closed-off areas. We're only interested in the biosigns. Clear?"

"Clear, sir," chimed in both marines, and we started down the passageway.

The halls were wide enough for five men to walk side by side, but we maintained a textbook single-file advance formation, staying close to the inside wall and then crossing to the outside every ten yards or so. In this way we were able to rapidly advance down the curved hallway with a minimum of our unit exposed to potential enemy fire.

Marker led, giving commands on an open channel. I took up the rear with only two men behind me, listening in to the advance and

chatter but keeping my own mic linked only to the command channel. I'd lost contact with Babayan seconds after we passed out of visual range. It was tempting to use a longwave signal, but I decided
discretion was still the order of the day, and I was saving that com for
emergency communication with *Starbound*.

Five minutes later, Marker indicated over the channel that he
had the colonel's team in sight. Another two and we were all gathered
at what appeared to be a large metal freight lifter. I scanned for biosigns.

"They're above us," I said, holstering the scanner. "This decking
does an effective job of blocking anything that would give us a defin-
itive ID, but I can still tell direction and distance with some certainty.
Colonel Babayan and I will go up, five men from each team with us.
Sergeant Marker and the rest of you, begin searching the rooms between here and the hangar deck. I want to make sure we have a clear
path back to our shuttles in the event of an incident."

"What kind of 'incident' are you expecting?" asked Marker. He
seemed annoyed at being left out of the party. "I should be there."

I shook my head no. "I want you here commanding this unit,
backing me up. You're damn good at covering my ass and I'd like to
keep it that way."

"But—"

"No buts! Colonel Babayan will pick a man to leave in charge of
her unit and then I want you to get to it. I don't intend to dawdle up
there, just get in, find our biosign, and get out. Clear?" Even through
the glass of his EVA suit I could see his frustration from his taut jaw-
line, but he was too good a marine to protest.

"Clear, sir!" he said. Then he started yelling orders to his men
while Babayan picked her five and left another sergeant in charge of
the reconnoiter.

"Let's go!" I said as our team of twelve gathered in front of the
lifter doors.

"Um . . ." started Babayan, "how do we open it?"

"Good question." I found an electronic keypad, but it was long burned out.

"There should be a manual override close by," I said, walking around to the side of the door and finding a round metal hand crank. I tried it and it held fast. "Give me a hand!" I motioned to two of the more burly marines, one Carinthian and one Quantar. The three of us stacked our gloved hands and slowly turned the crank until the doors gave way with a gush of stale air escaping from the lock. We turned it another full cycle again and it slid open quicker than I expected.

"Hydraulics," said Babayan. "Still working, too. Impressive."

"We can compliment their engineers later," I said, stepping tentatively onto the lifter deck. The ceiling above was open except for a flange a good twenty feet up just wide enough for a man to walk on.

"Gangway," said the colonel.

"Um," I said, thinking. I shined my LED up the open shaft. In the distance, a lifter hung crosswise across torn metal, suspended in the shaft by luck when it had been displaced, presumably during a battle. "Well, we're not getting up that way," I said. Babayan flashed her light to the back wall.

"Take the stairs?" she suggested. The stairs were in fact a ladder bolted to the wall that went up to the gangway.

"The stairs it is," I said. Two marines led the way and then I followed Babayan up. Once we got the detachment up to the next deck I turned my bioscanner back on.

We were looking down a broad, straight hallway with only a few rooms on either side of the wall. "I make it about a hundred yards to the biosign," I said. "Stagger left formation. Let's go."

A QRN marine led the way down the left side of the hallway, a Carinthian five yards back on the right wall. I came second on the left and then Babayan came up on the right. We progressed this way slowly, examining open bays that were essentially empty except for scattered equipment and empty storage racks. This was clearly a staging area for the hangar deck.

Once we were about halfway to the biosign I took another reading, then switched on the command channel to Babayan.

"There's no way this biosign is the crew from *Impulse*. At most it's one person, or a collection of small creatures."

"Or a big box of nanovirus?" said Babayan. I shook my head.

"All our nanoscans are clear. I'm picking up body temp, heart rate, what appears to be subdued brain function. Someone's either unconscious or very dumb." Babayan snorted in my ear.

"Do you use humor to get through tense situations?" she asked. I thought about the question.

"I suppose I do," I admitted.

"Well then," she said, "let's go find our moron."

We stopped in front of a closed door to an office or utility room of some kind. I turned my LED to the floor.

"Look," I said, "the dust layer has been disturbed, and recently. Looks like two sets of tracks," I shone my light further down the hall. "They came from in front of us, then went back the way they came."

"Which means whatever is in there was left for us to find," said Babayan. "What if it's a trap?"

"We came here to find survivors of *Impulse*," I said. "Our most likely candidate is just beyond that door. Do you suggest we don't go in?" She shook her head.

"I suggest we follow protocols and let two of the grunts take the risks."

I sighed in frustration, but asked for volunteers and got my two in short order. We backed off down the hall and crouched in defensive positions.

"Should we use our coil rifles, sir?" asked one of the grunts, the Carinthian one, with a heavy accent. I shook my head.

"Try the doorknob first," I suggested. He did, and it opened. They walked in without event.

"Sir!" came the private's excited voice over my com. "I think we've found a survivor! Looks to be female, sir."

In an instant I was up and bolted for the door. I swept through the doorway and into the arms of the mammoth Carinthian marine, who was holding me to keep me from floating off.

"You need to activate your boots, sir," he said. "Gravity's off in here."

I did as suggested and got myself firmly rooted to the floor again. The room was full of junk; wire bundles, discarded equipment, tools and metal storage boxes floated freely throughout the room. I pushed the junk aside as best I could.

"Where is she?" I asked.

"Up there, sir," the Carinthian pointed to a floating EVA suit near the high ceiling, about five meters up. The EVA suit could have been empty for all I could see.

"Get her down, goddamn it!" I yelled. The Carinthian marine handed his gun to the Quantar private and disengaged his boots, floating upward awkwardly and grabbing the suit by the arm. Then he got tangled in floating wires and lost his grip on her.

"Jesus!" I grabbed him by the leg and pulled him down, activating his boots on the way so that he stuck to the floor again. "Get out of my way!" I said, and pushed him aside in my impatience. I disengaged my boots, extended my toes and pushed off with just a slight feather touch, reaching up and taking the floating suit in my left hand, using my right hand against the wall to steer myself as I gently pulled her down.

I got to the floor and reactivated my grav boots, then took her out of the room and gave her to another pair of marines, stopping to look inside the helmet. It was Jenny Hogan, my Quantar astrogator from *Impulse* and Admiral Wesley's niece.

She was unconscious and still breathing, but it was sharp and shallow. Her eyes were closed and ringed with black circles, her face and lips strikingly pale. I checked her oxygen levels: forty-two minutes left out of three hours. I turned to Babayan.

"Whoever left her here hasn't been gone long. At most two hours, eighteen minutes. We have to assume they're still around. Let's get moving!"

She gave the order and we began our egress. Two marines hoisted Hogan between them. We were quickly back down on the main hangar deck level, our unit and Marker's forming up into a single squad, when Babayan turned to me.

"There's something I don't understand," she said. "Why did they leave her alive for us to find?" I looked at the colonel.

"Calling card," I said. "They want us to know what they are capable of, so they left us an officer of one of our most powerful warships." Babayan looked around.

"Let's hope that's all they left us," she said. "But where's the rest of the crew?"

Before I could answer, a streak of white coil rifle fire shot right between us, head high.

"Take cover!" I yelled, pushing Babayan down to the deck. The marines scattered and went to ground, quickly finding their bearings and returning fire. I rolled off of the colonel and looked up, drawing my coil rifle and blasting out a blaze of orange fury in return. Babayan joined my return fire a moment later. I looked back down the hall to find a dozen black-clad soldiers coming at us from behind, rifles blazing. I remembered the uniforms from my history classes, all black with a gold stripe on the helmet and shoulder epaulets.

Imperial marines.

"Break for the hangar deck!" I yelled into my com. "Get back to the shuttles!" Our units broke ranks as ordered and beat a hasty retreat from the advancing Imperials, running down the hallway. We'd rounded the last bend to the hangar deck, the doors only ten meters away, when we came under fire from the other direction.

"We're trapped!" said Babayan. "Form ranks!" she ordered. We pulled together, using what small wall space was available in the corridor as cover. The rounded curve of the inner wall provided some defensive angle, but not enough. They were going to mow us down.

"Now what?" asked Babayan. I looked at the situation—both sides of our line coming under fire, bursts of orange and white energy being exchanged. We were sitting ducks in this hallway. I scanned the walls and located a door about halfway down the corridor, directly in the enemy line of fire and farther away from the landing bay.

"Do you have an A4 charge?" I asked Babayan.

"Yes, but only for blasting bulkheads. You set it off in here and it could kill us all," she said. I watched a moment as one of the Carinthian marines fell in a hail of coil rifle fire. I stuck my hand out.

"Give it to me," I demanded. She did as ordered and I set the charge for a three-second delay. Another marine fell, this time Quantar. I got on the command channel. "Marker, I need suppressing fire to your rear for five seconds. After that, everyone hit the ground and cover. I'm going to drop an A4 charge. On my mark," I said, then switched back to Babayan. "When the charge goes off you'll have to collect your troops and get into that room. Then I want a dozen compression grenades in the hallway. And don't stop to pick up any wounded, including me. If we survive the A4 blast and the compression grenades don't kill us, it should buy us enough time to get back to our shuttles."

"Unless we're all unconscious too! That room won't protect us much if the door's blown off," she said.

"It will have to do," I replied as I hefted the A4 charge and switched back to Marker's channel. "When this goes I want your men in that room in a second flat, Sergeant," I said.

"Got it," came back Marker's stressed voice. I hesitated only a second.

"Go!" I said. The air filled with a hail of orange coil rifle fire as I broke down the hallway toward the door. A line of white return fire went past my helmet close enough for me to feel the searing heat through my visor. I ducked and dipped, then tucked into a roll and came up in front of the door, snapping on the magnetized charge and pressing the fire button in the same motion. I bolted back toward my original position taking one step . . . two . . . three . . .

The detonation sent me flying back toward Colonel Babayan and her marines. I spread-eagled in the air as I bounced off the wall and skidded several feet before landing hard. My head was buzzing as I felt someone grab me by my chest plate and drag me down the hallway. There was a rush of blurred activity, bodies streaming into the room I had just blasted open, then I was tossed down on a pile of marines as the second blast from the concussion grenades shook the walls.

I must have blacked out as the next sensation I had was of being dragged down the hallway by two marines, one in Quantar blue and the other in Carinthian green. I looked ahead as we made for the landing deck doorway. There was a firefight going on inside the landing bay, but the orange glow of our weapons was far exceeding that of the white of the Imperial marines' returning fire. I shook free of my escorts and started to walk on my own, wobbly though I was. Down the hallway, a couple dozen Imperial marines lay prone on the deck, out cold. For how long was the question. I came up next to Babayan at the entrance to the landing deck and stuck my head inside. Our marines were just finishing mopping up the Imperials.

"They didn't put up much of a fight," Colonel Babayan said, "given their rather legendary reputation. Do we finish them off?"

"No," I said, looking at the deck strewn with bodies. "We get the hell out of here." I ordered a full retreat to the shuttles. As we were filing back double-time Colonel Babayan stopped beside one of the dead Imperial marine's bodies. I watched as she knelt down over him.

"Colonel, we don't have time for this."

"Wait!" she said. I went over to her as the last of our marines streamed by me with Jenny Hogan in tow. Marker stood by the open hatch of the shuttle, impatiently holding his rifle.

"Almost out of time, sir!" he called. I bent down over Babayan and the dead Imperial marine. She pulled back his uniform, which had already been ripped open by coil rifle fire, and pointed to a tattoo on his chest. It was over his heart and still visible even though the rest of his body was badly burned.

"This tattoo, it's the double eagle," she said.

"The what?" I asked, not sure what she meant. She looked shocked. I waited for a second to give her time.

"The double eagle," she repeated. "Of Carinthia. Cochrane, this man is from *Impulse*."

"What?" I said. "That can't be." I looked down at his face. It wasn't familiar, still . . .

"Believe me, I know this symbol. Half the navy gets it tattooed on their chest when they enlist, over their heart, right here." She pointed again, then she stood up, clenching her fists. "Now we know what happened to the crew of *Impulse*."

I looked around the bay. A half-dozen dead men in Imperial marine uniforms.

"But what could make them change allegiance?" I said. She looked straight at me with those green eyes, now filled with rage.

"Nanotechnology. You experienced it yourself. The machine took you over, for a time. It must have been something similar here. No Carinthian would turn on his own like that, not willingly," she said.

"Commander . . ." came Marker's urgent voice in my ear.

"C'mon," I said, taking Babayan by the arm. "We've got to go, *now*." She gripped her rifle tightly, unmoving, finger poised over the trigger. "Lena, we can't fight whoever did this here. We have to do it from *Starbound*. Now we've got to *go*. That's an order," I said. She relinquished her anger then and I rushed her back to the shuttle and inside, then ordered us up off the deck. A few straggling Imperial marines started firing at us as we pulled away, but it was too scattered and too distant to hurt us.

"Do we return fire?" came Marker's voice over my com as I held onto Babayan in the personnel bay.

"Negative," I responded. "Just get us home."

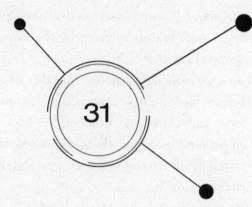

31

"Get me in touch with Maclintock," I ordered as I entered the shuttle's command deck.

"He's already on," Marker said. I nodded and activated my com, switching to the navy band.

"Captain, we have three dead and fifteen wounded here, but we recovered Jenny Hogan from *Impulse*. No other survivors. Colonel Babayan," I hesitated here, "Colonel Babayan believes the troops in Imperial uniforms that we were fighting were in fact the missing crew of *Impulse*, acting under some form of compulsion from Imperial nanotech. Do you read me, *Starbound*?"

"Affirmative," said Maclintock. "Put Colonel Babayan on with Commander Kierkopf. I have another assignment for you." I called over to Babayan and then switched to back the main com channel.

"Here, sir," I said. To my surprise the voice on the other end of the line was that of Serosian.

"Peter, you need to get back here as soon as possible," he said.

"We're on our way now. What's up?"

"We've located *Impulse*, and I need you onboard the yacht with me," he said.

"The yacht? Why?"

"Because we're going there," he said. "To *Impulse*. And we don't have time to waste. The dreadnought, that *thing*, is starting to move."

I switched the main shuttle display from tactical to a reverse angle. Sure enough, the dreadnought was lighting up, charging weapons, and starting to move slowly toward us, like a colossus trying to move in heavy seas.

I tried to swallow, and felt nothing but a thick lump of bile forming in my throat.

Thirteen minutes later the shuttle's hold was empty, the marines were offloaded, Jenny Hogan was on her way to the med deck, and I was back in space, the yacht pushing full bore for the abandoned *Impulse*.

"How did you locate her?" I asked Serosian. His reply was swift and clear.

"It's not important," he said from the control console. "I'll introduce you to the technology later. Right now I need you to focus, Peter. I need you to access the yacht's power core and prepare to release her HD crystal."

I was confused. "Now? Why?"

"You'll need it when you get to *Impulse*," he said.

"For what?"

"To refire her engines." I stopped.

"What?"

"I convinced Maclintock that I could get *Impulse* back in the fight. You're going to have to take the HD drive from this yacht and load it into *Impulse* to replace the one Tralfane destroyed. We'll make it back to *Starbound* on impellers," he said.

"Will it have enough power to run *Impulse*?" I asked. He nodded.

"It should, if we can survive long enough to install it. Now go." He nodded to the inner chambers of the yacht. I went in as he started the process of shutting down the HD crystal. After a few seconds, the doors to the inner tabernacle opened and the crystal began floating toward me with an appearance of intent that made me uncomfortable.

"What's our status?" I asked from the chamber over my EVA suit com. The line stayed silent for a moment.

"The dreadnought is closing on *Starbound*," he finally said. "Maclintock has it under control, for now. The good news is that it's not paying any attention to us."

"That sounds like we're getting lucky," I said.

"We're not," he said. "That dreadnought is on automated attack, most likely powered by the hyperdimensional drive stolen from *Impulse's* yacht by Tralfane. It has nearly as much power as *Starbound* has, with superior delivery systems. That's why it's critical—"

A wave of crackling energy came across the channel as interference. It was so loud I scrambled to cut off the signal, but it still left my ears ringing. I gathered in the HD drive and placed it in a protective case that Serosian had given me, then went back to the main console.

In the rearview display *Starbound* was being menaced by the dreadnought. White fire rained down on her in a blizzard of cannonade from the four massive coil cannons of the dreadnought.

"We've got to get over there," I said to Serosian. He looked at me, his face grim, but said nothing.

Impulse was a complete wreck, scarred and burned all along her main hull with large holes blasted in her midships. The conning tower and the bridge where I had spent so much time on my first assignment were gone. She was dark and spinning in empty space, a slow death ballet that both frightened and saddened me. She shouldn't have to go down this way, no ship should.

Serosian matched the yacht to *Impulse*'s spin and then came alongside her, aligning the airlock to one of her aft cargo docks. It had a small utility port that looked undamaged. It seemed to be the most likely place where I could get in and get to the galleria, the ship's central lifeline. From there I could access the forward engineering room and hopefully install the HD drive.

"You'll have to make it back out the way you come in. Once you fire her up you'll have to activate an automated defense protocol and point her toward the dreadnought. The tactical computer should do the rest," Serosian said in my ear as I stood in the yacht's airlock. "And we'd best use the longwave channel for communication from here on out."

"Acknowledged," I said, switching to the longwave channel. I was ready and emptied the airlock from the inside. The last time I had stood in a similar place I'd nearly killed myself by misfiring the cone jets. This time I strapped them on tightly, determined to get it right. I would have to, there was no time for a tether. I would have to navigate open space on my own.

I keyed in the code sequence and the outer hatch slid open. There was a tug as the airlock adjusted to the full vacuum of space. I held on to the handrails and then gently pushed myself to the edge of the doorway. I secured the HD crystal case to my suit, then looked across the abyss. *Impulse* floated some five hundred meters away from me, the sealed utility port door my only focus. I pushed away and fired the jets, just a small pulse to gently increase my speed. My EVA suit display gave me time and distance to my target, even recommended jet pulse timing and power settings. But I had to ignore them. They were designed for safety first, and safety was a secondary consideration. Time was something I simply didn't have enough of.

A flare of orange and white light flashed off the singed alabaster hull of *Impulse* as I floated closer. It was the glare from the death struggle going on behind me. I could only hope that *Starbound* was a better match for the dreadnought than *Impulse* apparently had been.

I was halfway now, breathing so heavily in my suit that the EVA controls were having trouble keeping my faceplate clear of the fog of my own breath. The crossing was taking too much time.

I recalculated time and distance, then adjusted the jet burst to cut the remaining crossing time in half. The suit warned me against such a course, but I shut the alarm off. My comrades were out there fighting for their lives, and I was determined to do something to help them.

I reset the jets for a six second burn, then fired them without hesitation. I accelerated toward *Impulse*, cutting the distance in half again in seconds. But then I realized I was off course. I was going to miss the utility port and splatter against the hull, or maybe just skid right along it until a piece of broken hull metal cut me into pieces. I only had one chance.

I pulled out my coil pistol and aimed it at the cargo door, now looming larger and larger with every passing second. I primed the pistol and fired it. The door exploded from within, releasing gas and air and debris into space, right at me. I rolled into a ball as a huge section of the door whipped past me. Small pieces of the door bounced off of my faceplate as I drove on, an out-of-control missile heading for an open gash in *Impulse*'s side. I reached out with my hand, desperately grabbing for a dangling cargo line. I caught it, but my forward momentum whipped me around through open hole in *Impulse* like a kite in the wind. It felt like my arm was going to come out of the socket, but I held on, grabbing at the line with both hands and pulling myself under control, finally killing my momentum against the padded cargo bay walls and then descending to the floor. I held on for dear life to a floor hook, then settled on to the deck.

After a few seconds to rub my shoulder and catch my breath, I floated slowly toward the doorway that would lead me out into the main decks, my heart pounding in my chest.

"Jesus Christ!" I said to myself. "What a ride!"

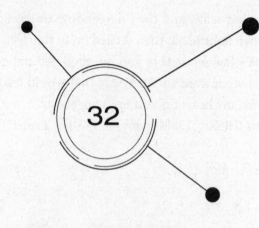

The Battle

I ran through the shattered main gallery of *Impulse* as fast as I could with my grav boots on, dodging fallen ceiling plaster and murals that had come undone from the walls. There was debris everywhere, but no bodies. I was making for the forward engineering room, where the main controls for Impulse's HD drive were.

I had been out of touch with Serosian for more than ten minutes, but in that time I'd picked up enough random com chatter to determine that the dreadnought was slowly beating down *Starbound*'s defenses, forcing her into a more and more precarious position with each passing minute, blocking her retreat to the artificial jump point. One thing was clear—for *Starbound* to make it out of Altos space, it was going to have to defeat the dreadnought.

I passed out of the gallery and into officer country, the dark corridor illuminated only by my helmet LED. I passed by the Historian's chambers that had been occupied by Tralfane when I was aboard. The doors had coil rifle burns on them, as did all the surrounding walls. I was sure the yacht, and Tralfane, were gone.

I made it to the control room, and pulled myself through the broken doorway. There was no sign of power anywhere on board. My grav boots made me cling to the floor more than I wanted, but I made my way across the room and to the main HD drive console. It was a mess, but the main panel, identical to the one in the Historian's quarters, was still intact.

I tried to raise Serosian on my com. It took four minutes before I got through.

". . . no time . . ." followed by crackles and waves of static was all that came through. Then suddenly the signal surged and I had to reduce the volume in my ear again.

"Peter! Can you hear me?" came the Historian's frantic voice.

"Yes, I can," I responded. The signal was almost crystal clear.

"I've diverted power from the defenses—" he was cut off by static again, then continued. ". . . got the crystal?" he finished.

"I've got it. I'm in the drive master control room," I yelled.

"Place the crystal—" static again, ". . . display panel. Do you understand?" I wasn't sure if I did, but I decided I had to act. I pulled the case out and removed the HD drive crystal, then placed it on the main console. The panel material began to swirl around the crystal and the panel began to light up with sickly yellows, oranges, and grays. I linked my com into the console to boost my signal and called out using *Impulse*'s main com system.

"Serosian! I'm here! I've got the console working, do you read me?" I called.

"Prepare to receive the code," he said.

"What code?"

"Peter, listen to me. I'm going to send you a key code. You'll have to call up the panel keyboard and enter it in exactly the order I send it. Do you understand?"

"I do. But what will happen when I enter the code?"

"If it works, we'll have access to the console and all of *Impulse*'s systems, at least the ones that still work," Serosian said.

"And if it doesn't work? If Tralfane has sabotaged the panel?" I asked. But I got no further response or explanation, only static.

The symbols started coming through to me on my EVA suit display. They were geometric in some way, and they appeared right to left. I swept my hand across the panel and a keyboard appeared with two rows of seven empty blocks each above the key display. I carefully entered the symbols in order from a menu, and each time I did a corresponding Imperial letter appeared on the panel, unscrambled, right to left:

VZVKZSK

VMBVZVK

I completed the string, then entered the code. The panel glowed orange and then went to a blank, deep blue as all the characters disappeared.

The panel seemed to turn to liquid then, absorbing the HD crystal into the console. It began glowing a bright red and then suddenly all of *Impulse*'s systems were coming back online to the degree that they could, but my communication line to Serosian was cut off. I checked the service inventory; I had one coil cannon battery, no Hoagland Field, and only half power to the impellers. All of the automated attack systems were offline, permanently. I had to make a decision. I swept my hand across the panel and powered up the coil cannon and the impeller drives. With a lurch that felt like it was going to tear the ship apart, *Impulse* started forward. I pulled up the tactical display and watched as the dreadnought pursued *Starbound* relentlessly, the two ships exchanging barrages of cannon fire. But the readouts were clear: *Starbound* was losing.

"Time to change the odds," I said aloud, then set my course and slammed the impellers to max—heading straight for the dreadnought.

The Imperial beast kept growing larger in my visual plasma display as tactical showed the distance between us closing. Soon enough I would draw its fire, but that would give *Starbound* a reprieve, and perhaps a chance.

I entered coil cannon range but the power curve was marginal. The cannon had taken hits in *Impulse*'s last battle and firing it without generating major blowback was a huge risk. I needed something more.

I called to Serosian again, with no answer for several seconds before he came through on a low-frequency line. The longwave was apparently out of commission.

"What's your situation, Peter?" he asked.

"Automated attack systems are out. I've only got a single coil cannon and I probably won't even dent the hull with that, assuming I can fire it without destroying *Impulse*," I said. I hesitated before asking the next question. "You have to give me something else to use, some other weapon," I pleaded, the dreadnought looming huge in my plasma viewer.

The line stayed silent for several seconds, then Serosian's deep baritone came through, crackling with static.

"Your only other alternative," he said, speaking slowly, "is to remove the Hoagland Field keeping the singularity contained."

I wasn't sure I knew what he meant. He couldn't possibly be saying what I thought he was . . .

"Are you telling me to use the singularity in the HD drive as a weapon?" I said.

The line buzzed and cracked, then Serosian's voice came through in fractured sentences.

"Peter . . . must open the hyperdimensional channel . . ." The buzzing from the ongoing mortal struggle between *Starbound* and the dreadnought blocked out the rest of the message. I was desperate with fear.

"Serosian, please repeat! You must repeat your last message!" I called into the com. His message came through in bits and pieces.

"Opening . . . drive will open the energy . . . singularity will grow. It will reach a critical level . . . will expel everything it cannot contain, then implode . . . close the channel between . . . otherwise . . . HD realm could consume everything . . . our dimension."

I pieced it together. I had to activate the HD drive without the protection of a Hoagland Field to contain it. The singularity would grow until it ejected the hyperdimensional energy uncontrolled into our universe, then nature's desire for balance between the two realms would hopefully collapse the singularity back in on itself.

An explosion of unbelievable force followed by an implosion of unknown dimensions.

"Will it be enough?" I asked rhetorically. To my surprise he responded directly and clearly over the com. I assumed he must have boosted the longwave signal again.

"Unknown," he said. "It depends on how large the singularity grows before the implosion, and how close you get it to the dreadnought."

"Oh, I'll get close," I said, determined now to avenge the crew of *Impulse*. "Have I ever told you the story of MacEachern's Run?"

"Peter, you can't sacrifice yourself," he said. He knew the story.

"I have no intention of sacrificing myself," I said. "If I did I couldn't enjoy my revenge."

A few seconds passed by, and I feared he wouldn't help me. Then his voice came cracking over the com again, bright and clear.

"I'm sending you the code to remove the field," he said. The code came across seconds later. I called up the keypad again on the console and typed in the characters.

"Peter—" another static burst cut him off. It was useless trying to recover his signal at this point. My decision was made and my path was set. I shut down the com channel and hit the enter key.

I felt the hair on my neck stand up as the enveloping Hoagland Field deactivated. A surge of power swept through the ship as *Impulse* started drawing on the unregulated hyperdimensional energy flowing through her. I realized as I took one last scan of *Impulse*'s displays that I was standing mere inches away from an opening to another dimension. The thought sent a chill down my spine. I shuddered, then returned to my task.

I set *Impulse* on a collision course for the dreadnought and locked in its tracking. It would follow the dreadnought if the Imperial ship tried evasive maneuvers, but so far the beast still seemed fixated only on *Starbound*. I looked to the chronometer display one last time. Six minutes until impact, an unknown time to the explosion. Time to go.

"Goodbye, grand lady," I said aloud, then made for the galleria as fast as I could.

I ran through the galleria, but it wasn't fast enough. I disengaged my grav boots and jumped, spread-eagled. I flew half the length of the ship in seconds. I was never as thankful for my zero-G training at the Academy as I was right then.

I activated my boots again from my wrist display and came crashing to the floor with a thud, but managed to keep my feet. I headed quickly for a utility lifter and found the shaft empty. I disengaged my boots again and with a blast from my cone jets I dove headfirst down the shaft three full decks, kicking up my speed with another pulse halfway down. I did a midair tumble spin as the bottom of the shaft approached, swimming through the shaft opening onto the missile deck, and hit the cone jets in reverse to decelerate as I approached the floor.

I arrived at the aft missile room and reactivated my grav boots, then went to the controls. The firing key was still in the launch panel and the missile ports were all wide open. The crew of *Impulse* had fired every missile they had in their arsenal. Whatever had happened, they hadn't given up without a fight.

I wondered for a brief moment about the rest of *Impulse*'s crew as I called up the launch sequence. Perhaps they were on the dreadnought, imprisoned where we couldn't detect their life signs, or even trapped here on *Impulse*. In either case I would be killing them all in a few minutes.

I put that out of my mind because I had to and focused on the firing sequence. I had participated in test firing a missile once during my Academy training. I hoped that experience would help me now.

I set the sequencer to auto with a twenty-second delay, then placed myself in the launch tray as it queued up, deactivating my grav boots again. I looked at my watch. Three minutes to impact with the dreadnought.

I gripped the edges of the tray and lay as flat as I could as the system auto-loaded me into the launch tube. I closed my eyes as the sequencer counted down, praying the HD singularity would hold off long enough for me to get off of *Impulse*, and hoping there was no debris for me to slam into right outside the missile port.

Then the launcher fired, and I was propelled down the length of the launch tube in a flash of seconds. It felt like my EVA suit would come apart at the acceleration as I passed through the missile port and then out into open space. I dared to open my eyes again, kicked away the launch tray, then rotated myself using the last of the propellant from my cone jets to try and get a view of the battle.

Impulse was already a fast-receding dot from my point of view, while *Starbound* was downward to my left. The yacht and Serosian were nowhere in sight.

Starbound had stopped firing completely and was backing away from the dreadnought, the purple glow of her forward Hoagland Field taking the pounding of the multiple coil cannon fire. I wondered if her field would be strong enough to hold off both the onslaught of the dreadnought and the HD singularity detonation.

As I watched, the dreadnought continued firing at *Starbound* but began the process of turning to face the menace of *Impulse* closing on her flank. It was already too late, though—the dreadnought would never be able to hold her off now. I'd done my job. *Impulse* would have her revenge. The only question now was whether it would be good enough to save *Starbound* too.

I watched the scene in near silence, accompanied only by the sound of my breathing, amplified a thousand times inside my helmet. *Impulse* crawled along her preset course, her midships emanating an orange glow as she tried to contain the HD singularity inside her. It wasn't enough.

Impulse slammed into the dreadnought.

The orange glow vanished in an instant as the containment field collapsed, releasing the HD singularity. It flared to life like a burst of sunlight in the middle of the darkest night. I tried to close my eyes, but too late.

I screamed in the deafening silence of my own universe, fully contained now in the EVA suit that clung to my body. I grabbed for my eyes, hitting the plastic shield of my helmet visor instead, clawing at something I couldn't reach. I took in six deep breaths to calm myself, then opened my eyes to utter blackness. I waved my hand in front of my visor—nothing. I fumbled for the switch to my LED on the outside of the helmet. It was in the on position. If the suit was functioning at all it would have given me an alarm if the LED had gone out, but it didn't, it hadn't.

I was blind.

"*Starbound*, this is Cochrane, can you hear me?" I called into my com. There was silence in return. Unless she had been damaged or destroyed by the dreadnought or the HD singularity pulse she should have responded. The EVA suit had a transponder sending out a location signal. If *Starbound* was there, she should have called for me.

I tried again to raise her, to no avail. I calmed myself. I was blind and drifting away from my only hope of rescue, lost in Imperial space on a rescue mission. I decided it wouldn't be a bad epitaph, but I regretted that my father would have to read it.

I closed my eyes and pulled myself into a small ball, almost a fetal position, trying in vain to stay warm. The cold I was feeling could mean only one thing: my EVA suit was failing. I was going to die not knowing if I had rescued my shipmates or destroyed them. Not knowing anything. In the cold of space.

Alone.

I spoke into the com one last time.

"Forgive me, if you can," I said to my lost shipmates. To Babayan and Layton and Marker, to Dobrina and Natalie and Claus Poulsen and Lucius Zander. To Derrick.

Then I embraced the cold, and faded into blackness.

Dénouement

There were sounds of confusion and frantic voices, some familiar, some not. I tried to answer them but I couldn't speak, couldn't raise my voice. It felt like I was floating in a warm bath, much more pleasant than the cold and loneliness I last remembered. I wondered if I were dead, or in some sort of transition from one life to the next, and when I would know for sure. Then it seemed I drifted away into a peaceful sleep, until suddenly I found myself here again, wherever *here* was.

I felt something warm on my cheek. It was soft and gentle and very pleasant in every way. I couldn't help myself. I smiled.

"Peter, are you awake?" I heard the words but didn't really comprehend them or who was speaking. I struggled in darkness, trying to determine if I was in this world or the next. I decided it didn't really matter. I raised an arm, or what I thought was an arm. It felt like lead. I decided that having a body was overrated.

"I think," I said aloud in a croaky voice that sounded nothing like my own to me, "that I might be dead."

"You should be so lucky," said the voice again. I even thought I recognized it. Then I felt the same pleasant warmth on my other cheek, and I decided that I must still have a body, or something similar anyway.

"Are you kissing me?" I croaked out. There was a small giggle, as if it were only meant for my unknown angel and me. Then the warmth touched my lips.

"I am indeed, Peter Cochrane. And you are still very much alive." I held up my lead-weighted hand and she took it gently.

"Dobrina?" I said.

"Yes, it's me."

"Where are we?" Again the giggle.

"We're in sickbay, on *Starbound*, docked at Artemis Station. You've been in and out of consciousness for the last three days, but this is the first time you've said anything remotely coherent. So far, though, you have managed to kiss me, Colonel Babayan, and Princess Janaan." Then she laughed again, louder this time.

"But not Captain Maclintock, I hope?" I said.

"No! Nor Serosian or Layton or Marker either, thankfully. Nothing so scandalous as that!" I shifted a bit in my bed, regaining feeling in my extremities.

"I can't open my eyes," I said.

"They're sealed shut. It will wear off naturally in another day or so. It's to allow your optic nerves to heal properly. Doc said you must have been looking right at the singularity when it went, without a filter."

"I was trying to see if we succeeded," I said.

"Succeeded? Peter, you blew that dreadnought into another dimension!" Then she kissed me again.

"So, Serosian's plan worked?" I said, after our lips parted.

"Serosian's plan? He said it was yours," she said.

"He's lying. What about *Starbound*?" I asked.

"She came through with some heavy systems damage, but minimal casualties, mostly burns. They've all been in and out of sickbay already. Serosian was true to his word, the Hoagland Field held. The only serious loss was communications for about a day."

"My com was out too, and my locator. How did you find me?" I asked.

"Well, that's a story," she said. "We didn't. Serosian did. The yacht was nearly blind from the singularity blast, but he just started a methodical grid search. Said he picked up a ping from your medical transponder and when he saw you drifting in a ball he swung in and pulled you into the airlock. You had five minutes of environment left."

"A close run thing, then," I said. I shifted my hand and she grasped it, our fingers entangling together.

"Very," she replied. "I'm glad we got you back." Then she kissed me on the lips, with more than a hint of passion this time.

The visits came quickly after that: Babayan, Maclintock, Marker, Layton, and even Janaan, who was polite but distant. I felt that I had good friends as well as comrades. Being blind wasn't so bad. I could get used to just smelling and touching the women instead of nodding and saluting. It was a pleasant compensation for being unable to see for a few days.

The last to visit me was Serosian, and I didn't have to see him to hear the concern in his voice. Something was brewing all right, something big.

He told me that this incident was merely the first act in a coming, much larger, conflict.

"It's now apparent that the old empire is still out there in some form and unwilling to concede its historical place in favor of a new Union of Known Worlds. And an empire under the influence of the Sri would be formidable," he said.

"Can we rely on you Historians, on your order, to provide us with the . . . resources we'll need to counter a resurgent Corporate Empire?" I asked. He didn't respond right away, then:

"You can count on us to help the Union in any way we can, and for me to be at your side, young lad."

That satisfied me for the moment. Then I had another thought. "Did Jenny Hogan say anything about the battle aboard *Impulse*?" I asked.

"We've tried all kinds of advanced techniques on her, but she remembers nothing after the jump through the membrane. We did find traces of expended nanites in her system though, and that is a certain sign of the Sri at work," he said. "Likely they wiped her memory for their own security reasons."

The conversation went quiet then, until I blurted out the biggest thing on my mind.

"Are they coming for us?" I asked. He sighed, loud enough for me to hear the strain that he was carrying.

"If *Starbound* had been destroyed by the dreadnought, probably," he said. "But your work with *Impulse* will likely give them pause, for now. They saw the destruction of their dreadnought, the flare of the singularity. One thing about the Sri and creatures like them, they are cautious. I expect them to be doubly so the next time they face off against Commander Peter Cochrane and *H.M.S. Starbound*," he finished.

That didn't really reassure me. I raised my hand to my friend and he clasped it.

"Thank you, Serosian," I said.

"Thank you, Peter," he said back. "You've done exceedingly well. Now heal quickly. I fear there will be much work to do in the near future and precious little time to do it in." Then he tapped me once again on the shoulder and was gone.

A few minutes later, I felt someone lie down next to me on the bed.

"You need to sleep now," Dobrina's voice said in my ear. I shook my head no.

"There's no time for rest," I replied.

She kissed my cheek, then snuggled down next to me. I found myself growing tired despite my best efforts, and I realized she must have been regularly dosing me with a sedative to help me heal. I felt consciousness begin to slip away as she leaned in close and whispered in my ear.

"There's time enough, Peter Cochrane. Just time enough," she said. Then the sweet scent of her faded as a last thought crept into my mind before it all went black.

Just time enough to rest before the next battle.